Fading,
My
Parmacheene Belle

Joanna Scott

Fading,

My

Parmacheene Belle

1 9 8 7

Ticknor & Fields / New York

Library of Congress Cataloging-in-Publication Data

Scott, Joanna.
Fading, my Parmacheene belle.

I. Title.
PS3569.C636F3   1987   813'.54   86-23031
ISBN 0-89919-451-6

Printed in the United States of America

P   10   9   8   7   6   5   4   3   2   1

For Jim

Fading,
My
Parmacheene Belle

ONE

Fading, My Parmacheene Belle

I WILL TELL you exactly how it was one day I said to my companion Gibble, "I am alone here, I need a wife," and he sent on the order without an adequate forewarning, he just breathed with a panting effort, those pockets beneath his jowls throbbing like the gills of a river bass laid out in a pail. I said, "Who are you writing that card to?" and he ducked his head to giggle, he reminded me of a schoolgirl from up Morania way and I told him so and got for an answer nought but a weakly, "Get on." Maybe if I had not been so indolent and out of sorts I might have suspected, and maybe I would have broken his pen and smeared ink across his filthy counter, but instead I had the asphalt taste in the back of my throat, and I attempted to dissolve it with a swallow of his Postum. I will tell you that if young Gibble had indicated what was to come I would have delivered this reply: *What reason have you trying to run my life for me when I got my own hooks, I need not rely on a mail-order bride, I go right to the stream whenever I want, I cast out my flies soft as thistledown they land upon the water,* and maybe I would have stopped these upheavals before they began, I would have gone on frying my own suppers at my pleasure, I would not have put a plank beneath the mattress, I would not have heeded woman advice or paid so dearly for angels on her pappy's tombstone, and I would have had nothing to do with her operations, whoever heard of a man supporting the gradual dismemberment of his wife? It is the same as calling in dogs to rip apart a suckling pig pink-hot from the coals.

I will tell you how the wife came to me, and I will describe our recent days, and you decide what effect a woman has upon a man after fifty-three years. The wife chooses to waste away like a pincherry tree in autumn—for repeated months she has been complaining of internal distress, yet we are in fact nearing the winter's end. Tomorrow morning the wife will be besieged again by the physicians, and how do you think she spends her last hours with me? She has in her the usual urge to rid the home of dirt, and as is her habit she makes it known to me that I am annoying her by following at her heels as she labors with the broom.

"Bothering you?"

I want to make it clear how she is mistaken. "You mean to say: Husband, I am sorry for obstructing your way fifty-three years," but still she wears a grin as if to let me know she is grateful to be leaving me tomorrow.

I say to her, "Well, you will be back, you have little left for them to take but they must find something, they will open you up and grab a handful of entrails and then send you home to me."

I have a promise to make to the wife: "You will be standing over the bed next week as you have done for fifty-three years." That is her way of waking me at dawn, there is no angel of mercy the likes of her, snipping away the threads holding my dreams to me, acting as if she has kept the command, high and mighty she thought she was when she came, with her pappy dragging and sniveling at her heels. I should have took one glance at the both of them and said, *That tart will have no place in my bed*, but I had no time to consider it, my companion Gibble had already cast out his reel, he had bought his pretty cousin a ticket inland from the seashore, a ticket one direction. I have never traveled on that train but I hear how you run through mountains and skirt along a ravine and climb peaks and then tumble down gorges, praying to God you do not lean too far one way or the other, like you are riding in a coal cart making for the bowels.

He brought his cousin into his sandwich shop on a Saturday morning, she sat at the end of the counter nibbling a biscuit, and Gibble said, "She has an interest in you, that gentlewoman do."

Of course I could not know then what he intended, but looking back I do understand. She was what we call a Parmacheene Belle—this is the most taking fly, made of feather and belly fin in the old-fashioned way. It wears out so fast we got to make use of it sparingly. A Parmacheene Belle draws the biggest fish and this is no secret. When the trout takes a notice of it skimming the stream he forgets his toiling and comes after the fly made out of his brother like nothing could taste so delicious.

I was a youngster when Gibble brought in the girl to be my bride, and I had no suspicion that he was drawing me ever closer to the net. When he directed me to his cousin and his uncle he was really dropping his most precious fly upon the water. She was the orange feather and her half-dead pappy the fin, and I, such a dumb spotted trout, I was sure fast to the Parmacheene Belle.

The next thing I knew I was studying the wrought-iron cock hinges at the end of the church pew, with my bride on my arm, and her pappy would not even release his fingers from her wrist, he was trembling and the bones poked through his suit, no wonder since he ate nothing but crackers and bean soup morning to night. I might have felt some true pity for him if he had been with dignity while he was sickly, but he had none of the perspective a man wants to flourish, he surely needed no one else's sympathy, he enjoyed enough of it from his daughter, my wife. He had no marrow, no courage, no pride, and the single time I at-

3

tempted to make an afternoon for him he stood knee-deep in the creek and moaned like a birthing cow, though I had him wrapped up warm as my own papa used to do for me, in a mackintosh down to his ankles and Hannaford rubber boots. He could not even lift the click reel, all he could do was bellow away, frightening the trout into the weeds, and on such a fine spawning October day I did not have a bite.

After fifty-three years the wife makes some grumbling that I cannot identify, but I have sufficient experience to forecast what she means to say, and I reply, "You think it is a saintly effort you are making, putting up with me. Well, Wife, I tell you I made enough sacrifice to pay our trip to heaven, remember who it was kept butter in our Frigidaire back when butter was so very dear."

Those were slim days when in the house we had but a couple of eggs, so what did we do but boil those eggs in onion skins and draw tulips on them with a needle, as if it were Easter in November, and with the warm weather come back for a day, we took our eggs—and yes we had crackers, some sweet cabbage and fresh butter—we took our meal to Josiah's Pond stocked so thick with fish it glittered, it might as well have been that city fountain she liked so much to waste her pennies in and make a wish. I remember our dinner was completed too quickly to satisfy, but we did not mind, this was shortly after we buried her pappy in Adenburg and we were becoming used to each other in a new way, she had begun to soften to me back then. I was considering, *There is to be some luck to come out of this*, while we wandered up around the rim of the pond. I was saying to myself, *I will be contented if I only stay in good health*, when the wife caught sight of a pair of trout in the shallow water, the she-fish was busy fanning out bits of gravel with her tail and the he was carrying away pebbles in his mouth.

I said, "I wish I had a jay fly," but the wife said, "No, it is my pleasure to watch them." I said, "What?" and she said, "They do not need to be afraid of me," so she waited until the male all sparkling red came waggling out of the water grass, she waited

4

while he swam back to fetch his brown-speckled lady, who was most reluctant. The wife asked, "Why won't she come?" and I explained, "She is like any new bride," which caused the wife some worry, she forgot about the fish and went to fold the ground cloth, pretending to be importantly busy, this has always been her fashion. I said, "Wife!" and she gave me a look not so different from the one she is giving me now, the look that means to indicate, *Husband, you are a fool*, and something else that I was never so sure of, maybe she thinks hard about her home near the ocean, her pappy's boardinghouse on the peninsula where on one side was the desolate bog and on the other peaks of sand. I have seen in the pictures how barren and forlorn was the wife's childhood home. But maybe for fifty-three years she has been thinking, *I hope I live to return.*

I try to convince the wife not to worry the dust on the wainscot, not to insist upon changing the sheets. "Why must you do this today, for you changed the bed Monday if I recall correctly." I say to her, "And the morning is nearly lost, I have been doing nothing but following you from room to room," which is my habit, while the wife says with her eyes, *Husband, you are in my path*, suggesting that she has been tolerating *me* all along like I were her guest on an extended visit.

Now I will tell you how I have paid her no attention for fifty-three years while she goes on referring to my faults, which is her favorite sport, it amuses her to blame me when the squash is none too sizable or when the roof takes to leaking. I am attempting to tease her when I say such things as, "Maybe I have a pact with the Lord and am intending to try you with temptation," but that is an untruth, I am more like Lot and the wife is looking behind, preparing to transform herself into a salt-crystal pole. I am but incorrect in her opinion, sometimes a nuisance and most times a millstone tied around her neck, she prefers to push me aside so she can wipe the stairway railing clean. I can do no right when she has the mood to expel the dirt.

"So hard working be you," I say to her. "If you indeed have the illness, why are you pressing that rag into the floorboards, why are you on your knees like it could be any day if the doctors plan to operate tomorrow?"

The day following she is to have her meeting with them so I must encourage her to leave the dust alone, to lie back on the mattress, to close her eyes against the daylight and I will tell her stories. I will have her live with me the night on Gorcum Peak when my brother and I filled our empty bed-ticks with wet straw, there was snow on the ground, and before we were long at the camp we had some good fortune. Brother aimed his slingshot at a squirrel, struck the first try, and provided us with our breakfast for the morning. I remember how I slept in a light worsted cap and a flannel nightdress, the blanket was a board of splinters rubbing against my bare legs and would not keep me warm, so I stayed awake, listening to the dark, knowing Brother was suffering but we both thought ourselves too old to complain.

After the fire turned to smoldering ash, I prayed that sleep would overtake me, for the wind was worse than river water in December washing over the edge of my boot, and suddenly I heard such a cry, a horrible witching sound of pain. We did not know in the middle of the night what had come after us, but we were in the same bedding by then, I wonder who leaped out and into the other's, I cannot recall it was so long ago, yet I do not forget how the stars were knocking against each other, nothing was still, but Brother had me reassured just by the warmth in his flesh, and I thought that if I could freeze the sky, say with my little Waterbury camera, if I could snap a picture of the night, I would have proof that there was a true pattern in the catapulting stars and the quivering branches, perhaps a constellation of a kind gentleman's face. Brother's legs helped the cold to subside and I had no doubt that I was safe, and when we reached morning we found the squirrel was still stretched upon the rock, the brains had leaked from its ears to form a blot, and the creature had some resemblance to a girl asleep in a hammock, her neck twisted, turning her snout to the sun. I tell you it came to me then what it was that had screamed in the night.

But here at home I do not have a respectful audience, the wife has no use for my adventure, she goes on scraping the grit out of the hearth tiles as if she were not a woman with the illness at all but a young bride trying to make an impression, though my wife was never one to alter her ways in an effort to improve a man's opinion. When she has her mind made up there is no affecting her, and I know how she thinks the operation will be different this time, she has suggested the possibility of trouble maybe to scare me. But she is trying to draw an apology from me when she makes such prophecy as this: "Man, it's a difficult chore the doctors must do, but you have yet to understand."

She is trying to blame me for her pain and the unhappy circumstances of her life, though she does not have a hard living now, she has television dinners for her convenience, she has cake as much as she can eat.

"Why do you whisper at your hands like that?"

Over at the sink she makes it plainer still that she has no interest in me.

"I will prepare myself for confrontation," I say to her, "if that is what you want. I have better time to spend than here on your tail as if I had become a child again, and tell me, do you truly have ears in your fingertips? Then permit me to listen with your hands thrust into the dishwash soap—do you hear the water suck into the drain? Is it akin to a gasp? You have made such sucking more than once, Wife, and do not pretend no!"

I am proud to be able to remind her how it was in our youth: coming home from the asphalt yard, I was all the time worn on my feet, she would set for me a piece of bread, a bowl of applesauce, and afterward we would couple on the bed kept firm with a plywood slice beneath the mattress.

She has never slept on a nest of pine boughs three feet thick, she has no experience of comfort, but I say, "Wife, I remind you how you sang your pleasure like this while I made myself into your body." I wonder if she has such recollecting as I, but how could she when all that is placed in her heart is a determination to play upon my misery, to frighten me with her complaints of pain, with the frenzy in her hands. "Wife, look at them," I say, for inside the filmy water they flutter and dance as if they belong not to her but to some spirited magician, it makes me uncomfortable to see the wife out of control when she has spent fifty-three years designing order in the rooms, perhaps she has always been expecting someone worthy to visit, the Alderman or the Pastor, but if she had only listened with her ears she would have heard me say, *No one shall come. There properly is and remains in this gray limestone house you as my wife, and there will be time, I do assure you, there will be time for us to walk into the orchard, the blossoms will be plentiful this season, it will look wonderful when the blossoms are spread.*

Yes, there are many things I would say to the wife if she listened. I would tell her again not to continue with her work but to hear some advice, I would say, *Wife, it will do good to lie on your bed and I shall offer you some of my facts, I shall teach you a compass's points and what is the best mosquito dope and I will forget how for our lifetimes together you have been identifying in me nothing but the worst, I will forget how you were Gibble's fly before you were my wife, and your pappy, he was all that made me scared of reaching old age, and in Adenburg there are angels weeping over his plot so dear they cost us our supper's beef for a winter.*

I still had hope and no suspicion when the wife first came upon me—how could I have known what a marriage would entail, how could I have known her pappy would be such a burden in our lives to last nearly a decade, and then when he expired he would leave a curse upon the wife, he would leave her with a bitterness that rotted her womb, so that our first boy was born an idiot and our second was removed from the wife before the babe was ready

8

to come out? How could I have known that from the beginning there would be such sorrow? Even now I have a reluctance to recall it, how the wife grayed at an age when she should have been ripening, how our idiot child suckled the strength out of her, suckled the fight out of her, so by the time I had a pension sufficient to pay for him to be installed in the upland school, the wife already had the illness. I tell you there are such workings inside womanflesh I do not understand.

Our surviving son is a subject that leads us always into argument and it is best to keep him out of our speech. I admit I have been hard toward him ever since I watched the wife failing and the Idiot extending in height, I admit I remain firm in my opinion and will not be influenced by proof of his good nature. I know how the wife makes weekly visits to the school but I let her keep at her private ways, I never give a clue that I have an intuition of her purpose when she takes off in the automobile for an afternoon; sometimes I think she favors him to me, he adores her and this is no lie, while she shows such affection for him she seems a stranger when we visit him on holidays. I watch the wife grooming the Idiot, clipping his hair, scrubbing his neck, I watch and I wonder if she would do as much for me.

"If I were the boy, would you be ignoring me so?"

I am unthinking, it is out before I can stop myself, and the wife in reply jerks her blade in quick strokes. What has she done? Paring the potato, she has blood on her hand. I tell you this is a revealing sign of disorder in the wife, for never has she wielded so carelessly, she who has a butcher's skill with knives. I do not remind her how it would have been avoided if she had been attending to me, I only take her hand and try to rinse the spittling blood in order to dress the wound, I tell her to remain still and not to shiver, her hand is so very thin, I might peel off her flesh as had been done to a figure painted on the upland school wall, his flayed skin in the mural is in a similar condition to hers, dripping, his eyes are like . . . I try to show the wife how the eyes of

9

the saint are stretched and hollow, I tease her to uncover a laugh, but of course she has no smile ready for me, she has nothing but gloom in her eyes. My temper rises now after I have made such an effort to solace, to comfort.

"If I am your bother," I tell her, "you may wrap the cut yourself. You know that be there any need for an argument, I am ready if it is today, so you express to me your words once and for all."

She turns, looks fierce upon me, and I see a face inside her face, it is the mid-aged wife in her full glorious fury.

"Get out!" she says to me with a passion roughing her voice. "Get out!"

The wife has an injunction, a forbiddance against me here? "Well, Wife, you know how you have been nothing but an irritation to me." I regret that I have said it but she treats me as if I were but vermin beneath the broom fifty-three years, and I with a compassion that wants to support her, and she with cold-chisel eyes. *Get out, get out!*

Well, I go but not without my pride, I leave the house but first I explain to the wife that I am taking with me only a kettle, a compass, and a muzzled ax. Yes, I go out of the house, my own house, but I attempt to make the wife feel a pressing guilt.

"I leave this all to you," I say as I gather my coat collar beneath my chin and prepare to make an exit. "I leave this all to you, from the root cellar to the attic, yours to the end. I begrudge nothing to my wife, but if at night you hear the knocker against the door, if you hear the latch rattle and the tired shuffle across the floorboards, remain inside your quilted coverlet, I warn you, for my spirit must perform a fanciful sight, lathering at the mouth and eyes abulge and skin the ashen color of a drowned man."

Now I am not being fanciful, I am composing a prediction to put fear in my wife, I mean to provide her with a suggestion of how it will be empty in the house without me, so I say farewell and I plunge into the chill weather. It brings me sadness to describe what the wife has no awareness of, the land that she ig-

10

nores, the sky asmoke, the ground crackling beneath the feet, soil laced with hoarfrost, the orchard trees gnarled like old men. The wife does not take pleasure in the cloud touching the lips on a winter morning or in the cock grouse rising from the bush, the wife is not influenced by the wind trumpeting against the ridge, the wife does not share the deepest love, she will not succeed in bringing a trout to the net, she will be but a sulking maid to obstacle a man, she will curse the mud on his trousers and never draw a gossamer gut across the water, slowly it must be done, for the trout have become educated by the tourist fishermen, the trout have grown wary, they anticipate a feather fly to be obscuring the fact of the hook, and on a day such as this they still enjoy a respite from the winter run so they can begin it again, the jigging and carousing.

I wish I had on me a penny whistle, for it is so quiet this noontime, an uneasy silence that extends far, my footfalls and my breathing make only a brief interruption but not what will last, and the wind cannot be trusted, it reaches to an end and I have the stillness around me again. I make my way down the slope to Josiah's Pond, where the water is a puddle on an ice saucer and the sunlight gives the pond the color of tin. Pulled onto the shore is a rough-hewed raft, the same raft that I made with my friend Gibble many years past, he displayed the mariner in his soul when he sawed two logs short of ten feet and between them placed plywood bound with withes. The raft is frozen stiff into the edge of the ice, I climb aboard it and rest here, observing the quiet upon the pond, thinking forward to spring, though it was Gibble himself who questioned such truths that apply to the weather.

He was a skeptical lad and by the age when a man should have a wife and a home Gibble was happily single, with a collection of scientific magazines enough to fuel a furnace through winter. From Gibble I learned an assortment of facts, and one returns to me now. It was a magazine that maintained: the very smallest particle of dust will not sit still and be measured, so when you try to make a location for it, it might be here or there, in the corner, in the middle, on the edge, you can never know for sure. The magazine insisted upon the information, and Gibble related it all to me. But on this day in March as I sit upon the ancient raft lodged into the ice, it is a fact too bothersome to mind. The spring means to be here one day—you trust if not the weather, then what? A turn in the weather is a prophecy of good luck—I should make this known to the wife, for she has been unnatural today.

My companion Gibble had my best concerns in mind, surely he must have been considering my wants when he sent away for his cousin to be my wife, but now it seems that Gibble is to blame for these fifty-three years, Gibble procured a mail-order bride who was not well suited to me, Gibble had secretive family concerns and it took some time to understand why he chose for me this wife and not another: he wanted to pass on the burden of his uncle who had no support, he wanted to watch his relatives thrive without bothering to shelter them. I know how cunning was Gibble, who preferred to remain a bachelor and a solitary man these many years.

It is a trick of the slope, I believe for a moment that I have seen the wife creeping by the hedgerow, though it proves to be but a corn husk bundle left through the winter. And still I have only silence flat upon my ears, nothing but the water and the raft. I shift my position and there is a tearing like the wife makes when she rips a sheet of foil to fit a bowl, the raft shakes loose from the border of ice, and before I can grasp a shoreline crag or bush I have floated away and into the middle of the pond. Far below, the trout stay wedged into rock crevices and in the sky the storm cloud hangs by a single strand. The silence weighs heavy as a bushel of stones, presses me down across the logs.

I remind you I am an old man and with the willow boughs scraping against my chin I am in sore distress. It is as though an invisible hand has a determination upon my fate, pinning me to the raft, tugging me farther from the shore; there is nothing to be done but lie still as death must be, floating, the raft slides along ridges of water, I wait beneath the quiet making a single word loud in my head: *Wife!*

It might be nighttime, so still is the air, but if I were upon our mattress she would pinch my hand to assure me I was safe. There must be waking and there must be sleeping, and I am somewhere in between, drifting from shore. My wife would navigate me home if she knew of my difficulty, she would wrap her arms around me, her bosom flat as the silence against my ear; she wears flannel pajamas at night and when I bury my face against her I sometimes imagine she is my own papa, he used to sing for me at the midnight hour when I thrashed and floundered inside a vision, he used to jiggle me free of my dream, tuck in the sheets and sing softly a tune to ward off the hunchback man, the old hunchback man.

Floating upon Josiah's Pond, I have such a fear of drowning I have never known before. Suddenly a crow erupts in a screech, no penny whistle that, it is the buzzard crow come to taunt a helpless old angler adrift upon the Gibble raft, snipping the threads of silence with its beak. It is unholy, the crow song, it must approximate the sound Gibble asked a description for: "Have you ever heard a rabbit scream?"

Certainly Gibble had learning, he had magazines for his closest companions, and he had a knowledge of how needles are fixed beneath a rabbit's fur, needles full of the liquid that makes the Frigidaire cold, and the rabbit strapped into a tiny chair makes a cry, there is nothing close to it, or so Gibble said, he had some ideas. "Have you ever heard a rabbit scream?" was the question directed at the customers who sat at Gibble's counter. It remained a problem for him to the end of his stay in our neighborhood and longer, he said he did not have imagination enough to hear the sound a rabbit makes when it has winter put beneath its skin. But I tell you now that a crow laughing while a man is near to drowning constitutes a song unpleasant to the ear. The crow song might be as a rabbit suffering, who knows? It is enough to encourage me to put my hands into the water. The cold wraps a muff of needles around my fingers as I paddle a slow return to shore. I use my hands as a garden trowel, the water yields, each stroke burns my skin to numb waxy red, and all the while the crow flaps in pursuit, cawing its mockery.

By the time I am close enough to grab hold of a thorny alder branch my fingers belong to me no more, and all for the wife it has been done. How I finally make it from the raft to land I cannot say, somehow I drag myself upright, somehow I step across the border of ice to the sloped shore. Maybe a man has a blind instinct compelling him to firm ground.

I watch the raft glide away across the velvet water and I wonder why I had such fear. I tell you I have no grand desires, only to provide the wife with boiled rice and coffee in the morning and packaged dinners at night. My pension is an accomplishment, she knows how I labored in asphalt yards, but she has always told me with her eyes if not with her tongue, *Husband, you are not as good as what I was used to*, like she did come to me not through a mail-order request but as her favor, and now to be pretending the possibility of trouble, attempting to use her suffering to make me regret the way I have handled her fifty-three years.

The wife wants no longer to endure me. But after being adrift and near dead inside Josiah's Pond, I have some forgiveness; if she needs to seek her private counsel I will not interfere, there are mysteries in a woman never to be explained, she has trouble on the toilet and deserves to be excused. I will extend to her a pardon, I will share my understanding, my sympathy, my love. I will reveal to her: *My wife, it is an awful thing to sink alone*, better than I no one could know, for I have come close to dying solitary.

I expect that the wife will harken to me and put aside her dust rag and sleep, a great wonderment is sleep when such silence is not to be feared, in retirement how warm the legs are, well do I know, and today there is a rest earned after a forenoon such as hers. I will put the stew to simmer and draw the shades, my wife will sleep even while the doctors come to nibble at her body, she will be adrift as before, many times over has my Parmacheene Belle been attracting the fish. How lucky it is for the wife that the physicians have such medicines to put her out while they perform their operations, her eyes will be shut against the pain, she will feel nothing and when she wakes again I will be there to provide a tulip like the one wrought in the weather vane atop the barn—there will be a slowing to respect, and we will have our days as before, but not with the argument, we will recall the pleasant and forget the daily tribulation.

Today I want only to be an influence of good, so if she is thinking hard toward her home of before, if she is seeing herself as a girl, if she is musing upon the angels guarding her pappy or upon the nuns at the upland school serving breakfast to her son, I will have her turn instead to an anticipation of the warm weather, it has been promised.

The angels must be restraining the four winds of the earth, damming breezes and the great river storms to make in the neighborhood a quiet everlasting. Our home is fixed upon the ridge, it stands with its eaves and its gables, ivy entangled upon its gray limestone face—it is my triumph after these many years. The creaking hinges announce my return when I push open the door.

"Wife, hello to you! I am back in time for dinner," I call out, and how sweet and comfortable is this smell, a welcome to my nose.

I have left the ax and the kettle at the edge of the pond, and when my wife looks at my empty hands I say, "I had a fright down there upon the water. My fingers will attest. I was stuck upon the Gibble raft, I was nearly drowned. But the adventure must wait, it is more properly a tale for some grim night by the fire, I will tell another time how I was almost lost inside the winter depths." I do not want to speak of my fear now, not at a feast such as the one prepared by my Parmacheene Belle, gravelcake and dumplings, enough to last through the week.

"The hands will be polished as the floorboards," I promise in my good humor as I climb the stairs, "the boots will be placed in the closet, the jacket . . ." I go into the bedroom and discover my suit, the brown-speckled wool, the vest, the trousers, all pressed and unfolded.

"Wife, why have you spread this out across the bed as if to prepare me for a special event?"

"Come away," she directs.

Come away I will not until I have a reason for this. "Come away." She tries to pretend calm.

Well, come away I refuse until I learn what is the meaning for it, my suit awaiting me. "You must tell me, Wife. I will not let go of your wrist" brittle as dry rope, I will not release her until she explains herself to me.

It is true I have never attempted to raise my hand against her, but a first there must be always. Ah, the wife will always defend herself, her palm is glass shattering upon my cheek, the old Parmacheene Belle has an effect to her yet, she is to remain an instrument of allurement and I have an urge to snap at her again and still again without considering the consequence, for my mad Parmacheene Belle remains a bait most enticing. But the temper disappears from her face and instead she has a pale luster such as you might see in a feverish child.

"Wife, why must you wear a disguise, why do your legs pretend not to support your weight?" I demand, and add, "You have inside you a true disobedience, enough to impair my mood," for I know how to hold the wife's attention. "You must do as I say, I will tell you what the proper manner will be for the afternoon," and as you might expect the wife shakes her fist at me, it is a true indication of spirit, a savage strike I make beneath the foamy current but she wheels around, staggers, clatters downstairs like a cascade of gravel loosened by a man's heel.

"Wife, you have been missing the seed and you must now attend with me—"

I pursue her to the kitchen but she does not wait upon my advice, with passion in her jolting pace, with uneven pride and fury, the illness must be weakening, it is my triumph, mine to keep her in a temper, to provoke, a smart slap she has given me the moment past and another I invite. But what is she doing? Settling upon her willow chair, buckling her knees, she sits but only for an instant, and then she struggles to her feet, overturning the chair, she fights, the moisture upon her face is morning dew and the color of her skin is lily white, she makes a cry, *Do not address me so do not pretend suffering* it is a voice I have heard, a sound newly learned, it puts a chill beneath my skin, *Wife, you are hurting me release me from those eyes* I order, I demand, it rises in her throat, a song to fill the terrible silence this.

TWO

The Burning Chair

THEY HAVE claimed her as their own. They stole away with her when I was wont to hold her in my arms, and they planted her beside her pappy, beneath the weeping angels. I keep my eyes fixed on the box. You know she would be less than proud of me today, but with the casket lid between us she cannot see how I am poorly dressed for her farewell—in ordinary trousers and a shirt with lilacs tumbling across my chest, and in respect of this new widowerhood I wear my green cap with my Parmacheene fly pinned to the visor, I wore it right into the chapel and into the field and have not removed it from my head. My brown-speckled suit has been left at home upon the mattress, untouched, yet I do not hear the wife berating me for my sorry appearance, I hear nought but the Pastor's dull speech and from far off a chainsaw taking down the forest. I have a restlessness in me that will not be subdued.

Now after fifty-three years I am familiar with the wife and I know she would be chafed by this public attention, she would not approve of ceremony on her behalf, so while Gibble and the others huddle with heads bowed I move away from the gathering, away from the open grave, down the cemetery lane, past my own automobile. I cut off into the woods. I will walk the whole distance home from Adenburg while birds cackle in loud reproach and the wind rustles budded branches, drowning the Pastor's voice with natural song.

Along the path there is the ordinary tourist trash—beer cans and food wrappers, spent slickers, cast-off galoshes—but on a grassy slope there is to be seen another kind of waste, the carcass of a deer sinking into the earth. It is a fact that during the season of my wife's death the deer coverts have suffered the effects of an epidemic surpassing any that has come before. It is a fact that the deer carry the plague across the high meadows, the illness advances and pleases to take with it many a fawn and paltry doe. And it is a fact that we have sciences and electrical dams and asphalt factories, but we do not have a cure to stifle the germ infecting our animals, we have only our eyes to set upon the tufts of deer fur and hunks of bone scattered over the mossy glade. In this fresh carcass the white worms are invading the skull, entering through her eye sockets, but this is not an unusual sight and has nothing to do with the Pastor's prayer, the grave, the wife, no, it is not uncommon these grim days to be strolling upon a woodland byway and to see uncovered another victim of the plague, a white-tail that might have been a mother but has become nought but a throw rug for the forest floor. The doe that meets me upon the path on my way home from the funeral has scores of cousins dead throughout the hills.

I have seen death spread unheeded before this. I have seen acres of bare snags where there used to be grand chestnut trees dropping their nuts at our feet. Brother and I would gather them for Yuletide, we would sit close to the range, washing down the roasted nuts with a swallow of beer while our mam raised her voice in holiday song, warbling, flushed from the drink, a girl again. It was a sad fate that befell the acreage of trees, the chestnut blight, the tree disease.

But I have a suspicion of the source. My papa, he thought it was the electrical industry contaminating the land, for it produces a warmth in the rivers, a pallor in the sky, it surely had some influence upon the chestnuts. But I say now: *radioactivity is worse, far worse*, it needs no wire to transfer it from one place to another, it is a force not easily diverted. Because of the blight I see only skeletons of trees upon the ridge as I come over the hill, and there will be no nuts to roast upon a pan. I predict the deer plague will have a similar spreading: it encompasses.

Now I do not have an innocence regarding natural ways. I accept the harsh realities, I know the deer stock would benefit from a certain reduction in their ranks. But you would not insist upon necessity if you had seen the devastation this season, it might have some comparison to the Big Ice that once spread across the woodland, ice thousands of feet thick, according to Gibble.

He came home for the funeral, but I did not acknowledge him, our bond has been time-altered and without the wife we are estranged for good. Still, I remember how he was a true scientist and had such learning, a singular man, but ambition took him, and he abandoned his diner, he abandoned his biscuits and his Postum, to live in the shadow of industry down south. Near a quarter of a century has been spanned since Gibble's betrayal and the wife's end. I have known hardship. I remember how Gibble once took a sheet of tin foil and he made a model of the Ice as it was in the years before my time, he explained how long ago the winter season repeated without a thaw and covered the woodlands in milky glass. He used a kitchen knife to crimp the foil into the shape of a continent upon the counter, he made a picture of the world as it was.

Now I tell you Gibble had mapmaking skill, he was a friend very dear to me until he took off and dedicated himself to exploit and plunder. Even as a young man he had an intellectual way, he taught me lessons in history and law while I drank his Postum that tasted like the burnt crust of a bread heel, I will never forget some things about my friend Gibble. He had a talent with biscuits such as we have never seen since in our neighborhood, and he was the last to sell sweetcakes without a plastic wrapper. Then, toward the decline of his middle age and the beginning of the wife's illness, he began to fall off into a sour mood, and when I stopped in on my return from the asphalt yard, he would prophesy that the Ice was due back, the winter would spread from pole to pole and blot out the great forests. I would ask him why he bothered to fret upon the future as I secretly dumped an extra portion of his fine sugar into my cup in preparation for the cold. I would sip and fortify my courage, and then I would ask for more information about this certain devastation. Usually he would reply with a dark, inspired look, and I would be left to imagine the conclusion myself.

But once I was bold enough to ask if the second Ice would bring *my* life to an end, which provoked Gibble's wrath; he said, "You are a coward if you are scared of the cold. If you had any wood knowledge at all you would understand how the hardiest trees survive."

He reminded me that the manly trees slept comfortably during the last Ice and after the Great Thaw they migrated north from the Blue Mountains and south from the Greens.

I know what he meant to imply: the manly plants were the survivors. They joined forces in our neighborhood and there was a mingling of influences among the vegetation, which brought to the land here an extensive variety, skunk cabbage and spleenwort, the Dutchman wearing breeches and jack in his pulpit. Manly plants—some are to be seen already this season of my wife's death, along with the tourist pollution and the doe upon the ground. The plants were not to be extinguished by the cold, and if the Big Ice comes for a second round into our neighborhood, if the spring brings perchance another winter rather than a hint of warmth, I know that there will be survivors. There are always survivors. There are chestnut shoots still growing from the crooks of the dead tree branches; there are deer that have escaped the illness.

And surely, somewhere, somewhere there are women who do not have a compulsion to die before their time, there are wives more faithful than mine, wives who make a fight against the illness, who forestall the end, who do not abandon their men. For if we are to be looking to the future, we must keep attached to each other—it is a promise made at the wedding, an agreement to resist such obstructions as death.

I am faithful to my vows. See how it is not the husband who permitted himself to be eaten by disease, it is not the husband who closed his eyes and retreated into the walnut casket the size of our Frigidaire. It is the wife. She has been taken by the blight, the plague, the Ice, she has been packed into the crate. I tell you if I had a suspicion that the wife would take such sudden leave, I would have prohibited our union, I would have found for my mate a delicious doe without a weakness in her bones, a wife who would not betray the wedding trust, for there is nothing to compare with the sinking heart in a man married fifty-three years as he approaches his empty home. There is only blackness behind the windows, only a vacancy inside, no one to greet me after a walk such as I have taken from the gentle slope of the cemetery hill where they carry on with the service.

Such a lengthy honoring they provide for her. My knees were suffering from the long effort of standing still, so I left my automobile in the parking lot and have come all this way from Adenburg through the woods instead of along the easy road. I have no concern for my Buick Skylark, it makes a death rattle and holds memories I do not wish to retain. They may bury the car with the wife, bury the fenders and the windshield, the muffling canister, the radiator, fill the automobile cockpit with clods of wet soil and let the white worms crawl through her and eat into her dashboard, her seat cushion, eat into the engine. They may let the worms coil inside the belly of my Buick Skylark, they may place a tombstone at the head of the grave. It is all the same to me, for haven't I unlimited freedom to wander now that I am alone again?

I have come all this way through the parkland where there is death upon the grass. I tell you the smell congeals in my nostrils, this scent of plague, the stench of radioactivity. The evening is already low upon the land when I finally reach my gravel drive; I stand at the border of my acreage and study the home. It does not welcome me with a string of chimney smoke and a glow between the shutters, the door does not open, the wife does not wait upon the step with a spoon in her hand and gravy spattered upon her apron. She does not scold me for leaving the cemetery before the Pastor had the chance to bring his prayer to an end. The wife is not here because she is behind me, dreaming inside the Frigidaire box. Now I wonder who will heat my supper on this night of the wife's farewell.

There are some people who talk of a married pair as being inseparable. It has even been told to me how among Indians the wives were sacrificed at the burning stake when their chieftains breathed their last. I expect the women must have protested as they were bound by the wrists and led up the path and attached to the pole. I imagine they must have had some regret that they did not expire before their husbands. For this is as it should be: the man ought always to take the lead into the shadows. This is as it should be. Perhaps if I had gone first, my neighbors would have looked toward the wife with a similar plot in mind, who can say?

As I stand upon the hillock the bluish dusk grows denser and I remember the solitude awaiting me. I tell you after fifty-three years you do gain an intimacy with the woman. She shares your name and you grow used to her presence on the mattress. But if the wife wants to proceed to the grave, if she wants to leave you to fend for yourself, then you must call an end to the union, you must prepare yourself for a long separation. The silence is not easily endured, so unlike the quiet that fills a room when the wife is here but with sleep binding her tongue, this is a watery silence that cannot be shut out. I should not fear the empty house. I am a widower now as I was once a bachelor, living alone in the family cottage after my own papa was buried. I knew days of solitude and I was not afraid there in the steamy valley where with the windows open the room was full of the good smell of rotting wood. I even had some kitchen skill—I could split a fish with my eyes pinched closed, and in a wink I could skewer it with slips of red willow, salt and pepper it and fasten it to a stick with a spruce root, I could secure it before the open fireplace and let it broil at an even pace. The fat would hiss as it dripped upon the hearth brick. And I remember when the tax revenuer came around for his collections, I would bolt the door, I would pretend an absence while he announced himself with a hard knocking, a sharp, insistent knocking. When he left I knew I had another season to keep my savings.

After pondering the past, I gather my spirits as an old-fashioned woman will pull in her skirts, and I go up the drive and through the back door to the kitchen, where, with the windows curtained and the sun sunk behind the hill, I cannot see to find the chain hanging from the light. I bump my knee against the table and exclaim, "Damnation!"

An odd sensation fills me when the wife does not reply. Not since my bachelor days have I cursed without expecting due reply. Living singly, I would gather my friends, a quartet of fine boys along with young Gibble, who was even then our leader, first in command. We would march off into the woods and collect green onion shoots and spend our Sundays eating onion ramps and drinking beer, ramps and beer, what a comfortable existence it was before Gibble made a recommendation for my happiness and sent away for the girl, his cousin, to be my wife. He wrote for her in April, and by June she had moved in with her pappy

24

and set out revising my home, moving the table first to the right and then to the left, positioning it at an angle that made for continual difficulty. I had a hope that when we exchanged the cottage for this grand limestone home, I would be able to avoid the furniture. Well, it has not been so easy, often I would strike my shin against the wood and when profanities escaped the wife would bark, "Man, watch your tongue!"

I throw the same vulgarity into the emptiness and still I receive no response. But the wife continues to influence me, she has positioned the lamps where I cannot find them, she has transformed my home into a trap, my own home, with jagged corners hidden, eager to trip me as I make my passage to bed, when I want only to stretch upon the mattress—I have come a far distance, fifty-three years, and need rest.

Now something has arrived. It makes itself known first with a short knocking upon the wall, or the table, it is difficult to determine the source of the sound, three sharp raps interrupt the silence, three sharp raps hidden by the dreary dark.

"What is this intruding without permission?" I spend my breath to ask, I cough, and persist, "Who is there?"

But this obstacle refuses to respond.

"A question from my lips expects a response," I say, thinking that perhaps it is a wayward child come to steal my food scraps. "Well, I warn you, I still have strength," though I do not have such courage, I admit I am sick with fear of masked thieves who slide in over the windowsill and unsheathe their knives. My fingers are not so supple as they used to be, my breath is stale, my eyesight poor. But I have spirit, yes, I have enough to overwhelm—the silverfax in the river know it. The tax revenuer knew it. Even the wife knows it, yes, the wife knows it best, for long ago I had a desire to enter her, it had been some months since we coupled properly yet still she tried to put me off, first with her steely hands covered with cake powder and then with her feet most ferociously kicking. I tell you it was not easy to hold her still. She protested while I had my pleasure with her, but I suspect she was less unhappy with the outcome than she pretended, old womanflesh does not always win the interest of a husband.

Such recollections revive me: "What is this disturbing my sorrow? Whatever you are, I warn you I will try violence when I find the light."

I wish I had lynx eyes that provide their own lanterns in the darkness, for this obstacle is invisible, it is not a fair trial, I have had no time to recuperate from the sudden separation with the wife. "I warn you, identify yourself!" Now my heart feels a hook lodged and tugging, and I announce to the night, "It will be upon your conscience if I am struck down."

This is enough to provoke him. The matchhead scratches the flint, the flame leans toward the candlewick, I see the face mottled orange by the light, like a speckled trout asleep on a lake floor. I approach and recognize the intruder in my home, I see before me my idiot boy.

"You. But I put you in the upland school. You are supposed to be residing there for twenty years and more. I told them not to send you for the funeral."

I circle him, grab hold his arm, my fingers find a solid arm to clutch. "Speak to me, then," I say. "Utter your purpose."

He greets me dumbly, this has always been his way, so I release his arm, I look upon my palm and shake it as if to loosen germs passed to me, I continue orbiting the boy who stands before me with head bowed.

"I see," I say. "I understand."

The son is not actually in my home, the son remains at the school and his presence in my room is nought but a dream-thought, nought but the result of fever in my imagination, nought but a fragment of my own self, I have always had this tendency to conjure nightmares, and the figure here is just my bad dream, arrived before bedtime. My fright settles inside me and I notice it is not I but he who is trembling, he who is afraid.

"Sit down," I say, motioning with my hand, and the Idiot sits. "Stand," I command, testing my authority over my dream, and the Idiot stands.

Well, it is a matter of pride when a man learns to discipline his nightmares without a wife's assistance. I finally find the chain to the bulb, I tug on the light, blow out the candle that the Idiot had used to reveal himself to me, and I look full upon my progeny. The grown child in my kitchen is hardly human, he has more resemblance to a ferret that comes to overturn the garbage pail— his is a pointed snout with wiry whiskers bushing from the nostrils, his are ungainly rabbit ears. He has a twisted mouth, a mouth that will not contain his spit, a mouth that refuses to speak. Hardly a boy, he has years of manhood already behind him, and I tell you as I look upon my son, whom I have not seen for all these years except at holidays and only then if the weather was acceptable, as I look upon my idiot son he seems the image of myself, the man I am, or was, transformed into a dream-vision. So when I speak to him I am in truth directing the anger, the disgust, at my own heart, for he makes me sorely aware of my failings.

He stands mutely and has such a fear of me that for an instant I soften, I take a kitchen towel and wipe the spittle from his chin. Until I remember that it does no good spoiling a dream-vision. He is a pitiful creature, adrift in my kitchen, motherless. I prepare to say to him such things as I have wanted to say all along but was inhibited by the presence of the wife. She did not permit me to mistreat the boy.

In the wife's absence my tongue is loosened, and I say to my vision, "You were never a figure of respect."

I say this and more, though I know his ears are sealed against me. "I order you: attend to me. I have much to direct toward you, now that your mother is not near for your defense."

I ask him if he has heard of her absence, but his milky eyes reveal nothing. "You did not expect to find her here, did you?

You, Idiot One! How did you make the trip from school?" Did he walk alone through the woods, did he see the doe sunken into the grass? My son. He was never a fisherman of skill. Now he inspires in me a discomfort, being the only product of the union that lasted fifty-three years.

But who is to blame, I ask you? Who was it convinced me of the wife's irresistible attraction, who said to me, "True, the girl has her father, but he will not intrude upon your loving"? Gibble was rarely caught fallible, but I tell you he wronged me when it came to a description of the wife's pappy, for it was the old man's presence in the house that tainted me with the gloom of age, it was Pappy's befuddled thought that needed the wife's constant attention. After a day spent nursing his confusion she was too tired to game as a girl should, and by the time Pappy passed on the wife's hard work and worry had turned her womb into a sack. It caused her such suffering that the doctors began their exploring, and they found a child developing inside her, they ordered the wife to keep at peace for the period, and soon the Idiot insisted on making his arrival, he barged silently into the world as was his way all along, he came with the drool upon his lips and no voice in his throat even when the doctor took to slapping him, I tell you this was the only time my son received a proper beating.

And the next year when the wife had pain again, the doctors insisted on removing her womb, along with the minnow who was to be my second son. Gibble made it known to me that a babe five weeks old in a woman's belly has fingernails, and ears to listen to a heartbeat, and eyelids sealed against the wet darkness. Gibble made it known to me that children five weeks old are like centipedes curled inside logs. They took my second child from me, the one who was to be my pride, and now I have no one to turn to, the solitude is vast.

"I tell you," I say to my son, though he will not understand, "I am no longer afraid of Pappy's condition. The rust. The rattling in the carburetor. I will shut off my ignition when I am prepared and not before. Understand," I explain, "our progression toward the end depends upon our attitude. You had a willingness to weaken, so you have become shrunken and cowardly long before the proper moment. The wife too gave up the trial early, she let illness steal her breasts from her, steal her womb, steal patches of skin from her face, leaving behind scabs that even the mosquitoes could not penetrate. Idiot, you did not have sight of your mam in her final hour, you cannot imagine how it was. But I am a proud widower, I intend to continue far into the future, I am a survivor. Such a helpless form as you no longer plagues me."

It is true, we share some qualities, he being the son and I being the husband of the woman in the box. We might be compared to a pair of landlocked salmon, attached to the same female and no easy route to the ocean. But while I am one to make a forceful rolling through the water, with fins enlarged and a clear purpose, my son is a smallish fish swimming about in an odd manner, as if he had his spine broken by a fierce pike, as if he cannot use his tail for fast propulsion. He is a crippled fish with such confusion inside him he cannot convey.

I do not forget a morning up Mungerton Creek when I took the boy traveling in a canoe. I had to paddle us through dangerous eddies and decapitate the waves while he shivered, wet from river spray, he was a skeleton of a boy in the fashion of his granddaddy, with hardly enough skin to cover his bones. Even now he has a closure to the past, he has no thoughts directed behind him, only around, only a notice of his distress, he cannot recall the still pool where we came to rest, where we settled in the quiet, he cannot remember how I let him use my second-best click reel and my own Jock Scott, and to my wonderment he had caught a silverfax before I even completed preparing my fly. It was a fish not much bigger than his thumb, and I made the recommendation to release it, but the Idiot did not comprehend and in his absent way he let it swim off, still attached to the leader. Let the boy be, I said to myself, and a few minutes passed when suddenly his reel arched like a cat's back, and I reached over to wrap my arms around him. I remember the feel of his ribs beneath the mackintosh, it gave me some shock to feel his wasted body but I had to address the fish struggling at the end of the line and I could not be concerned with the condition of his flesh. We battled and the fish fought hard against us, the canoe nearly spilled us, and with the boy moaning I had an impulse to release the reel and turn him overboard. But eventually the fish made less resistance and I was able to draw him close and scoop him with the net.

Surely the Idiot has forgotten the fish we worked to capture, a pike some six pounds, it had taken the silverfax into its gullet and the hook had slipped and somehow pierced through the socket of the pike's eye—from the inside, I mean to say, so the barb poked outward through the eye jelly. And I remember how my son sat with the net and fish and leader tangled upon his lap, and he heaved up and released a substance from his mouth like applesauce or like the milt expelled from a dead silverfax when it is squeezed.

Now as he sits in the kitchen on the afternoon of the wife's burial, I cannot resist confronting the boy with his cowardice. I tell him he is a weak silverfax such as belongs strung upon the leader, I tell him this with a ruthlessness, I come close to him and say, "Boy, you look like you belong either in water or in a packing crate."

He might be manacled to the chair for all the freedom he enjoys, he might be a prisoner awaiting the sizzling expiration. I know how it is done: in the river rapids they have a millwheel that turns and makes the current even stronger, and they direct the electricity into the prisoner's chair, and from there into his bones. It roasts him if not at the first attempt then at the second, though I have heard of men who make such resistance the electricity must be switched on thrice.

"How about you, Idiot? Have you a desire to feel the thrill rippling beneath your pasty skin? Would you like to feel the light put inside your body? There are ways," and though I know the

30

boy does not comprehend, still he has such a fear upon his face I regret the way I am abusing him. But if the boy is not sitting here, if he is just my dream-vision, what harm have I done except to myself?

I am considering these alternatives of dream and fact when the bulb blinks suddenly off, and with the light out I cannot find the cause, I meet only darkness behind, darkness before. I hear a scuffling, then silence.

"What is this? Idiot, do you have an influence upon the bulb?"

Now all the while I am assuring myself that this confusion in my home is no more, no less than a dream; I do not have an unreasonable fear of ghosts, of demons sweeping down the chimney, of unnatural things. "You come and demonstrate yourself to me."

If what is outside is nought but an eerie echo of my past, as a nightmare echoes the day, then I need not worry over the consequences. But I hear a voice, a gentle trill rising from a corner of the kitchen.

"We were on a return from a long journey and had exhausted our provisions altogether . . ."

It is such a soothing sound I believe my own papa is to be the next ghost, and I wait, impatient for him to declare himself outright. He tells how we came down from a lake along a trail, he revives a past sporting adventure, and before long I perceive that there is no close relation to me hidden in the dark, neither my papa nor my brother revived.

"After making a considerable portage across the rocks, we set down into the water and went sweeping into eddies, along the great rapids, buffeted and whipped around by conflicting currents." The words come all the while from the corner, I cannot say why I mistook the voice so familiar to me—even without the light I am able to make out my man Gibble. "The river was breaking across the boulders like huge combers . . ." He is describing a northern fishing expedition we made an age ago. "Our voices were lost inside the roar and one of our canoe men signaled his discovery with his fingers. He had seen for himself the dorsal of the great salmon, he had spotted the school inside the swirling cauldron where the waters from separate byways met. If we had not seen the fish for ourselves, we would not have believed it, for who would have thought the *Salmo salar* would swim in such turbulence."

This is my Gibble, as learned as ever, but with poetry in him unspoiled. I have lost my urge to strike out, I forget our estrangement, and I take up the tale breathlessly: "I remember it was some hard paddling we had to accomplish, snaking in between the tops of submerged alders, then making a traverse, pointing upstream until a current caught us and spun us half around."

He says, "Now it requires a quick hand to distribute flies across the river."

And I interrupt, "To approximate their location, to encourage your switch-cast to drop the fly upon the lucky point," and in this manner we continue:

"To hook the fish," says he.

"To lower the tip" is my reply.

"To keep from smashing rod and tackle in the exhausting fight."

"Silverfax make a strong resistance."

"*Salmo salar* are not easily appeased."

"Yet they are a priceless food."

"Artfulness and patience triumph."

"In a battle with the silverfax. It is you, truly. Gibble."

He switches on the brass lamp bolted to the kitchen wall and in a moment we are in each other's arms, locked in a hard embrace. Old Gibble. In whose company I have caught many worthy salmon on our journeys northward, in stretches of swift water, in quiet pools, in shoals, beneath the raging falls. The same Gibble who bound me to the woman, whetted my appetite with a contaminated bride, and went to worship the industrial plant far away south, at the point where three rivers meet. He has been absent more than two decades.

I back away and say with reservation, "We have not heard of you for years. I thought you had lost interest in the countryside." "I am the same, or no?"

He is Gibble, I declare uncertainly that it is a pleasure to have him in the kitchen, and I beg him to provide an account of his last years.

"You must be older than the century, man," I say, "but first you will be my guest and share the pear wine here, it has ripened while the wife was disintegrating, it was for years she despaired. She deserted me to descend into the grave beside her pappy," and as he is nodding solemnly I make an effort to improve the pall, I start collecting glasses to contain our wine, and then I stop, look toward the Idiot still lodged in the chair, look back to Gibble and wonder again whether this experience is true.

"The wife did not speak of you," I say to him, "I thought you lost concern for us." I pause in my speech. I have power unheard of in this neighborhood, if Gibble is here, but not. "I do not recall making an invitation to you. Nor to him," I say, indicating my son. The wife would be displeased with these intrusions into a half-cleaned house, for even at the end she had a strict pride in appearance.

Now Gibble is making a motion to indicate fatigue, so I wave him permission to sit, he reaches to upright the overturned chair, the wife's own chair that I have left upon the kitchen floor. I cry out and rush over to hold him back.

"Not there, no, that belongs to the wife," that is where she fled from in her last hour, that is where she was sitting, enjoying our conversation, when she felt the final restfulness approaching. I have not dared touch it since.

Now the Idiot wants to make an impression upon our guest, as if he had some comprehension of social rules. He rises from his chair and offers it to Gibble, who accepts without a signal of thanks, and I feel fierce toward the man not only for appearing unannounced on this day of sorrow but for uprooting my son

33

from his place. I would lash out in a sudden fury if I had pride enough, I would say, *You smell of deer rot, you smell of horse piss, you smell of leeches and the pint of flies to be discovered in a fish's belly. Gracious God, man, I know what you smell of. You stink of radioactivity!* Without the wife to oversee me I possess two voices—one raging ever on inside and one performing out loud.

Gibble does not hear my inner complaint or if he does he is not dismayed, he responds with a yawn, and says, "It would be an improvement in my health, sir, if you offered me again the wine you were always famous for."

Old Gibble. He has a talent to appease with his compliments, but I am not like the wife, I am not susceptible. I pour a glass for him and one for myself, and I wait for an explanation.

After a deep draught he says, "I went directly to the church, my friend, as soon as I heard of the wife's end."

"That was gentle of you." I mock his concern, remembering the walnut box containing the wife, knowing that any comfort short of the word that would revive her is useless to an old angler.

"I said to myself, the husband needs Gibble wisdom more than ever now; it is a fact that you are solitary after so many years."

"Fifty-three years," I remind him.

"After fifty-three years," he says. "I was there in the back of the chapel but you paid no attention to me, you seemed to find a fascination in the flowers"—irises, and there was one with the tawny petals lapping backward like a dog's tongue curling.

Gibble's words have recalled for me the service, the box, the wife, her sharp tongue and my lifetime spent involuntarily.

I return to him, "You are nought but a traitor. I bid you gone. Go to Adenburg, go join your cousin. You were always so familiar with her, there was no space between you for me. Gibble, I have left my Skylark in the parking lot, you may claim it as yours if you do as I bid. It is yours, man, and now take leave of me."

I dangle the keys but I do not yet pass them over, Gibble clearly intends to remain, he rambles on in false compliment of the organ song that flowed as honey into the ear, and this descrip-

34

tion of music leads him to say, "Friend, I have explained to you the inner workings of a cricket, have I not?"

Such a rare scientist, but I have no interest in his philosophizing this afternoon, I have been beset by tragedy and need time to recover. He wants to make known to me how inside a cricket there is a creamy yellow membrane, soft as the fish gut we use for our leaders, it provides a curtain to the two hollow chapels inside.

Gibble goes on about the cricket and then he stops, looks toward my son, and says fondly, "I remember when you were the size of a large rabbit."

It makes me sullen the way he pretends feeling for the Idiot, and I say to him, "If you are at an end of your wine, you may excuse yourself from here."

Then I turn to my son, and with my hand around his wrist I remind him of his responsibility to me, for even if he has a mind impaired, we still share the blood, the name, the history, even if he produces in me nothing but disgust, I still claim him as my property and I do not want Gibble to interfere or influence the boy. It is I all along who have been paying for the special caring he receives up at the school, I who pay his bills, so it is not right that Gibble should come in and treat my son with fatherly devotion. Gibble who was my companion and the Idiot who is my son have been absent from my home for nearly an equal time, they have convened because of the circumstances of my wife's burial, and though I mistook them for nightmare phantasms they have no reason to pass as friends to each other.

As I am considering, Gibble explains the insect workings to my son, who surely does not understand, he describes how the wing cover must be snipped to lay bare the pairs of stick and tambourine that are responsible for the ticking sound so common to our summer nights. I would lead him bodily from my home if I had sufficient strength. Instead, I interrupt his lecturing. "What is the purpose of your visit?"

And he replies, "To bring comfort in these trying times."

But I have a suspicion he has been sent by *her* to bring me back to the cemetery, maybe she has an anger because I did not remain for the whole burial service, because I did not watch the soil being raked upon her flat bosom, because I did not return to the church and attend the mourning feast in her honor.

He wonders why the cricket sings at an everlasting rate, why the suitor need make such persistent declaration. Who, he asks, would be drawn by such a racket? The cricket song remains a mystery to this day, yet it is a mystery Gibble conjectures upon: in his opinion the insect is deaf to music but can feel the vibration of the notes as a man feels the trembling sheets of a hymn book. It might be that the voice of love laps like waves against the cricket's shell.

If this is the actual Gibble in my home, it is appropriate that he has arrived now; even if he did not spring from my own head as a fish leaps from the falls, the challenge is no less. As with the Idiot I have plenty to say to my old companion. "Gibble," I venture, then lose firm grasp of my words. I ponder the iron loop handle on a cupboard door. I wonder how many times this handle was gripped by the wife's indifferent fingers, how many times the cupboard door was open and shut, canned goods removed and replaced. I wonder how many times the wife yanked the bulb chain or scoured the floor or arranged two plates upon the table. There is nothing here that speaks of the wife—no ornaments, no photographs, no pink-frill curtains, no paint upon the plaster walls. It is as though she never passed through. Except for the chair, yes, the overturned chair is her last testimony.

"Speak, man. Explain your disapproval," Gibble breaks into my sorrow.

"It was fifty-three years ago you had an impulse to deprive me of my freedom, my solitary nights, my private ways," I begin.

"A wife was your suggestion."

"You sent for your cousin knowing full well how she would handle me, you filled my heart with desire as you filled my head with your prophecy of doom, all along you have been in command and I never knew."

"An obedient wife, yes?"

I point to the Idiot and ask if he is truly the product of obedience. Gibble has no answer for me, I have stumped him here.

"It was fifty-three years ago that the Pastor decreed our union," I continue, "and it has been for fifty-three years that the wife has repudiated my passion, she has no interest in the wilds and she scolds endlessly for my bad habits. In spring I track in mud, in autumn I drag in leaves and twigs, in winter the windows do not have a seal sufficiently tight against the wind. The wife has no patience."

Gibble says, "*Had*."

I look at him, confused.

"She *had*. Not *has*. They buried her today."

I warn him not to interrupt. I tell him that I mean to speak now of his role in my misery.

"As it pleases you," he says, but I have lost my place and he must prompt: "Fifty-three years . . ."

"Fifty-three years I have suffered the woman's tongue. And her pappy, he made for great distraction even after he was dead. The wife had a conviction that she was a poor daughter and a shameful mother, and in trying to amend her faults, she neglected to be a good wife."

"But she's gone now, and you are alone."

"Do not force your facts on me! I have you all here for company." The house is not well used to containing such a crowd, not since I sent the Idiot to school.

Now Gibble has no interest in my fury, he is swirling the pear wine in his mouth, his cheeks bulge beneath hoary stubble, his silver hair billows to his shoulders. He says to me, "What is your plan? What are you going to do now? Now that she is gone, I mean."

"I tell you, do not interrupt!"

"Forgive me, man. I have come to offer condolence."

He knows me well enough, he perceives that I am not immediately accustomed to solitude, but I will learn, yes, I will adapt myself to the empty home, I will prepare the television dinners without her assistance, and I will let the dust thicken upon the wainscot. The sympathy that Gibble comes to bring me is not the kind I prefer, he has a gloom upon his face suggesting that my sorrow is his, that he not only understands my situation, he shares the loss, he too has seen into the fearful emptiness ahead. It is true he was family to the wife, sometimes I envied him the shared blood and name, and on occasion they did not include me in their conversation.

He murmurs, "Would it be better to follow her, man?"

I slide away from him and say, "What is the meaning in your words?"

To sleep. Anyone can drown. I assure you this is what he implies, he is an ugly presence in my home, and it would be best to have him rid from here.

It is clear to me what Gibble and the Idiot have come for— they want to lure me away, to hasten my expiration so they can have free run of the home. I am an old man but I intend to hold my own. I am a lively silverfax prepared to fight and I have some thought about the river: I know there is a quiet pool ahead. The torrents have been rough so far, but surely the water will calm, it always does. Gibble has come to lure me back to the wife just as he lured me toward her long ago when he sat behind his counter and gave a girl, his cousin, the instruction to wink coyly in my direction. She would not be ignored. A fly most enticing. A Parmacheene Belle.

"It was not much suffering you had in fifty-three years" is his opinion. "But it is over."

He hangs low his head so he has a posture nearly identical to the Idiot One by his side. I look upon them both, the weak men of a fallen line, and I say to myself; *I will not go with them. Pit every fly, every dodge, every tack against me. I will make a firm defense. I am no squaw to be burnt upon the stake.* My knees have taken to teasing me with stabbing pains. The wife always knew what was best—a water bottle for warmth and Bufferin to make me forget, a drink of hot milk and half a cheese sandwich. She had a spirit admirable in any antagonist, until the illness began, crept across her body, ravaged so.

I announce to my companion Gibble, "I have wanted to consolidate my tackle and fish north again. In these latter years I have been assigned to domestic life."

He shakes his head and explains, "You are still a youngster in your heart."

I do not have an innocence regarding natural ways, I understand how bodies must make their transformations. But I have been left behind and it is the solitude I am not entirely prepared for, the space inside my arms where once I held the wife. If Gibble and the Idiot have come home, why won't the wife make one final visitation? I have left the Skylark in the cemetery parking lot for her convenience. If it were true that my head holds powers to summon spirits, then I could order my wife's appearance, command hot supper laid upon the table—boiled beef and yellow pudding—I could direct the door to sweep open and my wife to shuffle across the floorboards in her ordinary dress, it was always overalls that she preferred and a shirt more fitting for a foreman in the asphalt yard. Sometimes it seemed to me that she was the husband and I the wife. I have in me an agreeable disposition and she had stern authority.

"If you intend to make prize of me, if you want to snag me on the hook, if you want to distract me and bind me in the net and carry me to the wife where she is sleeping, I tell you I will resist."

I have tasks to keep me occupied and I have a freezer stocked with stew, a cabinet with macaroni cans and in the Frigidaire she has saved for me the lemon meringue that bears resemblance to the ridge in winter, a turbulent mound covered with snow. But

39

the spring season is upon us and like the vegetation I am ready to enjoy the sun. I make it known to Gibble that with the cold behind me I have an investment of strength.

"It is warm in the waters near where I live," he tells me, and I am struck by the implications of his words.

I whisper to him, "Repeat yourself!" for I know how the wading angler casts—a well-placed fly will bring a fish to the net.

The man, my friend, the wise Gibble, who had been my support so many years, holds up before me a handful of colorful hair ribbons.

"What do you flaunt at me now, old man? Dried onion ramps, the first of the season? Or is that a new kind of leader?"

He drapes the ribbons upon the Idiot's head, he wraps the band of yellow around the neck of my son and says, "Do you remember how to work the salmon into the net? Do you remember which colors provoke an interest from the fish?"

These are the ribbons the wife wore on the day we met. These are the ribbons belonging to my Parmacheene Belle.

"Man!" I cry out, "you are nothing but an exploiter of the past."

"Red is a color dismissed by salmon. Better, the combination of yellow and black. Above all, beauty is required to bring them in. You will handle a large fish on the tackle with the proper arrangement of colors. Then declare your patience with the fight, and sooner or later your antagonist will bite. Now the two choices are before you: you can exhaust him with the back of your paddle, punch him with the gaff, and for supper he will be sizzling upon the coals. Or you can tear him off the hook and throw him live back into the water."

By the end of his speech my son stands like a female. I circle him, I look at him from the back and from the front. Truly he is the wife, altered by disease yet with youthful ribbons on her balding head, the wife as she was both at the beginning and at the end, the wife who sat at Gibble's counter and blushed to attract my interest. And it is the wife ravaged by the illness, the

40

wife without bosom, without hair or teeth, the wombless wife who was less a woman, more a man at the end. It is the wife past and present. I look upon her, I see how she has faded, yet the colors in her hair are as bright as ever. My Parmacheene Belle.

She has an interest in you, that gentlewoman do.

I stroke the shoulders, caress with the back of my hand the nubbed cheek of my son. The aged wife had hair upon her face—even in the final days she had a strength sufficient to heave a garbage sack upon her shoulders, and she retained a talent with the electric lights, it was always she who would climb upon the chair and exchange the old bulb with the new. I did not know for sure whether she had become what she was not, it seemed I was yoked to a husband in the final days. A flat-chested, balding Parmacheene Belle was my inheritance. A manly wife. But this is a contradiction, for manliness should have made her a survivor.

"Gibble," I say, "tell me why my wife lacked the fortitude to endure through the thaw? Why did she depart from the house in such a hurry? Why am I here while she has succumbed? She has betrayed our union, she has chosen darkness over light, she who would handle the lamp so tenderly, as if it were alive. If she were truly less a woman, more a man, why did she leave suddenly enough to cause the chair to overturn?"

"It is as I expected, man. You have a wish to join her. You have a yearning to rest with her inside the cemetery hill. How do you intend to make it there, alone?"

"I want only to understand."

"It is Gibble wisdom that the man needs. Only Gibble wisdom can provide peace."

"You have a knowledge of this matter, then? You have been holding information concerning the wife? Gibble, remember when you took the foil, and you showed me how the Big Ice spread through the neighborhood? Remember how you spoke so bleak when I asked about the conclusion of such devastation? Remember how you made it known to me that there must be survivors. There are always survivors. Tell me, then, why did

41

the wife lose her strength, her courage, her proud ways? Gibble, explain to me the disappearance of the woman, a woman who had mettle uncommon to a female, the woman you chose for me . . ."

He lets my words hang in the dense silence for a minute or more, and finally he replies in a voice so soft I can hardly make out the meaning, "I have an instinct, my unlucky friend. I have an intuition. I have a suspicion that the clue to understanding lies in the chair."

"The chair cast aside by the wife?"

"The same."

"But it is charged with her spirit. It is the only evidence left of the disorder in her body. The wife decides where the furniture will rest and I have no influence in the matter. If the wife chooses to overturn the chair, I will not object."

"Man, you need Gibble to bring you from the past into the present. You must be like the suffering wife, and then you will understand what you have lost. I will teach you to mourn. And then I will take you to a faraway place where your needs will be cared for, your beef cooked thoroughly, your bath water drawn for you. Gibble will install you in a house where there is no possibility of danger."

He motions to my son for help—it is as though they share a language of gesture foreign to me—the Idiot is comprehending all, and though I try to protest he has uprighted the willow chair that belongs to the wife's final hour. "You must do as I say and be like your wife. You must be as she was at the end. Pretend it is happening inside you."

"You speak in puzzles."

"You will be tamed, my friend, when you accept what you have lost. You will beg me to take you away. And I will oblige. I will take you to a special home in a fine suburb where the chill in your bones will subside, and the food will improve a poor condition, fade liver spots, help defeat a sluggishness of temperament. The house will have a positive effect upon your nature.

Listen to me, friend. I made a promise to the wife long ago: I declared that I would look after your wants."

Now I see his sinister purpose, I see how he means to defeat me with his science, he means to coax me into indifference and then with all manner of destructive engines, sewage, refuse, he means to poison me as they poisoned the wife. With radioactivity.

"Do not try your modern ways on me, Gibble."

"Settle in the chair, friend."

I resist.

"To understand the wife," he says, "to understand, you must be now as she was in her last moment, you must sit in her chair."

He takes hold of my wrist and though he has weakened some in old age, still his strength is superior to mine. He leads me over to the chair, positions me in front of it, pushes me down. "I think you should be sitting," he declares. "This is the promise I made to my cousin: that when she left, I would come back for you, I would come back for the boy, and I would take you both to a home near me, where care would be dependable. I have an obligation." He holds me in place. "Relax, my friend, transform yourself into the wife as she was. You are weary, the chair provides heat. Imagine you are the suffering wife. What an awful thing it would be to find yourself solitary at the end."

I struggle, but Gibble holds me firm. "You have turned your wisdom to a devil's purpose," I hiss.

I know how it is done. Radioactivity will generate the current that will charge the magnet, igniting the motor, propelling the locomotive forward, carrying me back to the cemetery to be with my wife. I see what I must do to resist him, I understand how I must make the separation final and declare my independence once and for all.

"I say now, the wife is but a faded lure," I whisper, the words like gravel upon my tongue. "I say now, she is but a fossil in Adenburg, dead, yes, dead, and I am alone here, in the silence everlasting, but I say now: I am prepared. I do not need your

43

lights, I do not need your heat, your bulbs, your wires, I will accommodate myself to darkness, I will not invite the poison into my blood, no, I will not lose my skin in patches, I will not vanish gradually. I declare now, I relinquish the wife!"

"You give much sport."

"I renounce the wife! I tell you I have no desire for a reunion, I fear your sciences, Gibble."

"I agreed to take responsibility. It was a promise I dare not break."

He backs away from me, gripping the Idiot's gangling arm, leading him to the corner as if I were contaminated, as if I were branded to be denounced and expelled. I try to make a resistance but I seem to have leather clamped around my midriff. I know how it is done. It is a fact that a conclusion will most certainly be reached, as long as the charge is sufficient in intensity and duration.

Situated upon the chair, the very same that the wife had loved so dearly, seated in the middle of the kitchen, I look upon the scientist who had once been a friend and now means to force the wife's fate upon me, I look upon the Idiot who had been my son, I see them there, together, I see them there, the reflections of each other, I observe how the lips upon the Idiot's face match the Gibble orifice, and I have the final understanding: Gibble, the wife, and the Idiot One. I have the final understanding of their family loyalties and my exclusion from them, fifty-three years and I have no place. Gibble, the wife, and my idiot son. I get up from the chair, I break the bondage of wedlock and title, I seize the wooden legs and with a rising of rage such as must stir in the earth's bowels before a quake, I fling the chair toward the shadowy pair in the corner, it misses Gibble and like a fanged mouth swallowing a ball it engulfs my son, he folds over the rim and sinks with a pitiful wheeze, crumpling to the floor. Gibble is soon crouching over him, tenderly brushing the hair ribbons from his face. I see the rust dribbling across the boy's fractured brow, the eyes pinched closed and the pinkened spittle upon his chin.

44

THREE

Wandering the Elements

DISAPPEAR into the dusk, stumble down the hillock, sink into the orchard, *hide, Shadow,* in the camouflage of timber and bush. Who is this sorry hunchback making his way along the path? Who is this phantom stealing through the night? Could he have some relation to the man so recently a husband, a father, a companion? Could he share a name with the man who slayed his false son before the eyes of his false friend? This is the consequence of the invisible power that will not be contained: to be alive, and dead. To be mad, and shamed. To have a home, to give it up. To be an aged man, to be alone in the dark wood. I cannot identify the hunchback stumbling and fussing along the path, I would abandon him to his wanderings if I could shake him off. But he is now my burden, and together we are fleeing the slaughter, giving up the home, following the rutted trail in thin leather-soled shoes that do not keep out the cold. I doubt I will survive the long night stretching ahead; I wish I had a wool blanket, a bed-tick, a dutch oven, I wish I had a mattress pushed close to the radiator and then I could be sure this bad dream would pass and by morning this new knowledge would lose its significance. In my sudden departure I have left behind my rubber war bag that contains everything a man wants to survive—a toilet case, a knife, mosquito dope mix of pine tar and castor oil—so now I have nought but ingenuity to defend myself against the night, and a man who has lost his personal history as I have is liable to be in some confusion and to forget tactics helpful in the wilderness. I do remember this: when you venture on a long expedition it is best to wear woolens, and like a simpleton I chose this morning flimsy, colorful dress to improve my spirits, I chose flashy polyester instead of the brown-speckled suit, and now I suffer the cold because of my foolishness, the wind reaches with ice fingers between the buttons of my mackintosh, pries open my jacket and cruelly scrapes at my chest.

Wife! I ask you how could you have deceived me, pretending love when all the time you were plotting my captivity? I wonder what passion passed through you, woman, when you envisioned me chained to a crib, relying on nurses to feed me my meals, as if I were more babe than man, incapable of feeding myself.

The thought of such dishonor makes me sour inside and from the deepest grotto of my soul there is a stirring, I feel it rising, I cannot swallow it down, the thought of the wife and Gibble devising my imprisonment brings the mulch up through my gullet, and with a heaving I expel the rot, I let go fifty-three years upon the forest floor, staining perhaps a toadstool or the frond of a fern. It is so dark here, there seems to be an arm locked around me in a firm embrace, squeezing once and then again and again, causing me to make such groans that thunder through the night, fifty-three years and I have nought but waste to show for it and no roof to divide my room from the sky.

You know I have heard of fish that have a language to express their discontent; in southern swamps there is a species that will shriek and scream when drawn from the water and teased open with a knife blade. And in the tropical jungles rare fish hum cheerfully beneath the surface of the water, though you will not hear their songs unless you suffer to plunge yourself into the river up to your ears, for the sound does not carry into the air. I wonder how far my bullish grunts travel through the night. There are lights to be seen through the leafless branches, kitchens where folks gather to talk over the day before retiring, and I expect they do not hear beyond the walls of their home, just as fish do not hear beyond the surface of the water. You may bellow and curse and fill the neighborhood with your ire, yet the fish will remain placid inside the stream, but dangle your toe in the water, make a gentle plash in the reeds, and the fish will dart and scatter.

Do fish actually hear? you might ask if you do not have an intimate knowledge of their ways. Do fish see? Do fish taste? I answer that a fish has senses refined inside the water. Some fish have a wary skill to match an angler's art, but outside the water they are soon dead. We all belong in our proper element, an old man needs to retain a roof over his head just as the fish need water surrounding them.

I struggle onward and the forest grows ever darker, how long I have wandered I cannot say, I know only that I must put a distance between myself and my crime. I have a recollection of a glade far into the wood and I wander in that direction, weary enough so the thought of the wife's betrayal is not a sproat hook ripping my gums, it is more the tip of a gaffing pole in my side as I hobble along the path. My legs are weak from this effort of flight but I remind myself of the punishment assigned to men who murder their sons: extinction by the burning chair. The thought urges me on beneath the snarled canopy of beech and oak, and the trees find it amusing to lift their roots from the ground, causing me to trip, to flounder, but I do not fall, they will not bring me to my knees. I have enough passion in me yet along with spare time for a new beginning, and if I had but wool upon my chest I would be content, and perhaps a flask of whiskey and a box of hardtack and two pounds of salt. With these supplies and a coverlet, a slipcase to fill with weeds, my lance-wood rod and a gut leader, I could wander the woods for a season or more.

I am an old man and it is true I have the additional burden of my crime, but I have skill that comes from long experience and would not be afraid if only I had adequate provisions.

Even Gibble used to remark upon my wilderness talent when we made our journeys north in search of pike and silverfax. I remember well how the ungainly Gibble used to stand at the edge of deep water with his trousers rolled up, and when he hooked his prey he would flap his elbows, boots slopping in the muck, and when he finally brought the fish to shore he would deliver a lecture in scientific gibberish, he would show off his technical knowledge as he was extracting the hook from the jaw of the fish, yet I was the one who could dance my fingers upon the wire and have the hook dislodged quick.

But why am I considering the scientist when he is no longer a reality to me? He remains a bad dream in my kitchen, attending to the boy whom I once mistook as my son, while I have been cast out, and if I am sure of nothing else, I know that I must stay warm until morning, toward this I need direct all my efforts to survive this bitter March cold. The soil is jagged again beneath the toothy frost, the trees are grainy in the dusk. Behind me there is blood, ahead only night. I climb the sloping path with heavy heart. Such a chill must surround the box containing the woman, my wife, she is underground by now, embedded in satin cushions. I will not tell how much I spent to provide her final comfort, I wanted only to make sure she had some protection against the winter still lingering in the earth. But why am I considering the wife when it has been revealed to me that for fifty-three years our marriage was not true?

I have read such fantastical things in the supermarket newspaper, tales of mermaids attacking divers, and infant sons joined at the breastbone, but there is one that comes back to haunt me, I wish I could forget. The paper told of a man who roams the mountains, he travels miles each night and because of bunions and corns upon his feet there are no shoes misshapen enough to fit him, so he remains barefoot through the winter, and there are people in Utah, Wyoming, Alberta, who have seen his prints in the snow. Who knows but that he heads eastward? He imagines himself a king, he has an aversion to wanderers because he suspects that every passing individual means to strike him dead and take over, he is skittish in the wilderness and rarely spotted, but there have been incidents reported when woodland travelers have been found mauled, and the doctors have attested that the savagery was done by human teeth.

If I claimed such political power and was all the time fearing for my title, I too would come down hard on individuals who trespassed into my territory, and on a night such as tonight, with the moon rising and the birches pale troops assembled, the barefoot king might be close by, observing me from behind a shadbush, he might hear my shoes snapping frozen twigs along the path, he might hear me panting. It would be best to trot light as a deer but my body does not move according to my inclination, I shuffle and stumble and drag through dead leaves, I make a racket to wake the forest. Surely the wild king is near, surveying me, and soon . . . but up ahead I see some sort of shelter, a cottage or abandoned coop—no, it is only the dented carcass of a truck, the side windows shattered, the windshield intact but webbed with tangled cracks. Now if my recollection is dependable there is a road not much traveled on the ridge above this glade, yet how the truck flew from there to here through the resisting brush is a miracle. Perhaps the victims are in the back seat even now, motionless bodies, blood-crusted, staring ahead. I must make a careful approach—it is no lie that a man whose eyes meet the eyes of the dead will not live to the next dawn. I peer through the side window and see only clods of dirt, beer cans mashed squat, cigarette butts, and upon the torn seat cushion bits of broken glass.

Now I wonder what became of the driver and why he needed to travel so speedily along the ridge road. Likely he was on his way from Franklin City, you know the saloon keepers in that town can spur a man to madness with their sweet berry brandies and their anecdotes of love. I have heard such fabulous descriptions of the activity in second-story rooms—females knotted to bedposts, clad in nought but seashells and lace—I have heard tell of ladies who agree to brutal impalement, sometimes I do not understand womanflesh. Newly wedded, I would sit fixed upon my stool and listen rapt to the speaker behind the counter, and afterward, outside the bar, the streetlights would throb blue and red, I would confuse my time and place, I would wander like a stunned soldier or a king dethroned.

I do not forget how one night I walked the streets until sunrise, and I tell you, when I found my Buick at the curbside where I had left it I made a silent vow to stay true to the wife in vision as well as in practice thereafter. When I reached home I found her making cake from a packaged mix—she had no patience with old-fashioned cooking, she had learned to prefer canned foods and easy mixes—so that morning she was pretending to bake but I knew she had some worry for me, we had been married three years and a month and I had taken off to town to forget my debts. Those were troubled days when I did not know how to meet the bills, and though the tax revenuer no longer came knocking on the door, still he sent .his invoice by mail, and the wife always agreed to his high price. She submitted to the government while to me she was forever resisting, as on that morning I arrived home, she pretended I was but a passing shadow. It is true I had been unbalanced by the abundance of drink in town, and when I came into the kitchen and found my wife beating water into gingercake powder I showed neither irritation nor desire, I still was preoccupied with the awful possibilities of saloon love. I did not acknowledge her and she did not acknowledge me, I crept up the stairs, threw myself upon the mattress and when I awoke in the afternoon I still wore the same soiled clothes. I tell you it took more than a week before I was able to split the wife with spirit, and I am not sure if she entirely forgave me for my long absence, always she was disapproving of me, I could do no right, and now there is no chance left to repair her opinion.

Tonight is yet a wide river to cross, and if the pickup truck is not an inspiring home, still it offers shelter, and on the seat is a tarp that will serve me as a coverlet. I pull open the door and climb inside, wipe the cushions clear of rubbish and post myself lengthwise, squeezing my head beneath the steering wheel and my knees beneath the dashboard. I will bear drought and blight, I will accommodate the return of the Big Ice, I will endure the plague, rather than allow myself to be snared by the law. I have savage instinct, I will fight through to the end. If you could look upon me you would see blood splintering my eyes, you would see my lower jaw thrust out, the lip sneered to reveal the remaining incisors—truly I have enough of a bite to wound an intrusive hand. I would like to sink into the Gibble flesh, I would draw blood, though he is an opponent of daunting strength, he is a devilish pike, built solidly for lightning speed, holding his own in the tumultuous current. I have seen a boiling cauldron of fighting pike, I have seen two shadows below the choppy surface swim at each other with open jaws and lock their mouths together, lashing their tails and twisting inside the water, backing off, then rushing forward. I have found two fish dead, so fast bound together I could not pry them apart, nor did I have a wish to, they stank of rot though I could see how in their time they were handsome fish, before they were marked with the severe battle scars across their bellies. Yes, Gibble is a true fresh-water shark, he has no discretion, the quality of his food does not matter, and he will take into his mouth anything alive, anything digestible, even if it be an equally voracious opponent. I know now why he was so eager to help in my search for a wife, to pass off his cousin as a mail-order bride. I would pay her bills and be as a slave to the family tribe, always on the outside; they could stay a merry group free of vulgar influence. No, I was never good enough for Gibble, he is a sharp-eyed sly fish and I wonder if I will ever see him sink; he grew into a noble-looking scientist in his elder days but I hope he suffers the ravages of slow disease.

What I do not understand is the wife and why she did not stay at the seashore if for fifty-three years she would despise her home, why she traveled inland to find a mate, for she had a beguiling charm in her early years, a cheerful puck with some rough edges, surely there were coast fellows who walked with her across the sands, made eyes at her in the faint moonlight. If the wife as a girl had a hope of fine living, why did she permit herself to be married to such a silverfax as me, who had no pretensions and no ambition to be more than his own papa? Why did the wife take the silverfax as husband when her desires were likely fixed on the sea shark? I tell you there are workings in a woman's heart I will never understand.

If only sleep would come to me, these passing thoughts are dreams that will not permit me to wake, thoughts holding me tight as a gimp snook binds a sproat, visions of the wife as she might have been but never was in the peach orchard, the wife on her back with grass tickling her cheek and mine for we could have been close, our tongues at work in each other as if we were jointly sucking a lemon drop. I have visions of the Idiot One nestled upon my lap, plush as a couch cushion with a quiet in him I mistook for wisdom. I have a recollection of my man Gibble carving a trout freshly fried over the coals, Gibble in the northern woods, his face tangerine in the firelight. These memories crowd to come to the front, they are bothersome as black flies that sneak inside the bed-tick and suck blood from your neck: *Gibble, the wife, and the Idiot One.* I see the Idiot leaning against a teacher dressed in nun's habit, gripping her Catholic hand. I tell you if he had still been residing in my home he would have received a sound lashing for such hand holding, I tried and failed to inject in him a perception of the Catholic way, how the path forged by popes and saints points the believer to the end, making him forgetful of the here and now, it is a path that leads the faithful along the steepest gully in an effort to quicken his ascent.

I announce to this cold night, "The grave is not the goal!" and I receive no reply, not even an echo to bounce the fact back to me.

Now my mouth does not hinge properly, and my eyelids hang heavy as steely torpor takes over, I would gladly sleep if only I could be assured that my reason would return to me at the dawn hour—but without the wife how can I be assured of waking evermore, how can I tell whether this sleep is not the slow solidifying of the ice in me, how can I trust this fatigue? Maybe the enemy Gibble has tracked my steps, maybe he is intending to spring when I am off guard. You might be wondering why I do not creep back home to discover Gibble asleep, you may be thinking that the brave act would be to draw the kitchen knife across his gullet. Well, I have no intention of triumphing unfairly, any angler may use a dozen trolling lines to conquer a pike but I do not care if he has been plotting my captivity for fifty-three years, his Satanic Majesty is an enemy who deserves honest sport and I will make this vow to last a lifetime: I will never charge my enemy asleep, no, not even in the most desperate straits.

It pays to plot cautiously. In my boyhood the fish in our pond feasted upon our birds, so one day when a young fowl met an early death I took a wad of duck down and strung it onto my lure, I pushed my raft away from shore and drifted out on the water. Not a minute passed before a covetous pike tried to swallow my duckling decoy, he took the hook into his gum and tore off beneath the water. Now I had no experience with such a foe and I let my reel whir, there was green milt upon the pond from the plants sliced as the fish dragged my line through the water, rippling the surface like a tunneling mole. It took some time before the pike was played out, but I finally felt the resistance lessen, and just when I thought I had him near enough to swat with my paddle, he shot off again, and this time my raft tipped and dumped me into the lake. It was a lesson hard earned: never trust a pike until he is dead in the bucket.

This was just the beginning of my career. I do not forget paddling myself to the lakeshore and there was Brother awaiting my arrival, grinning at my bedraggled state. "Got your first strike?" he called out to me, I must have looked like a new hatched hen bird and he took advantage of my defeat—"Took a dunking?"— though truly a pike is no small task for a boy. "I saw you fussing about there, I thought you were diving for frogs," he said. "Papa will wonder why you let a fish take advantage of you."

You do not tell him, Brother.

I shall tell him whatever I please.

Adrift in this cold night, I want Brother to be my comfort, to be my friend, a most wonderful friend would Brother be if he were here.

You do not tell him. My brother as he was, a gangling youth with yellow tufts of hair cropped close to his skull, in this moonlight he appears balding, one of the ancients, from far away you might mistake him for the hunchback man.

You do not tell him.

He leans across the hood of the truck, pointing a gnarled stick at me, no, not a stick but a weapon he has found, from here it looks to be authentic in the boy's hand. Well, I must put a stop to his dangerous gaming, the smile he directs toward me means to suggest: *Brother, you are a coward.* He is practically aglow, so pale is his flesh against the blackened forest, he means to mock me, to frighten me with his rifle and then tear off to Papa and tell him, *Your son is a coward.* I will not permit him to spread such rumors, it is time to prove myself once and for all.

I peel my body off the seat and push open the door, step to the ground, and I am nearly swept off balance by a wind, a sulfurous draft, it might carry the scent of the wife as she dissolves into the earth up in Adenburg.

My brother laughs when I have endured such a complete loss

that I have nothing left but my body and even this is not as reliable as I would prefer—while Brother has retained his youth, he has a sparkling in his eyes and a slender chalk face like a young girl's. He is nearly bursting with hilarity, his cheeks bubbling with excess air contained in his mouth. I am going to put an end to his ridiculing. In the passing years I have gained the advantage of size.

With some difficulty I scoop from the ground a handful of sharp-edged stones, and these I prepare to hurl at Brother, though first he lets off a cracking shot, the glass cackles as the bullet pierces the windshield, luckily I have removed myself from the front seat. I heave the rocks one by one toward the figure who is my brother as he was, they hit their mark one by one, demonstrating that I have retained an agile aim into my old age. Now I wish it were the traitor Gibble ahead instead of my brother. The boy attempts to block the cascade but the rocks find access past his raised arms and strike his head, split open his brow, his face is ribboned with blood and soon he is felled, he is on the ground, curled like a centipede inside a log.

I approach him. I go to him while he lies motionless, I study him and see how in his open mouth there are no teeth to be found. As I bend over him he makes a slow exhalation, the wind leaks from his throat like air from a balloon, I thrust my finger between his lips in an attempt to plug him, his gums are smooth as pudding but still breath seeps out from his nostrils, his ears, the pores of his skin, here before me he is shrinking even while I try to pinch closed his nose, enfold him, I do not have enough hands to save him, my brother, the only one I might have trusted all these years, the only one who would have been a loyal companion to me through this long life. I had such respect for him not to be matched by a fondness for the wife, for Gibble, for my idiot son. If I had been given a capable child he could have received the love floating like an aimless line upon the water after Brother made his early abandonment of me, after he took the wanderlust into him nearly three-quarters of a century past, climbed up the power pole, and clutched the wire. I saw him fall, I saw him sprawled upon the ground, but I did not understand. All through my youth I was expecting him to return. Finally he has appeared in the dark forest, he has appeared only to vanish and in his place I have nought but a patch of rubber matting, all that remains of Brother, whom I loved so dear despite his mocking ways.

No loss is ever suffered once, I have endured my brother's death over again. I return to my truck and settle in the rubber swath, I try to put the vision of him away. I keep company with the darkness and when branches rub and creak I fear it is Gibble come for me, or the barefoot king.

During the long night winter returns, emblazoning the windows in silver, it is designed like the glass chips inside the scope that the wife once bought for our son. A stiffened tarp hanging from the rear flaps, the metal rings clang against the bumper, a haunting sound, a pendulum tick. Even to draw air into my lungs causes pain. I have but one desire left: to find a lively flame inside a furnace, to sit close to it.

There is a chance that the knowledgeable Gibble was right in his opinion—there might not be a perpetual returning of spring. I am no coward though I am not certain I can resist this interminable night, I am alone *Brother I am afraid, tell Papa I am afraid* of the blight, the plague, the Ice, I have forgotten how to survive, I have grown dull beneath the wife's watchful eye and do not remember how to forage on my own. I have been seduced by the electrical heat and I do not have flesh to insulate me properly, so my heart is frostbit, gray is my skin.

I wonder if he who incited me to murder my son is resting peacefully tonight, I wonder if Gibble is settling upon the mattress. He must feel a proud lordship now that he has taken over my limestone home, purchased with years of hard labor, day upon day tending the huge cauldrons, heating oil into a glossy liquid to mix with chemicals to make the asphalt to pave the countryside, a bubbling heat would put an end to my distress. If I had Brother to keep me warm, if I had Brother as company, this solitude could be endured, I would survive, alone I cannot, I sink feather-slow to the bottom, my breath wheezes and sputters, alone I cannot, but now from far off between the branches I see a slice of dawn, a purplish blur, it has come too late, I am descending to the silty bottom and here there is no pain as long as I do not let memory intrude—*Gibble, the wife, and the Idiot One*—as long as I do not consider my history—*Brother, see how it was for me fifty-three years*—as long as I do not think of what has been lost or what waits ahead, see how I have chosen the cold over the furnace, darkness over light, it is not a lowly descent I am making, I have reason to be proud as I take leave, but the winter, the silence—*the grave is not the goal*—I remind the phantom who shares my body, I must not allow a cowardly ending, I will fight. With a mighty effort I pull myself from sleep, from night, and I enter the morning, where winter is already melting to teary splotches upon the cracked windshield, the trees shuffle and yawn, and sparrows flit in the brush. It is a woodland welcome enough to revive a man's interest.

Then I see the face, the wife, she rises on the opposite side of the glass as if the window were a mirror and the head my own distorted image. An unkempt wife, a spectral wife, she has come to haunt me, both the young wife who blushed her introduction at the Gibble sandwich shop and lured me through fifty-three years of disgrace, and the wife who has been to the grave.

No, this face belongs to a stranger, a child, a girl with hollow cheeks and tepid flush, you would not say she has beguiling charm. Maybe it is the minnow, my daughter as she would have been had she been given a chance to develop. No, the girl outside the window has no resemblance to me or the wife. She is studying my form greedily, as if I were a mutton chop and she a carnivore looking through the butcher shop window, she swings open the door and without glass between us, I fear she means to take advantage of me, I am an old man out in the cold all night and she has her fists raised, leaves tangled in her hair, eyes puffed as with bee bite—so mad, so crazed a girl I have never seen before. If I kicked out my foot would pummel her, but my leg is frozen and she already has the advantage. She observes my weak form, plans a strategy of attack, opening her mouth wide, revealing her teeth, but she makes no move to chew upon my leg—it is a yawn escaping her, she does not even cover her orifice to keep in the devil, she does not have a courteous manner proper for a girl. I see she has no impulse for violence, she is looking peaceably upon me, reading me as if I were a book in a foreign language she does not understand.

I try to direct a bold look back, until her lips curl upward and her eyes sliver and she says to me with a gurgling that I take to be laughter, "Old man, I thought you were dead."

FOUR

Chapter of Perfection

DARLING, she names herself, but I have a better label to attach to this intruding vision, I will call her the mermaiden, after the murderous she-fish in ocean waters off Panama.

Do not ask me to repeat the waste that has already spewed from her mouth, I dare not repeat her reaction to my suggestion of "Get off with you, away!" neither will I detail her manner of wiping her dripping nostrils with her sleeve cuff. I will merely wait for a quick draft to snuff her out as easily as the day gave birth to her. But she insists on sharing my shelter with me and I can do nought but oblige, the girl claims ownership of this battered vehicle and who knows, she may speak some truth. A scrawny, bandy-legged youth, she has eyebrows plucked to resemble two geese rising in flight, she has patches from the rough winds upon her face and thin painted lips so busy making speech her mouth will not hinge shut, and on her midriff a puckered line runs from the bottom of her blouse into the waist of her pants, a scar the color of clover, an awesome scar—as if the girl had been cleaved into two pieces and sewn whole again. She has climbed aboard the seat with me, she steals a corner of my tarp to cover her knees, but even in this close vicinity I do not know for certain whether she is real or another one of Gibble's dressed flies.

When she has finished with her vulgarities she sets off on an account of her most recent adventure, jerking her hands as if to catch an invisible ball. "It was like this," and off her fingers go, gesticulating, wavering like insect antennae. "I was orbiting this clearing for half the night, trying to find my truck, but I got tangled in the constellations and last night turned into one space-age show." Floundering in the night wood, adrift in the dark. She rocks restlessly to and fro as she tells me of last night's plight, the cold, the confusion, the distant stars that punctured the haze. "Were you watching the sky, old man? Did you see me skipping across the galaxy? I walked to Pluto, I spanned eighteen sextillion miles, blew right through the rings of Saturn on my return."

I wonder if she is a member of the Franklin tribe. I have heard tales of how the boys of that tribe stone old men to death, I have heard tales of how the girls carry germs and pass disease to men who pay for favors. If this mermaiden truly is a female with the disease I do not want her company, I have been close to woman sickness enough for a lifetime, I want to watch no more. I do not suffer from desire and would rather make a quick parting from this girl if she did not have such a singsong voice, a voice running ever on through her story of the night spent out in the universe, it might be the same voice my daughter would have owned had she escaped alive from the wife's womb. She pauses for a moment while she spreads tobacco upon her trouser leg and rolls the particles tight in paper. She offers the stick first to me but I refuse, I know how plagues are passed through the lips.

"Suit yourself." She shrugs, the match flame flickering for an instant, casting evil light upon her face. "You old pirate. Tom Trouble. You're just a toper on a bender, eh?"

She wants to identify me but I will find her out first, I want to know her reason for appearing, I want to hear the cause of her belly scar. I interrupt to ask, "How old are you?"

She has the talking trait, so different from the wife, who spoke sufficiently with her eyes and needed words only infrequently, so I learned to sense her meaning, I knew always what the wife meant to say before she said it. I wonder how these fifty-three years would have been different if my Parmacheene Belle had had a larkish voice.

I suspect a lifetime spent with this young girl would prove entertaining, she may be a slippery prey but so is the sleek, irritable mink, and consider her fine pelt. I wish I had a residue of youth in me, I would have a go at this lure who has come to me as the wife would—in the morning, marking the night's finish, causing sleep to drop away. Staring at the purple vein that travels like a string of smoke from her ribs toward her crotch, I cannot help but consider how it would have been altered for me had I chosen a wife less severe, had I chosen a wife properly coy, a wife who would have remained in good humor for a lifetime, a wife who would not have made the transformation into manliness, giving up her parts to the doctors as she gave up my paychecks to the government. I wonder what adventures I might have had if the wife were a mermaiden with spirit.

How old? She tells me to look at her and guess, she claims she is preserved entirely, like petrified wood, like dried bacon. "I'm about as perfect today as I was when they buried me, the bones of my body, my teeth, my hair, intact," she says with emphatic certainty, like the neighbor child who came to my door one late evening to tell me how the moon had drowned in the pond when it was nought but a reflection in the dark water.

Mermaidens and children share this quality of opinion, they are correct in their statements always, there is to be no reasoning with them, they believe what they want to believe. She claims a mummy's years, and my weak response to her is a chortled "Go on," for it is best not to incite her. Whether she be lady or relic, flesh or wax, if this truly is her vehicle then I am caught trespassing.

So they buried her, she continues, leaning aside to observe her reflection in the rearview mirror, tracing her lips with her forefinger, they buried her with her baubles and rings, her magazines, her boots. But she escaped, left everything behind—except her make-up and cigarettes. She refused to leave her face in that musty hole, she refused to abandon her smoke.

Now she has the aspect of a worldly bard sitting in the truck cab puffing upon her cigarette stick, she appears to be trying to put on a look of wisdom, furrowing her brow, studying the hood, and I recall with a start that this youngster is a stranger to me, for all I know she may be a decoy for the law, they may be surrounding me at this moment, preparing to slip manacles upon my wrists, drag me to the jail and at the midnight hour roast me in the chair. This female is a cunning foe, a rare species, unlike anything I have met before, and I must not linger. I make a motion away from her, I fumble for the door handle.

"Major," she demands, "where are you going?" all the while smirking at her own reflection as if she were deaf and knew my actions through vibrations, as a frog knows sound, feeling it upon a string of gut—a frog has no ears and a woman has no understanding of men, but there are special methods built into both species for gaining information. "You, old soldier, you don't mean to leave me here?" She leers, unleashing her impudence. "I thought we might become friends."

Soldier, she assumes, *friends*, she mocks. Well, I tell you I will not depart until I try my authority on her: if I were a screen star I would throw her upon the mattress be she hobbled or free, I would have my way with her if only I retained sufficient muscle. Who knows but that I might have ability to take advantage of her anyway, for she is a wasted thing, maybe her declaration is true and she has been in the past both alive and dead.

"I will do as I please," I tell her. "It is nobody's business. And you—you find a proper term to address me by."

She reminds me that this vehicle is her property, she advises me to stay compliant and agreeable. But I will not be treated with such disrespect. "You would be best to call me sir and then I might forget how ill bred you appear."

Now she forgets her image, she implores the sky, requests from the heavens an explanation for me, an old codger she has found asleep in her broken-down truck deep in the wood. She directs her speech above as the wife used to do when she reached a point where a description of my faults became necessary, she reminds me now of her late hardship, her night wandering, she tells how she planted the vehicle here before she was entombed: she drove off the highway into these backwoods, assuming the trees would keep her truck safe until she could come back for it, the weeds would keep it camouflaged. "I meant to return in a month. And then the centuries passed, I lost track of time."

Well, she is back, the truck has sat patiently but I am here to complicate the reunion. She stops, fingers the webbed windshield, murmuring something about the precision of the pattern, the marvelous design.

Now do not ask me for her meaning, as usual there is no sense in womantalk, she is one who prefers the sound of her words above the content. The child needs discipline, you would think she was whelped by a wolf, she is all instinct and no poise, likely nought but a loose Franklin girl. There are no females to be trusted—they all have their loyalties hidden and their surfaces are designed to draw attention from a man, to steal the weekly paycheck and the seed from a man. I tell you women are false.

"We might find we have something in common," she says, as if she could hear my private thoughts.

I make no reply, I can see she is preparing to ensnare me, she intrudes without invitation, claiming this truck as her property, she has been speaking fantasy and is indifferent to my condition since her first acknowledgment—she thought I was dead, little would she care if it were true. Now she has gone ahead and filled the cab space with her tobacco smoke, for she has no consideration for an old angler, this is how it is with girls today. They seem to be suffering the modern condition—as the land becomes cultivated and the air thick with poisonous activity, so do the females decay. Looking upon the mermaiden, I predict she will suffer a fate similar to the wife—her face is flushed with rosy talcum, animated, the girl is of brighter hue but underneath the artificial color she has the same poor quality of flesh. And such a scar that shows she has already been carved and mended, just like the wife. Still, if she were scrubbed, polished, fed a hearty meal, her charm might take on an exciting nature, a dangerous nature, she looks like she could be trying sport.

"I mean," she says, "here we are. In the interior. Me in search of my truck, and you running away from your Miss."

Truly the woman is a siren! I see the foul intention glimmering in her eye as she makes this slow circling toward my crime. "Yeah, an old man running away from his Miss."

She is trying to yank from me a full confession, she might be one of the school nuns in disguise, or maybe she has been sent by Gibble as my torment. I shall warn him: *Gibble, you will smash your rod unless you lower the tip.* I wonder if he would understand the true nature of my advice. I am a stubborn fighter and must be given a hard blow to be defeated, the man must have strong killing powers if he wants to make me his victim. I will lead Gibble to the verge of rapids, I will entice him out into the deepening water and laugh aloud as he disappears inside a broad patch of foam.

"You must have slipped soundlessly away," she charges. "No bags with you, no blankets. Do you even care that you've left her behind?" Well, she will soon find out I will not be taken easily. "You're not sophisticated like Tom Thumb," she assesses, "not so hefty as Fatty Mack. But you're an oddity all right, a curiosity, an old man running away from his Miss."

I bear the onslaught—the girl has knowledge of my deed, there is nothing to be done but to let her announce my guilt, her power is like the electrical current that steals muscle strength, her accusations unnerve me. I must collect my scattered defense, prepare to turn and make a sudden strike.

She says that likely my woman is sorrowful, likely the wife has a mug of cocoa waiting there on my bed table. "But you don't care. Gather round! Come see! A faithless old man captured with great difficulty, brought to this country, a one-time-only exhibition!"

However she chooses to display me, announce me, abuse me, I see now she does not know the facts, she does not know of the wife's condition, she has been inventing my state and now her version does not match up with the truth; she has finally missed the mark, drifted further into a faulty account.

"And right this minute the jilted lady is mixing pancake batter, squeezing oranges . . ."

Not only is she wrong in her suggestion of the wife's existence, she is also wrong in her description of the breakfast meal, for the wife never slaved over the stove for me in the early morning, she would do nought but shake me awake, set out the kettle, and make a fire down in the cellar, returning to the kitchen with coal dust smudged upon her brow. She thought the fire was enough of a morning task and she would take her own breakfast at her leisure, leaving me to forage among the cereal packages for sustenance. Only on Sundays did she take the trouble to fix a pot of boiled rice with syrup for her husband, who was all the time worn from industrial labor, even after retirement my limbs remain weak, maneuvering about the house demands an effort, and you must have some idea how this long night has come close to leaving me drained eternally of spirit.

"Your fairy tale does not impress me," I proclaim, which produces a reaction as if I had poked my thumb between her ribs, she rattles away, laughing something about my constitution, how I am truly an antique grandpappy, which is more incorrect than anything she has expressed so far, for I have no heir except the Idiot One, I mean to say I have no heir at all. I still am confused over my loss, I forget that my son does not belong to me and my

65

home will nevermore accept me back, I am a wanderer without a destination, not a Dutchman plant fixed upon the forest floor but a Dutchman ship adrift upon the open sea.

The sea. *Landlocked* as a description of the fresh-water salmon is not accurate. It implies a restriction upon the fish's return to the sea, but I know well enough how every silverfax in a cascade, a quiet pool or foamy rapid has access to the wide water. I know well enough how every river turns to torrents which turn to placid headwater which empties into the ocean. The ponds full of fish food are connected to the salt water by stretches of swift river. There is to be found no true lake that does not flow toward a more encompassing body.

"I mean to travel eastward," I say, hastily deciding upon a destination.

She looks treacherous as she reaches into her mangy hide of a jacket and from the pocket she pulls not a kitchen knife as I am anticipating but a bar of drugstore candy; she unwraps the paper slowly as if it contains explosives, she makes a line across the chocolate with her ragged thumbnail and then she splits the candy, twisting each half to break the string of caramel.

"Here, old man," she says to me, "for breakfast."

I accept the offering and watch her gape as she did upon her first awful sight of me, she takes the entire sweet into her mouth, the chocolate seeps like blood between her lips and she makes such sucking noise as she attempts to dissolve the candy that I am reminded of the youthful wife when we went vigorous at the loving. I have not nibbled into my piece before she swallows the last of hers and turns hungrily upon me.

"If you don't want that, I'll take it back. Yeah, I'll take it back," she says, so I indulge, be it poisoned or hiding a barbed hook I do not care, it is all I have had since the previous forenoon and I am near starved.

I attempt a fast digestion but my mouth does not work as strongly as the girl's, I am like a dog attempting to chew a tarry bone, it does not pass easily down my throat but I tell you the morsel sets me in a passion, I devour and all the while the girl smiles at my feeble masticating effort. With the last swallow I feel a small stone sliding back along my tongue, passing into me before I can spit—it was not the internal spine of the candy nor a snare lodged by the girl, it was one of my own teeth, I do not have enough to spare. Now on my top gum there is a tiny cavern, a useless space, I can locate the gap with the tip of my tongue, I taste the salty fleck of blood, foul as a swallow of sea water, I am near to drowning in this girl's abuse.

"Good?"

She is ignorant of my misery. Already I have less teeth than I require, and when I have nought but rotted gums how shall I sustain myself without the wife? She used to prepare my suppers according to my condition, our final days were full of applesauce and quick mashed potatoes, stews and custard pies, the wife had an understanding of my needs while this girl means to disarm me with her caramels. But I will not admit the truth of my injury, I will keep the extraction a secret, for the girl must not know of the damage she has done.

"You should appreciate it," she says, making imitation of the wife, commanding my opinion.

Appreciate it, she tells me, for that was her last morsel for today, perhaps forever. And now, predictably, she wants to know if I have cash to share, she declares that she is famished, she insists that she will die. She clutches her middle like she has internal suffering—all these women have to make a dramatic show of their discomfort, to pretend pain in order to win sympathy—she even glazes her eyes with tears. Now the wife never had such ability, the wife could not invoke tears suddenly like this. In fifty-three years the wife never wept, not even after her pappy was buried in Adenburg, not even after she lost her bosom to the illness. I wonder what the proper advice is for a girl clowning sorrow.

"Sickly?" I inquire, for if she admits to the woman disease I could be rid of her, germs would be enough of an excuse to cut short our mingling.

But she denies disease, she says she has suffered a long famine. She is near hysterical now and I do not know how to appease appropriately. They gave her bread and water, water and bread, she maintains, choking upon her words like they were the nourishment she demands. This truly is a reversal, five minutes past she was a jocular space traveler, now she is but shriveled bait upon the sproat. She lived on such a sparse diet that it was only a matter of time, according to the girl, before she could slip between the bars of the iron grille and escape into the night while the warden slept.

Was she incarcerated then? Was she entombed? Is she mummy, is she flesh? I do not follow, I insist that she explain herself, she has a delicate persistence like she were carrying an urgent war message across a mined field.

"Old man, you want to know who I am?" Her voice is high-pitched, quavering, I find myself clutching her arm, hardly more than the diameter of the Idiot's thumb. *"Backstage U.S.A., authentic slut, she'll make you blush, no cameras please!"*

A streetwalker!

"Contain your words," I demand, releasing her.

"Now I have your full attention," she says, a conclusion restoring her foolish pride. "I have your full attention."

"Tell me the truth: where are you from?" I whisper.

My interest is excessive. If this girl has a history of prostitution, and if she escaped from prison, she would have a need for secrecy. She would not dare provide an account of my hiding place to the authorities, she would not dare make a proclamation of my whereabouts, for that would mean her own surrender. This female clearly is, like me, in flight from the law.

"Where is your Miss?" she snaps back, but I do not feel compelled to answer. "You didn't cut her up and bury her in the back yard, did you? I know about you rustics."

I warn her to contain her accusations, I address her with a glower fierce enough to diminish any foe, but from out of her gaunt face the slitted eyes reflect my rage right back at me—we stare at each other, we drift like two pike jaw-locked with the current flowing overhead. Finally there is a softening between us, it might be the girl responsible for the truce, it might be me, or it might be both of us making equal acknowledgment. This wild thing is a streetwalker and she is impudent, but she has shared half her sweet with me, though she is near starved. We have a need for food, we have a need for secrecy. Arising in my head is a proposition: we would benefit from a partnership. With her talk she could provide entertainment for an old man, and I could be a protection to a young girl, and traveling together we would be in disguise, for Gibble or the law would never think to find me in the company of a weak tart, and who would look twice at a young female beside a hunchback man?

"You . . ." say she and I in unison, our words bumping like two passengers at an autobus door, I wait for her and she waits for me until I see how it is necessary first to inform her of my own crime.

"I made a transgression, and that's all you need to know," I explain to her, feeling inside me lingering unease, for I have lost trust in womankind, and it demands an effort to put aside suspicion and take the girl into my confidence.

Giggling, she delivers her reply: "Say the same about me. A transgression, right."

She falls silent, contemplates her confession, then she goes on to say how she is planning to travel to Tomorrowland, to use her skills of contortion and somersault, to earn her keep as an acrobat, a starlet on a high wire.

All through her talk I feel in me a rising interest not in her ambition but in her flesh, I consider her night occupation; the mermaiden wears denim trousers and a flimsy lace blouse but beneath, beneath—I start to unpeel her, the dog-hide coat, the shirt, she is truly a skeleton but her bosom is ripe and the moss upon her belly is soft.

69

How would she meet me? She might settle back against the truck door and make no resistance as my hand took that spidery slow journey up the womanthigh soft as salmon gut, she might even grin, yet I regret to admit there is a reluctance inhabiting my fingers, I have some reservation though the girl is a showcase of flesh, I am shy as I was upon the first occasion with the wife. In fifty-three years I have not entered any unfamiliar crevice, I have not known another's touch, and now with the possibility I find that my spirit of adventure has slackened some, the wife is a habit that will not be easily shed. I remember how it was with her upon the marriage bed, how for the wife it was an obligation, and when we were through she turned her back to me and slept sound beneath the coverlet, and in the morning when she had risen I looked to find the spot of virgin blood upon the sheets.

Now I do not clearly remember the morning, I cannot recall whether the marks to indicate the change from maiden to wife were there or not, I cannot envision the mattress nor recall the blood to prove to myself that my bride was intact. During the course of a lifetime troubles arise to preoccupy a man and I have had enough worries without the additional concern over the wife's innocence. I will never know, though I have late evidence that she was capable of deception. I wish I had confronted her long ago and demanded, *Wife, what do you mean to do with me in my old age?* How it would have been different if I had known the wife was but Gibble's lure and I had taken this journey when I still had my youth. How it would have been a whole lifetime ahead if I had left the house in my early manhood and ventured out upon the path and found a mermaiden with an appetite not to be appeased by any drugstore candy.

With the admission of disgrace between us, the girl and I have a powerful connection, and I prepare to make my proposal to her. Putting out of my head her naked form, considering instead how I may use her, I say, "Madam?"

She grinds her cigarette into the ashtray, and I proceed:

70

"Madam, for every piscatorial species there are different methods of casting; for every representative of salmon, trout, pike, or river bass there are appropriate flies and manners of working in the fish." She studies me with curiosity, so I press on. "If you understand the techniques of fly fishing you can transfer your desire from the river to the bucket and earn for yourself an ample supper. I have in my tackle basket at home a Queen of the Water. I have a Professor and a Grizzly King, and I have learned through this long life that be there any interesting fish inside the water, a well-chosen fly, a smooth cast of the leader, and an amount of patience will bring him to the net. What I am trying to say to you is that I am a seasoned angler, and I see before me youth untried, and as I am about to throw my line upon the water, hoping that a sizable fish will bite, I am making a proposal that you accompany me upstream. You seem to be a female of uncommon intelligence, and we both share interest in similar sport."

There is confusion upon her face. Clearly she is no female with practice in the fine art, but slowly she puzzles out my meaning, she understands I am proposing a relationship and she starts like a truck engine, chattering, protesting, not even a streetwalker wants to comfort an old hunchback, no, not even a strumpet will take him in her arms.

I add, "A relationship strictly sporting. I have the experience and you have the youth and together we are an expert pair of renegades. Be it chance that we have arrived together in this forest glade, or be it fate, we may benefit from each other's company, perhaps find for ourselves some digestibles and meanwhile be avoiding the law."

I see the girl's interest perk. I tell her how we would go unnoticed as a pair, but singly we would not be free for long, and with the mixture of our skills we would be shrewd adversaries in both woodland and city. Now I take a few minutes to come to an end of my speech, and while I am still progressing toward the finish the girl draws from her pocket a silver key, which she taps against the dash in rhythm to my flow of words like a bell buoy tossed about by frolicking waves.

"So this is what I am asking you: will you be my traveling partner upstream?"

I outstretch my hand and the girl shows her palm in agreement, we shake upon the business and she says to me, "I get you. We're going to take a trip. A parade to the Fun Zone. So move aside, old man!" as if I were a dog upon the mat, but now that we are partners I am determined to stay loyal, and to show her how I can receive commands I push open the door and step out of the truck onto the running board and make my slow descent to the ground.

"Watch this." She waves the key before my eyes. "Hup! A mad ride ahead for us . . ." but the truck engine responds with only silence beneath the hood and for a moment we are an abject pair.

Now I could have told her that this rotting vehicle would not be easily revived, no mind to me, for I prefer mulch paths to asphalt. But the girl's disappointment hangs heavy in the air; there are conversations between the birds, far away a dog barking, and upon the mermaiden face—defeat. I cannot help but reach up and tap her elbow, she ignores me and declares in a flat voice that this was her last hope, she had come all the way for nothing. She had left the key in the crook of a parkland sign that warned all visitors to *Take only memories, leave only footprints*, she had come from a lightless cell to find an old angler sleeping in her front seat, she finds that he has some reason for flight, and just when we are growing familiar with each other, when we are ready to make the escape good, hope is extinguished.

"I dreamt the truck was polished and waxed, the engine repaired. I dreamt the forest opened to let me pass, there was nothing to stop me." She is not so distraught as she was when she declared her hunger, she speaks in a single pitch, a dangerous calm that must be a cover for rising emotion, just as a smooth stretch of river leads to the falls. "Nothing to stop me—" she repeats, and finishes her speech by pressing hard upon the truck horn, and while the key would not activate the motor, there is still spirit contained inside the steering wheel, and the sound of the horn blasts into the forest grove, bouncing back and forth against the trees.

I seal my ears with cupped hands, wait for the girl to stop humoring herself, and when she is through there is an inspiring peace and far off the hounds have begun barking, a pack of them. The girl shifts attention from the dead motor to the canines, shouting her gutter curses as she pushes and pulls upon the wheel, trying to yank it from the stem.

"Why must you disrupt the forest so?" I demand.

She declares that the dogs are on her scent, fast approaching, eager to dismember her limb by limb. She must be mistaken, but as partners we are equally vulnerable, and I can see the mermaiden is not making light of the situation, she truly believes that the law will be upon us. I tell you we have more than crime in common, we have both lost what we trusted: she has lost her truck and I have lost my wife to the winter cold, and it is the lasting consequences of our losses that resound through this parkland. If the hounds had no knowledge of her whereabouts so far, they surely have been given sufficient clue by the truck horn, and I know we had better depart from the grove, we must be spritely as fish darting from the sound of the angler's boot. I tug upon the girl's fin, I command her to act according to my instructions or soon she will be feeling the electrical current internally.

"Come away," I urge, "come along with me."

She hops onto the ground, impulsively she hurls the key far into the shrubbery, vows never to trust a dream again, and together we follow a path into the wood. Now my legs lack the strength to meet the demands of flight, so I slacken my pace and make bold enough to catch the girl's wrist and lean into her. We are an awkward pair—she has no experience in the hobbling gait and we move like runners on a fair track with ankles tied, as if we had but three legs between us.

Still I hear the hounds, they are speaking of yesterday's catastrophe, reminding me how it came so suddenly. I cannot help but feel unsettled, I want to blame a woman, any woman, so I turn to the girl and mutter, "Why must you drag along when we should move at high speed?"

She assumes a superior, exasperated manner and hooks her arm tight around mine. Now in the daylight I know these hills with a blind instinct, I know the deer paths and the wood chip trails, I know the swamps and the meadows, so I lead my partner onward. She does not ask about my plan and I do not venture to tell her, for it takes all my concentration to trace back through scores of years and remember the route I want to follow. Meanwhile the girl tears a bladder-nut pod from a bush, rattling the seed cluster in her hand like she were the Idiot One and the pod a special toy. I do not counsel her on the proper attitude of a refugee, I do not warn her to contain the noise during a fast flight, she is ignorant of woodland strategy and nothing I could say would improve her.

We progress upward along the slope; far off, the hounds have stopped their racket. The bladder-nut pod still trembles in her palm and she takes no notice of the light falling in silk slices from the trestles of beech and pincherries, she takes no notice of the patches of green vegetation marking the forest's awakening, the girl has lost her circus spirit and now even the wood scene sparks no revival in her, the girl trudges beside me, and from the weight of her arm it seems I am providing *her* support.

I did not know that the law makes use of hounds to retrieve a streetwalker, but we are not certain the pack is after her, more likely word has spread through the land that last night an old man struck dead his idiot son, word has reached into the corners of the valley and the mob has been aroused, they are coming at me with pitchforks and axes, no, they approach me with metal bracelets to secure my arms, leather straps to bind me to the chair.

Such thoughts distract me so I lose my instinct for direction, and now with this new responsibility fixed beside me I feel as I used to when my bank funds dried up and the wife had to sell her fine porcelain to pay the bills. I remember how she would take a shepherd or a milkmaid figurine upon her lap, she would cradle it there as she used to hold the Idiot, she would keep dusting as if she were intending to rub the object invisible, while I remained in my sitting chair across from her, blaming myself for her loss. In truth, all that mattered to her was that she give the pawnbroker an impression of her clean ways. The wife did not mind forfeiting her inherited articles, just as she was indifferent while her womanparts went one by one, but she minded well the impression she left on strangers, she wanted them to be sure they noticed how properly she arranged her dress and furnishings.

"Old man, where are we? Where are you taking me?"

My breath catches upon the back of my tongue, I cannot exhale properly, and I am in a hacking fit, my lungs are worn from industrial fumes, my gullet paved with asphalt dust, and the coughing comes on violently. I depend upon this girl to keep me upright. *Where are you taking me?* she wants to know, and I would answer, *To the Haven of the Persecuted,* if I trusted my recollection enough to be sure of the direction, but now I am just wandering indiscreetly along the parkland paths with the girl beside me starting to recover her spirit.

When I am not so stricken and able to speak again, I grope for an explanation, come up with nought but "We are lost, is where we are," for as a pair of refugees it is important to be honest as well as loyal to each other.

"Lost," she echoes dully, but she does not release my arm.

At least we are putting behind the forest glade, the pickup truck and the hounds afield. If I were sure of myself I would describe the haven where my brother and I would go to rake the soil for old-fashioned trinkets—pottery shards and iron crosses— a haven high up on a mountain ridge, a haven where a damp limestone refuge was carved into the earth.

If there is any place nearby where spirits linger, it is in the

Haven of the Persecuted, where long ago a tribe of European outcasts came on a pilgrimage to wait for the Final Day. They were named the Chapter of Perfection after their flawless square tabernacles built of cedar wood. I know the history of this cluster of outcasts, I know the facts from my brother, who during his short life had an interest in the distant past. He explained to me how the forty brothers considered themselves on an exalted expedition when they set off across the ocean. Forty brothers settled atop the ridge, implanted iron crosses in the land, read fortunes for the valley folk, and summoned spirits from the cemetery hill. Forty brothers went on waiting for the Final Day, and the Day came and went and left the Chapter still intact, and one by one the brothers came down from the ridge and disappeared into town, one by one they left behind the Chapter of Perfection until only one member remained.

He was the Gibble of the Chapter, the worldly one, the intellectual who could do such things as put a piece of wood to flame just by looking upon it, and three hundred years later he was still residing in the limestone cave when my brother and I went to find him. Brother claimed to see his shadow upon the wall, flickering in the light cast by our lantern. It is a limestone cave not far from my boyhood home, the front is marked by a stone slab. It would be sufficient shelter if I could locate it, and if the spirit of the hermit still haunts the cave, he must leave room for us, we are far gone on an adventure that will not be reversed.

She insists she is near to collapsing, as usual the female is first to announce her misery while I have no time for a torrent of complaints, I am busy devising strategy for survival as the mob comes ever nearer and the wind hums with danger.

There is a legend attached to the last brother of the Chapter of Perfection, a brave man who had suffering in him but did not speak of it. The story was told that the hermit kept all his secrets in a small wooden casket, and just before he died he tossed the box into the river and as it splashed into the water it burst into flames. My brother had a fear of and an interest in all kinds of mystical wisdom, for in his last year our nation was at war across the sea, and Brother worried that the enemy would creep like a wild beast into his bedroom, when in fact our foes were nought but the descendants of the ones who had stayed behind when our own forebears sailed west. When we wandered to the secret sanctuary on the ridge we were looking not only for the garbage of the Chapter, we were scouring for pieces of the splintered casket that might have blown back upon the bank by a strong wind. I remember as if it were yesterday how my brother did not bother to swat mosquitoes that drank his arms' blood as he dug, he squatted upon his haunches and drove a stick deep into the soil.

I would not be frightened of that hermit if I were to confront him today, for I understand what it is to be solitary, without family or companions, knowing the world will end if not one day then another. The casket remains fixed in my memory; as it was a closed box lost before it would reveal its mysteries, it shared such qualities with my brother, who died with all his future still contained in him, the years forthcoming locked inside when he was struck dead by electricity.

Now I wonder if the wife was a similar object, with the future sealed. I will never know how she would have replied to my temper if I had let loose on her once and for all, if I had brought my discovery to her attention, if I had said, *Wife, I know what you mean to do with me.* Maybe it would have been an occasion when the wife would not outdo me, or maybe still she would retain authority and order me to aim my slander for the toilet bowl instead at her, I will never know for certain how it would have been now that the casket is locked and the key thrown away.

So you see these woods are patched with ghosts. There are towering pincherries that were but saplings bent backward by Brother and me as we made our trips to the Chapter's refuge, there are fossils of the night crawlers that shared the forest with us, and somewhere there is a limestone cave. It might be that I am leading my partner astray instead of toward it. I have some doubt now that my fifty-three years have proven false, now that I am back at the beginning, now that I have to make up a lifetime: *Why did the elder brother burn and the younger survive?* I have no reply, I do not understand why I have survived and Brother, who showed such promise, left off during his middle youth. I do not understand why it was Brother who climbed the pole and I who stayed firm upon the ground.

I wonder if, on the day that my brother was roasted, a mistake was made; I wonder if all the while I was supposed to monkey up the stake irons on the power pole and reach to the wires to find out for myself whether there was a current flowing fast inside. Surely, had Brother survived he would have been a decent man, surely, he would not now be making his way through the woods in disgrace. It might be that the world has a plot arranged for us and sometimes we interfere; it might be that there are digressions to snarl the plot, shaking events out of proper order; and it might just be accident that the younger brother intended for death still lives, while the older brother intended for glory died before his time.

The forest does not treat me kindly today. We can see ranch houses between the trees, and I lead inadvertently through a tangle of bramble and trumpet vine onto a strip of narrow back street. I try to withdraw, for nearby there is danger of the law in search of us. But the girl has lost patience with the twigs catching at her sleeve and the thorns lacerating her flesh and the mud sucking at her soles, she is ready to take to the street, where her passage would be easier. We will dodge cars, she says, and we will advance toward neighborhoods, find food and drink. I have a suspicion that her wallet is as empty as mine and how she intends to make lawful purchases I do not know, so I think it best to stay in familiar territory. I may not understand this female but I do have wood knowledge, and I am certain it is safer than the pavement, shrubbery disguises but the open street reveals, and without a reliable automobile we have no means of quick escape. I would rather be starved than fixed upon the chair, but the girl does not see what trouble lies ahead along the pavement, she forgets that we are refugees, she knows only the hunger in her belly, like a dumb trout she is ready to snap at any lure, ignorant of the hook hid by the feather. But I have a sense that can foresee danger, and I know what is the safest route—we may be lost inside the forest, but that is better than to trust ourselves to civilization. The girl is a stranger to the region and does not understand how the neighborhoods are full of Gibbles and idiots who are either cunning enough to snare us or dumb enough to stand in our way.

"I tell you we best avoid the road," I insist, and the girl makes some choleric mutterings, but after taking a moment to consider, after tucking back her wiry hair that looks like a tangled leader wrapped around a spool, after digging her sneaker into the soft grass beside the road and shaking the bladder-nut pod as if it were a rabbit foot, she obliges and adheres to my decision.

We retreat into the forest like two smart silverfax avoiding the cascades where anglers wait. There are enough paths to be found in the parkland, so that we do not wander far before we stumble again onto a wood chip carpet, we head along this until I advise a detour, then we move back into the forest, making our trail up the hillside. This is wise maneuvering—to keep off established ways and cut our own path. We hear no hounds, no mob shouting and crashing through the rhododendrons. I feel safe inside the shadows here and though we are approaching noon and I have a thirst enough to cause my breath to stick upon my tongue, still I hold up my pride, for I am responsible for our isolation: we remain free. And if we never find the hermitage sunk into the hill, if we are caught again in the night cold without shelter, if the girl repeats her complaints about hunger or the bitter wind, then I will remind her of this fact—we remain free—and that shall be enough to silence her.

But she has taken to producing strange sounds, an imitation of a cricket, clicking and whirring. I see she is again articulating her distress, complaining of her discomfort. I tell you she is made up of two—one stares vacant-eyed and does not often speak, and the other rises to high pitches of emotion. I wish she were not so much a female, it is difficult to think when I am having to look after her. Somewhere close is the sanctuary, somewhere close is the shelter where we could hide for weeks, feeding upon the canned foods left scores of years past by my brother, and if she would allow me to attend to the direction, I might soon find it. I have the woodland mazes in my memory, and in time I will find us a place to put up for the night, it will be a magical place crowded with spirits, there will be a hermit murmuring and there will be my brother yelping at me to *come along, come along*—he was always the one in the lead as we climbed the path.

This could be the same creek bed we crossed, though now it is empty, a cracked mudflat with an assortment of pebbles. Yes, this is the same gorge we used to crawl up, even then it was a struggle, now it proves a nearly insurmountable task for an old man, and I rely on the girl to drag me toward the top, she takes hold of my wrists and heaves me upward, we clutch saplings growing at odd angles, we dislodge chunks of clay and stone. When we finally reach the top I am exhausted, but I am so thrilled by my familiar surroundings that I rush across the mossy glade.

"Here Brother and I would set for our noontime sausage," I cry. "Here Brother and I would go digging for artifacts."

It is a sanctuary full with my history, a clearing that has grown up with me so now there are weeds waist high and bramble hedges and bloodroots showing their buds. Thinking myself young, I increase my pace to a canter, I leap onward and my knees buckle, my legs leave off supporting me and I am flat upon the ground with the grass washing over me, my face rubbing the earth.

"Old man!" the girl calls out to me, "old man!" reminding me I am an ancient, not a boy.

But I pull myself upright and stumble forward to the refuge, it is overgrown with suckle vine and on the stone slab to the right is chalked foul graffiti. I tear open the curtain of vegetation and in the dim light see inside not the orderly rows of canned foods we left behind but instead the waste of youth—cigarette butts, broken bottles, a flattened inner tube, a cluster of charred rocks—all left by vagrants as was the stench of piss and decay now clinging to the walls.

The girl asks, "This is what you were trying to find?"

This—the garbage, the spoor, the disorder of youth. The children have driven the hermit spirit away, they have broken up the Chapter of Perfection, they have left me nothing to return to but their slum. With aching despair I begin to straighten the clutter; for the first time in my life I have the urge to be as the wife, to arrange objects in order, to wipe away the filth. This was my last refuge and it has been turned into a dumping ground, they have made a final devastation, polluted my past with their revelries. I rage when confronted with such abuse, I am like a cloudburst sprung up sudden, blowing out of the dark limestone cave all the rubbish that has no right to be here, and the girl keeps after me, "This is what you were looking for? This? This?"

With her voice persisting I am reminded of our contrasts: she is womanly, she is young, she is one of the tribe that has been wrecking the sanctuary, defiling it, and though we share similar fears I am sickened by her, this girl who abandons trucks in a quiet forest glade, this girl who sucks open-lipped on a drugstore candy, this streetwalker who is better off caged, who is all vice and has been nothing but a burden to me during my flight. I am holding a dried article that looks to be a peach pit covered with dirt, and this I whip hard at her, it strikes her face and leaves a smear upon her cheek.

She cries out and lunges at me, she grabs my shoulders and starts shaking, rattling me like that bladder-nut pod until I am feeling my very soul swell, I am ready to retch upon her coat front when she finally lets go. She pulls back and observes how I have already surrendered to her, for though she is a smallish mermaiden she has a strength superior to mine. Now she measures the damage she has done to this old angler, she sees how I am sagging, ready to topple to the ground, she understands that soon the limestone refuge will be my sepulchre, and she mumbles something of an apology. She is a carnivorous mermaiden truly, and I am weak with shame, dizzy from her anger.

I am inside my final hour now, so cold here in the dark, but she reaches out with a tender cast upon her face, repeating, "Old Tom Trouble, poor old Tom." She secures my arm tight around her waist and leads me out into the fuzzy light splotching the weeds, she leads me down the incline, away from the sanctuary, and I mulishly oblige, for I am so dazed from the assault that I would not even feel the current if I were locked into the chair. This must be similar to the silverfax sensation when the knife splits wide its belly, this must be the numbness that sets in after the hook sinks into the jaw. When so much is lost so quick, I doubt the silverfax feels anything at all.

FIVE

Obligation to the Eggs

IF WE HAD an appetite for worms or midges or water striders there would be food abundant for us, the day has brought in spring and the insects are congregating in celebration, in the creek beds the catfish will be crawling out of the mud and in beeches the yellow warbler is caroling. Surrounding me there is renewal but I have no place here, I would be disintegrating in the pickup truck or in the limestone cave or somewhere on the path if it were not for the girl, she has shared her own spent spirit with me, chiding me to attention while we amble onward, she has taken charge and I will do my best to prove worthy, for I have nothing left to lose.

It is her intention to take to the street and travel south to her fanciful city, where we will be greeted with fanfare and confetti. As we push through wet hedges and briar she tells me, "Pile granite on my stomach, crack the blocks with sledgehammers, I won't wince. Just wait, Major, wait and see what I can do." We will have hot baths daily and plenty of food, silken garments, a television set. "Trust me," she persists as we struggle through the bracketing hedge onto a road. "Trust me." She leads along the winding strip of tar. When the velvet curtain is pulled aside, I will see her stretched across a bed of nails, I will hear the audience gasp. Well, I will let her choose our way, for my nerves are raw after the night spent worrying about kings and cold and the morning lost trying to find a violated cavern. "In no time we'll have—" rubbing her fingers to indicate wealth as I strain to see ahead on the curve. "I'll buy you laurel wreaths and lucky skulls," she says, but I admit it is a sorry lot for an old angler to depend upon a sentenced streetwalker, fate can truly impoverish the man, catastrophe can paralyze.

I do not look forward to elegant accommodations and vaudeville entertainment, I have no interest in her curtains and trials, no, I do not look forward, yet I dare not peer behind. I had best attend to our present danger, and while I rely on her to keep me upright, still I remain sensitive as a catfish with his slick tube running along his side. He can feel the touch of things far away: he feels frogs waking in the pickerel weed, he feels a minnow dying, he feels the spring coming. And he is the only fish that hears the sounds external to the water: he can hear a grasshopper biting upon a leaf just as he can hear the trout arranging pebbles in a shallow spawning bed. He has whiskers to distinguish the taste of weeds and snails as he glides along the pond floor, sampling a variety. I tell you the catfish is the most human of fish, with his beard made of fleshy barbels, but the male is an oddity, for he does the chore that is proper to a wife, he holds the egg clusters inside his mouth for weeks, keeps them warm until they hatch, and all the while the catfish cannot take in his own suppers, he suffers a long famine because of the mouthful. I assure you I would never perform this most womanly of tasks, I would spit the eggs into the weeds if the wife tried to plant them in my mouth.

There is another catfish quality that must not be forgotten: it is a fact that the parental instinct turns murderous as the minnows grow, turns to cannibal desire, so the catfish try to eat their little

84

ones swimming in near vicinity, they attempt to take back their hatched children as if they longed to hold the eggs inside their mouths eternally. I wonder whether I suffered from a similar change of affection when I struck down my son. I wonder if there are other fathers who look upon their progeny and want to devour them. But no, I forget, I am the victim of betrayal and was exacting revenge upon Gibble, who did as much as announce his alliance with my wife, pretending tenderness with me when he wanted nought but to lock me away. *Gibble, the wife, and the Idiot One.* They were all of one tribe, while I was their victim to be exploited. Well, experience has made me cunning, and I have learned to smell out lies, to feel danger.

It is true that for the early years of my marriage I had no suspicion that the wife planned to have me confined in an institution, but when the knowledge finally came, it came full, and I saw the truth inside the wife, I saw how she had designed my end at the start of our fifty-three years. Now I am able to look upon a friend and recognize him as my enemy, or I may look upon a girl and know how to make good use of her, I have the ability to see past curled lips or the eyes algae-green and placid. There is no treachery in the world that escapes my insight now. I see through the electricity poles disguised as trees, I see through the traitors disguised as friends and the idiots disguised as sons, I trust neither wind nor light. The country surrounding me is polluted with deception and I have only the company of a strumpet for support; we can find no refuge in these hills, no one to trust, so we must journey far, we must lose ourselves inside a city, for there is nothing left in the wilds.

I dare not bring to the girl's attention the sight of a doe upon the grass, a mound of fur some yards off in a horseshoe clearing. Another doe, another victim of the plague, probably the maggots are already making an entrance into her eye sockets. I know the girlish fear of decay so I do not attempt to show her how the deer plague eats into the weak and defers to the strong. I do not attempt to instruct her upon disease, for she would soon be trembling at my description of the slow rotting process, no, I do not want to enfeeble my support. Right now she has a strong arm and a firm direction, she is the nearest thing to family I have. We cannot trust the woods, for they have been ravaged; we cannot trust our homes, for they may be staked out by the law; we cannot trust our loved ones, for they have the mixture of passion and evil in them enough to incite them to betrayal.

Yet the girl has announced her plan to lead me into the bowels of the city, she means to earn our keep with her carnival exhibitions, she will endure brick and nail, whip and chain, it seems she will do anything for the sake of survival. I tell you the laboratories have disrupted the order of the world, everywhere the past is demolished and there is no shelter left for us—this unlucky girl beside me is tainted by nameless intruders, even within her there is no clean sanctuary. Her touch reveals a hard center—she proceeds as decisively as the wife, who would come down to the pond at suppertime, seize my lancewood rod and carry it home with me in pursuit—but there is also a gentle cast to the girl, a plushness to her form that belongs properly to a maiden who has not yet known a man. Although the mermaiden is no longer intact still she has potential for repair, it is my duty to protect her, to see that infection does not weaken her resistance even more. I must prohibit her from traveling to the city, Gibble's lair, that metropolis bounded by a triumvirate of rivers, for I know its trappings, I know how industry corrupts. I must direct the girl as if she were my own and we were poor immigrants in a foreign land.

Now an automobile is overtaking us, and before we can run the distance into the shrubbery the car has come round the curve, there is no time to pull the collar of my jacket over my face, no time to hide, too late, we are undone. Instead of abandoning me and dashing into the wood, the girl raises a suppliant hand, points her outstretched thumb toward the car, signals to the driver, and the vehicle clatters to a stop up ahead. Why the girl called attention to us I do not know. She spurs me toward the car as if she were eager to turn me in, as if she were greedy for bounty. Yet it seems she has some canny intention, she mutters instruction as we hurry along the gravel shoulder of the road to the waiting car, she tells me I must pretend to be someone I am not. "Don't despair, old man, just listen," and she unfolds her plot. In this scene I am to be her grandpappy, we are traveling south to be with the wife before she expires, we must hurry if we want to bid her goodbye.

"I do not want you to ridicule me so," I say, angered at the girl's handling of my recent circumstances, though she could not know how close she is to the truth.

"Just do as I say," she hisses. "We have no money, hear me? We're coming from the north. Hear me? Going to the hospital."

We are nearly upon the automobile, a squat beetle-black vehicle streaked with bird droppings and sticky seed copters from maple trees. We are approaching the test of our disguise—this strain I can barely endure, I am weak with the imminence of peril. But will the man in the vehicle know me for who I am, or will he mistake me for a harmless old hitchhiker out on a Saturday expedition? And what next? South? The facts remain: south is industry, the industry is poisonous, the poison is invisible. But I, I have a knowledge of masks, I know better than to trust the geography that has been Gibble's home these past two decades. Those rivers that drench the bolts and cudgels of the blast furnaces, those rivers that connect the city to the interior, those rivers carry disease, yes, they scorch the neighborhoods with fever. Gibble and his compatriots, try as they might to dam and sluice, filter and divert, cannot sweep the rivers clean of their scum. It is too late, the damage has been done.

I will not follow the girl's scheme, for I have a better one, I have a safer destination—we will travel east, to the ocean, I will look upon the water before my end, I will see it full and I will watch the sun rise out of the surf. In the past I had no desire to stand at the Atlantic's rim, I could observe it adequately on the television screen, and when neighbors journeyed to the coastline, Gibble and I turned inward and carried our rods and tackle to the northern lakes. For fifty-three years the wife longed for the sea, it held power over her and she wanted always to return to it, though when I offered the occasion she refused; her reunion with the ocean would have to be permanent, she would not set eyes upon it for a short period and then take leave again. Well, I shall see what her nonsense was about, I will have a look at the ocean and decide for myself whether the wife's infatuation was justified.

We approach the waiting car. I have revealed nothing of my decision to the girl, but before we reach the back door I mutter, "To the cemetery in Adenburg. We must go to the cemetery in Adenburg to pick up my automobile. I left it there in the parking lot."

She stops. "You have your own car?" There is no time for anger, but I see the girl is on the verge, she is distraught over the inconveniences of foot travel.

"I left my Skylark in the cemetery parking lot. We must go there."

She has her fingers upon the door handle, and for a moment we are two outlaws nearly divided, she has lost trust now that she has learned of certain valuable secrets contained in me. "Adenburg?" she demands, and I can see the spectacled driver inside twisting impatiently upon his seat, so I answer, "Ahead," with a nod, though I cannot be sure, the sun indicates where the east direction lies but it does not tell me where I am, the cemetery could not be a far distance yet with such confusion in me I cannot even navigate through my own neighborhood. The girl opens the door and shoos me into the car, into a dense fog, a cloud of perfumed smoke, I keep my face averted, my hands upon my knees, while she settles herself in back and unfolds, so demure, so enticing.

"Hey," she says above the coughing, sputtering radio noise, and the driver sucks upon his cigarette stick and looks into his rearview mirror for a glimpse of her. He must be equal in age to the Idiot, he wears tinted glasses to hide his eyes and a tie with river bass stripes, he has a meager build without the plumpness in his cheeks common to local lads.

"Hey," he returns the rude greeting peculiar to the young. "Where are you headed?" He has a rumbling voice, a voice that could belong only to an honest man despite his shaded eyes and annoying fumes, already I am confident he will not betray us, he is groomed like a gentleman—perhaps he is a doctor, which would be a good thing, there is a scarcity of honesty in that profession, what with the physicians eager to steal pieces of flesh to use for their experimenting.

"To the cemetery down in Adenburg. We're going to put some flowers on Grandmama's grave."

I turn to observe the creature responsible for the swift fable, but all her attention is directed toward the rearview mirror, watching our driver's face as she spins her tale. She explains how we depend on strangers for our transportation, we do not have funds sufficient to buy a bus ticket so we stand along the roadside and wave down passing cars, this has been our way ever since we buried the wife.

He announces the coincidence of direction; Adenburg is on his way, he will take us as far as we want. "Heard this before?" He fiddles with the radio knob and the car fills with a troop of motorboats, it is an action enough to influence poorly my opinion of this young man.

"Profound!" cries the girl above the noise, but the driver must be privately considering me, for he has already adjusted the heckling song to a quiet murmur, relieving my ears, disappointing the girl, who can no longer hear the particles of song from the back seat. "Profound," she mumbles, sullen now as a pike on the lake floor after a close defeat.

He revives her with: "Say, as a matter of fact, don't I know you from somewhere?" and though she assures him they have never met, he persists. "I'm sure I've seen you before—I'd never forget *your* face."

Maybe so, then, she says, or maybe not, but she is clearly flattered. He expounds upon the nature of the world, how size is deceptive, the circumference vague, and while there is great opportunity and virgin turf, still a man his age is bound to circle back upon acquaintances, and does he have acquaintances, renowned companions, people with connections. A veritable braggart, this one, I do not feel such affection for him now. And the girl has fallen for his ploy; truly he deserves only condemnation, but from her coat pocket she takes a small brass tin, opens the cover, studies her face in a mirror the size of a trout's eye, then snaps it shut again, satisfied.

"You gotta know people. You gotta know the right kind of people," he says.

There is intimacy established between these youngsters, he has lit a cigarette for her, she perks at the offering and that puckered rind upon the driver's face must be his own version of a grin. Do not ask me about the content of their conversation, for I cannot follow them, they do not bother to make their meanings clear and without a better knowledge of their subject I cannot fill the gaps left in their speech. I wonder why youngsters must ravage everything they use, be it a language or a limestone cave or an old man's mouth, they must do harm and leave holes and wounds and rubbish to mark their passage. I wonder why they must carve their signatures upon property that does not belong to them, pretending the world were some contract that needed their names to be made binding. I pity this girl, she never learned the value of innocence, never savored chastity—a streetwalker she is, an acrobat she wishes. She has made such boasts of immortality, such claims of superhuman strength, yet I cannot help but conclude that the only method of protecting her is to keep her indoors, for she has not learned self-control and soon she will defile her body so it can nevermore be inhabited. What then? Where will she retreat to when she knows there is no refuge at the end of the road? It is a good thing I am aged and will not live to see her on the Final Day.

Now the girl is gambling upon this fellow's friends, predicting that they have "leads" to fortune, she challenges him and he mutters a fractured reply about how she has thrown a good pot shot, she has guessed right, and he affirms again his individual importance, using still his bearish tone, though he has lost my respect, there is a devil in him, villainy in that voice. He has influence, he maintains, he has connections. Babe, he calls her—why he needs to address the girl so vulgarly I do not know, I thought he was an honest soldier, now I wonder if he had something to do with the destruction of my sanctuary?

She laughs at this phantasm behind the wheel, calls him a Hercules, but I assure you if he had ever trespassed onto my land I would have been quick to chase him off. The girl is busy making romance, I see clearly her intent, she has forgotten we had other plans and have no time for detours.

If the driver observes her reflection through his tinted glasses he will see her coat split wide, her blouse with the unbuttoned collar, her meaning could not be mistaken, and if I could forget my crime then I would turn and set upon her, for she has no right to be soliciting, to be flaunting. It is not fair that such a sluttish creature is young, with her future ahead, while the wife is dissolving into the hill, the wife who was always discreet and properly mannered and knew how to thin my paycheck so it would last an extra week. The wife belongs here while the girl should be replaced in her cell, who could have been careless enough to let such a wild harlot slip out into the night? *But man, you forget the wife was disloyal*, the wife was false, she intended to put me away, fifty-three years and I was her burden. Like a teaspoonful of asphalt dumped in boiling oil, the wife grew hard and would not be convinced of my good nature. While the girl here who offers herself wholesale has years ahead for reformation.

He wants a suggestion for diversion, he wants her to define the game, and she replies, "I like perch acts. And pyramids. Can you wind iron around your biceps, twist a horseshoe with your thumbs?"

So brash, a streetwalker, unripe. This was why she chose the tar to the soil, this was why she preferred the highway to the wilderness—to incite propositions, to provoke.

"How capable I am, you'll find out," he proclaims, but I tell you, amphibian is what he is, his leather covering is a frog's cold green skin and his tongue flicks fast enough to catch a strider skidding across the pond.

These youngsters are good for nothing but to serve as pall-bearers, meanwhile the roadside slips by and I do not know for sure if we are closing or increasing the distance between me and my Skylark, I cannot help but look with longing at the hills. We are ascending a steep curved road and the driver does not attend to the limit signs, he lets the needle creep up until from my position I cannot see the tip. I am close enough to the end and need no accident, I will go when I am ready and not before, though with my dependency on this tart I do not have full control.

"I got this friend," he declares, paying no attention to the many deaths lurking at the bottom of the steep ravine. He has a friend, he says, as if confiding a treasured secret, a friend who vacations south for the winter, goes south and returns with armloads of valuables. There is a telling silence such as must follow the finish of an execution, with the audience gathered behind the iron door, listening for some sound to mark the end, waiting for death to speak.

I see he means to use the girl's appetite, he means to tempt her with promises of delicacies, but I tell you I have some claim to the girl now and I will not let her be abused. Having recently suffered the threat of captivity, I know what it is to fear a strong foe, I understand how the world is ruled by the carnivorous—I have insight into their methods of shooting and casting, I know the difference between a lure and a digestible, I know better than to snap at a pike's eye floating among the lilies. And I see how the driver of this vehicle is dragging his line soft across the surface while the girl does not recognize the threat, she is waggling fast to his Grizzly and soon she will be split upon the grill. Meanwhile we rush furiously ahead, there is the possibility of accident and I fear that I will not have a chance to rescue this mermaiden if I am too soon drowned in the rapids.

"Slow this automobile!" I cry out, my fingers taloned around the dashboard, and the car fills with squawkings and chuckling, it is the scorn of youth, they are making fun of my fear. I am but a tumbling arena clown, the girl calls me a sorry old bear while the boy does not bother with a description, he howls his mercenary laugh and it is only luck that we stick to the road. Let them laugh, it is nothing to me, for now he obliges, his foot lifts off the pedal and we glide safely around the next curve. Let them laugh at an old man, for they do not understand natural law, they do not perceive how elements such as time and speed are to be respected: do not attempt to extend the day or you will lose track of your course, and do not dare the higher speeds, or you will greet an impact far worse than any collision you might imagine— it is a rule that once a destructive pace is set, the dissolution will not be reversed.

I do not worry for the boy's survival, but I must attend to my own well-being if for no other reason than to protect the girl, who knows but that she would be mangled and bloody from the jaws of the hounds by now if it were not for my urgent appeal to leave behind the dead pickup truck. Who knows but that it was more than chance that we were thrown together.

Since the wife became manly and the Idiot grew full-sized, I have not had the opportunity to be tender, and I have oft wondered what my function is without a woman and a child to look after, all these years working to make the asphalt smooth and durable and for whom if not for dear ones less capable in these tumultuous waters? And then for the wife's cousin to come and tell me I have no place left but a dank, stinking corner in a southern institution . . . It is an awful thing to be homeless but it is even worse to be nought but a caterpillar upon an institution bed, with two orifices, one to take in and one to expel. There is the girl now, a young thing in flight. I have only fragmented knowledge of her criminal past, but whatever she has done, whatever dreary back way she has trodden, whomever she has held, I do not care. Yet listen to her mockery, hear how she ridicules: "The old man isn't used to convenience, you see. He still thinks you can just dig your heel into your filly's side and giddy-up, *voltige à la cowboy*, they call it in the trade."

"And you stay on with him, when there's the whole world?"

But what is the world to her, she asks, maintaining that someone must look after the ancients, and why should she wander when she has friends back home and this is what matters, friends she can count on. "I do tricks, I'm their entertainment. They drive their motorcycles across my body and hang from balancing poles propped on my nose. It's been said I'm as talented as Pinky Lee."

"I'm not much for show. I prefer," he presses his tongue against the crevice in his teeth, squirts a drop of spit onto the dash, "I prefer a private viewing."

"Well said, Gladiator. You're clearly a man willing to pay for the privilege."

It is as though they are caressing in the mirror glass, such is the intensity of insular emotion present in the vehicle. They debate obscurely, I am left out while the girl markets herself and the boy adjusts the value.

"I admire the form," he says, "I admire the structure."

"I like feeling my lungs balloon. So tell me—and be honest— tell me what you think I'm worth."

Is she teasing, does she mean what she says? he demands. "Just for the hell of it." She shrugs. Well, then he must look at her in detail, he must assess. "Just look?" she asks, amused. To look, that is correct. She insists on knowing more about his tropical connection, his friend, the currency, the surpluses, what does she want, what can he give, where shall they go, they could make a temporary detour, *temporary*, she is insisting, and he has implied, *All I want is to look upon the landscape*. *Privately*, he says, privately she agrees, jiggling about, scraping her thumbnail along the window. *Nothing else, just to look? And in return?* A percentage of the total. *Promise me again: take only memories, leave only footprints—promise me.*

There is some more wrangling over the bill, I do not follow them completely, though I have a suspicion, there is carnal exchange occurring, they barter like greedy hawkers at a fair and when an agreement is finally reached the girl turns, proclaims that I appear near exhaustion and the best thing for me would be a brief retirement. She addresses me as if I were a hound or an infant, as if I did not have adult sense, while she is the one bent on destruction. I do not know exactly what has been decided between these youths but I do know the girl has sold cheaply—sitting beside this driver, I can see his lips pale with the thought of the carnival ahead.

We have turned off the side road to an intersection, the driver hesitates and I shout, "To the right!" for I recognize our whereabouts now, we are not far from the cemetery, the Skylark, the wife. I want to be rid of this intruder, to be fixed behind my own steering wheel with the girl beside me. We will follow the interstate east until we reach the sea, I will have a look at the water and then I will find the wife's childhood home and take a look at that, I will discover the source of my wife and know whether she had reason for spending fifty-three years all the time turned backward, longing.

The driver steers as I direct and we proceed through territory familiar to me, to the left are barren cornfields with brown husks limp and rotting, and to the right are the foothills behind a mesh of azure haze. I have not forgotten that the hills are responsible for so much recent terror and discomfort, still they are full of promise. But now, instead of heading on to Adenburg, the driver sets his foot upon the brake, we slow to a crawl and a car hurtles past. Perhaps it was old Schell in his Plymouth, for he lives up in these parts. He might have snatched sight of me and is on his way to give a statement to the police.

"Hurry on," I urge, but the driver has a new intention, he turns upon a dirt road back into the hills, I do not know where this will lead. Why does the girl oblige him? She must have forgotten the existence of my Skylark, our only hope of escape and we are being diverted from it.

There is a conspiracy; again I am the outcast, I am put aside because of my years. First the wife arranged for me to be swaddied like a newborn, and now the girl is devising some similar plan. Tuck me away, she thinks she will, well, I tell you as soon as this vehicle stops I would bolt like a rabbit loosed from a snare if I had reliable legs, legs that would carry me back through the hills to the cemetery. But this is a world full of dangers that will overtake the poor foot traveler, this is a world where a motor is essential for survival, so now I am but a dry leaf to this windy bombast in control, and he decides where I will go.

We bounce over the gutted road and begin a slow ascent, tail pipe rattling, chassis squeaking, and we finally come to rest midway along the slope. The driver shuts off the engine and for the first time since our journey together he revolves in his seat to stare directly at the girl, undressing her with his eyes, pinching a wrinkle of his lip between thumbnail and forefinger. She does not squirm or blush beneath his gaze, she neither buttons her coat nor ducks her head, she faces him squarely, a fierce invitation she extends, no bashful maiden this, you might compare her to a mad dog foaming at the end of the street and were I a spry thing I would run from this female whose hands are already gripped into fists, she seems preparing to beat our driver to pulp. This is the manner of courtship these days, saloon love, the two sexes approaching like wild beasts, full of hate and envy, as if the lovemaking were meant to destroy.

"So," remarks the driver.

"So," repeats the girl. There follows a moment of old-fashioned awkwardness until the girl gives a nasty laugh like the crumpling of an empty can.

Then she is out of the automobile with the boy after her, and I watch her backside as she leads away from the dirt road, I watch her stumbling over shrubbery like a swimmer wading to deeper water. Well, at least they hide their barbarisms from me, I have no urge to go in pursuit, I am sickened by these damnable children and I would take this car and drive it down the mountainside if the key were left in the ignition, but the driver must have an inkling of how shrewd I am, he must know better than to give me any opportunity. So again I wait in a stalled vehicle in the woods. Another female I have trusted, and another female has abandoned me. I should never have been swayed by that girl's cajoling, I should have made an early departure and purged her from my heart, but now I have an obligation to watch over her, she is my responsibility however wayward she be, I must ignore her tendencies and defend her as if she were pure, untainted. She is not an idiot to be turned over to a special school, neither is she a wife dissolving from me, she is a girl vulnerable to vagrant males, she is with appetite, misguided, yet surely she deserves a second chance. If she were truly a relation I would not be fixed here in the car, I would be on my way through the woods, I would catch them before the damage was done. I prove myself a coward and do not attempt to rescue the female, I remain impassive and who knows but that the driver plans to take advantage before brutally ending her existence, he may have a dagger hid in that frog-hide coat or he may just grip his fingers around her slender throat.

I exit the vehicle and take off after the lovers, I follow their

97

careless track into a grove of evergreens, it is hard traveling through the dead branches tangled ankle-high, and sometimes I do not lift my foot sufficiently, my toe catches, I lurch forward but luckily I do not fall, a collapse might be the end of me—I am a tottering, fragile construction now and I must take extra care. Finally I see the pair standing on a bed of pine needles, like a poacher I crouch behind the trees, I spy upon the youths and the view is enough, there is a stirring inside me, hope revived, the wish—long since forgotten—that the wife would one day submit to me deep in a forest.

The day has warmed with a tepid draft but still it is dangerous to uncover flesh, yet on the ground is a mound of matted fur, her coat. The driver's back is to me, he blocks her from view but I can see how her elbows are flagged out as she unbuttons her blouse, I see only fragments of her behind him but it is enough to glimpse the chocolate tip of a breast, I am reminded of the wife as she was before she birthed our son, her bosom intact, indeed it may be the wife spirited back into this forest glade to perform for me a type of loving we never knew. The children here are stationary but I tell my wife could have been different, she might have circled her palm over my chest, cupped one gentle hand around my trouser bulge, yes, if she had agreed she would have drawn her face close, mingling her taste with mine, leaned back and for a moment we would have looked unutterable things toward each other—it is the wife as she would have been if she had attended to me, I told her all the fifty-three years how she must be as the carnivore and not as the meat, still she resisted me on the mattress, as if my loving were an incursion and the act obscene. I am not sure whether the tickling on the back of my legs is the touch of her fingertips or the breeze spiraling around me. But it takes a mere darkening of the sky as a knotted mass of clouds passes before the sun, an abrupt shading, for me to see the activity with new eyes.

Still the children face each other, an arm's width apart. I look upon them and understand how it is without love, the two bodies are used as fleshly currency, high prices paid for the visual exchange. I tell you the world is poisoned and the young people do not understand, one day they will be covered with malignant sores, their spines will curve, the fish will die, and the rivers will turn to blood. The children will scatter in fearful confusion, they will become stooped wanderers and will gnaw upon tree roots and bugs for sustenance. What an awful thing to be a youth during the final storm, to know that the future is forever denied, to lose all time, to feel the past float away while the present sinks, dragging down the last survivors. Such loveless activity will speed the catastrophe forward and if I have any influence remaining I must drive these children apart, I must take hold of the girl and make off with her. If she were my daughter I would show a temper far exceeding the maddest pike that ever sucked the trolling bait behind a boat.

I am compelled forward through the evergreens, the racket warns the youths of my approach, and they cut short their gaming, the boy sputters ugly language while the girl stands in display. There is not the thunder I was anticipating, only the boy's mutterings and my panting breath. I want nothing but to hide. She draws her blouse about her, shields herself with her coat bundled in her arms, kicks at clods of dirt. Finally I find a voice, a weak voice to mumble "Come away" to the girl. "Come away."

I am the fool for interrupting, I have no authority over these two, they may dance and flaunt as they choose, for I cannot influence young lives, and here in the glade fragrant with rotting pine, here on the sloped clearing where I might have coupled with the wife if she had been a different sort, here I have drastically aged, I have been thrown out of my time into another. I tell you age is but a blight, you earn nothing but contempt as you grow old—once the youngsters have control you are stuck in their opinion of you, they will not retain interest in your past, to them you are useless rubbish, you are helpless and you signify nothing but the bleakness ahead.

I turn my back, I dare not repudiate them, I want only to go on as before. I keep my eyes down while the girl buttons her blouse and the boy rages about the glade, ranting at her as if my ears were sealed against him. He is blaming her for me: "This is a fine setup. The pair of you. Save me the pissing inconvenience!"

She returns the outburst, barking that it is not he she needs. Then she softens to a plaintive whine, for it seems she still wants this speculator's judgment. "Tell me what it's worth—top to bottom, skull to toe."

They argue in whispers as they tramp back to the automobile. The girl demands, "I trusted you." He replies, "I'm an honorable guy," and I trail far behind, sheepish as a beaten hound.

In the automobile the driver plucks a hair from his head. "Your market value—this," he says, passing the strand to the girl.

So the deal is decided, the contract settled, he has declared her to be worthless, it is too late for her to reclaim what he has taken. I shrink into a corner of the back seat, ashamed for the girl—she earned a single strand of hair. I tell you she has much to learn about a young man's motives. But she holds up the fine thread as if it were a blue ribbon, a necklace of pearls, then she pushes in the cigarette lighter, in a moment pulls it out and touches the stub to the tip of the hair. The string of brown curls, shrivels, disappears. Now I am not so sure who is victorious, I cannot say who is more disgraced.

The driver pays no attention and in a moment we are rolling backward down the hill, I feel the sloshing in my stomach though I am empty except for acids, there is nothing in me to relinquish, I am a hollow old man and there is no freedom possible with such a leaden obligation.

The girl is a catfish egg in my mouth. I cannot fool myself and believe in her good intentions, I know what she stands for, but still I am committed to her and when she makes invitation I have a twofold purpose: I must prohibit her activity and I must bear her shame—it is my duty to endure her guilt, as if she were sprung from my loins, as if she were my own creation, for it appears that the girl does not have the faculty for self-disgust. She may unclad herself for a stranger and feel no compunction, she may use her body as a commodity and show no discretion in her choice of mate. I suffer to think that had she a mother like the wife she would have grown into a refined maiden with beguiling beauty, and I would have had no purpose but to sit and observe her flowering. Had she the wife for guidance she would have been immune to depravity, a bright, cold beauty, she would have been my pride. But as it is now she has no blood connection to me, only the connection of crime, and I must keep her close. I know the boundaries of my influence. She is mine and unlike the Idiot I cannot send her away, instead my goal is to keep her from captivity. The vision of her naked in the wood evaporated when she burned that strand of hair, I cannot recall the image of her standing cockeyed with her coat heaped in her arms, I am left with nought but the female as she exists here, along with a sense of my loss.

Our driver hunches behind the wheel while the girl whistles an appeasing tune. We turn off the mountain onto the street that will lead us to Adenburg. Docile as a plow ox now, he takes us directly to the cemetery, and at intervals the girl flexes her fingers, stretches her legs, reminds him of their recent exchange: "That much, yes? Priceless, yes?"

The driver does not answer but there is conviction enough in the girl's voice, as though he had made a spectacular payment while in truth she has nothing but a mark upon her reputation. Like any game fish she fell for the artificial fly as quick as she would spring for a live caterpillar impaled on the sproat.

They are known to me here, the old haunts in this Adenburg township—the barn I helped raise when I was young, the fields that are barren now but were once lush with cattle corn, the cemetery where they buried the wife. The girl promises to send him an autographed snapshot, he chews upon her words as she declares, "You've given me confidence, Gladiator. You've given me hope. But now we must get to the grave. We loved Grand-mama, you understand," fashioning the wife as her excuse to extricate herself from him. Well, she may use my woman as her alibi, it is the only innocent purpose she has left to claim.

The driver pulls the car up short in front of the wall and I wait while the girl tugs on his rubbery ear and slips out, a wisp that will not be contained, I struggle after her and slam the door behind me, we link arms, I lead her away and do not turn to see the vehicle jerking forward. I am full of indignation and she with insolence, the cemetery resounds with her laughter, she means to mock the dead, there is nothing sacred.

"Consider what you have lost!" I demand. She stomps the sod and I say to her, "You might as well have sold him your bones." She shrieks, I warn her to contain her hilarity in this solemn place.

"That's right," she says, "he bought my bones, he bought my skeleton. He paid with this—" thrusting before me a small package, a plastic bag, she shakes it close to my ear, it is an herb pillow, a fool's toy. With one hand she squeezes the package and with the other she balances me over the uneven land. "I drive a tough deal," she sniggers, and slips the bag into her pocket.

The girl has sold her skeleton, so she declares. For what? A bag of seed she must have stolen from the driver. She does not exaggerate the extent of her loss, she has sold her dignity, marrow of the soul, and though she may sow these seeds tonight, though she may tend the plot carefully, I am certain no stalk will sprout tomorrow and carry her aloft.

Now I cannot help but wonder what the wife must think as she watches me stroll across the cemetery in company with this young tart, the wife surely mistakes my intention, so to give her clearer indication of my relation to the girl, I take hold of her wrist and drag her across the slushy lawn past tombstones all with familiar family names, we ascend the rise and soon I see the new mound indicating the wife's plot. The girl has quieted now, surely she senses my loss, she falls silent, finally respectful of the dead. I would take her to observe the memorial, I would point out the costly weeping angels marking Pappy's site, but there is a stooped figure beside the grave, a man in a brown cap and a mackintosh, leaning heavily on a silver cane.

At first I mistake him for a monument, but I see him exude a long breath, a loving sigh, as he shifts his cane to secure himself on firmer ground. It is a stranger conversing with the spirit of my wife, a stranger gazing endearingly upon her place, joining the angels in their sorrow. Who is this man and how did he serve her? I want to know, but instead I lead the girl away, I stagger backward and veer off so I am heading for the parking lot, furious at this additional betrayal.

"Why did you leave your car here, old man? Has someone died?"

Has someone died? she asks, naïve child, *Has someone died.* As if she needed to be told that there is an end to every beginning.

"No one has died," I say.

From a safe distance I turn to observe the man, even from here I can see how he grovels in adoration, he is solitary in the cemetery and has come to speak privately with the wife, and I tell you I despise this stranger, my eyes blur as I consider how there was adequate time spent apart from the wife, time available for her to convene with adulterers. I convict the nameless figure, I blame him for my fifty-three years, I detest him until I see he is not so much a stranger as I had thought.

With concentrated effort I bring the bowed legs, the mackintosh, the stooped shoulders into focus: it is the cap that provides sure identification, for the cap is the brown worsted that belongs to me, the same I left at home. *The man is me.* I am here, in my fishing cap with my Parmacheene fly pinned to the brim, and there, in my brown worsted, both with the girl and at the gravesite of the wife. I tell you I want to go to the man who is me, I want to reach out to him, for he is no longer an adulterer, he is a dedicated mourner, he wears my own gray mackintosh among the rows of tombstones. I want to take my place beside him, for I left early from the funeral ceremony and had no opportunity to say farewell. I would go to him, but I expect he would not acknowledge me, his stance suggests a relentless worship that will not be disturbed, he will remain beside the wife while I have upon my arm a young thing of bones, sinew, and flesh, and I do not have time to waste accompanying the man in his grief. I will leave him to watch over the wife while I attend to the girl and we continue. After all, it is the fault of the wife that I am forced onward, so I feel no compunction for my haste, let the other man who is me suffice. I have a responsibility to life while he has come to dwell on death. I grip the wrist tightly, I will not release her and approach the wife, no, I will not travel across the sod to mourn.

I direct my eyes away from the heaps of scalloped mud blanketing the box, I press on toward the Skylark that is waiting in a corner of the parking lot. I do not feel such regret, for I have not left the woman alone to grow cold inside the soil, no, I am attending to her even while I force my influence upon this girl, even while I find my Skylark upon the crumbling pavement and take the key from my pocket, unlock the door and hold it like a gent for his madam, she slips inside and gratefully curls upon the seat.

No, I am not abandoning the wife when I try my Skylark, it falters, lets out stale exhaust like the breaking of wind, springs to life, and soon it is jigging us along the gravel drive away from the wife, but she is not alone, no, I assure you I have not left her alone, I am attending to her even as I drive on toward the sea.

SIX

A Witching Day

TRUE, we depend on the current, I understand the internal workings of this vehicle, I know full well that we are perched atop a metal chassis charged with electricity that runs from starter to plug, lighting a colorless flame beneath us, propelling the crankshaft. But I am master of this power that would melt us as if we were wax figurines, would turn us to a colorful puddle upon the road if it escaped. I do not enjoy aligning myself with the current, I would rather be a swift-footed woodsman, loosed upon the land, but there are demands put upon old men and now distance is of some concern to me, so I must depend upon this motor which despite its internal treachery, has always been honest, a trustworthy servant these many years.

It is best to proceed tentatively, for you never know what obstruction might spring up around the next curve or at what moment my indolent passenger will take it into her head to leap free. She has drawn her knees beneath her and sealed her lips, she searches the roadway ahead for what I do not know, perhaps another fellow who would pay for her unveiling, perhaps a drugstore where she could charm the clerk while she pocketed his chocolate bars.

Now I would like to make conversation with the girl but still some unease lingers in me after witnessing her performance, and I do not know what is best: should I pretend forgetfulness and steer our talk toward sport, should I provoke a dispute over cast bait for a pickerel, arguing for the fry of the silver chub minnow against the shiner? The girl could defend the opposite opinion and our debate would keep us entertained as we wind through the countryside and leave my homeland behind. Or should I remain silent and let her perceive how I profoundly disapprove of her recent exchange? She has no sense of consequence, no understanding that today's tricks will fuel tomorrow's slander. It is impossible to untangle her snarled logic, she ignores the philosophy contained in men such as myself who have been through a lifetime of conflict. I could advise the girl on her ambition, I could help her distinguish between the false and the true, I could point out how her politics are flawed. I would help her to fashion herself upon the wife, I would list the tasks and merits of that good woman and help the girl to catch an honorable lad, I would stand beside her while the Pastor united them, and I would bequeath to them my limestone home high on the ridge, dark and abandoned now but someday it will be warm with furnace fire, swept clean again.

How I do fool myself! Truly the home is lit with lamps worked by Gibble, he is busy ravaging the cupboards, depleting the hot water, he claims my possessions as his own, and the wife is no model for a girl, the wife cared for her man not at all. It is best to proceed eastward, to leave the home behind and carry the girl to the coast where the wife was raised, where she should have stayed put, where, if she had remained, I would not be a wanderer upon the road. It is late to lament my mistake but once more let me express remorse, let me say: How I wish I had remained solitary these fifty-three years, how I wish I had never formed an attachment to the wife, for now I function no better than one of her physical parts severed and discarded.

Enough pity! We have come far. I have never traveled this direction and I should not dismiss such adventure as this, a vacation without the obligation to return. There are possibilities ahead for the girl, we will change her hair and her contours, ply her with meals until she has a voluptuous build, she will not be recognized as the criminal she is, she will have a new beginning in some picture postcard seashore town and I will station myself nearby, I will hire myself out as a lighthouse keeper and fill my solitary time with chores, I will feed upon salt pork and beans and I will listen all night to the surf careening against the continent's edge. At dawn I will descend the steps to the cliff, I will cast my line far over the water, the arch and spring of the rod will tell of the unwilling captive, an ocean perch or bass to be wrapped in muslin and sent to the girl's home so she may enjoy a fresh breakfast. You know it is remarkable how an old man may weave a hopeful dream from nothing, even I, who never had an interest in salt water.

"It won't be long . . ." cuts in the girl.

She has grown impatient with my slow pace, she wants immediate gratification as if I were her own bottle genie, subject to her whims. Well, it seems we have both fled without money, so our hunger must be bravely borne until we can earn a day's salary. "I'll be nothing but bones, bones, old man, bones that don't even belong to me," she insists, shifting her weight impertinently upon the seat, attempting to distract me from the road. "You think I'm joking? I do what I have to do to get by."

How could I possibly help her now that my pockets are empty, what crossroads store would give us a package of rice, some john-nycakes, raisins, coffee, for the price of a sincerely uttered thank-you? After her interruption the only dialogue is her fingernails upon the windowpane, her rattling cypher, there is no communication between us and I pay no mind to her.

But our trial is not over yet. I glance into my rearview mirror and see that sinister tank, that automobile all too familiar to me, following at a safe distance back. I have no doubt that the driver is he—the one who valued the girl at nothing.

"Look behind," I whisper, "Look behind!"

She twists to see, then smacks her fist against the dashboard.

"Fly, Pirate!" she shouts, *fly*, as if I were capable of wizardry. "Save my bones, old Trouble!"

She toys with me as a cat will paw a mouse paralyzed with fear, she pretends that the man behind us desires what no man should ever desire—a woman's skeleton without the flaxen hair and ruddy flesh. But I fear losing her, I must keep her near me, this is all that matters now. I turn onto a side street and urge us into higher gear, luckily these are gentle dips, obscuring the pavement ahead but still of easy rank for my Skylark. I turn left onto a timber drive that curves round to the main road, I set the engine at idle and ignore her while she pulls at her knuckles. The few cars that clip past are all a blur to me, so I wait until I am sure he is long by, and just as I prepare to drive on the girl begins pretending tolerance, relaxing, expressing her interest in this place.

"Why don't we stay here? Maybe we'll get lucky and discover some remarkable two-headed curiosity. Yes, maybe we'll get lucky."

There is something in her manner I do not trust, I am afraid she might bolt from me and hide herself in the woods and I would be alone again. Without a word I put the car in gear and take us back to the road. She makes no protest though I am wary of her changeable mood. She fingers the packet inside her coat, casting a sly glance my way as if to tell me the seed is poison she means to dump into my ear when I am fast asleep. I must remain alert, I must not give her the advantage.

On the highway I take notice of the fuel gauge—now this is a concern I did not anticipate, we have no funds and I doubt the merchants would extend credit in these foreign parts. I do not make my worry known to the girl, maybe she would try to sell herself again in order to obtain our gas. It is poor luck that we are unrelated by blood, for if I had the right of discipline over her I would improve her attitude. Now she is settling back against the seat, perhaps she will sleep and I can proceed with concentrated caution.

But she cries "Stop!" with such frenzy I fear we have come close to crushing a rodent beneath the tire. "There, Navigator, turn in there!"

She has spotted a lunch sign flashing, an aluminum trailer, windows jaundiced with grime, a tin-shingled roof, a diner afloat in a swampy lot. We roll in and to a standstill before I can think to protest, and the girl lunges from the car. I shut off the engine and slop after her, past the Skylark hood shuddering gratefully for the respite, and as I struggle up the steps the gutter flow of thawing ice drips from the roof onto my cap and shoulder. I take this as a portent of misfortune; there is something awaiting us in this diner, something cruel, something hostile, cold as the frost water dripping on my mackintosh. But the girl has already passed inside so I have no choice but to follow, I pull open the glass door and it seems that the half-dozen pairs of eyes present in this restaurant are all fixed upon me as I hobble along the aisle to the booth where the girl is residing, already absorbed in the plastic menu. I squeeze in across from her, I remove my cap and use it as a fan to disperse the stink of hamburger grease mixed with coffee and fried potato, and I watch the girl's eyes troll back and forth over the menu while the six mean-looking pike consider us. There is a seventh and that is the cook, a woman so expansively hipped she is double the width of the mermaiden.. She is indulging in a cigarette, enjoying the last sucks above the filter while the girl moistens her lips in anticipation of her meal.

"But I have no money," I whisper, hoping my confession does not travel to our audience, and the girl replies, "I have a fortune."

A fortune, she says, which is hardly credible, for why is she clad in such a ragged coat if all the time she has exceeding wealth and why was she eager to perform for a stranger when she has sufficient funds to buy her wants? No, the girl must have an empty wallet, but it is too late to make a discreet departure, the cook is pressing her aproned bosom against the far side of the counter and drawling, "You all decided?"

Now I know there are different methods of serving but I do not approve of this woman, who lacks the style cooks need to set their customers in a congenial mood. The girl recites articles of food, and referring to me again as her grandpappy, she selects what I will eat, sandwiches and slaw when I would rather have boiled beef with filling, though I do have hunger that blurs my discretion. If she has a plan I must trust her, though I tell you there will be no naked dancing, no loving performed at any price, whatever this girl intends it will not be an act to shame me, my connection to her is artificial but still there are many people here to be fooled by our disguise, to be passing judgment upon me for the girl's behavior.

It is a fact that this girl has an inviting manner, and the cook, a dark-furrowed mistress, has already softened, the dimply folds of her face smooth as she unpeels leaves from a lettuce head. She carries on a conversation, asking first about the weather behind us and then about our home, and the girl has wit quick enough to draw up a tale about a cruel stepmam who wanted to send her daughter into the coal mines, and a grandpappy who came to rescue her, to steal the girl away one midnight past.

"He shook me awake and said, 'Let's go off together,' that's all, no explanation, no direction, 'Let's go off together,' but the old patriot doesn't have a penny so he puts me to work. I got a knack for contortion. There are postures I could do that would amaze you. I've already earned more than I'll ever spend." She slaps her coat to indicate an imaginary purse hidden inside. "So I made up my mind I want to see Disney. I'm going to spin around in a few centrifugal barrels, swing in cages suspended from the sky, and then I'm going to get a job. Do you know that beneath the games, beneath the rides, they have a hidden city? They keep their greatest performers underground. We'll live in the underground city for a while with the sewer rats and the off-duty clowns."

Now I am not certain whether the cook believes this fanciful mermaidish story, but the girl has related it convincingly so even I am nearly taken in, a carnival above, survival underground— rafters dripping in lightless rooms, bats clinging to ceiling beams below this magical Disney where aboveground young lovelies strut in continuous presentation and the working class keeps sufficiently hid. That is the way in cities, there is space for a percentage of the population and the rest carry their homes in sacks, taking shelter below and emerging at night to rake park fountains for wishing coins. No, I will resist such a fate, I will not drift in urban sewage, I prefer a home high above the water. The lighthouse is a proper location for me, solitary and austere, and I will have duties to occupy me, I will keep the lights burning and suffer the proximity to electricity, for there are lives that need to be saved, boats that need to be warned away from submerged snags and reefs.

It would not be appropriate to describe here the girl's bestial manner of chewing and swallowing, grunting and gulping, I have conveyed already her indulgence in chocolate and it is with similar appetite that she devours her lunch, glossing her lips with slime, ignoring mustard flecked upon her nostrils. I try to focus on the plate to spare my eyes, chew slow to spare my sore gum. I do not know what food I am digesting, every bite tastes of the hamburger grease and brackish tap water. When the girl has finished she pulls a tuft of napkins from the dispenser, wipes her face, then slips out of the booth, leaving me alone in this establishment, so quiet it seems as if my ears were impaired. The men are arranged haphazard at the counter and doubled in a booth, but there has been no talk since the two females lapsed back into silence, and I am reluctant even to dislodge a bulk of congealed spit from my throat, so still is the atmosphere here you can hear the buzzing Lunch! sign as the electricity lopes on through the coils. The girl has ordered me milk but today I would prefer a fizzle, yet I cannot bring myself to speak aloud and order soda pop. *Suffer on, old man*, I tell myself, *this is only the start*. But am I too old to make a beginning, am I not more properly suited to the cemetery hill?

I have opportunity to long consider this, for the girl stays forever in the washroom, I am wondering if she has slipped out a back window and left me with the expense of the meal when she finally appears, her face paint renewed, her hair bound back with a rubber band, her eyes aglitter. I think to myself, *Well, it is a good thing, she is glad again*, a young tart needs nourishment, now she will be tame and we can proceed without scandal. I rise to go to the facility myself, I aim for the front door but the cook barks, "Don't ya want your check?" and I have to announce my desire to pass water. Now this draws a response from the reticent pike, there is a ripple of laughter as the cook directs me to the interior bath. You can be sure it is a closet stinking of human waste and a strange, acrid, woody smell. I cannot find the bulb chain, which is a good thing, for the opaque window mutes the light, veils the filth, and I do not have to ponder the encrusted basin. I can imagine myself at the woodpile at home, and there is the wife puttering in the kitchen, scouring the cast-iron frypan in the water, ice cold, that was her stoical way back when coal heat was so dear and my paycheck was slim.

But it is best to attend solely to the road ahead. I step out of the privy to find my girl distraught, pale-lipped, the cook massaging her shoulder. I approach, thinking that the weeping indicates a confession, expecting that her shame has burst, she has admitted all. She says to me, "I lost it, I lost the money," with such despair I am powerfully moved. "Everything." She spits the word out to be rid of it, and I do as the cook, I rub her shoulder, clasp her hand in mine. It is an unjust world that deprives a girl of her last fortune, there surely are other victims more deserving of the loss, individuals with reserves to fill up their wallets, while the girl has nothing and now we do not even have four dollars to meet the restaurant bill.

But the cook is making a generous offer, declaring that the meal comes free and enjoining the various pike to take up a collection for this pair, this girl and her grandfather, poor wanderers but rich in loving affection. Well, when the dollars begin floating upon the counter before me I want to object, I have been impoverished before and have never accepted alms, not even during the scarcest year when Gibble offered a loan to forestall the debts, no, I never borrowed and I have always paid in full my monthly mortgage, there remains no bill unreconciled behind me and I need not worry about any bank slandering my name, for I have remained respectable despite the troubled years.

But the girl whose eyes brim with tears has already begun to collect the cash, sighing, "Thank you, thank you so much."

Such emotion I do not want to puncture. I allow her to accept this exchange, these gifts are not generated by sordid motive, the men congregating here seem kindly steel-mill laborers, and such a family feeling runs among them I look with pleasure as if they all were my brood mingling after a holiday meal, with my granddaughter the hub and the spokes revolving generously around her.

"I must have dropped it," she explains, and the cook shakes her head, clicking her tongue at the misfortune.

But I have greater insight than the girl and it occurs to me with a shock that the thief remains free upon the road, the fiend of a driver is making off with our last penny.

"No," I cry, "get on the phone to the police!" without thinking of our own position. "It was that devil, that driver . . ." There are questions thrown at me, the men demand "Who?" and "Where?" at bullet speed I cannot answer, all I know is that the girl has been deceived by the man she stripped for, I want him apprehended and brought into court to be properly sentenced. I stutter an explanation of our hitchhiked ride, but the girl resists the idea, she insists that the wallet was lost and not lifted from her pocket, she is truly a gullible soul believing in accident, rejecting intention, unwilling to admit that the stranger is a crook.

113

The cook struts toward the pay phone but the girl pleads, "No, I tell you I dropped it, I'll drop anything no matter if it's glued to my hand," and though I am riled by our recent abuse the facts of our situation come back to me and I recall how we are criminals, fleeing the authorities. The girl has an agility I admire, she asks for directions to the headquarters and persuades her audience that it is best if we gave a complete report in person.

Wrapped in our outer gear again, descending the steps to the mud lot, I remember the icicle drops streaking my mackintosh, and I admit how this is once when the foretelling was incorrect, the evil in the diner never arrived. They were a kindly group inside and we have come through our difficulty with compensation. I am drowsy from the food and drama; I direct the girl to the driver's seat and wave her permission to work the automobile if she pleases, and she moves eagerly into place behind the wheel, she is all quick scuttling motion and short laughs now that she has satisfied her hunger, and I tell you I admire the girl for her good humor despite our recent loss.

But she has the impulse to proceed at a smart pace, ripping out of the dirt lot, my Skylark is not used to such demands and I warn her that she will short the connection if she does not use more care. She proclaims me bad—bad, she says, and I admonish her, "I do not need to remind you who is responsible for the theft."

She erupts in a hard-hearted laugh as if she has shown me up as a fool again. "Theft!" She chokes upon the word, spins the steering wheel, we lurch toward the shoulder, veer back, steady, move on. "Theft? Don't you understand? I never had money, you know that as well as me. Old man, we didn't have a cent to buy our food."

I am not so backward that I am ignorant of her meaning, no, it is all coming clear to me now, her deception of the kindly cook and the six pike. I am appalled. There was no wallet, this was a lie she threw upon the water as bait. Now there are different ways of catching fish of low intelligence, fish such as the pickerel—you may impale a mouse or a frog upon a hook, or you may cut a slab of bacon to resemble a minnow, and this will bring the fish to the net. Such disguise is artful. But there are cruder ways to go at it, there is the method of trolling ungainly hooks from a boat while you sit upon an armchair in the stern, and there is the buoy method: you cut mullet into pieces chestnut-size and for three days you thicken the water with excess bait, and on the fourth day there will be such a mass of fish feeding that you need only plunge your hands into the water to catch one by the tail. With nearly a lifetime behind me I have a clear vision of right and wrong and no matter how pressing my desperation I would not play unfairly. Prostitution and fraud are an abuse of the sport no matter what degree of discomfort this girl has suffered. For these long hours I have dismissed the fact of her crude manner, but with two strikes against her it grows ever harder to forgive, I would rather suffer my hunger than participate in such a devious game. She is jumpity and upstartish as a puppet, so refreshed by sustenance she can hardly keep still behind the wheel.

"You nearly ruined us, old man," she accuses, turning to observe me instead of the road, "when I was in the middle of my act. Tell me I was stunning. Tell me I was chic. What you must remember first, above everything else, is that an experienced contortionist should astound, never disgust. That sap Hercules didn't understand—the beauty is in the movement, not in the frame . . ." babbling on, such a spritely tart now, she seems to have exchanged personalities. This renewal possible in youth is remarkable, while I feel fatigued enough to sleep but I will not permit myself to lose awareness, this girl is careless with my Skylark and she needs me to remind her to use caution. I wonder how much money she has pocketed, whatever the amount she is joyful and proud of the booty. "How about it," she chortles, "Disney and the underground. We're going down, old man, that's right, downtown, and we'll make it there by nightfall."

But the carnival city will not be our destination. "Steer us east!" I command, and the girl sucks in her breath, glowers at me through those eye slits sunk deep in her flesh. "I have another preference," I say with authority that will not be dismissed. Still the girl looks resistant, and instead of providing a lengthy explanation of how southern cities are not to be trusted I remind her that the Skylark is my possession, as the woodland truck was hers, and if I want to direct the vehicle toward the sea, the girl has two choices: to accompany me or to desert me.

"But south . . ."

Yes, south they built the glorious industry, the object of Gibble's devotion, and I have heard how all the trout for miles around float belly-up along the rivers, dead. Around the city there is no skill needed—you need not even tease the fish with feather or worm, you can simply skim scads of corpses off the water with a whirling spoon. "Eastward," I repeat, and she shrugs, acknowledging defeat. This journey is fast depleting my stamina and now that our direction is assured I can attend to the girl with my ears and rest my eyes for a moment.

She begins upon a series of questions I do not have strength to answer, she wants a history from me, an account of my abandoned Miss, and I wave my hand to indicate my fatigue. So she carries on about herself, not much minding whether I am listening to her or not, she is a charged wire and wants to tell, which satisfies me, for the voice keeps me from descending into murky sleep. She describes a home in Pitshole, an odd location, Pitshole, as I know it is nought but a ghost town, a fossil of the mining industry. So it was Pitshole where she spent her winters hopping over frosted foothills and her summers cutting her way through field grass as tall as she until a night. . . What is she saying?

I can hardly make out her words now, she seems to be speaking through cupped hands, murmuring, with a wide distance between us. Something about the rolling of side drums, the audience's hush. Something about a ladder, powdered rosin on her hands, the bar, the kick-swing to gain momentum and the slow revolutions inside the circus tent awash in white light, her body suspended, turning over and over. I see the girl as a bathing beauty somersaulting in the air, her scrawny tadpole of a catching partner stretching out his arms, groping for her wrists, now she dangles from him like a slab of venison from a hook, but with gravity against him he cannot hold on forever, his grip loosens, she falls, bounces safely in the net.

It is as though I dream, adrift in a canoe, float and dream, solitary or perhaps in the company of Gibble; it might be dawn and we drift upon the velvet water, that was a gilded hour when strange light transformed the shoreline trees into human forms descending to the lake. The acrobats may be my own creation, I cannot open my eyes, it is as before, I fall into dream and need the wife to shake me, I need the wife to say, *Man, it is morning! Wife, what a strange dream this is, I will tell it to you when I awake, I will explain how they buried you beside Pappy and I was swept off with this mermaiden, a poor example of a female, Wife, she could have stood some of your influence, but I was loyal in my obligation and I kept her near me, we were both criminals, Wife, it was a witching dream I tell you, out of control, I wish you would come to me and I will explain to you my relation with this girl—why I took her as my ally—for in the dream I killed our son, yes, I struck down our boy when I was aiming at Gibble, who was back for your funeral. He intended to lock me away, that was your wish, Wife, in this dream you were the one who set the catastrophe in motion, I am sorry to say, and now I travel with the girl, trusting her with my Skylark, I wait anxiously for the morning hour when you will proclaim, Man, it is time to get up!*

Now I feel the vehicle slow, drag to a halt, I hear the girl leaving me. With my last ounce of strength I blink open my lids and observe the gray scenery. A gas station it could be, yes, the girl is inserting the nozzle into the car, a good thing she attends to the dials. She gossips with the uniformed attendant, hands him a few dollar bills, then cuts short her bandying and returns to me.

We continue forward, putting my home behind along with all my possessions but my cap, my Parmacheene lure, and the flimsy clothes upon my back. This dream has arisen from a conversion, I have come to know the wife for what she was, no, that is part of the dream, I only thought I knew. I must not claim certainty in any matter, not tonight, I must remember that from the eyelashes upon the mermaiden to the discomfort in my knees, all is part of this vision and has no truth. *And when you finally wake me, Wife, you will no longer be complaining of internal pain, you will recognize the illness as something to put off, we will laugh together at the dream of this young tart in charge of my Skylark, we will laugh at the powers of my fancy, for surely in the passing hours I created a convincing image despite my ignorance of girls.* I designed such a daughter that might have developed from our lost minnow, though I assure you I would have kept her from straying.

I have lost track of time but we must be hours from the diner, for the terrain is flatter, interrupted by a few jagged peaks, not the comforting foothills of home, the automobiles wagging ahead seem to move without design, the roadside billboards announce banking cards and lotteries. A change in our speed has jarred me alert—the girl has another reason for stopping, she turns off the highway and pulls into a barren lot, shuts off the motor, puts out the headlights. She has a need for rest, of course, a girl needs sleep, she will die without sleep. It is good for her to relax, and perhaps this termination of motion indicates the end of my dream drawing near, I feel already a renewed control, soon I will be free of this paralysis of fatigue and I will take the wheel and by dawn the wife will set upon me with a smart shake, we will go on as before. I will keep my brown worsted cap always on my head.

"Bastard!" Her sputtering curse—what have I done?

She lands a slap upon my grizzled chin. I have offended. I wake cramped, stiffened by the cold, we are nowhere on an asphalt plain carved into the forest, no streetlights to illuminate the land, only a moon floating in red fog and stars blurred by the mist, the heavens provide light sufficient to give shapes vague outline. A pale hand clings to the steering wheel, a shadow quivers against the door, the girl's eyes glint with mad fear. She renews her attack, hissing, striking at me in the darkness, but I raise my hands to fend her off and her fingernails scrape the back of my palm.

Then her door is open and she tumbles out, flings the door shut behind her and disappears. She has fallen overboard, plunged into lake water, sunk beneath the surface. With her curse resounding, the sting of her hand upon my cheek, I acknowledge the girl's distress, she is needing help despite the murderous assault. I bend my legs fettered with sleep and go out in search of her, all the time treading on sharp quills, for my feet have not yet woken. I find her crouched upon the hard surface, her curved spine touching the front tire, from here she resembles a ghostly motor with a poor carburetor rattling inside.

"What is wrong?" I query in a soft voice, for though we are nowhere I cannot be sure there are no eavesdroppers close by.

"Go away," she tells me, "leave me alone."

But what does she mean by this? We are committed to each other, she cannot wake at midnight and order me away, she has brought us here and I am lost without her. The stars are drifting inside the night haze and I cannot use them to locate myself, they will not hold still for me, the whole sky seems to be flowing by and we are here, fixed on some island. I can make out evergreens on the periphery, and behind them I am not sure if that mound is a storm rolling in or a cliff. My breath takes shape in clouds drifting from my lips, everything moves past or toward me yet we remain stalled here upon the asphalt. I cannot abandon the girl, it is a flood of one kind or another approaching, a deluge of fog and shadow soon to sweep in and dissolve us.

"Go away," she says, but I am an old man and need someone to attend to me, how can I find my way from here and what then? "Get on. Get out!"

Out, as if there were an exit close by. I would not mind if the authorities fell upon us now, they could bind my wrists and commit me to prison, then I would not have to endure the cold; I may not survive another night away from home. Think of it: for fifty-three years we kept our bodies pressed close to share the warmth, even if we went to the mattress quarreling and turned our backs to each other I would wake and find my arm embracing the wife, my legs wrapped round hers, even when we were resenting each other we could not stop the loving in our sleep. And now to be cast off upon a strip of asphalt, some deserted parking lot or playground, to be sent from here, alone . . . Where would I go? But the girl's plea is so desperate I cannot find in me the impulse to deny her. I do not often give way to youth but how shall I decline? Away, then, into the car, I will close my ears to stifle her frantic sounds, I will open this door, assume my proper place behind the wheel, solitary, in control, and I will drive on through the night.

With the key readied in the ignition, my shoe upon the accelerator, I am prepared to carry through with the separation craved by this girl, I am prepared to leave her on the asphalt, but I venture one last glimpse at the feeble thing hunched by the tire, I give a moment over to reflection, drifting upon this desolate place in profound meditation. Never before has the final dissolution seemed so easy to me. It is as if particles of my body were already lost, evaporating, I am becoming the breath I take, the night air is becoming me. Now I know how it would be to float upon air currents, for here in the car each sliver of draft seems to break off a chunk of me and the pieces are bounced hither, thither by the nearby highway sounds, to human ears it is a soothing hum but I know how the harmony is false, the sounds disguise the violent source, traffic music is not natural and now it comes as a multitude of tiny fists beating hard upon me. I would remain here rather than drive on, the journey does not seem to matter now, but the girl has made her demand so I will go, I will go.

I will not. Our contract is broken, but I cannot stand to be wrenched from a woman a second time, with my body disintegrating I will soon be nothing but a rotted husk to be mowed flat into the land. So in this last segment of a lifetime I must cling to what I need, and if that is an unagreeable tart I still must stick fast to her. I have seen her unclad and I have seen her invent falsehoods, but if indeed the hounds are coming after us, I will spend my final moments with this girl, I will not be left alone.

I search for language to lure her back to me. Through the open window I puff out words like seeds of a broken pod, *I am sorry*, an apology not easily uttered, and returning to me is her demand: "What?" and again, "What did you say?" before I can reply.

She stands now, dusts her trousers, pinches pieces of gravel from the matted fur of her coat. "You had your hands all over me!"

"I?"

"Don't pretend you didn't," she warns, but I see her spirit reviving as she comes out of her dream. "You had your hands on me here when I woke," she says, less with trepidation, more with ridicule now, gripping her bosom to indicate where I transgressed. I cannot determine whether this is a lie she has constructed or if there is some truth. My hands do not remember the touch of her, no, I have not explored, I was asleep against the passenger door while she was fabricating such involvement.

"You are telling a dream," I mutter, though my meaning is probably lost to her, my tongue is dry from doubt, I cannot be certain whose recollection is accurate and whether I truly trespassed onto her. I think not but I do not know and here the girl is convincing me how I went at her while she was asleep. No, I did not, I think, but it is possible, for I have the habit in me to sidle close to warm womanflesh at night. The girl has forgotten her plea for separation, indicating that she is ready to take her place behind the wheel, so I grab hold the dashboard and pull myself across the seat, leaving ample space between us.

It must have been her dream for she is composed again, declaring without fear how I put my hands on her, then pausing to reconsider, "Least I think you did. Maybe not. Maybe I made it up. It could be after all I made it up . . ."

We cannot know for sure one way or another, but she is warning me to keep off her and I am telling her both how sorry I am and truly I never did such a thing. There is no evidence from such a crime, all we have is our memory, which is not so trustworthy in sleep. The girl starts the motor and we spurn this asphalt, we take to the highway again, it must be near dawn, for eastward there is a glow behind the mountains, blessed light, sometimes I do not know how our days become nights, our nights days.

SEVEN

Gut Makers and Gut

SOMEWHERE the tide floods in around a seagull's legs, but it is not here. Somewhere there are stretches of white sand cornered by high bluffs, salt mist to tingle a man's nostrils, somewhere there are traces of the wife but here you will find nought but brickface, tar, withered saplings groping for the sky. The light I mistook for day is merely the dome of electrical glow surrounding this city, our direction has not been eastward and our destination is not the sea. These night hours I have been trusting her while she has been steering me ever deeper into Gibble's own terrain. I ask her what she means to do and she ignores me. I dare not grab for the wheel, such progression I will not disrupt, I have too great a fear of collision as well as a respect for all forward movement. Even now there seems to be some logic to our direction, there seems to be a force independent of the girl, independent of me, a current directing dead branches and wanderers down the left fork of the river instead of down the right.

Inside all mechanical motion there is a natural spirit, a spirit that does not depend on any artificial plug, a spirit that makes the current possible. How would a boulder loosen from a crag, I ask you, if there were not a breeze to chide it, a quake to dislodge it, or a boy to push it? And whence comes the breeze, the quake, the child? How would the electrical current flow and how would the smallest particles surge into activity without an agent transferring the power from one object to another? I do not have much science, only what comes from Gibble, but I do know that nothing begins without its having begun before, there is no true origin inside a body, be it mechanical or biological, there are only wheels, veins, lines, wires, livers, to seize the motion, contain it, make use of it before it is passed on. And here in these midnight neighborhoods that show no signs of awakening, here there is still the need to go forward, to grow ever older, to flow toward the city's heart.

But this fact of motion does not have significance enough to silence me; I grumble protest and still the girl drives on with some secret destination intended, a sweetheart's hideout, a carnival, a television room. She has a marble face and the female talent for resistance. Sometimes they do not seem alive, these painted women, with their wants invisible beneath their decorated fronts. Now she steers into a ward of foundries and dilapidated shacks where on street corners men vagabond through the night, we pass one group that makes sport of throwing bottles against an old hostel, I hear the glass shattering against the brick and I cannot help but wonder if this is a threat directed at us, we are bumpkin travelers here and I wish I could color my gray hide temporarily brown, for there may be rites planned for the night that need sacrificial victims and I know well how white flesh makes a colorful sight with blood streaked upon it.

I am not ignorant of urban ways, I had an early vision of the city from Gibble, who designed for me a landscape with pepper shakers, forks, and sugar bowls, a city framed by lordly waterways, a city arousing Gibble's passion so he could not stand to worship it from afar, no, he had to snuggle in its bosom, he had to retire to its foul bed. I always suspected that Gibble's city was a false city, a creation of his own fancy and ambition; the truer city announced itself in newspapers, on television, boasted of its hospitals and orchestras yet could not stop the plundering and slaughter in the crowded river wards. I know well how city nights breed an unrest such as what troubles me in my sleep—inside me the cowardly and the stalwart, the wrathful and the peaceful make such confusion I cannot even keep my hands off a young girl's bosom. Inside the city there are similar contraries that clash and cause unspeakable transgressions, it is best to stay secure in a truck in a wood glade rather than to try and make your way through these back streets.

The girl is intent upon the road, retreading some bygone path, perhaps she knows of another Chapter, another sanctuary full of brothers proclaiming the end of the world. Well, I will join them, for I have an intimation that my end is approaching, and I would rather be in the company of men than survive alone, I am weary of mingling with opposites—friends with false intentions, girls with rude instinct, ungainly spirits, coarse strangers, wives such as mine who break off the leader and float downstream before their time. I wish I belonged to a loyal fraternity, brothers forever defending each other with the bulk of strength that comes from the union of types, we would cut ramps on a Sunday afternoon and in winter we would drive north, carve into the iced lake, dangle our lines in jagged holes and run backward.

It was with young Gibble I shared adventures of ice fishing, we would travel by bus and by foot through the woods, we would bravely endure the winter in a rough-hewed cabin that had a flat metal roof and iron crossbar windows without glass, we would near to freeze every night but every morning we scrambled from the bed-ticks to fish in the dawn, forgetting our discomfort—this is always the way with sport, you must suffer before you win your trophy. There was one day when a four-pounder rose out of the hole at the end of Gibble's line, skidded far across the snow-crusted ice, such a beauty, I have yet to see its equal. We let it lie upon the frozen lake through the forenoon, then we brought it to the camp grill, where a formidable Canadian was willing to prepare it for lunch as long as we gave her a share, so Gibble and I sat pondering the lovely while the cook went at it with a hatchet. We were shaking our heads at such stricken majesty when suddenly, as the woman positioned it for the beheading, I saw the gill quiver. I said, "Look at it there," and Gibble demanded, "Quiet, man!" though I knew he had seen. "Look at it move," I said, and the Canadian paid no attention to us, she was quick to gut our prize. I never proved that it was still alive upon the chopping board though years later Gibble admitted he too had noticed the gills fluttering, he too had seen the dead fish live again. Just as I have not come across that trout's equal, I have not met a man who would be a lasting friend to me as Gibble would have been if he had not changed his habitat so late in life. I lost Gibble to his science, the Idiot One grew ever more simple, and the neighbors took to avoiding me in my old age. True, I threatened to poison their hounds that polluted my lawn, but the neighbors all had been mightily influenced by television and they had no patience with me; the other ancients covered their balding heads with wigs and pretended a foolish youthfulness, no one wanted to look upon an old man who took pride in his age, who did not worry over the fact of the grave, who was too involved in the angling sport to waste hours bemoaning the strong current dragging us all downstream. No, I have not met my match and in these wards there is no possibility of earning sympathy, there is no one who shares my love of the fish, no one who will trade tales with me, who will mingle his voice with mine.

Across the river, buildings with unblinking windows keep a watch over the streets. I will tell you how money passes hands there to pay for construction of electrical plants enough to wire every tree in every forest with a bulb. Imagine the woods always aglow, the night blazing—such light would bring an end to mystery, there would be no darkness to give shrubbery forbidding shapes, dreams would be mere daytime thoughts, we would lose the conviction that gives nightmares their influence. In the city I would never be afraid, for there are streetlamps to shine through window blinds, there is light from passing trucks, from hallways and neighboring windows—how would I sleep at all, I wonder, with eternal daylight and such chaos trumpeting? Traffic and sirens, faraway explosions imitating war that I know are only the internal workings of the city. How would I find sufficient rest to gather my strength if there is to be found no place of mute darkness? I would rather endure fear in order to rest, endure nightmare in order to sleep, relinquish control of light in order to pass from today into tomorrow.

But what does she mean by this—slowing, dragging to a halt in this district of warehouses perched in piles of mud plowed against the curb? Why has she stopped here in the burnt-out remains of Gibble's dream?

"Wait for me, old man," she directs, and then she is out of the car and scurrying across the street, glancing around her as if to assure secrecy.

She goes down a stairway into the basement of a squat building and soon I see only her head of unkempt hair bobbing above the concrete, then nothing at all, and not until she has disappeared from sight do I understand how the girl continues to abuse me: she has stolen the key from the ignition, so wherever she is, she retains control, and I am adrift, alone, with the city gurgling restlessly. These massive structures and the lamplight staining the buildings lemon, this strange sweet waft of raisin mixed with river rot, the naked trees, all is but a spoiled dream, a vision sprung from an embittered mind. This carnival of asphalt and industry has gone all wrong. I know how Gibble has something to do with my misery, he means to mock my worst fears by depositing me in this manmade disaster of a neighborhood. He is the crow that flapped over Josiah's Pond a lifetime ago, and I still float upon the Gibble raft. I do not know how I passed into his dream or where I may leave, there is nothing to do but wait for him to release me. I tell you he will grovel before I forgive him this game. This is a dream of world-record length—I have grown old, how did it happen? Long ago I was embraced by my friend's affection and made his slave, knotted with his cousin and dreamt through fifty-three years.

I long for Gibble to end the intriguing, I yearn for this mind to return to the laboratory so I may conjure up my own images of timber and lake, which would improve this landscape of abandoned buildings, names writ upon plywood knocking in the wind, streets empty of movement except for the newspaper sheet whipped by the breeze, curling, unfolding, rising, then plummeting like a bird with its wing scorched from shot. Who knows but that this very page tells the facts of my crime?

My humiliation is to be prolonged. A man staggering along the street—a languishing, intoxicated bum—has taken notice of me and approaches the Skylark. What does he mean to do? Lurching across the pavement, he gains momentum as he draws near, so I secure the door lock, pretend interest in the empty street ahead. He bangs his fist upon the glass, a shudder passes through the car. Why will he not leave me? I am as the wife was in her latter days when I pestered to have entrance to her private opinions, and she was all the time refusing me, deaf to my queries.

This man has an alfalfa beard and though his overcoat seems a quality make I can see from the corner of my eye how his sleeves are secured to the shoulder with safety pins and his cap is bound to his head with a worn woolen scarf. This, then, is one of the poor, a specimen of the underground tribe, this is one of the city vagabonds who has come upground to see the granite-faced castles and the gothic spires while the inhabitants sleep. He examines me through the window as if I were a zoo reptile. But I feel no fear now, only pity for this aimless spirit, I look at him and think, *This could be me;* I am thankful for the good fortune that spared me this fate. Scratching, clawing at the glass—what could he want from me? He does not even have a streetwalker who will take care of him, a streetwalker with a charmer's rare power. But I do not mean to imply that I approve of her methods, I put up with her only because I have no other. Yet here is this individual ambling through midnight streets, stoical enough to stay solitary while I have surrendered to depraved dependency. He wheels about, trots off like some kind of creature who has come close to sniff at me and is assured I am harmless, he returns to the city, a white man, an old man, a friendless man.

Enough. "Wait for me!" I cry, flinging open the door, but the sound of my voice frightens him and he scuttles around the pyramids of garbage sacks, he runs, an agile spirit, I would not have expected him capable of outdistancing me but he must have such fear coursing through him. He turns down a cobblestone street and I am after him, with one hand I press my cap down upon my head to keep the wind from prying it off, I huff onward and before long I lose sight of him. Still I pursue, expecting to round one corner or another and find him waiting.

He is gone. I am alone at a quiet T-junction. Across from me, in a deserted lot, dried weeds hum around a charred vehicle. I do not recall what streets brought me here, whether to turn left or right at the block behind, I have lost direction and there is no moss-covered tree to point me north, no sun to pull me east. The wind is sharp as a wife's hand against my cheek, my trousers flap about my knees, and my knuckles are swollen from the jaunt. My labored breathing does not immediately repair when I count backward, but I understand how this is not distress, this is a change of perspective, so while a minute prior I was frantic, now I am indifferent, numb as a man trapped in a snowdrift. I have always known cold to be a penetrating, cruel intrusion, but now the cold itself helps to weave a cocoon, a coverlet, and I am not so afraid as I was. I am a fish egg sealed against the night. I move down the street, not caring whether I head north or south, not minding the barbed draft.

But still there is a disbeliever in me. Is this a new religion I have got so quick, or is it politics persuading me how I am not an individual but a particle contributing to the whole? Is this a false calm, the eye of a storm? Whatever impulse arises in me, always there is one to challenge it, to battle and subdue it, so now that I am finally secured inside my mackintosh, sharing in this city as if it were my home, still there is an antagonist disturbing my peace of mind. *Do not forget*, he says to me, *you are a solitary, lost in the streets, surrounded by wharfage, without rod and tackle, without compass, without wife.*

I go on. Ahead, three forms congregate around an ash can fire, and though I remain afraid of strangers, I am compelled by curiosity—they are white-skinned vagabonds up from the underground. I turn the corner to avoid confrontation, they would see me first as an intruder before they understood me to be a friend sharing their city. I cannot forget the stories I have heard of how ruffians douse ancients in kerosene and put a match to them. No, I will not serve as entertainment though they are civilians like myself, suffering the cold. They shall be my companions from far off, I will position myself by this brick cornerstone and peer around the side of the building and watch them as they hunch close to the flame, their wool hats pulled down to their eyebrows, their hands thrust in their coat pockets. Surely these men do not have wives to care for them, their home is the sidewalk, their furnace is the ash can and their family is each other. From afar I may be one with them, imagining the heat soaking through my sprouting beard, and I could tell them all I know—how to dress flies and knot the leader to the hook, how to choose between live bait and an artificial lure, how to make a rent cane rod, how to be self-sufficient and fill their tackle baskets without the help of a department store. The true angler is not the sort of man who has everything done by others or who has only unskilled fancy and no knowledge when he goes to string the line. Life is too short, there must be a foundation of experience before a novice can search out haunts along the shoals, and I have a compassion in me that wants to share my talent with these men.

Slowly I approach, trusting that they will do me no harm before I declare my peace. I creep close to the buildings, preferring the shadows. When I am past the last stoop and away from the iron railing the mutter of conversation dies and three heads turn to examine me. Three men, three city strangers, shift wordlessly to make room. They must understand that I want to forget our differences of origin, for we are all men neglected, without shelter, cast off or abandoned; we are all men sustaining ourselves through the night. I shoulder my way in between the one who is solemn as a wood Indian and another, with ragged beard, he is familiar to me, he might be the same man I so recently pursued though he does not acknowledge me. We watch the flame in silence, they keep their words inside them and I wait, anxious for an introduction. I do not often long for recognition, not since Brother lay prone upon the earth, not since the wife toppled from her chair, all I ask now is for some sign, some indication that I am one with them. But I understand why city dwellers are reticent, they cannot know who means to game, who means to destroy.

No word from them, no greeting, though they have lit a cigarette and are passing it between them. I feel such brotherhood swell in me I can hardly contain it, yet I can only wait for one of these brave men to initiate the talk. There seems to be some glances passed, a covert message, you know I think they mean to jump me, bind me, use me as fuel for their fire. Now this foxish man on my left is chuckling, wheezing, now the one on my right giggles like a schoolgirl, now all three of them laugh, howl at me as if I were scantily clad or inserting my finger in my nostril, I am a joke to them, a buffoon, as usual an outcast. They intend no assault but the mockery is worse, everywhere I go I am ridiculed for my sex, my age, my crooked back, they are all in league together, they do not understand how I have such profundity in me deserving a listener. I would have given them my wealth of information if they had not taken to this drunken revelry—ingrates, all three of them. I am through with this city once and for all, I am through with brotherhood, and with the portion of sky seen through the buildings gilded with dawn, I do not need the companionship of strangers, I do not need another soul. I strut off from the ash can fire, keeping straight as possible, a proud withdrawal, I show no shame.

But around the corner I must slow my pace. Already the air filters in smoky morning, the cityscape assumes a dream quality, reminding me how I am trapped, and I try to predict what Gibble will do with me next. I still long for company, though I have given up mankind. I had hoped the city would accept me as one of its own, and I miss such comfort however false it was. In the primal hour blood runs sluggish in a man, he is susceptible to delirium, he cannot always tell true from false, and being a pilgrim in this ward, I am not as convinced as I was before that I remain myself, I fear this lightheadedness is the symptom of transformation.

Still I go on, harboring a kernel of hope yet wondering if I need waste emotion, for if I am changing to spirit I should not fear what the city might do to my flesh, there is no possibility of pain if I dissolve, and maybe around the next building I will discover the man himself, the man in charge from start to finish, old Gibble, who has yet to bring me to my knees and keep me there. Age falls away in changing light and now my feet do not feel so heavy, my bones do not ache. The wind teases me along, tugging at my cap, and I assure you it makes no matter that I am solitary, for I am hardly more than a dandelion seed adrift, I am content to let the wind carry me until down one street or another I encounter him.

I draw back when I see ahead a policeman raising his club, he stands outside a bank building and at his feet there is a lump of spun gray wool, some huge butterfly's cocoon. I want to touch it, unpeel it to see it asleep, who knows but that it is the wife huddling against the cold, her gray brows knit with crystallized sea salt. Gibble might have set her here as bait, still I would be grateful for our meeting, I have much to say to her. But the officer means to take her as his own, to make off with her. I will not let him abuse my woman, I will put an end to the violence; though he has greater bulk and muscle and a firearm strapped to his belt, I will stop him. A cautious approach is necessary, he might turn on me, beat me to a pulp if I jump, and then I would be useless to the wife. But this bundle does not have womanfeet, the crude rubber galosh and trouser cuff sticking out of the coat belong to a man, I am sure, the foot bespattered with mud is not the wife's. Now the officer shoves the huddled form with the toe of his boot, tapping rudely at the appendage with his club, urging him to wake and rise.

"Move on," he commands, "move on," ordering the cocoon back to its underground haunt.

Roused at last, the vagrant rocks to his side and breaks out like some lazy monarch. He is colored the glowing brown of a night sky before a blizzard. "Get up, move on." *Do as he says!* I would suggest, I want to help, I want to interfere, but still I do nothing. The Negro holds the club that has been prodding him, he uses it as a crutch and pulls himself up while the law remains staunch, sullen before him. He is one-legged, the other limb is cut off at the knee, the trouser end knotted closed. The knobbed cane upon the ground must be the one he uses to make his way along the sidewalk, but he does not intend to travel a great distance, he hops backward into the doorway and grips the handle.

Such defiance maddens the officer, and he readies his club to use as the weapon it is designed to be, he swings against the half leg, and I hear nought but a dull thump at the impact, no splintering bone, no outcry from the Negro, who clings ever tighter to the door. The club swings wide and hits again, still the stubborn black man keeps silent as a flopping, expiring trout when it is struck with the paddle and heaved into the canoe. But the law has succeeded in dislodging him, he holds his arm now, dragging the blanketed bundle toward the intersection. The vagrant cannot make equal stride, he skips forward but the law must pull him faster, still faster, the law has no pity and does not understand that a man left out in the cold all night must be thawed gradually. Only after they are a distance away do I remember how I am in flight and have been hovering here hardly three yards' distance from the uniform, feeling the blows as if they were rained upon me, feeling my half leg smart, feeling not like the wispy spirit that the dawn made me but instead a meager construction of flesh and brittle bone, near collapse.

I follow this street past tiled squares, across intersections strung with red winking eyes, beside barren garden plots caged by iron fences, I pass other officers who wander with their visors pulled low, their weapons belted to their trousers, I hustle along for I know this is what they want—a solitary man is free so long as he does not linger. I keep on and the office buildings give way to foundries, the parks to vacant lots, I keep on and the molasses smell grows stronger, the rush of the interstate louder, I keep on until I find myself beneath a railroad bridge where iron slabs are propped on stunted cement blocks. Nothing dares to grow in this desolate place, here under the tracks. I would go quickly through but I am caught by some strange babbling hum, a soft purring, a gentle draft, a sound unlike any I have heard before, a secret voice, you would not think the city was capable of such sweet song.

I cry out to it, "Hello!" Again, "Hello!" and suddenly there is a roar, the cavern resounds with it, the noise of a great blast furnace, and I am surrounded by countless multitudes, pigeons, a huge tribe of them, a maelstrom of white, birds descending like a handful of gravel flung into still water. I see now I am standing in a carpet of their powdery dung, I see now the crushed feathered carcasses scattered over the ground. The whirring of the flock is overwhelming and how I manage to stumble from this roosting place I cannot say, how I move backward yet stay upright I cannot tell, how I am able to find the street again I do not know, and though I leave the bridge behind, I cannot put the drumming of the roused flock from my head.

This is Gibble's trick, I know how it was he who lured me here and set the pigeons loose. I do not forget how two decades past when he boasted of this city he told me of the silver birds that were to be found in such numbers almost to surpass belief. Well, I do not envy Gibble his scientific faith—there are no woodland havens left, no forest where the persecuted may take refuge, so the poor will go on plundering, the law will assault, and the vagrants will be displaced. Whoever designed this checkerboard of tenements and jeweled bridges should be put away, for he is to be blamed for the unrest. I tell you this fairy tale city is no good.

Day is pressing but I have no interest in the pedestrian traffic, the vendors, the girls, the families dressed for church. My head is filled with a thousand beating wings and I am near the end of my strength when I finally come upon the Skylark, still moored where I left it. I want urgently to leave Gibble's nightmare behind. I have always thought that to comprehend a place you must greet it at dawn, you must watch the sun ascend, transforming watery night to day; now I know what the city contains, I know the secrets, for I have watched it awaken, and I am prepared to put this bubble of raucous sound and rank smell behind me. In these slum gutters there is sodden cabbage, grapefruit, orange rinds disintegrating upon the asphalt, stomped by pedestrians, smeared into a carpet of filth, unable to dissolve into the earth. If I had such insight at the time of the wife's burial I would have kept her out of the casket, I would have made sure that she was wrapped only in muslin and planted in the soil, for it is not natural to delay dissolution with an asphalt sidewalk or walnut box. I regret having spent my strength thickening the oil and dust into the substance that has become the surface crust here. I regret having a hand in the production of asphalt, for now I am responsible, as guilty as the next man for the warehouses where there were fringes of willow, the office towers where corn once grew.

The ignition slit remains empty, the Skylark stalled against the curb. There is nothing to be done but to go and seek the girl, we have another destination and I worry that time will interfere, we must be on our way. Tonight we will find some hostelry where she can use her sex's wiliness to our best advantage, she shall not fabricate or undress for a stranger, she shall simply coax a shelter for us; I do not think I could stand another night confined in an automobile.

I recall how the girl descended the stairway across the street, so I follow her route, I take the quick, cautious steps down the stairway into a concrete shaft where a single door is propped ajar by a cracked snakeskin sandal. Quiet as fog I push open the door—until I locate the girl I am a trespasser, I have no excuse for intruding here without first announcing myself formally. The ceiling is low and a single bulb casts sickly light upon the spastic wall scrawlings, it is a cavern of foul rot, piss stench, excretion— even my worn nostrils are offended. Where this girl is taking me I cannot say. The corridor leads directly to a narrow wooden door, and I would enter if I could. But this door resists me, I hear the bolt rattling but it will not budge, I struggle with the blue-chipped porcelain knob but it will not give. *Hurry, man!* I sense the stealthy arrival of the law, I hear their feet padding down the concrete steps, soon they will be upon me and here in a ward basement even my white skin will not save me, they will recognize me as a bloodless criminal and I will be through.

"Open the door!" I hail desperately. "Open the door!"

All the while I am vaguely recalling how this dream has been devised to torment me, I am a mere experimental rodent to the Gibble mind, he is sending the authorities after me, keeping the door closed, laughing from above at my distress. There is no direction to retreat with the law pressing in and the girl refusing me, surely she is behind the door, she is the reason for my predicament, there will be no release because of this girl's foolish tricks, soon it will be over, they will take me away, and I doubt the girl will long regret my disappearance; she is one who lives only in the moment, without respect for the past.

Now, just in time, the door opens wide and I stumble into a room, dimly lit, cramped by low ceilings. It is quiet here except for my breathing and the purring of radio music turned low and the warble of the strange woman greeting me, brown but with tufts of hair a rich copper color and eyes, her eyes, even in the poor light they shine like discs of shale on a rock summit. She extends apology for the delay while I am trying to find speech to explain myself.

"I am so sorry," she says. "I was back in the kitchen."

She is sorry. Well, I tell you that is not good enough, I have been poorly treated by this city and I expect compensation, I want my girl returned to me.

This woman—I survey her coldly—is a bejeweled spirit, she wears a skullcap with gold baubles dangling over her hair, a pearl chip embedded in her nostril shows like cartilage through flayed skin, her felt robe drapes below her knees. A magnificent Negress, her pigment glistens like plowed earth in the rain. I understand at once how I have made a mistake. But she encourages me, surely she does not suspect me of violence or else she would be resisting—no, the girl, wherever she is, has kept the secret of my flight and I am safe here, anonymous.

The woman actually takes hold of my wrist in a familiar way, saying, "We've been expecting you."

I do not know what motive compels her to this kindness, but I will show her I stay loyal to the wife and will resist provocation. What does she mean to do with me? I have survived a tumultuous night and a sitting room should give me satisfaction, but already I am prepared to return to the road, I cannot be contained in a basement where the walls are cluttered with strange objects, sheaves of straw, iron grids, rope hanging in poorly tied knots— there are no porcelain shepherds here, no practical chairs, only floor cushions and a low sofa, no proper place to sit.

I see I am not meant to rest. The woman makes such demands though I do not even know her name, she leads me across the room to another door ajar, she gestures, prods me gently to peer inside. I oblige—what else can I do? I survey the second room lit in a night-lamp glow, a windowless chamber where it is forever night. The children upon the mattress are stretched in sleep, two underground runts clad only in white panties, sharing the mattress with my own mermaiden—the coverlet is bundled at their feet and three pairs of legs are entangled. So ghostly pale between them, I wonder if she still lives, but the children would not be curling toward her for warmth, no, my harlot sleeps and even when a little one stirs quietly she does not wake.

I look upon the bodies stretched beside each other and recall the worms grown in Spain—worms bred specially for the silk gut used to make the toughest leaders—and though I have never seen them alive, it has been described to me how in country homes beds are built of bamboo sticks and the worms are arranged in rows and fed with a covering of mulberry leaves laid over them. They sleep, gorge, and dream until they are ready to spin their cocoons, and then they are stolen from their beds and dumped in vinegar, their entrails are pulled out, boiled with soap, bleached and strung upon hooks dangling from the ceiling. No, I have never seen these worms alive but I have used the gut leaders and they have never failed me in any battle with pike, trout, silverfax, no leader has ever snapped or withered though you can be sure I tended the valuable gut with beeswax and wound it properly on the drying spool. Now consider how the worms feeding upon mulberry and sleeping a full three days at a time could not know what lies in store for them, they have no inkling of their fate. I envy them their ignorance.

But why must I be distracted with Spanish worms? There are strategies that need to be devised, escapes to plot. When the girl wakes I must tell her the secret of the city night, I must describe what I have seen, and we will go on together, as before.

EIGHT

Fancy a Woman

IF I DID NOT see my hands with my own eyes I would not believe it possible that these fingers grip peeler and carrot and go at the chore as though I had behind me a lifetime of experience. I am at ease here, you would assume the underground had been my only home through this long life. The Negress recites facts of the weather, how it means to rain tomorrow and wouldn't it be fine if she had a patch of earth where she could plant okra and peppers, never mind the cost of an upground plot, if she had the money she would purchase a bamboo hut and decorate it with bunting and watercolor pictures. I mean to tell her of my plans to work a lighthouse but there is no occasion to insert a word, the lady who calls herself Magrass has such a wealth of talk in her you would think no one else ever invited her to speak of her dreams. What with her broken language and her fanciful subjects she is lucky to find an audience like me who knows that we who have ears should attend to speech however foreign it sounds to us, for sometimes there is wit and contrast to enjoy, other times it is ribaldry stringing sentences together, and the wary audience will improve with experience, his ears will become attuned and the aged man will have a quick intelligence to discern between voices of friend and enemy. She trades one task for another, she seems governed by a compulsion that diverts her from sausage to boiling rice to onion slices upon the chopping block—this is not the wife, who knew how to prepare a meal one dish at a time, first boiled beef then gravelcake, or a television dinner complete in its package; this is no upland dweller who knows how it is best to stay single-minded, to select the proper fly designed to attract one species, not all.

But like the wife she longs to have her childhood back, to have a view east and west, to be situated high on a hill, to watch the sun rise from the valley and sink into the sea. It seems she is a long-time immigrant in this country, but still she has such nostalgia it troubles me to hear, for she does not consider the impediments of station or remark upon chance—she has a well-insulated American home, her children sleep comfortably naked, truly she is lucky to have a warm enclosure while I, an old man, a citizen from the start, have neither a dollar in my pocket nor a house to call my own. She prefers the past to her present good fortune, but this is always the way with women.

"Food there was," she says, "like you never see here—pumpkin soup and curried goat, callula, turtle steaks, and the birds, they do sing enough to wake the dead, nightingales and parrakeets, and the bee bird, fawny ball of fluff . . ." This is the usual manner of women who do not appreciate their lot, they are always looking backward, missing the adventure of today. "Mada never was used to the bee birds dead. All day they banged into the window back of the house, Mada was one unhappy lady at the bee bird accidents. She made me hold one dying in my hand, a bee bird maybe big as this button on your shirt. 'Gal, you watch it, you keep it live,' she says to me. 'But Mada,' I says back, 'you give me one sick bird. Now one dead bird.' Absolutely dead, its tiny eyes open, watching me, tiny claw hooked like a baby finger, like it wanted to stay with me, hold my hand forever." Magrass, what do you mean trading talk of improvement for a consideration of death, why must your fragmented speech travel this way, from dreaming to dying, as if there were but one direction? Still, there is something to be said for an underground Negress who spends her Sunday preparing an elaborate meal for an old angler who is a stranger to her, an old angler who might have some terrible secret, indeed, an old angler who might have struck down his idiot son. To this female I am a companion to the girl, and that is all she needs to know to trust me, and though she travels rapidly from hope of how things might be to the truth of how they were, and though she has tasks to keep her occupied, and though our coloring is opposite, still I cannot help but note how she has grown attached to me, treating me like family though I am penniless, accepting me into her kitchen as if I were a peasant from her island home. She is committed to my girl but still I do not understand how the relation developed between black and white, between immigrant and native girl, between a mother and a common female—the Negress has given no clue and I will not inquire, I do not wish to establish a pattern of exchanges or soon she will be wanting an account of my journey and I have no talent for fraud.

Now she praises me for my peeling effort and I confess I feel a small swelling of pride at my performance though this is such a lowly task; I do not forget how the wife used to put the Idiot in charge of vegetables when he was a boy, I do not forget how he sat upon a kitchen stool, keeping his eyes wide as though awed by my shadow upon the wall. He would scribble figures to his mother upon a pad, he had no need to communicate with me and could never comprehend my directions, with oversized ears you would think he would someday acquire powers of discernment, but no, he remained an idiot and sometimes I would find in the wife's pocketbook his pencil scrawlings, malformed trout taking the fly or stick people embracing in crude affection. Once I discovered a sketch of what must have been the wife though she was made grotesque by the Idiot's hand, she too had mulish ears and gaping mouth, she was the wife transformed into the Idiot, the Idiot in the wife's disguise. I do not know why she chose to keep the drawing in her purse—maybe it served as her vision of what she would someday become, ravished by illness, monstrous, aghast at the thought of the end. To look forward without hope will hasten life, well do I know, and when I am more familiar with this Negress I mean to give her some advice in payment for the meal. Already my stomach contracts in anticipation as I survey the assemblage of sausage and rice, surely this is more than I can contain inside, still I shall try, for though my spots have turned a purplish brown and I have grown sluggish from the struggle, though I have suffered some loss of condition and my teeth are weak as low-grade asphalt, I have not lost my disposition to feed.

But it seems the surplus must be shared. The Lady is off to call her young ones, leaving the rice to congeal upon the counter, leaving me alone in the kitchen with its coil fluorescent light that tints a white man's skin to a ghostly emerald shade, the plaster walls to tallow. Now I would like to prove a gentleman, and in these private minutes I contemplate my form from my shoes to my trousers to my lilacs shirt hanging as if beneath it there were a scarecrow, misshapen with straw. My knuckles are calloused from industrial labor, it has been three days since I last brought the blade to my chin, my Parmacheene feathers are discolored with soot, and my clothes have not been washed, I must smell foul as a spoiled silverfax but I cannot discern my scent, I have grown used to it.

There is an oval mirror strung upon the wall and I rise from the chair and force myself across the floor. The face of what I used to be is doughy folds beneath a bluish beard. But with my fishing cap pulled low to shadow my eyes I do not boast to speak of a respectable quality, a certain majesty, with my mouth closed I might resemble a foremost politician, who knows but that I might have been a leader if I had done things differently, if I had taken education past the tenth grade, if I had avoided Gibble and fled from my homeland at an early age. I might have been prominent in the world. Not a poor quality—prominence, recognition—instead I am a miscreant. If I had influence I would make sure only honest men directed the electrical current and there would be no place in the region for a scientist like Gibble, I would banish him. But I do not want power; well do I know that whatever possession you treasure most will be lost—a wife, a home, a position—all will be apprehended by youth eager to assume control or seized by your competitors. To own means to rival, while to disown assures you liberty, and surely there is a refuge somewhere for a man unconnected by name to family or by contract to industry.

There is no time for more meditation. The children, identical brats dressed now in knickers and rags, clamber into the kitchen, pummeling each other to enter first through the doorway though when they see me they stop their gaming and insert their fat thumbs into their mouths. They are followed by another child, a breathless elder sister. She bounces in like any floozy expecting attention to follow her along, she takes my chair and assumes command, high and mighty she thinks she is in her overalls and turtleneck, with her man's light copper hair and the same bewitching eyes.

Magrass returns and explains me to the youngsters—I am nought but a companion to my strumpet, who remains deep in dream, I am identified by my connection to the girl, not by my home, my skills, my profession. It would be too much of a task to instill awe in these minnows, they are underground worms and I can see from a glance how they are of a destructive nature; already the daughter has knocked a plastic cup and sent it bouncing across the tiles, and the twin chub surge forward, they take off one after another and race round the table in proud performance. And now there is a fourth child, a boy a shade darker than the others, clopping along in heavy boots, he makes a wide arc around me, leans back against the counter, bundling his sleeves up his forearms as if to show off his fighting power. Now the chub are yanking upon my trousers, demanding if I need to make my pee—that is their question truly—and I cling tight to my belt loop, trying to shake them off my legs.

Magrass is busy with the foodstuff and when she finally sets the plates upon the table she makes no reproach, instead she winks at me as if we should both be pleased members of the audience. She directs me to a side chair and the children shift their attention to the rice heaped upon their plates, they assault the food with their miniature incisors, chew savagely through their dinner while I take dainty swallows of beans and wash away the tingling with gulps of water. There is such peculiarity of feeding habits here and such spice on my tongue, soon my stomach rebels, refuses to receive more. I set down my fork and knife discreetly, I have no desire to offend the Lady, and no one notices my displeasure except the elder boy, who remains sulking in the corner, his plate upon the counter. This must be the common dinner organization—the other small fry ignore this wary dunce, as if it were not unusual for him to stand counterside. A single empty chair is saved for the sleeping beauty, still I can see the boy would refuse to sit whether he had a place or not. All through the meal he directs toward me such wrath I am sure a flush rises to my face, though I assure you I feel no guilt, I cannot help it that I am white and have come from the country and that he is colored, obliged to remain underground. But if he is a night wanderer he surely has a suspicion of the dangers, and what am I to him but a backsettler king who does not suffer city confinement?

I endure the boy's indulgent hate and I ponder the Lady, who devours like her children, as though the food will be snatched away. She is still in her robe, but I wonder now whether it comes from a nearby Woolworth's, the red cloth has worn thin at her elbows, the triangle tip of a paper tag peeks above the collar. Why she sits in bedclothes for Sunday dinner, why she does not govern her brood with firmer hand, why there is no man at the head of the table, I do not know—this is a strange sanctuary the girl has brought me into and when she wakes I will urge her to depart, though I tell you I will be sorry to leave, for the Lady, Magrass, she has a quality of rare kindness.

The children do not dawdle, they are up from the table, scampering off. When we are alone again Magrass turns to me with those tinted eyes, twists a finger around a strand of gold bauble, and she asks how I happened to be traveling the road with a girl. Now I am a stranger here and choose to remain so, nameless, without explanation. How shall I disclose part of the truth without telling all, how shall I confess our introduction in the battered truck without revealing who I am? Who I am. I will not say. But it seems Magrass has some of the facts already. She admits, "She told me she found you sleeping in the truck." Well, if the woman suspects I am in flight why does she still expose me to her family, as if I were a dignified visitor instead of an unshackled murderer, why is she so gentle with me when I am but an object for contempt?

She sighs, dabs her lips with the napkin, murmurs, "Makes no matter how you met. It's awful anyway," as if she has true sympathy for my affair.

I mumble agreement and while I consider my predicament I watch a collection of insects crawl out from behind a table leg, tiny red ants searching for a drop of sugared milk, a cake crumb. I have heard of roaches that carry disease, seek out sleeping youth, nibble upon their exposed infant flesh—it is no wonder a city child turns rabid, hateful, irreverent, with a fever in him burning continually, burning night and day, devouring and infecting like the plague inside a doe.

"She came in early this morning and told me make room for two. But when she went back to bring you in, you was missing."

Now I want to explain what I have seen, the secrets I know, the dull flapping of a thousand wings in my head, but I am reluctant to offer more than simple replies, for when my tongue starts waggling there is no stopping me, I travel back and forth and if I am not speaking of the land then I am speaking of myself. I do not yet know all that the Negress has learned from the girl. She reminds me that nights here are not safe, she was brand new to the city when she found out for herself—over a dozen years past she left her island home, came to our great land with high ambitions, she arrived aboard a train in the last hours of darkness and set off on foot.

Miles she walked before a man stopped her: "Some old sugar weeble, he asked me if I enjoy myself dog way or missionary way, so I tried laughing him on, but turns out I was supposed to make a better reply." He took her to the police station and she spent the morning locked with three lawless females, three painted dames. "They the real dishes, not me."

Prison—this must be where Magrass and the girl crossed paths, the girl was one of the incarcerated trio. I would feel safer with this brown lady if she admitted the truth—even an old hunchback deserves to know the facts of a woman's past.

"Is this where you were introduced to the girl? In jail, Magrass?"

"She?" A trickle of laughter squeezes between her glossy lips, she folds an arm across her chest, propping up the mound of her bosom, and I do not hear whether she has said yes or no. The giggling falls fast away, there is but a small repository of joy in her, she taps fork prongs against her plate and I am reminded of the old beggar who rattled his fingers upon the glass.

"She says she is never going back," murmurs Magrass. "She says her fada means to kill her soon as he gets his hands on her."

"Do not game with me. Say what you mean!"

"Her fada, the man who bred her!"

This is the girl's life she has kept hidden from me—a home, a parent—all along I have been traveling with another man's spawn

146

and did not suspect. Magrass continues, "She says nothing to you—how she's run away, how she's looking for a hideout? She says nothing about the accident, or about her fada, how he quarrels with her? She makes out like the man is no good. If he wants cooking she does it for him. If he wants fumming she goes out and finds him a woman what will play up any way he asks. It sounds like she got tired of the work."

How I am able to ingest what she says I do not know, but as she reveals the girl's secret life I piece together the puzzle—she is one of the rat-packing youth let out into the streets, she had a papa and a place, she traded home for prison. What crime she committed to cause a man to abuse his progeny I cannot say, unless it was his bad nature. I doubt it was his nature—she has proven herself capable of fraud, theft, and exposure, she carries in her such audacity to make her do unthinkable things. I conclude, "He discovered her. That is it! You say she has been mistreated. Well, who, I ask you, would stand to have the family name defiled? I tell you she is not innocent. She is a streetwalker!"

"What you say to me?" The Lady seems on the verge of fury, as though she had some stake in the girl's reputation.

"He found her out. Maybe he spied her in Franklin himself, maybe the truth was gossiped through the neighborhood. One way or the other he found her out for what she is."

"Ideas you have, sa. But watch, that child never speaks true about herself."

"Do not defend her, woman! I have seen for myself how the girl shows herself off, I know well how she bares her bosom for anyone willing to pay for the view."

But what stories she has been telling me, how I am wrong! I must understand that the girl is full of nonsense, indeed, she told Magrass that out in the automobile there was—here the woman pardons herself, she means no insult—"some creature, half man, half brute, something better for a cage."

"You want to know the truth?" I interrupt, a choked sort of

gurgle in my gullet which might be a laugh. "You want to know the truth of my life? I had a wife fifty-three years, she is dead."

Always the truth is sobering, the truth is like a multitude of pigeons sweeping down from the dark girders. The Negress apologizes as if she were to blame for my injury, but I wave away her complicity, it is not her fault that in the eyes of youth I am nought but a beast, a rare species.

"Guile and cunning!" I utter my judgment and think to myself, *Man, get away from that girl before she is your defeat.* But I do not have strength enough to rise and leave this basement home, I am comfortable here and would be pleased to stay another hour.

"But sa, you stay from blaming her. If you knew what she's been through."

If I knew what she has been through—surely neither war nor natural famine, and anything else is but minor suffering shared by all, her past does not excuse her from adhering to the rules, the past does not absolve her.

"She says her fada, he'll do her in for sure if he gets hold of her. She needs to keep quiet, she comes here, we're the closest she got left to a family."

Yet she is spritely enough, she would not allow herself to be abused. I do not want to hear of mistreatment, probably yet another twisted tale. I do not want to listen anymore.

"She loves the marijuana. You know she loves the weed, don't you?" Of her habits and preoccupations I am ignorant and choose to remain so.

"You see how she enjoys her smoke?" she persists.

"If she has come to you for a temporary refuge, tell me where she intends to go next."

"Who knows? Maybe she's after more weed."

Drug. I want to believe as before that we are partners with the similar need to put our homeland behind us. If the girl is merely wandering away from abuse, if she is an injured silverfax and can only swim in circles because of a misshapen tail, if her troubles cling to her and will not be left behind in the home, then how do I know she will adhere to me, how do I know she will not prefer a man who will satisfy her habits?

Drug she is after, weed, the lady says. Hemp. "Don't you understand? A child needs two things: a home and something sweet. She's about ready to call it quits, she says to me, 'enough is enough.' But there's the weed, that makes her happy. And could be she's come to me just for a hideout. Could be she's feeling the need for a permanent place."

"She told me she escaped from the tomb."

"Sa, you been fooled." And with this she whirls from the sink basin, takes to lecturing upon the drug sensation, no pleasure survives forever, wakefulness must give way to sleep and pleasure must give way to craving. She recites such symptoms as a peculiar cast to the eye and mottled flesh, but I do not attend to her speech. I am already saturated, for I have seen such sights—office buildings with crumbling entablature and pediment, bridges harboring winged vermin, river wards with windowless homes; I have seen such episodes—beatings, bottles exploding against brick; I have learned such things and now there is no room in me to contain more. I do not want to know the workings of the girl. I do not want to uncover her, and I do not care if internally she is polluted, there are allowances to be made for trouble inside a female, and as long as she does not drag us farther off our track we will have good sport together along with the satisfaction that comes from reaching a far destination. An addict, a streetwalker, a runaway, an acrobat—I know nothing for sure.

But I always say it is best to put the fly where it will do the most good. The girl has proven her worth and belongs beside me, I have come to depend on her budding ingenuity and she need only be directed by a man such as me who will help her circumvent the snares. But what do I know of drug except what I have seen on television and in the wife when she would address me in a sleep-thick voice as she woke from one operation or another? It was rare to catch the wife groggy, she was always a woman to spring awake, alert at the first streak of dawn, but in the hospital they injected enough sleep to stifle her so she could murmur only at slow speed. A drug that bloodies eye whites and staggers the pulse I do not understand, the girl needs no incitement, she is high-strung enough and why anyone would relinquish control of the body I do not understand. If on occasion the drink has brought me a sensation worth renewing, still I do not dare increase my intake, for a man must live as if at any moment his enemy might spring upon him from behind or as if the house might burst aflame—we are like spaniel pups swimming in pike-infested waters, beneath the surface there are unspeakable threats. Making it through a lifetime is no light task and how I turned into an old man I do not know, it seemed a single moment of transformation one day, as though a spell had been cast upon me, aged me overnight. In truth I have traveled all these years and the distance come is a glorious achievement, no matter what trophies have been snagged along the way.

"She's fifteen years, just a baby," the Lady says. "She thinks she's lived too long."

Fifteen, and I put her in charge of my Skylark, I let her order my lunch, now they will hold me to kidnapping as well as to murder. Fifteen she is, when I was thinking her older every hour, I assumed her twenty in the wood, twenty-five upon the asphalt last night, surely that was a woman's terror she showed, not a child's.

"A baby, sa. Pity her . . ."

Well, pity her I will not, there are individuals in the world who do not bring misfortune upon themselves while this infant addict is willing her own gradual disappearance, like the wife who sought a drug to make her drowsy. Resignation is as good as invitation. Once your defense is down, the intruder—be it ice, germ, or vermin—will make its way into you and it will be too late, there is no one to help you and you will suffer the fate of the wife, you will lose yourself piece by piece until you are hollow and disfigured. This is surely why the girl is tainted with craving, already the hemp is working to empty her, and with caverns expanding inside soon the intestines will leak and the organs will turn crackling dry, unfed, unwatered.

"But now she's here, what do I do with her? You're welcome to stay tonight, we're not as good as a palace, but we're okay. You know, I better send her home tomorrow. Like I said, a child needs a home and something sweet. Her fada will be changing his mind. A man goes mad, he forgets his trouble the next day. He will be missing her. He will be sorry. But you stay with us tonight."

"Woman, if you knew who I am!"

It is out before I can withhold it, she is the kind of female to cajole confession from a man and still I want to go on, I want to tell her everything, I want to pass the catastrophe to her like a bad dream, to narrate and then dismiss. My son upon the floor, cradled in Gibble's arms as if the Idiot were still pint-sized though he must be—have been—nearly four decades old or more. "I did . . ." The sentence will not complete itself out loud though internally it resounds: *I did strike him dead, I did strike him dead . . .*

"Sa, I don't need to know," she says, though surely if I could tell her she would be glad to have the truth out, she would take back her invitation once she realized that it is not safe to keep a man like me when there are children about. Who knows, I might reach for another chair, raise it high over my head and fling it at the boy who silently charged me with my guilt. I belong in a locked room where the furniture is bolted to the floor—I am no longer responsible for myself, there are stirrings and whisperings inside, I am inhabited by strange spirits and I do not know how to respond if I am provoked again. The instinct that compelled me out to dangerous shoals has released itself upon the land, there is tumult in me, I do not like to think of it. Why now, with my strength waning and my shoulders stooped, why at this time in my life do I begin to lose control? Surely the wife had an early understanding when she resolved with Gibble to put me away. It was an accident—the tragedy—I must not forget it was an accident, yet I tell you I cannot promise to keep myself from a second murderous outburst. Maybe it will be Gibble next if I ever meet up with him, maybe it will be the girl while we are parked somewhere beside the road, my hands will not reach for her bosom but for her ivory throat, they will grip the vital passage until my fingernails glow white as maggots.

It is an awful thing for a man to understand his capabilities, they are always in stock whether he makes use of them or not. Maybe a similar awareness turns a teenager to hemp. Once she knows chemical pleasure it will be neither forgotten nor fully recalled until it is invoked again, maybe when she has the far-off look in her eye she remembers the drug dream and hopes to soon relive it. Here is something new we have in common—an instinct that will not be restrained. I tell you, never live long enough to commit a crime that cannot be undone—how is a man like me to contain knowledge of himself? The least I can do is to keep continually in motion, for when I stop, the thoughts collect like fish around a baited buoy until I am frantic with fear of myself, even now in this good woman's kitchen I am cold as window glass during a blizzard and she can surely see what kind of man she has let into her home.

She has turned away from me just as the wife used to do when I approached her with arms outstretched, this lovely Negress has decided that murky soap water is an easier sight to bear, which is the usual way with such females, preferring dishwashing to confrontation. Yet how different she is from the wife, who had access to my privacy. Even when I kept dark thoughts out of my speech she knew always what hid behind my performances, while the Negress sees only an aged man, a feeble stranger, she cannot guess at my meditations, and I can flutter and dance madly in my mind as long as I keep indication off my face. How desperate a man used to a wife becomes when she is lost, no matter what plans to betray him she had made secretly. But I do not want to sit here like a walnut casket with grim ponderings inside me, I do not want to stay unknown to Magrass, who might have vague resemblance to the wife if she were a different age and a different color, I can only imagine such a transformation, I cannot replace the wife with her, she is so far off in appearance they are near opposites.

"I need sleep," I mutter, as if fatigue were an adequate excuse for my halting confession, as if all were false, merely occasioned by my weariness, and there were no finish to the sentence that began with *I*.

"Course you do," she says, but she does not move, and I wonder if already she has made the smart decision against accommodating such an unpredictable, unsightly visitor.

There is nothing to be done but to watch her sing quietly a sad dirge while the water runs, a tune of failed love, the woman knows what it is to be heartbroken. Her thumbnail scrapes a fleck of food crust off a plate, her robed knees shift weight from one foot to the other. A worthy female beneath the velvet, I can see from here, and though this is a troubled city still I wonder if it is such a bad thing to be deposited underground with the Lady for company. "Are you married, Magrass?"

A gentle snigger. "I lived with a man sixteen years. We went for each other like pickpockets to money. Then one day, two summers back, he left. But listen: if he's not dead, he's coming home."

Exuding goodness while all the time she is full of sorrow upon the spawning bed. If I had sufficient funds I would take this velveted Negress away from here, I would let her test the spring of my best rod, the tautness of my delicate line—this is surely a woman who would appreciate the angler's art. We would fill a sack with dried peaches, johnnycakes, roast coffee, and I would show her the secret quiet pools carpeted with lily pads, soon the trout will wake and be competition toughened by a hard winter, they will provide good sport.

She keeps her back to me as she draws a steep breath, enough to fill her with air to suffice an hour or more; she says, "A man grows up, he thinks he got to do double-time."

"A man must learn patience," I agree.

"That's it, he got to take time out and watch things around him changing."

"He can't be worrying about tomorrow's supper when today's is still full in his belly."

"A smart missus knows she better go after something she can reach. A man thinks he can love whatever. So here's a sad story about a boy who wanted too much too fast. Sit there and I'll tell you. You see, I have four children, you count them at the table? Celia, Joseph, and the twins. So there was five at the table last year." She pauses, her tongue is reluctant to continue. "I had another boy. He was young, in prime, when he took to wanting a fabulous treasure."

As she talks there appears at the doorway a tousled, spectral visitor with eyes swollen from sleep, my mermaiden roused, listening to a mother's loss described. Magrass does not turn from the sink, there is a peculiar dryness to her voice and I want to advise her how a swallow of water mixed with a teaspoonful of soda will wash the sand from her throat.

"So I says I was going to tell you one sad story and here it goes. You know, some men think they live in a land beyond the sky, a country full with birds of rainbow beauty." She waves her arms as if in this grim kitchen, this underground, there were indeed such flocks of richly colored birds, an open sky. "Now my Gus, my oldest boy, he was a fine hunter, he liked to go after the birds, he liked to wear their scarlet feathers in his hair, the green feathers on a string round his neck." She must stop, steady herself before she can go on. "And then one day my Gus, he saw a bird more beautiful than any he had ever seen before. It was like a rare jewel in flight, that bird. And my boy swore he wouldn't return home till he took her. His most tender love for her I cannot even say. He went after her. He thought it was so fine, the proud crest of hair she had, the plumage. So one day she settled on a branch, and my boy crawled forward, inch by inch, holding his breath. He let his arrow loose, he watched her go down and disappear into the grass. He pushed aside the thorn bush, the sword grass, tore away the weeds in search for the bright bird. He looked all over, couldn't find her nowhere. Instead he found a hole. A hole, sa, leading to another world, oh, a world of savannah and green forest, deer and fat tapir. And you know what? My Gus, he bent so far forward to look into that hole, he fell through."

Now tell me where is an aperture such as this, how is it possible for a boy to plummet through the earth, what most ardent love can she mean? A boy after a bird in a land that does not exist makes no sense to me, an old angler who understands better than most the dangers lurking in the forest's depths. I look to the girl for an answer but she has the glassy eyes of a sun-baked trout— her collar is half folded down, the lace upon the blouse washes like laundry suds to the edge of the lake, her ungirdled nipples show through the translucent cotton, and on her lips are red crystal scabs. No, I will get no explanation from her.

"My boy is gone to the better world, call it an accident of love. And that bird, she was hurt bad but not completely done for. She was all I had left to remember him by—the bird that drew my son away from me. Call it an accident of love. I went off to find my son, I found the bird instead. She was lying in the grass there, with the arrow in her heart."

An accident, she says, but tell me what she means: he went after a bird, tripped in the bramble, and fell. It makes no sense, this womantalk.

"My son is gone from me in this life. And his fada doesn't even know. The man hid himself so good no one could say where he was. He still doesn't know his boy is dead."

Dead. Now I understand the meaning here, her son is dead, I know how that is and I would not like to be a father with such ignorance, I prefer the event clear to me. Her son is dead—a firm fact that may be hooked in this eddy of wild fancy. But what of the birds, the arrows, the sprawling netherworld? Who will interpret the Lady to me, who will explain what she means? Not the girl, who purses her lips as if readying to spit, then disappears from the doorway.

"Like to see a picture of him?" offers Magrass, and this is enough to finally distract the woman from the sink, from her lore, from this tangled tale, she wipes her hands on a towel and leaves the kitchen. Out in the sitting room I hear her exclaim, "You're awake. Then come on and eat. I saved you some, you're in my house, you do as I say," though there is little insistence in her voice, she knows it would be foolish to try forcing her will upon the young rebel.

She returns not with the girl but with a snapshot set in a frame of brass—first she must worship it with her own eyes, caress it with her fingertip, her son, dead, what might I say to console her? She hands the frame to me, and I look upon him, one brief glance is all it takes, a flashing image like a silver shiner darting from the angler's boot. I turn my head away, shoving the snapshot across the table as far from me as my arm will reach.

Let me assure you I have no interest in young romance, let me make it clear I care neither one way nor the other. And if the girl were not accountable to me I would feel nothing at the snapshot. But there she stands, a little bathing beauty upon the sand, with his arm snaked across her bare shoulders. Coal-colored and tawny, opposites entwined. So the mermaiden caught first a Negro. I mutter my appreciation of the boy to please the woman, though in my heart I prefer a son such as the Idiot, who would not dare transgress. Now I wonder what compelled them toward each other, the white girl and the colored boy, I wonder how youngsters can come from two antagonistic species and fall into love, how it is that youth may both indulge in the world and still ignore it, be like the Idiot, thickheaded but with a mouth continually wanting to be filled, how a child raised law-abiding with manners instilled in him can stop, midway in his teenage years, and cast off tradition. Whoever claimed that an old man transforms into a youngster again in his final years is a fool and did not have a lifetime behind him and could not understand that between the young and the old there is an unbreachable gap, there is no easy visiting back and forth between the regions and only outcasts are willing to work together in order to survive. I am a lawless wanderer not because I have aged backward, but because I have lost my last fifty-three years and my family and am forced to live as a child and with one until I make a new home for myself. Still, I do not understand why they must violate merely for the sake of fond emotion—if they had seen what I saw last night they would think twice before posing for the Polaroid.

The girl is a fool fish when she is hungry, she would jump at a bare hook and now she must have some sore regret for taking a sweetheart who was not well made for her and who would have been gaffed early anyway if this strange hunting accident had not first done him in. But it is the mother who must bear the brunt of their folly. I look upon Magrass, I think of what has been lost to her, I think of the charred vehicle I saw in a vacant lot last night amidst weeds singing like mournful women, and I understand: the girl is the ghost of the Lady's son, all that remains of him.

The mermaiden has followed Magrass back to the kitchen—her belly will be her shame, she must ask for the meal that a minute past she declined. The Lady cubs her on the ear to jiggle her full awake, and the girl smirks forgetfully, causing her cracked lip to bleed a dewdrop. Now that they are together, they shall not be separated—death has made a covenant binding them as mother and child. The girl is here to replace the son. I see how there is no room for me, all the time I have been traveling away from my home the girl has been traveling forward to hers, she is properly installed now, still with her childhood to live out, she does not belong on the road so I will leave her and go on alone.

She does not yet know that I have released her from our contract, she turns to me and declares, "You, old man . . ." sputters an echo, "you, old man . . ." like my own earlier statement, unfinished, unutterable. You, old man, are a murderer. "You—I told you to stay put," and to Magrass, "he's faithless, freewheeling, he's running away from his Miss."

Magrass interrupts, "But the wife, she's passed away."

What do they mean discussing me as if I were a spectacle for them? Let their talk stick to subjects unfamiliar to me, I do not want to be tossed back and forth between these females, jostled and unwrapped, I do not want them to consider me.

"Passed away?" The girl is disbelieving, she thinks it is not possible for me to contain secret suffering. "I thought—"

"He says so. His wife, she's passed away." Do they think I have no ears, no voice, do they think I cannot proclaim the fact without their assistance? "But he kept calling out to her last night."

"Called her? Called who?" rises up from me, another voice that is not my own, for I am somewhere hiding from the girl, I do not want to know what I confessed in my sleep.

"You were calling for your wife last night while I was driving. You kept shouting, you wouldn't shut up. She's dead? Why didn't you tell me the truth?"

"The truth! You are one for the truth, you who have set one lie atop another, prison cells and hounds—"

"What do you know about me?" she demands, and to the Lady, "What have you said?" She forgets my loss and confronts the Negress responsible for this unraveling, secrets shed, snapshots displayed. "What have you said about me?" and to herself, "Never mind. Because I know what you said."

"You know I says what?" There is some bristling between these two females, and as I have already made up my mind to go, I would best leave quick before the battle.

"I heard you tell the old man how Gus thought I was a special item, you implied that I'm to blame."

"Child, it was an accident. But he's my boy, and I do what I can to make some sense out of it all. Listen to me: I want you to stay here. You stay in my room, we put him on the couch. I have to leave the babies alone half the night since I work the late shift now. They took away my day hours and okay, what do I do? I keep at the machine. So you watch the babies for me, and you go on home tomorrow."

"I've tried to make you understand—it was no accident. We knew what we were doing, and it was no joyride, it was no *accident*. We meant to keep going straight when the road curved. Do you hear me? We meant to do what we did."

"To do?" I am trailing behind, I can hardly make sense of her words.

"To drive the truck off the road."

"But why?"

"Because, old fool, we wanted to commit an unforgettable act. It was supposed to be the ultimate performance. But there is no justice in this world and I survived, don't ask me how."

The girl is death! That is her secret, she survived because she is death—the ibis and the peacock disguising the hook—she is what draws a silverfax to the surface, *death*, I tell you, she is all that causes a man to forsake his element. Who was it who brought me here, who was it who dragged me from the mossy earth onto the pavement, who was it who took advantage of me while I slept by driving south instead of east? She has caused me to turn from the woodland, just as she lured the boy to collision.

"Vicious talk," says the Lady. "Listen: you must rest, and take a look at him, he's wilting fast. Stay with me to tomorrow. And I'll put you on a bus for home."

Home. A casual condemnation, she cannot know that home is hell where a colorless flame burns day and night—if I go back it will be the end of me. I tell you I would like to settle underground in Magrass's realm forever after, but she does not want to shelter the girl who caused the death of her boy—I do not blame her.

And she does not want to care for a man who struck down his own idiot son. But there is some truth to her assessment, I cannot keep pace with the high-speed mermaiden as she traverses, springs forward in broad sweeps, stops and starts. Maybe I am not meant to complete this final run. It would not be such a bad thing to remain here with this queen of the underground attending to my needs; there are the children, but I have seen how they are easily dismissed and I can think of tasks to occupy these greedy feeders hours at a time, lines to untangle, knots to learn, snooks to secure, I will teach them to be more properly respectful while I live the life of ease, claiming this family as my own despite our different colors.

Yes, maybe this was meant to be, a side track to a festering ward, I am destined to spend my last days beneath the surface of Gibble's city. What a short effort this expedition has been, though it was the same back when I set off for a wife and searched no farther than the end of the counter in Gibble's sandwich shop before I found her, a well-dressed fly, awaiting me. Now with the snow water flowing the journey would be swift, but I am not so eager to work the lighthouse high above clay bluffs, I am content to feed on the fry of silver chub. Here is a way to make these children mind me, I will threaten to impale them on the hook like a frog or a piece of fat pork and dangle them in deep water, yes, here is a way to make youngsters docile. I will spend my last season under Magrass's command, I will make the children worthy, and if I am not shut in a room with a window overlooking the sea, still I am closer to the wife as she was. I will be content to remain even if upground there is no chapel to hold ceremonies, no bell house to announce meetings and no cloistered bank to guard my pension. I will not miss the cupola and railing, the weather vane and gambrel roof, but it does not matter to me what lies above, for I have no desire to see the sun again, I will turn inward with a purposeful roll, leave this shoreline, and dive. I have passed through the rapids and evaded the island obstructions so there is nothing to be done but go down. There are worse places to wait for the end. I do not need window glass and a view of the sky, for there is a good, free-running past behind me to consider, I have fifty-three years to work through again.

"We need a place to hide"—the girl makes this pitiful plea—"pretend I'm a photograph, all that's left, a photograph of me and the old pirate. Put us away in a drawer somewhere, keep us a secret, and we'll go when the coast is clear." Death is always pitiful, a mere ratpacker's wish for a home.

The woman politely resists so I say quick, "We can clamber along rocks on a portage through the countryside. We can ride fast along the asphalt and undress ourselves for strangers. Or we can stay here with you, if you will have us—"

The girl interrupts—her voice must be like an ocean wave, a crashing that drowns the song of seabirds and a man's whisper, she kicks at the cupboard and I see her before me as if she were stripped not of her blouse but of her lies, I see her homeless, excluded, hungering for drug. She raises high a fork with food bits clinging to its prongs, she holds it above her head, makes a motion as if to plunge it into her eyes, then freezes. "Your Gus left me behind."

Here is death threatening disfigurement, death preparing to blind herself while we witness the deed. Well, I promise you we will not stand by and do nothing. I look toward Magrass and tilt my chin, I brush back my gray locks greasy from the long journey and I let her know with my eyes that we are in league together, Magrass and I, we have nothing to fear and will do what we must to subdue the girl. The Lady has clearly read my intent, she is taking a new tack now, calming the girl, cajoling down the fork.

"Let me think about this. You sure can stay here. I say you sure can stay, you're good as family to me, so is your friend. Now you relax and give that over to me." A smooth cast, we are soothing the girl, we will appease her, and when she is asleep again we will bind her with reliable rope.

She has settled in front of her plate and rudely she stabs a black bean fat as a tick you might find behind a dog's ear. She is mumbling, "I need time, that's all, just time. Mags, you always welcomed me, why does it have to be any different now? What would Gus want you to do? I promise you we'll move on when the coast is clear."

We watch her, Magrass and I, pretending nothing certain is decided while in fact the decision has been made secretly between us. The girl who aimed for destruction will learn to prefer life, I shall teach her to be reconciled to lost love, and if the lady keeps directing questions at me soon I will tell all, yes, it will do good to confess. I will explain how Gibble was controlling me and I never knew, I will explain the murder as the accident it was, I will describe the wife—not only the faded wife but the wife when she was ripening, when on winter mornings she could still lug crates of coal dust from the cellar and tamper with a cold car motor to set it running and chase away hounds pawing around the garbage pails out back, she could do this all and more while I rubbed sleep out of my eyes, she could do this all and still wear ribbons in her hair. I used to sneak up to her when she was in her chair, with a quick hand I would give a ribbon a single tug, unraveling the bow, but she always kept a stern expression that compelled respect even when I teased her, she would retie the knot as if I were but a bothersome mosquito droning round her head, though I tell you sometimes I wished she had greater pluck and drama in her, sometimes I wished she would have shrieked at me.

Still, she had so many talents, it will take time to recite them all to Magrass, fond Magrass, who promises to be a patient listener, I expect she will have a broad interest in the wife as she was, I expect she will want to know everything and when I am through she will lean back against the kitchen counter, shake her crowned head at me, her skin shining like lake water in sun, the gold baubles on her skullcap clacking, her nose chip the tip of her jeweled soul peeking out, she will shake her head in disbelief even as she says, *Fancy such a woman who could do all that.*

And more! I will cry, remembering still some other commendable trait or maybe just the way she appeared on those rare occasions when the drug gave her a sluggish temperament and with her flesh unwrinkling into the pillow she became ageless. I would touch her closed eyelid and still she would sleep, I would put my lips to hers and still she would sleep, sometimes I would gently unbutton the pajama and finger the brown rinds left of her bosom. Surely this woman will know what I mean when I describe the wife, and if I lack the means to revive her still this woman will understand what is behind me, she has been attentive and maybe with time and long speeches I will transform her into the wife, she will learn to make fire and cook dumpling stew by listening to me and one day we will couple properly upon the mattress. I will have the wife back once and for all. I have come far across the mountains to find the shape containing my lost bride, and though it will take an effort to coax the transformation I am well used to a long wait, floating and dreaming, dreaming and floating. I tell you this is no banishment I suffer, wherever I go I come to my own and even here, underground, there is good.

NINE

Gaffed, a Minute to the Pound

I WARN THEM to attend to me if they want to learn the sport. I assure them no great northern pike will snatch a fly lazily cast.

"You must go out in search of him, try channel banks and rushes, submerged tree knots, dismembered logs."

I challenge Joseph to name me the bait that works best in a furious eddy, and he makes imitation with his fingers of a minnow impaled on a gimp snook, you know I have trained him well, already he has knowledge of the rudiments. I have turned the Lady's sullen boy into a seasoned angler though he has never held a live fish in his hands, never felt the short line go taut, never felt a lake bass twisting and shivering inside the water. I have found my calling late in life now that I have an audience of youthful heads unfilled, uninfluenced, ears ready to listen and voices eager to repeat me. Where the late days have gone I cannot say, for time moves slowly underground, little is lost, the end is long in coming but I do not mind the wait. No, little is lost when there are children to mold into cunning sportsmen; the hours do not pass, they pile on top of each other and every day I feel closer to the sun though we have not been ascending, no foundation has been raised, no platform built, we remain below the asphalt and if you look at our reflection in the mirror you would think nothing has changed. But I have gained lodgings without putting out a cent, I have a Salvation Army chair and a sofa that suffices for a bed, I have new shoes brought to me by the girl, and when I stroll through the parks I wear the children like they were tree ornaments, they cling to my sleeves as we march in a cluster along the cobblestones between triangles of new sod, and there is such admiration from passers-by I understand now what a young hussy must feel when all eyes are upon her.

"Joseph, you learn well and I tell you I do not envy the luckless fish to be attracted to your bait."

He swipes at my own Parmacheene Belle, he makes a playful threat to rip it off the cap though I know he will do no harm, I am a rambling old snake in his opinion, he begs me for angling lore and it is all I can do to diminish the adventure as I relate it, for who knows how long it will be before he is set free. I have easily won his spirited affection, my only competition here is the television set, which tries to lure the boy away from me with its slow-motion film of a leaf bud unfolding. Even now he releases my hand, his jaw drops. But I have not spent a lifetime improving my ability for nought, I do not give up early, I press on with my talk, I speak of contests that kept on hour after hour when I was still a novice and did not know how to play the fish right, how to strike with a simple, quick turning of the rod handle.

"None will resist the accomplished man, there is no walleye nor trout nor muskellunge that cannot be brought to the gaff in the time equal to his weight, a minute to the pound: five pounds should be yours in five minutes, and a better weight should take no longer than a half hour."

The sister Celia on the cushions chews her thumbnail, her eyes fixed on the television screen though I suspect she catches my every word, she, too, imagines herself wading into a deep stream, sees herself in a felt hat and a mackintosh with only the laughing water for conversation, she, too, hides along some back stream shoreline, a would-be expert lady angler. I should soon wrest her out, I should remind her how we are underground, governed by restrictions. My wallet remains empty though I have supplies sufficient for a lord, and I am not so limber as I was, slowly I am rusting into this armchair, I am learning to sit patiently and wait. Maybe this is the training most important through a lifetime—to learn how to wait upon the cast line, to sit in a canoe and glide along the current without making a sound, and when the time comes I will not exclaim aloud, I will not overturn the chair, I will be as stone. These children all have much practicing to do before they exhibit the skill of immobility, always they must squirm, clutch, leap upon anything that moves, race hither, thither, they will have to discover what it means to be patient.

Yet I envy these little minds their well-lit corridors and bright, unfurnished rooms, they can think only of filling themselves, they cannot conceive of an intellect like mine able to fit no more. It is a good thing I have the children to take in some of the excess contained in me, there is so much, a dazzling array, in all these weeks beneath the city I have not yet ordered my thoughts, I have not formed firm opinions, nor have I resolved the question: why did the wife do what she did?

She draws ever farther away, and if I do not think first of her upon waking in the morning, if I do not bring her to the front of my mind, then it is difficult work searching through the clutter to find her again. This is the true illness the wife suffers, the first has proved a trial run of what was to come, she dissolved piece by piece before my eyes and now she does the same inside me— which is worse, much worse than the witnessed illness, for once she leaves my head she is gone forever, and just as before she does not attend me, she does not wait upon my direction, she fades though I would have her stay, and there is such a racket inside me I cannot think clear, it is Gibble's influence, his great flocks of pigeons will not return to their roosting place, the wing flapping will not be still.

It is best for me to sit upon the chair and speak softly of adventures past so the children will have no suspicion, I cannot let them know what lies in store, I want to keep them looking forward, to keep the little ones full of anticipation for the late summer days when the street sycamores begin their molting. And then the fall—we are planning great outings when the weather turns cold enough to poise a cloud upon our lips, we will dress in woolens and at the first snow we will all of us go out into the vast white and write our names with our tracks, yes, I will game with them and never let them suspect how the wife is slipping from me and the birds do not disperse. I will not share my troubles with Magrass, for though she is a gentle hostess still she has not satisfied me, she has not sent an invitation, she remains another man's favorite and refuses to share her mattress, so we live as strangers to each other—I, a fossil of a man, and she, cast off, dulled by nights spent attending to factory machines and days spent scrubbing floors, wiping the counters as if any moment she expected the surface to break and up spring some prize trophy, some welcome visitor.

And then there is the girl, not so charming as one would prefer, still she has served her purpose—to Magrass she is the specter of the lost son, to me she keeps close at hand the fate that means to be here if not today then tomorrow—we are bound to her. It is a good thing she is so useful or what would be my reason for inhabiting this sanctuary when I am connected neither by blood nor name? If it were not for the mermaiden I would have no cause to remain. She does not talk of leaving anymore, she does not talk of hiding, this is home now, she is a part-time working girl at the Woolworth's and gives half her earnings to Magrass. With the other half I suspect she purchases hemp, for she returns from work with red-splintered eyes, the weed scent clinging to her, she clatters across the wood floor in her new lady-heels, wearing blouses that show her midriff and the purple dribble of her scar, with her face painted like one of the porcelain dolls the wife kept on the mantle. In the evening she turns greedy, she would eat her supper plate if her teeth were strong enough, but this is the way with a paltry female, daily she diminishes, nightly she must replenish herself, nightly her eyes bleed and she evaporates happily into her drug dream, nightly I lie upon my sofa bed, waiting for her to strike.

But if I have such worries, still I appreciate good luck, I know well what it is to be without a roof, without a home, I know well how an expiring angler must take what he can get. I am not one of those whose opinion is tainted with prejudice, no, it does not matter to me that we have differences of skin as well as of sex and age, it does not matter that I have flesh graying like cardboard stained with damp rot and the family takes after the brown-speckled trout, though if you want me to be honest I will say there are times when I miss my own kind, boat partners and fly fishermen who will put up good argument over the quality of rod—ash wood or bethabara or split bamboo.

But I am grateful to be here, and if I cannot hope to venture away, still I will teach the youngsters how to escape when need is pressing, I will share with them my wood knowledge so they, too, can survive on summer berries and wild turnip, river bass and silverfax, for no one should rest easy in civilized dependency, though I think even I have not done poorly in finding a replacement for my past. This is a rough basement but secure, the children keep me warm while I rest, the twin chub gather on my Salvation chair and curl like a brood of puppies upon my lap to watch the flickering TV blue, their lips brush my cheek grizzle, their snouts press into the hollow beneath my chin. I only hope that on the night when the sleep continues and the dreams continue the children will stick with me and keep me warm, for it is the cold I fear most, the spreading Ice, and I must train myself to sleep through without waking. I do not have the courage to repeat the wife's end, I do not have such fortitude to meet it on my feet, full front, but if it arrives in my dream then you will hear no outcry from me, you will hear no pain, it will come just as the TV tiger ripples through the tall grass. I must learn to sit firm in my chair.

"Switch-cast—drop the fly!" erupts Joseph at the next commercial, turning his wrist to lower his imaginary rod.

He springs to his feet, rushes across the room with Celia close behind him. These fry do not make discreet departures, they seem trained for another element where walls would not hinder them. They are off to run wild in the streets, and I make no effort to detain them, I do enough by schooling them in American history and fishing lore, for you know it is a mother's job to discipline, a man's to educate.

Now you would think with such ruckus continually disturbing me I would treasure these rare pauses, but I confess there is too much worry in my mind, I have no peace when I am left alone, best to keep involved in prattle and forget the nagging troubles. I pretend interest in the TV drama but when the knock sounds on the door I am grateful for the company though I am not so pleased to have to rise from my chair and play host. Deserted by the children, it is the old widower who must unhinge his stiffened joints, straighten his bent back as best he can, and move off to take care of visitors.

"Hurry up," I mutter, "hurry up or you will miss the TV adventure, that is the way with the screen, it does not shut off and wait."

I do not mind if no one can hear me and make sense of my words, it is satisfying to complain aloud. I shuffle across the room and try the door, but with this resistant knob you need a college education to open to the outside. "I am coming, I tell you, I am right here!"

They are impatient, whoever they be—the children, the Lady, the girl—knuckling the wood.

"I say you're all I ever cared about—" he splutters, stops upon seeing me.

He is a man I would ordinarily steer far from, his woolly blackness fills the entranceway and his hand is raised, he means to assault me though I am an ancient and he one of the young giants, the type who roll sleeping drunks and beat vagabonds, he is one who should be stationed at a tavern as sentry, good for nothing but to stand in as a representative of power, yes, some pitiless commander's foot soldier, he must be enlisted in Gibble's regiment, I have finally been found out.

"I say I'm back, do you hear? I say I didn't do right going away like that!"

Trained to cripple an old man's spirit, he is as loud and rude as the pack of hounds we left behind in the woods long ago. He lunges toward the center of the room, turns circles, tears at the belt loop of his denims and I am reminded of the pigeons in wild array.

"I want you to know just this: I'm sorry, do you hear? I'm sorry."

He will not understand why I am dumbstruck, for he is no hunchback cruelly accosted, he is no widower challenged to reply to abuse. Joseph and Celia took to the streets in anticipation of the intrusion, they left me alone to suffer this violence. The creature before me flings aside couch pillows that still show indentations from a child's elbows, he squats to peer under my own Salvation chair.

"If you're Gibble's man, you need not rage, I will make no resistance, do with me what you will," I manage to utter, for in these long weeks living beneath the city I have been preparing for my summons, I have been practicing dignity and stoicism for just this—the final contest. So it is time. I need a moment to gather my wits. It is time. I am not ready. But it is time. "Gibble," I plead weakly, "another minute."

"Who?" returns the soldier. "Who do you take me for?"

"Gibble's man—"

"I am no one's man, I am my own. I'm here for—"

"For me."

"To ask forgiveness, do you hear? I say I'm sorry, do you hear?"

Could this be true, is this a treaty, Gibble's gesture at reconciliation? Well, I tell you he will not soon be shaking my hand. Gibble has been sponsoring the catastrophes of my life and appeasement will not be earned so easily.

"Do you think—" I address the ceiling, not the man—"do you think I will be tempted by your messenger? I am wiser now so do not expect to win me with your passionate apologies. I have had enough opportunity to consider your influence and all I have to say is: Gibble, leave me be."

Now I am repulsed by this soldier and yet I am an admirer of his bulk, this is a man who has murderous instinct and does not try to stifle it, this is a man who would feel no compunction were he to injure an old widower. Above his denims he wears a T-shirt stained with arcs of armpit perspiration, and above his shirt is a head too small for the proportions, a round eggplant set upon the Goliath hulk, dark goose-down tuft upon his chin, the shadow of mustache, mudwater eyes. His face is that of a child.

"My own home," he mumbles, "and I'm a stranger. My son— buried while my back was turned. My wife, where is my wife?"

"The Lady is out, she will be back." Curtly I utter it before I fully comprehend. "They all are upground," I explain, though I am ill prepared for the truth.

I return to my chair, wanting nought but to retain my property; he may take his position on the floor or he may wait outside, I have little concern for his comfort. Now that the storm has passed over and I can be sure Gibble is nowhere near, I need not hurry to converse with him. I stare toward the screen, the narrating voice speaks of scarce water and seasonal change, I listen to these facts of foreign weather and ignore the intruder while he examines the wall objects, familiarizing himself with my room— at night the sofa serves as my mattress, the embroidered sheet my coverlet, but I assure you it is only a matter of time before a man loses his last refuge. This is a sorry world run amuck, with mad husbands pursuing their wives and children disappearing. I have the power to slander the Lady who belongs to this man, I might pretend that she is my new bride and sever his connection to her, yes, a wedding announcement would send him away. He will see I am not easily dismissed, I am not so ready for the end as I once thought, I am the fisherman in charge of this basement, there is no need to hurry out.

"The Lady and I, we are . . ." I begin, but hesitate. It is not easy to imagine him throwing his weight against me.

Now his eyes have alit on the snapshot of young romance, Little Death and the boy arm in arm inside the brass frame. The man erupts in an avalanche groan, he seizes the picture, shakes it before my nose, and says, "Remember this: a black man turns his back, the white bitch sneaks in to steal his boy."

So the father knows how his child took the dressed fly, swallowed the sproat. A dead son—I understand how this is. I feel deeply for the man who has suffered a similar loss, and if he means to blame me for the mermaiden's powers of seduction I will make no protest.

"I am sorry for you, friend." I would like to assure him that his is not a solitary grief.

"Then there's two of us. Maggie, we say to you we're sorry!" he cries, clapping the snapshot face down upon the table.

Over a year his boy has been dead and he must have but recently discovered the fact. I see now he is not here to deliver my destiny—he has not touched me yet and will not, I am safe. Perhaps he is the boat companion I have been seeking, a man with many talents and many interests, a man of my own kind who would not allow a pike a foot of slack line, who would know how to play the fish without letting him drag the hook off into the weeds. He forgets how he has frightened me, he turns toward the screen, together we watch and share the sympathy springing from our pasts—I warm to him. I do not mind that he is in my refuge without invitation. If he is the lawful husband he has more right to the Lady than I, though he will have to keep me on for I have nowhere to go, who knows but that there will be time to wander upstream with the man and try our flies upon the giant muskellunge. It has been years since I gamed with one, but if they are still to be found in the water despite the pesticides and tarry slicks and laundry sud, if the muskellunge are there I will have a go at the rare species once more before there is no time left.

We wait, and tigers prowl across the television screen. "I have been watching over your home," I offer as a way of introduction. "I have been seeing to it that your surviving young fry do not go astray. I have been keeping an eye on the woman." I wink.

"I say a black man turns his back—" he plumps a couch pillow and sits.

"I too have suffered the death of a son."

"I say a man belongs plugged into his wife. That's what he's made for, yes? To populate the future."

"To spawn. To reproduce his own kind."

"But a black man turns his back and he loses his son."

"I tell you I understand how it is—" I want him to know what we share.

"Then there's only one thing left for him to do."

"To accept the loss," I suggest.

"To take his place between his woman's thighs," he declares, "to start over again." And he is right, for I ask you, who is nobler, a father who defers to death or a husband determined to extend his lineage?

As long as there is the possibility of birth, there is purpose. Perhaps this progenitor is not to be blamed, he abandoned his family but he hoped to return a better man. He has learned the ways of the world, the impediments, his strengths. He has been thinking hard toward his home, and he must know by now that it is wrong to cut off communication, a man and his wife must speak the words aloud, for they are like television film, even when they are closed, the volume down, still the programs run on through complications and resolutions, there are shows progressing continually inside a woman's head.

Fifty-three years should have made me more familiar with the wife, it should have given me full access into her, I had a glimpse of secrets flickering inside but still she kept so much private, there were dramas in her life I did not suspect, so when the wife fell from me I saw nought but a stranger upon the floor, fifty-three years and she did not include me in her transformation, she did not prepare me for the final blow. It is best to make a marriage with the habit of talk—breakfast babbling like a shallow stream and night whispers across the wide mattress—this is the style of marriage I would have preferred, a dialogue back and forth instead of my heated requests for attention and her stony, silent replies.

We are two who have suffered similar loss—we wait for the Lady to return and now I am willing to hand her over to this ponderous, powerful mate. Every young man needs to feel the exhilaration of traveling with a stiff wind at his back, but every young man must return sooner or later to the place he left behind. This man had the wanderlust, now he wants to rebuild his little nest among the gravel, he had his excursion and now he will have his wife. I see how the variance of coloring takes on a marked difference during the breeding season, and though the Lady might have had an interest in me, she has been all the while waiting for one of darker hue. With her ova well developed and with a gnawing emptiness left by the son, she must have a great appetite. I wonder if this man can fill the Lady's hidden grotto, I wonder if he had any suspicion while they coupled on the mattress that her thoughts were far off. Likely all the time he split her she was longing for her island, a woman remains hungry for the past. Then after he stole away from her she wanted nothing but to have him back, yes, it is no secret that a woman wants only what she has lost. Now he is home in full splendor of rage and sorrow, addressing me as if I were accountable, and if we did not have a share in a similar tragedy I would not easily excuse the man.

I wonder how it will be for me. We have had some suppers that I will always remember, a plenty I have never known before, curries and rice, stewed chicken, yes, there have been memorable gatherings here though I needed only to cast my eyes across the table and look upon the mermaiden to perceive that my joy would not last forever.

Still his family remains above, still the TV narrator drones on, I am readying my testimony when I hear someone trying the knob, and the door opens to the hallway, to the paper bags encircled by brown arms. She does not know what awaits her. If there were time to make a warning, to wave her away . . . The man has turned his murderous look upon her, she peers over the rutted edges of the bags, there is a moment when nothing is exchanged aloud, both of them trying at once to accept what they cannot believe—and there is fear on both faces, yes, even the man seems to shrink from the sight of his wife. But the moment passes, he explains in haste, "A stranger—I never learned his name—he stopped me on the street in Chicago, asked if I was ready to hear bad news. He told me everything—the girl, the stolen truck. He said it's a judgment against me."

She snaps the door closed behind her and erupts in broken gibberish though clearly it is no surprise, she has been expecting his return all along. He seizes her by the waist, causing groceries to spill onto the floor, and among the spice bottles, dishwash soap, bathroom paper, I see a jar of applesauce rattle across the planks and come to rest in the middle of the room.

I will tell you how there is one sure way to make a man worthy and that is to put a bowl of sauce sprinkled with a pinch of cinnamon before him. Nothing could compare with the young wife when she had her arms submerged in a bowl of mashed apples and molasses, her hands never tasted so sweet as they did coated with fruit sauce. I would begin with the little finger and nibble my way across to her thumb, it was a most wonderful treat, so what if we had nothing else for dinner but two crackers each and a small piece of boiled beef? As long as I had applesauce I was content, as long as the wife let me feed on her I was content. If there was need to work overtime I had only to think of the wife's applesauce and I would have strength to meet the task. Then one Saturday I was tasting my young wife, she had the sauce nearly to her elbows and I took my good time licking her clean, sucking the fruit from beneath her fingernails, savoring her boney wrists. I stopped neither at her forearms nor at her shoulders, I moistened her neck, the hard line of her jaw, and it was then that our eyes met—she did not have the dreamy glaze I was hoping for, instead she had a look of farewell, you would think she was even then preparing for our separation though she was to be my company still for forty years and more. I wonder what caused her to start looking forward to the end—it could not have been the illness, which was still long in coming, it could not have been her pappy, for we had already buried him. But she bid me farewell that day when she should have been saying welcome to the Idiot, who would be entering the next summer though we had no clue then that he was on the way. You know it was this same season when the wife learned the convenience of packaged foods, she had better things to do than befoul herself with shredded fruit, especially in our latter days when my teeth began to rot and I needed applesauce as some men need tobacco.

Now I know the sauce upon the floor has been brought for me and I cannot describe what I feel as I gaze upon the container and listen to the voices, barbed damnations flung out and returned quick from woman to man and back again. I have never heard her speak this way—it is not anger, neither is it love—it is somewhere between the extremes—she has contained in her a speech I do not understand, her voice is like water rushing over the shoals, the meaning clear in the sound. What of the dead son? They do not mention him. And where are the children? A good thing they are gone, they must not be allowed to learn from this.

I push myself out of my armchair a second time, I turn my back on the battle and retreat to the children's bedroom, leaving this married couple to their war, unaware of me. I will have none of it. The room is empty of bodies but full of spirits, that brown bear on the corner of the bed might well be the girl chub, her finger rooted in her mouth. Were she here I would say, *None of it is true, little dame, this bad dream will pass, you will awake, it will be as before.* But I am alone, without influence. This is what I would have had to endure if my wife had access to such language, thankfully she had a quiet nature and there were never riots in our home.

But what does this new silence signify? An unnatural peace— there is danger in the pall. I wait for the voices to rise again. There is shuffling, clacking glass that must be spice bottles knocked against each other, then silence again. It comes to me, the meaning in the stillness—beneath the abusive words, the violence, there has been propulsion. Silence. The current surges on through diversions and transformations. They may be taking kindly to each other but do not forget: between them is a year of absence and a dead son. The man means to claim his wife, to overpower her, he has the advantage of size and the woman does not have strength to make adequate resistance. Who will aid the Lady if not me, who will protect her, who will see to it that she is not violated if not me?

I leave the children's room and return to my Salvation chair. The Lady and her mate have shut themselves up in the other bedroom, and were it not for the impediment of age I would turn the knob gently, making no plash, no disruption, I would push open the door and witness the act—he with trousers crumpled to his knees and she naked altogether with her dress draped over the headboard. He on top, she with fingertips pressed into his fatty buttocks, he carving into her so viciously her head would knock against the board, they, panting, he, one hand squeezed between their bodies, gripping her full bosom. I do not like the thought. I settle into my chair and await the conclusion, I imagine myself so far into the sealed bedroom that it is very nearly me doing the bait casting, holding tight the cork grip, pressing thumb against the flange of the reel. I can feel him crushing her, such a stoical lady. Is it a loving that will recover the lost son?

Springs squeak, headboard taps the wall, a long exhalation from the woman, but he will not let up on her, he will not give her a moment to repair herself, he is at her and then loose inside, spawning, clutching her, traveling into her womb, him to her, my God what a rare monster might be fertilized inside the bedroom. Silence. Now they must be lumbering together, and if I were spying through the keyhole I might see a portion of her lip in view, a telling grimace, a deep sorrow. The sucking sound, the extrication. She is glossy with his sweat, bubbling with laughter now, she has made him hers again, she is content, most likely she is thinking of the new son promised, surely a child has been promised. I must not let them suspect what I know.

As I rise from my chair I catch sight of Joseph, panting, flushed from his run. So he has been audience with me, to me, I am not sure what he has seen but he wears a smirk indicating it is enough. I lunge for him, grab his collar and drag him into his bedroom, he giggles like a drunken tart, and I foam at the disgrace. I will discipline this boy, I tell you I will make good for what he has done, watching a solitary man taking his pleasure.

The boy recovers himself, looks soberly upon me for an instant then breaks up again, he might laugh at a vision of his own death if it were revealed to him. He has witnessed me, yes—but what of the bedroom door closed to him? When he learns his own papa is back and that he will soon have a new brother to replace the dead, he will not be so prone to hilarity. If he knew how his world has been disrupted, he would not be mocking me.

178

The boy grows impatient, unpeels my fingers from his shirt and assumes his post on the floor, flipping through a sporting magazine, laughing off and on. But I assure you I am not ashamed. I button my trousers and I give the boy a slight cuff upon his ear, that is enough to explode him, he turns on me, this Joseph, this one I trusted, he insults my age with descriptions of pig and mule, he swats his magazine against my shins. Not since my arrival here has the boy treated me with such disrespect. I would not stand for it if I did not have insight into this young fellow, if I were not sure that the slander directed at me will soon be diverted to the man who has usurped my place. I will make him hear me when he is through, I will remind him, *Joseph, time and circumstance have locked us to each other, no?* I will ask whether he is ready to stick to his account of me, for I have been an honest dweller here, no? I have been without prejudice, with only fair, discerning judgment, and that is no lie.

I can do nothing but watch this family perform their contradictions, they are full of the particles of dust Gibble described to me, the dust that will never be still, inside them there is such fluctuation I am hard pressed to predict what they will do with me next. I thought Magrass meant to stay an independent queen, I thought the boy was a companion who would spend his summer lying among the weeds, listening for the kingfish and the warbler. This has been a false calm here, I have been deceived and in fact there is no communion, we are all of us injured and are seeking reparations: the children have their youth, the girl has her drug, and the Lady is too preoccupied with necessity to hold a grudge against the man who abandoned her. While I, I am left to mull upon life, to ponder the scenery, and though I have discovered what would best remain hidden it is too late to retract, I have seen what I have seen.

Now I would prefer to be invisible and take my pleasure without fear of interruption, though I tell you I am not ashamed. If the wife is not here in body she is still real enough to incite me, sometimes late at night the thought takes shape and I am nearly she, there have been occasions on my way into dreaming when I am doubled, split; just before I fade into sleep I am nearly the wife, nearly but never completely, no, a solitary man is never enough to himself. I am condemned by the boy, neglected by the Lady. But I am not ashamed. I have my chair and no one will take this from me, I have a place to protect, so I leave Joseph and go out into the sitting room, I resume my seat and I cannot help but overhear the bedroom voices, the husband's repentant babble, the woman—"Don't let it make you crazy. Just don't let it make you crazy."

They mean to send me away, to turn me out into Gibble's foul landscape, but they should know and I will tell them I do not care if they exclude me, it is all the same whether I am in family company or not. I have spent a lifetime educating myself in sport and need not fear my solitude. I will not lose ambition, I will not be as the men by ash can flames with nothing to do but watch smoke take weird shape in the air, no, I will always be in flight and will not soon adore another woman. I prefer to be near the finish than at the start of such a struggle, and I do not envy the creature to be born to her, surely it will be a furious infant without my own son's quiet way, no, I assure you I prefer my idiot, who was ever mindful, always attempting to please. If he were still at the school I would retrieve him from the nuns and bring him home, I would bathe him, smooth and pack him in hugs as if he were a clod of wet earth to be troweled into a garden plot. I have seen enough this afternoon to appreciate what I had once, and I regret the damage done, yes, I regret—not a fine feeling to absorb a man in his final season. Now where is the girl responsible for my misery? You know, maybe I would prefer to be as she, a little painted acrobat with my belly exposed, indulgent, indifferent to danger, rather than to be looking behind me, regretting the journey and the choices made.

"I was meaning good for you, that's all—"

In the far room there is such sticky sentiment, the man declaring, the woman reassuring, and now the front door opens, it is the other children back from the playground, Celia first, then the twin chub, then the girl returning to what she does not yet know. Well, she will learn soon enough though I shall not announce the bad news. Magrass appears in the bedroom doorway, her braids mussed, her frock disheveled, and a hand emerges from behind, a man's hand, rubbing her cheek fat toward her ear.

"He's come back to me," says the Lady, but I assure you her eyes show she is ill pleased. She need tell no more for he has appeared beside her, they stand there and it is clear, even I can interpret the pantomime.

The children leap upon their papa, pawing, tugging as they used to do with me, he has come home, there was some trouble but it will be all right on the morrow, the trust is magically repaired. I had it so fine here, and now I am ruined, but that is always the way, no sensation lasts forever. For a moment it seems the man means to crush the girl, Little Death, with his widespread palm, so full of anger are his eyes when they alight upon her. She stands like a window display in a darkened store, he looks away but she continues to keep her chin high, her shoulders square. Now Joseph has come from his room to investigate the commotion, he stops when he sees his papa and I tell you I would like to take the boy into my arms, but it is too late, the man has extended his hand, Joseph stares as if he were not sure of the gesture, then he offers his own hand, they shake not only in greeting but in awkward acknowledgment of a new bond, that special intimacy shared between a father and his eldest boy. The family moves off like mayflies swarming thick over a patch of foam, but I tell you the reunion is wrong, and I would like to comfort the girl, though clearly she needs no consolation, no reassurance.

"He just doesn't know what actually happened," she says to me when we are alone, *he doesn't know,* she believes, but he knows too well how the girl is to blame. You can be sure I will not argue, and I will not point out to her that she has been willfully ignored.

"He doesn't know the truth, and I'm not going to tell him." With that she struts toward the privy, where she can be assured of an audience—that single spectator, her own reflection in the mirror glass.

Where the hour goes I cannot say, the children gather in front of the TV, the newscasters talk of the weather and war but they do not announce this basement revolution, there has been a take-over today yet no one proclaims the new rule.

There is nothing to be done. During supper the man does not speak, he eats heartily, masticating open-mouthed, the gaps between his rugged fangs filled with meatloaf. Silence in respect for the dead, a full meal to replenish the living. He cannot know how lucky he is to have a fertile wife and young fry who admire him. Afterward he leads back to the TV, the girl wanders upground, likely to smoke her hemp, and I stay in the kitchen, watching the Negress's back as she washes the dishes. Now I do not talk of tomorrow though I am already plotting—it is time to take my longed-for journey to the coast, I will set out driving and never turn back, though if the Lady offers I will stay another night. Surely she will not turn me out so quick, without notice. I shall remain another night. From supper it is a short run to bed for the children, to the factory for Magrass, she plants her bauble cap on her head and glides from the closet to the front door, pecking her husband's lips, he clutches her as if he means never to let go, but she seeps from his hands and does not give me so much as a nod before closing the door behind her.

I have nothing to say to the leviathan, I am silent with him even when we are alone. I try to follow the TV stories while he dangles his cigarette stick, letting his feathery ash grow inch-long and drop to the floor. In the bedroom the children have likely forgotten the changes, they will be not fretting in their dreams. I am disappointed in the Lady for putting up such feeble resis-tance—that is the way with wives, they submit before their time, and I want nothing more to do with them. Tomorrow I will ask the girl for the key to my Skylark and I will drive eastward as I was intending before this riverward detour, I will leave Gibble's city and confront the ocean and find out why the wide water was so magnificent to the wife while the mountains were nought but impediments.

When I hear the new papa shut himself up in the bedroom I turn off the television, settle upon the couch and wait for sleep. But I am every bit awake and can do nothing but stare at the ceiling, black as an ice-fringed pond, the reflection of night on still water, the lightless sky. My brother atop the power pole had very nearly reached the heavens, how far he would have risen if he had not touched the wire I cannot say. And after he fell he refused to answer even when I called out to him, even when I took a twig and poked at his arm. I squatted near and watched the cord of black blood draining from his mouth, I looked at him for a good long time until he was not my brother but a stranger. After studying him so long he turned unfamiliar on me, I could not remember who he was, still I understood that his body had trouble, and somehow I managed to find my way not home but down the ridge to an old gristmill where a widow lived solitary, her name I do not recall, nor what happened next, only it took years to be convinced that that truly had been my own brother prone upon the earth. I could have cut short these long years of affliction by daring with him to climb rung by rung and seize hold of the wire; it cannot be long for sensation to numb and then I could have taken my single flight and be done with it instead of traveling from that day to this along the ground.

Still, there will be an end, there must be an end, so dark, I would not be able to find my way even if I tried. No whispering in either bedroom, no suggestion of life. Tonight no city noise seeps underground, no traffic, no sirens. If I held my breath, or if I tied a sock around my neck, knotted it tight, or if I struck my wrist against the wall tack holding up that rope, if I took that rope, if I clamped shut my lips, pinched my nostrils, if I willed the end, I wonder what would come next. If it makes no matter. When it makes no matter. Soon the Ice. It will be the modern sort: winter put beneath the skin, a sudden shock. There is already an infant growing inside Magrass, a boy to replace me. My will is not my own, I am Gibble's slave, I am not responsible. It makes no matter what a man does with himself, to himself, if he is not responsible and he has no one left. I have come to this, a far cry from the years when daily the wife would rouse me and send me off to labor, feed me and arrange the bed, rouse me and send me off to labor, and without the propulsion from behind I slacken, without a woman urging me forward into the day I waste the hours and despair. But this was the way in the beginning, with the wife not behind me but ahead—a lure trailing across the Gibble counter, an invitation. Now I understand: she has slipped out from behind, she has struck on again, my course lies in her wake. I must follow the easterly path—it is my task to find her out, to uncover her. I am ready to proceed, and if all the while that I go forward I am dissolving, so be it. If while I hurtle on I become the air, that is better than to fail at a standstill.

Man! Her voice, even now I hear her voice. She expects me to rise from my bed—"Old man—" instead of waiting for dawn she insists that I wake, come away, yes, this must be the wife, always impatient, not permitting me even a night's sound rest before I have to move on again, her hand gripping my shoulder, her arm brushing mine, her skin eiderdown soft.

"Come on . . ."

"You just wait, woman, I have things to do." I take my good time fumbling along the floor for my trousers, pulling them over my shorts. "Where is my shirt?"

The bundle is thrust into my arms, she urges me to hurry, she helps me secure the buttons. My fingers are not supple enough, gratification she wants now and not later so she is even on her knees before me, slipping on one shoe and then another. Well, if I come away it will be at my pace and not hers. I cannot see the

184

wall, the door, she guides me across the room, not allowing me a moment to collect the other articles, my own mackintosh I leave behind, my hat, and how I would like a cup of milk but there is not time, we are out the door, slinking through the hall lit by these lamps burning all day, all night. Slight wisp of a mistress yet she has a firm grasp on me, I cannot pull away. We climb the concrete steps into the street to my Skylark, you would think we were young lovers slipping into the night. She takes the wheel and I am beside her, the car coughs once, dies, the woman curses, the engine obliges and we are off, prowling forward through unfamiliar streets, past warehouses, over the river, past the blast furnace, out the end of this grim city, Gibble's own construction, his bad dream.

I will miss the family, I will miss the young fry, I will miss the girl. The girl beside me. The same, she and not the wife. I am deceived again. I have been thinking this midnight departure occurred at the wife's insistence, but here I am still traveling with the mermaiden as if the time spent underground did not take place, though I do feel the effect, this separation is not easy and if I were in control of the wheel I might still turn back. Yet it is true the family wants no longer to include me, I have been cast out and at least I have direction again, I have a guide even if she is a mere runaway whose face shimmers with neon as a screen receives images, the lily skin cascades with shadow and light as we leave this wasted land behind.

Well, it was a strenuous fight but we gaffed old Gibble good. I am proud of the girl, I had thought she was sent to be my death as the wife was sent to be my bride, but she has proved her worth, yes, we gaffed old Gibble good, I do not know how long it took to overcome his influence but we have triumphed, we are free, and now there is nothing to stop us from reaching the ocean. But what will become of the Lady, what will she do without the girl who stood in place of her son, the angler who was as king? Will our disappearance trouble her, will she be grieved? And what of the man she has readmitted to her home, what will he do to her now that there is no one left to interfere? These stoical women are delicate inside.

"We must go back, we must not leave her alone with him!" I cry out, but the girl cares nought for the Lady now. "We must return!" I direct, but she will not obey, she has her mind set.

"You wanted to see the beach, old Tom, you'll see the beach."

How easy to shrug off our responsibility when we are far removed, how easy to ignore disaster that we will not witness: a woman abandoned and we are to blame, she will not survive beneath the asphalt, she will not endure in a home where there are no windows, no back door.

TEN

Dread World Unraveling

I WILL NOT describe to the girl how age grips ever tighter around my heart, I will not admit that even in these last days, though I have prevailed, still something has been lost. I have grown used to my underground Salvation chair, I have given up some muscle in exchange for the peace that breeds in lengthy, stationary hours, and there were times when I rose too quick and stumbled, the colors washed aswirl in my head, the ceiling glittered with pinprick lights. No, I am not the same, I have left behind my cap, my only Parmacheene Belle, and there are slight twitches affecting my fingers as if I were wired with a mild current. And now, traveling east again, I am more dependent on this green youth than ever before. I have a talent for nomenclature and named her right when I selected *mermaiden*—she has demonstrated her speed and her ability to attack, she is not one to fool with in deep waters, she is not one to trust with an account of my pain.

"Old Trouble," she says, "understand: we're not wanted anymore. But in the seaside wonderland we'll make a name for ourselves—a two-member Congress of Freaks, Tom Trouble and the twenty-five-thousand-dollar beauty. I'll learn a few songs and practice my body bends. It won't be long before I master shoulder dislocation. We'll be a hit. You, Pirate, did you always know for certain that fishing was to be your peculiar talent?"

What does it matter to her whether I nurtured one specialty or another? At her age I was surviving almost independent of the manmade world—*survival*—yes, that is my talent, the skill I have shaped and modified through this long life. What I did not learn at home I learned from the lake, the swamp, the stream, the pond, the cove, what I did not learn from water I learned from Gibble—technological facts to get by in the world—and lastly there was the wife to fill gaps with certain kinds of practical knowledge helpful to a man. Such was my education over the course of my life, most of the time I kept in good health, I was too young for the first war, too old for the second, I owned property, grew peaches and squash, I secured the house against seasonal change, I kept the wife in sturdy dress, I gave her my seed and my paychecks, I labored in the asphalt yard and carried my rods and tackle north. I have nothing extraordinary to report, there was some joy and sorrow, little that is unusual over the course of a normal man's life. Now behind me is vague history, and ahead is the wife. Do not ask me what I intend to do when I find the woman—hers is not a fertile womb nor a moist, receptive haven, and I am no young man determined to replace the son I have lost. If I have any purpose it·is entangled with this girl, she speaks of some imaginary vaudeville and I must see to it that she does not offer herself as a public spectacle.

While I was underground I watched two females, one abandoned, the other cast away, I studied them closely and I saw in the one, the Lady, an attitude of innocence unspoiled by experience or exploit, I saw a purity her man will never appreciate, while innocence in the girl has been buried deep beneath a crust of deceit and drug and prostitution, but I assure you she can salvage the quality, I will do what I can to uncover her.

"Sing for me then," I say, but she snorts as if I were making some indecent request, though music was her idea before it was mine.

"I don't think I want to after all," she replies.

I see it will be hard work reviving innocence here, but I will keep after her, whenever she flashes beneath the surface I will drop the line, one of these days she will swallow the bait and go off on a tear.

"Do as you wish," I say to put her off guard. I will not let her think I have an interest, for the girl has a tendency to displease me when I am wanting a result, she is like one of the weather demons my own grandpappy would describe, woodland spirits that darkened the sun when we wanted it bright, chilled the air when we wanted it warm. In the olden days they used hexes to ward off ill treatment, today they use persuasion, but neither seems to have much influence. Now I am not one to credit superstition, I do not carry a rabbit paw or protect myself by hanging circles inlaid with stars from roof gutters, still I am wary of forms invisible to the eye: a man who believes only in touch and image is a fool.

I watch the play of light and shadow upon her face while she accelerates us away from Gibble's asphalt ruins. It is a fact that though I dare not bring up the topic the girl is still bound by law to her progenitor, it is a fact that I would be held for her wrongdoings, so I have reason to stay alert. She is mine—I have grown used to the idea and do not want to relinquish her. Along the road balsams have replaced split-level homes, we head south or east, I am not sure of our direction, for though the city lights have transformed to broad, heavenly scapes of constellations and a moon three-quarters full, I have lost my talent for celestial navigation.

We drive on and I stall encroaching sleep, I wait and keep a watch upon the girl. I do not forget the woodland auction when she pretended to lose the rights to her bones, done to mock me, a burlesque meant to taunt a wifeless man, I do not forget her abuse of the matron in the highway diner, and I do not forget how she laughed as we stumbled over cemetery sod. I have gained some understanding of mermaiden ways, I am familiar with her appetite and her abilities, nothing she could do would surprise me anymore. Now it is not long before her eyelashes begin to flutter, I see her grip weaken upon the wheel—one hand lazily knots strands of her hair, with her attention wandering who knows what she might reveal.

"It will be light soon," I say, and she murmurs acknowledgment. "I intended to walk out to the river to see the late-blooming dogwood," I tell her. The girl is already elsewhere in her thoughts, so I proceed. "A solitary dogwood." The girl is elsewhere. "I meant to return for breakfast. Perhaps Magrass will buy crullers on her way back from work. But you and I will have no sweets." I must keep an even voice, draw my words lightly one after another. "It promises to be fine weather when the sun rises. I said it promises to be fine weather when the sun is aloft."

"I hear you, Trouble," she murmurs in a limp, indifferent voice.

But still I must use care, I must not let her outguess me. "I intended to set the kettle boiling for Magrass. And Joseph, Joseph thinks he's old enough to drink coffee, Joseph thinks he has no more developing to do now that he has no elder brother to admire." I pause, then creep on. "I wonder if there is any catastrophe worse than a brother's death, be it by accident, illness, or violence. No, I can say from experience the loss of a brother is very nearly the loss of oneself. Be it accident, illness or violence. Now the untimely death of Magrass's son was no accident, neither was it disease. You yourself said it was no accident, you yourself told how—"

"We turned over and over . . ."

I nearly have her now. "You intended to do what you did."

"And the sound of crumpling metal, it was like a surge of applause."

"There was one person who could have saved the boy, one person who could have cried *stop!* Can you tell me who she is?"

But I have learned mermaiden habits enough to be sure of her complicity, I do not need to wait for her reply. "You were in control of his fate."

"Who?"

Now this is false ignorance poised on the girl's lips. *Who?* she asks, pretending she has not been following me after all.

"You," I hiss. "And your young Negro. Why did you encourage him to prefer death, why did you allow him to drive out of control?" I shall make plain to her what I know: "I do not doubt that you were the one to convince him that the only way to protect romance is by seeking a quick end to it. I do not doubt that had he been a wiser lad he would have gone his independent way. I could have warned him, *Boy, a fast woman will destroy you, she will draw you into the whirlpool and swim away as you sink beneath the foam,* for I tell you I know how it is to be left behind."

"It was no accident," she says agreeably, "and you know it wasn't Gus who steered us into the ravine. It was my foot on the gas pedal, my hand on the wheel. Maybe he would have protested if I told him what I had in mind."

"You told him nothing!" I cry out, aghast at her indifference. "You mean to say you drove him off the road without sufficient warning? He would be alive if it were not for you—he would be there to assure the Lady of peace, he would be his mother's trophy, he would be her pride. Never forget who is to blame, never forget who is responsible! Explain to me why you wanted him dead."

But even as I rage I lose my conviction, I do not believe so readily in her guilt, who knows but that this confession is yet another feather hiding the sproat, a lie, of course it is a lie. Her claim is not to be believed, he is dead, this is the single truth, it is all I need to know.

"Because," she replies, "because I'm sensible." She seems half

191

asleep, weaving a dream aloud. "Because I know it's better to jump rather than dwindle, better to leap than crawl."

The girl will not give up the tale now that she has begun it, but I tell you there is no violence past, the girl was not capable of such a deed, she knows as well as I how death makes such a cry that will haunt whoever overhears. Whether it be in the form of a woman collapsing, an idiot bleeding, or a small boy burned by electricity, a man can never shut his ears to the echo. Now the far-off peeling of car brakes on wet tar reminds me of the dreadful voice of a fading woman, no one knows better than I the sound of the fall, the thud of impact.

You wanted her dead.

"What did you say?" I demand.

"I said because I'm sensible."

"Not that, the other!"

"To jump . . ."

"The other."

"That was all."

What compares with this evasive prey? She is here and there, darting from bank to rapids, full one minute of confession and the next of accusation. *You wanted her dead,* she said to me, I heard her and now she claims ignorance. She will not keep consistent, she pretends it is I who deserve damnation. I wanted her dead? "Repeat yourself!" I say, she begins again her declaration, I order her to be silent. This web of words, I do not know what I want to say or what I am denying. I wanted her dead?

"Whom do you mean?" I mutter.

"You—" she begins, but I do not know who is the predator, who the prey, the girl has caused such convolutions soon I will be confessing to murder, she will have me uttering some grim account of how I crept up behind the wife and pushed her from the willow chair. The girl toys with me, batting me to and fro, she has me enacting a crime that never occurred, she has me imagining I assaulted my wife. Would she have grasped at my arms, would she have known as she fell that it was I who had toppled her? There was the slapping sound as her hands met the floor, hardly more than the splash of an unskilled angler's fly upon a still lake, and the cry, cut short, but loud enough to resound evermore. *Because you wanted her dead.*

"But we were talking about the boy!"

"Who?"

"The boy who was courting you."

I say you wanted her dead.

"Be silent!"

"Old man, you are under the influence. You must be under the influence, that's the only explanation."

"Do not speak to me! Do not utter another word. I have no ears for you, I will not listen anymore." She presses her lips together, mute as my idiot, she does not dare go on with her abuse, for I have come down hard.

"You shall not speak to me again," I say, "we are through with words."

I am forever closed to her, the drug has unraveled her logic so that I do not know what to believe. Simply sitting upon the car seat, I have been implicated, somehow I have traded places with the girl and I am just now recovering from the murderous passion let loose upon a sickly woman. I am in delirium, I cannot be sure we are moving forward and not backward, upstream instead of toward the sea. I still have an urge to look upon the sea, I know this if nothing else: I have a wish to look upon the sea. The girl is a muzzled shadow now, we do not share a common language, there is to be no mingling, no effusions, no demonstrations—she keeps her thoughts, I keep mine.

I see we are traveling east—the sun has made a slow ascent ahead, yes, we are driving into the morning, away from the night, drifting on some broad, crowded highway. Cars flit past us, but the girl does not take sufficient caution, who knows but that she wants to repeat the collision that caused the young Negro's death.

Is she capable of murdering a boy or did he accept her high speed, did she spin the wheel without warning or did he volunteer to die? There can be only one version of the of the event but the girl has confused me, proposing multiple accounts: at one bend in the guardrail she is confessing to murder, at the next curve she denounces me, and then she denies the facts I spit back at her. The girl thinks she can redo the incident by relating it with different words, for pluck and suppleness nothing compares with her, she is one moment guilty and the next naïve. How remarkable to have such control, to turn and alight backward through the same deep lakes and up nearly insurmountable falls.

Well, it is easy for a young female to ignore realities, but for an aged man the facts will not disappear, I am here, neither behind nor ahead, my wishes cannot influence the weather nor re-create the past. I expected death to strike when I was underground, yet every morn I woke refreshed, and I admit I grew fond of the Lady, who had a place in her home for me but no place in her heart. When once or twice I made an effort of intimacy with my eyes she rebuffed me, lifting her proud chin, stalking away. Would it have been a grand chore to return my loving with some mere fragment of affection, an indication in a raised hand, a slight tilt of her lovely head? Perhaps there were occasions when we came near to colliding but ended up gliding past each other gently, who knows but that all the time I thought I was alone the Negress was adoring me, hoping my unquiet thoughts would calm, yes, all the long, solitary hours under the city I was not alone. I wanted to transform the woman and waited for her to accept me on the mattress when she was loving me in another way, worrying like a mother for a soldier, a nun for a dead sinner. I shall never forget her splayed cheekbones, her ripened lips, the braided rivulets of hair descending from the lattice on her scalp, her hefty bosom beneath the robes, how her teats would have swayed if she had mounted and took me in—I was sick with love but how could I have invited the Lady to look upon my store of dry bones and scaly flesh? No, I knew well enough I was not fit to receive her. Still it pleased me to imagine her visit, with my eyes closed it was the wife, yes, with my eyes shut I could hope for the Lady and wait for the wife. This mighty longing fed upon itself and nearly gave me the wife back in vision, yes, I very nearly had the wife back. Now, at liberty upon the road again, I have lost hope, I have lost inspiration.

"It won't be long," says the girl, ignoring my demand for silence. "The ringmaster retires and the side drums begin to rumble—"

I outstretch my finger, rap upon the dashboard and remind her, "I said I have no ears for you."

I too can dream, I too can remember as I please. I can have the Negress embracing me, the wife with a hardy appetite, the girl as my offspring, the basement as my own bedroom and instead of a plaster ceiling above there will be the cloud-spattered sky, Gibble with a Jock Scott pinned to his cap, the Idiot, my first-born son, limp upon the floor, bloodied from the impact of a chair cast his way, the Idiot, with Gibble kneeling over him, brushing aside his tangled curls, the Idiot, sucking in air through nostrils wet with blood, the Idiot's rattling breath, his fingers rubbing his stinging flesh, a lump rising beneath the welt on his cheek, eyes watering, but the Idiot *alive*, yes, I can game, I can tell the tale differently, I can pronounce the Idiot alive, recovered from the onslaught of his aged papa's wrath. I can say, *Look at me—I am guiltless and this flight unnecessary.* There would be no consequence, no appointment with the executioner, if I did not cause death. I can say, *Look at him, he survives. True, I struck him down, but as soon as I was out the door I tell you he arose, and Gibble prepared an ice poultice to ease the swelling on his brow, the Idiot groaned but in an hour he was nought the worse for the attack. Look at him—you would not know he had been harmed.* By now he would have lost memory of the assault, he would not remember the wife's willow chair thrown in his face, and if he dreams at all it is not of terror but of

195

the weeds bordering Josiah's Pond, the breeze caressing him, his mother's warmth as he rocks upon her lap and drinks her frothy milk.

Such a rare talent: I want my son to live again, I make him live. He is fixed in some special school near Gibble, tended to, watched over, moving carelessly through his middle years, blind to age overtaking him. Now that he has recovered I can wonder how it would have been for us if I had brought him home after I buried the wife. Together we could have spent these many weeks arranging the furniture as we chose, moving the squat table in the corner of the sitting room to the center, lengthening the kitchen bulb chain by two inches, letting mold spread on the wainscot, grime collect on the stove burners. Consider: a return.

Man, there is nothing left for you!

Hush and consider this: a home intact. Reliable, practical chairs, a hard mattress, a television, cabinets stocked with instant foods, potato, oatmeal, gravelcake. My idiot, asleep.

Man, she is rotting into the soil, fodder for the white worms.

I do not fear. Consider the world inside a fleck of insect membrane, the insect gut, the wonder of insect digestion, pellets of gristle and flesh. The mystery of the world inside that tiny parcel is enough to fire a man's imagination, he can fancy up the minute structure, he can fancy maggot opinions, maggot habits and preferences, he can ignore the appearance and imagine the secret life.

Man, the flesh is flayed, shredded, clinging to dry bones, the jaw is agape. And the white worms. Making their way into her.

I do not dread. Consider maggot oblivion. He does not care about the former occupation of his foodstuff as long as the body be dead, he holds interest only in the nonliving and knows nothing of the world. I ask you, is a man so different from a maggot? A fellow can fix upon any object and burrow his way into it, he can travel far into the silverfax and yet go nowhere, he can revive the past and yet need not live through it again, there are so many possibilities both behind him and to come, more than he has time to consider. So I will design my life as I prefer it, I will revive my son, I will bring him home. I rest easy, knowing what I may attain.

Man, nothing is left for you.

There is this: consider the empty house, yes, the solitary nights, the spirits lingering, the remnant rags still draped over the banister, the dishes stacked as she arranged them, the suit still spread across the bed awaiting me, our mattress, her willow chair, her coats still hanging in the closet, her wool jacket with her own fragrance clinging, yes, all arranged by the wife, abandoned by the wife, my own house, built with my blood.

Let me tell you how it was when I threw the chair at my son— I saw him dead because it was the easiest conclusion and gave me reason to leave my home once and for all, I saw him lifeless when he was merely sulking upon the floor, I imagined his condition without taking a second look. It was my excuse so I could depart from the home haunted by fifty-three years. Now who knows how far back deception goes? As far as the first stirrings of love, so that I persuaded myself of a fondness felt toward Gibble's dressed fly when in truth there was no love? I have remained alone though I fooled myself good, now I am a widower, floating in a vast space yet so convinced by love's deception that I have made myself forget the solitude a man must endure.

These are thoughts coming from great depths and I would prefer them to sink away from me, I find no joy in a consideration of my powers. There are few events with easy explanations: *He is dead, alive, how did he die, why did he die, or live, or fall into a loving that lasted fifty-three years, was it fancy, was it fact, did he love the wife, did he ever know a wife who was not his mere daydream full-bodied?* And when it is all behind how can I adhere to my opinions if I cannot distinguish the truth? If only I could revive the credulous child inside me, the boy whose imagination worked upon the world until there was no world to be known separate from his dreams. For drama I could make a dead squirrel scream in the night, for comfort I could turn my brother into a stranger so I would not have to acknowledge his death. But a man is educated to prefer the world unmuddled by imagination, and I am too aged to have my understanding shaken by this girl beside me, I thought I knew what to believe but now I am sure of nothing.

Well, I will do as I please, I will go on gaming with the girl, insisting upon imaginary truths, but I will not be so caught up in the artificial tale that I forget I am inventing all. While I construct a new version I will retain a perspective. So if I announce the existence of my son, I will know the fact is only a wish, and if I declare that the Negress gave me nuggets of affection, I will know the claim is only a desire, and if I call *Wife!* and hear a whispering reply, still I shall not forget how this is a sport on the verge of tremendous rapids, there is no solid earth beneath me, I can be sure of nothing.

But I am glad to be released from the underground, away from the city, even the pigeons have stopped their dull flapping. I am grateful to be other than the Negro who has resumed his place at the head of the table—at night he will be one of the city wanderers, hovering beside an ash can flame, sucking upon cigarettes, laughing, taunting, knotting aluminum cans to the tails of stray hounds. Well, I hope young Joseph follows my advice, I hope someday he will make his own way out of the city up into the hills, hike north along a riverbank until he comes to some broad pond spattered with lily pads, he will set up camp in a quiet glade and he will live year round, foraging for food, catching bass and trout, trading trophy fish for provisions at the market. His sister Celia will fill out into a rounded woman after the fashion of her mother but even softer than Magrass, and she will know the satisfaction that a ripe girl must feel when she is savored. They will soon be forgetting us, by tomorrow they will no longer wonder, by the next day the long stopover might as well never have been.

But I, I am an angler who leaves homes in quest of greater bounty, I did not stay content with the brackish water of Josiah's

Pond, and though there have been detours, I am on my way again toward the sea, a life of hard work behind me, glory ahead.

Now the mermaiden has taken it upon herself to put us off course, steering down a ramp into the parking lot of a roadside cafeteria. Respecting our determination to keep silent, she offers no explanation as she shuts off the motor, she just leaves me to grow old alone in my Skylark. I watch her parade along the sidewalk in those denims so tight nearly every ripple of her arse is visible to any passing stranger who takes the time. I watch her pass through the entrance doors, I wait a good five minutes longer before I reach over the seat and grab her little beauty bag. I search among the brow pluckers, hair pins, nail scissors, scents and special soaps; I do not find the drug but that most likely remains with the girl. Instead I take out the many colors of grease paint, the carmine stick, eye pencils, the powders and shadows; I collect the decorations in my hand. The girl has a supply enough to last a lifetime—showy female, one day she will not be able to peel the mask from her face. I dampen my fingertip, dip it in a disc of waxy red, and press the color to my tongue. Well, it seems no more noxious than a child's crayon, but I know the truth, it is a foul substance and will transform a girl into a tramp.

I open the door and pour the plenty onto the asphalt, emptying my hands entirely, and though I intend to replace the bag just as I found it I catch sight of a tip of paper hidden inside. I do not commonly pry into a female's secrets, but consider how we are connected—it is my duty and my right to look more closely at the snapshot. It is the image of the Negro boy and Little Death arm in arm, the picture that speaks of impending tragedy. If I had seen the two on the beach I could have said then and there how the romance was all wrong and would end in death, this is the only possible fate for mismatched lovers. I pocket the snapshot— the girl stole it from Magrass so I may justly claim it as my own. I shall keep it with me in my trousers, for you know it tells a story similar to mine—I was married to my opposite, the wife went on ahead and it is I who have died, yes, I who have suffered the impact.

With the paints spilled beneath the car, the photograph hidden, I return the bag to the back seat and drag myself out the door and into the restaurant. I look about but I do not see the girl in the crowd of highway travelers lingering in the lobby, I do not see her by the gum machines nor by the road map display. I find her where I might predict—at the candy counter, selecting caramels and suckers from cascading rows, purchasing one of every item. I would go up to her and remind her of sweets' ill effect on spirit and teeth, but still we are not speaking to each other. I position myself where she is sure to see me—a few feet away, beside a rack ornamented with stuffed rabbits—I watch her and wonder what inspired her to make that desperate romance. She has seen me for sure, but she will not acknowledge me, so while she exchanges money at the cash register I approach and stand as a henchman beside her. Let people stare, let them imagine what the girl has done to offend me, yes, I am embarrassing her. She hands over an allowance of two dollars, shoving the bills toward me as if I were a pavement bum, and I make no attempt to thank her, for the money is fair pay.

I wander off to survey the icebox cases, I select a slice of cream pie, an ample slice with what looks to be a molasses syrup glaze, and as I draw it out of the case my elbow is rudely knocked, the pie slides to the edge of the paper plate, teeters, drops upon the floor. People step around me, jostling me against the glass case, smearing the dessert, churning it to a muddy mess. It seems the entire world wants to pass me by and no one has taken notice of the accident, so I remove a second slice of pie and cradle the plate next to me as the flow of tourists forces me on. They are all buying egg sandwiches and coffee, no one cares to take notice of me, and though I would like a cup of milk, still I do not dare try to balance the plate with one hand, I must be content with what I can manage.

When I reach the front of the line the dame at the register glares at me as if I were a disgrace in this slick highway restaurant with its stained chrome and its donut-shaped electric lights, I am in clean trousers and a flowery summer shirt but the lady looks me over like I were scum upon a pristine lake. She mutters, "You going to pay for that other piece?" nodding in the direction of the dessert icebox, disguising her command in the form of a question so that though it is unfair I see I have no choice, I am obliged to pay for the slice swatted from my hands by that fat man or that lad or that woman in tinted eyeglasses. I announce that I will pay, but when she rings the sum it is a figure almost double the amount I have in my hand.

Where is the girl? She has abandoned me, left me to flounder and starve in this mad competition for breakfast. I tell you there is one general principle working in this establishment and it is *maul!* Maul your neighbor, maul your food, turn wholesome substance into trash, masticate, discard. Nothing to do but give up the piece that is rightfully mine and pay for the sludge on the floor. Surely the woman can see I am an honorable man, I, a wizened, beardless man, honorable and proud.

"I shall purchase that slice," I say, "and return this one."

Dull female, she sees there will be no conflict, her green eyelids slip back to their half-raised bored position, she takes my money, gives me pennies for change, and I attempt to backwash through the line but none of these vacationers will give me an inch, it is no easy passage holding the pie and maneuvering. When I finally reach the case the crowd has closed behind me, blocking the dame from my view and I from hers.

Now I have an idea, not an honest idea, nor brave, but I have been training in devious mermaiden methods, I have been mastering her talent for achieving satisfaction regardless of the rules. Instead of returning forward I continue back against the crowd, I clutch my plate and slip around the corner of the slatted divider into the patron seating area, I make my way through clusters of

complaining infants and old women until I reach the entranceway, only to find two policemen inspecting the crowd. Now I
have not forgotten the one-legged man who was beaten in the city
dawn, I have not forgotten the savage face of the law. Cradling
my sweet in my forearm, I back away and push through the
privy's swinging doors, where inside three men are splashing
wordlessly. There is one place left for me to occupy in this world,
and that is on the closeted john. I close the door, secure the latch,
and here, with the smell of waste and cigarette smoke spicing my
meal, I devour my sweet in great gobs, I use my fingers as a spoon
and scoop the cream from the graham crust. The thin syrup icing
crackles, flakes off. I do not wait to swallow the last morsel before
I gobble more, my lips and cheeks are sticky with chocolate pudding, the crumbs cling to cords of my hair.

Soon there is nothing upon the fluted plate but streaks left by
my tongue. I sit upon the toilet, breaking wind and wiping my
face with the rough bathroom paper, I sit here, sleepy now, peaceful, indifferent to the profanity writ upon the wall. I could remain
an hour if this were a more solitary enclosure, but there are voices
of youth gabbling by the basin, and I am reminded how this
public bath is but a temporary refuge. I take the opportunity to
do my business—it seems I am excreting what half a minute prior
I heartily enjoyed, and I cannot help but wonder whether the
theft was worth the trouble. You can be sure I check that my fly
is buttoned before I leave the compartment, I keep my eyes fixed
to the floor. I do not want a stranger to remark upon my shame,
to see the ignominious criminal inside me, the same criminal who
played truant as a boy, spending the school day at a brook, bringing back poor specimens of sunfish and eel strung upon a withe.
Such spirited adventure produced no fame, always I ended the
day a fool, with a few scant spiny-rayed fish instead of a salmon
or a trout trophy.

It takes a determined effort to stalk past the law, even though I
have revised the assault behind me and have brought my son to

life again. My deceit offers no security—if I have absolved myself and made my son live, still the world may not agree with my version of events, the law may insist my son was dead and remains so. I maintain a humble stature, easy enough for an old hunchback, nobody notices an old hunchback. I walk past the police into the parking lot, I crawl on, fearful, anticipating the outcry: *Stop!* But I am at the Skylark, a free man still, and the girl is inside chewing caramel, staring ahead. It seems she has not discovered the theft of her paints, nor does she suspect I have pocketed her image—she has not checked her beauty bag, a good thing, for the colors are visible beneath the car, a pyramid of clutter waiting to be mashed into a pancake by the tire. The girl still has no voice though I am weary of these rules, I want to announce my cream pie adventure, I want to boast of my most recent crime. But if she insists on sulking then I will make no effort toward reconciliation, I can snub her or converse with her just as she pleases. I shall occupy myself privately with anticipation of the possibilities: the ocean bronze-cast at dusk, the ocean sparkling at noon, the midnight ocean. The wife wants to share with me the surf foaming against monumental rock, the gulls wheeling, laughing, the schools of perch and blue churning the surface; the wife will not soon forgive me if I delay.

You see, I am an old man but I can anticipate carnivals and a future that has no end, I can hope with a young girl's vigor, I can steal cream pies and drive to distant places. Were it not for the photograph—a stiff paper square against my leg, an emblem of how the world goes awry—I would be carefree. But the snapshot reminds me: *Every romance has its destiny and when opposites are matched, that destiny is sure to be collision.* I can fancy false accounts, I can pretend that the woman crying out to me on that chill March noon was not the wife, but the illusion soon evaporates, and when I remember how I am alone, when I admit that all the adventures following these losses in my life spring from the dead like green shoots from a new grave, then I grow indifferent to the gaming, the sport becomes a trial—the flights, the digressions, the causes and effects, all have no meaning apart from the dead. I tell you it was I who fell when my brother burned, I who collapsed when my wife cried out, I who bled when my son was struck by the willow chair. And now I make no passage forward, my journey is but the slow sinking of a battered man, a corpse.

ELEVEN

A Black, Formidable Tail

BUT BRING ME a hundred yards of cuttyhunk line and half a crab and I promise to have ready a boiled, well-spiced dish of salt-water fish for our supper. It cannot be long from here. The street is crowded with row houses pressed shoulder to shoulder, homes wrapped in drain pipes, veiled with porch screening. Well, it must be a glorious sight ahead or why would all these bathing beauties and slack-chested men be making their way in such a hurry, columns of them marching along the sidewalk like ants intuiting the rain, with automobiles creeping slowly along and children tugging squat wagons? Any moment the sea will be before us, the open water where huge schools of carnivorous blue leave behind a wake of mangled fish parts. Now I have seen a dead blue stretched upon the table and I have tasted blue, but I have never been inclined to go out after these barbarians of the eastern waters, these ravishers. There is nothing the likes of them in the fresh water of home—their gluttony is renowned, their savagery and indiscretion. They do not spare their victim, be it a promising adolescent or a mackerel bloated with spawn, they seize the unsuspecting fish and devour the hind portion while the head piece floats away or sinks. It was Gibble who told me how a school of blue is a chopping machine that will not be interrupted, they are to the ocean what the deer plague is to the forest. It was Gibble who swore that on record is an account of how a fish swallowed whole by a blue nibbled his way out through the stomach wall and escaped. No, I never had inclination to go after blue.

I am in the wife's domain though I see no sign of the wetlands, the juniper, the wind-swept grass, I see no sign in the streets of the wife's past as I have imagined it. I know from Gibble how she would dance alone over stretches of white sand, she must have been a lively terror, and I wish I could have been introduced to her before she put away her youth to become my wife. But where are the balding dunes, where is the marsh carpet surrounding her childhood home, the grass full of seabirds that would, Gibble said, erupt in squawking cacophony and attack the wanderer who trespassed among the nests? It was Gibble who spoke of the wife's girlhood, for she remained silent on this subject; it was Gibble who told me of her fear of roosting terns and the handful of stringy weeds she used to ward off an attack. Imagine a young girl leaping madly above the sea, or a young girl on a winter night, a face behind the rain-streaked window, watching the wave summits boil, the black sea heave. My salt-water wife, she never renounced her first love, I was always second in line to the expanse of ocean outside her childhood home. Now all I want is an intimation of the majesty that preoccupied my woman, I want to see how the water earned her devotion. The wife had little need for my conversation, she had her Atlantic for companionship, and he had such a resounding voice to make me jealous long after she left him behind.

The wind carries the scent of sun-dried fish, but still we have no view of the sea. I do not know how the girl has found her way, perhaps the direction eastward is instinct in a woman, perhaps they all are drawn by some colorful lure. In this last hour we have shared no conversation, we might as well have been traveling underwater. I wonder what she is intending next, she must have friends here, another family we can claim as our own while we grow familiar with this town and find work for ourselves. She could serve suppers in a fish diner and I could purchase tackle gear and stand knee-deep in the surf—we will have sheepshead in the morning, marlin at noon, sea bass for supper. I will make this girl robust, this sultry, silent girl who does not yet know how I have outwitted her, probably she is anticipating her next smoke, hoping to invigorate herself with drug and paint her face. But she is due to rest, a young girl will die if she does not rest, while I, an old angler who has earned his retirement, I have lost my capacity—during my stay in the city I had no chores, no tasks at hand but to teach myself armchair patience, and I have stored up enough sleep to last until the final night. Weeks, months, how long I remained underground I cannot say, I have lost track of the date and the seasons changed while my eyes were closed.

What will I do now, how will I fill so many waking hours? I shall ponder that body which served to entertain the wife all through her childhood—I trust that it will live up to my high expectations—fifty-three years Gibble had me convinced I was not as good as my wife's first love and all along I wanted nothing to do with her Atlantic. But now I am not so envious of the salt water, instead I am prepared to honor the ocean, to pay my respects.

But is this narrow strip of landfill the coast, and the flat water ahead in truth a fertile breeding ground? The streets drag the bathers toward the water like determined shallow rivers carrying all the effete material from inland to dump on the sand. The girl turns our Skylark onto an avenue running parallel with the public beach, she pulls to the shoulder, sets the engine at idle, and from the patch pocket over her breast she takes a twig of a cigarette. She plucks out the car lighter, presses it against her stick. I am no fool—that is not nicotine incense, it is the rank smell of hemp, the girl has lost all discretion and will not even spare me the sight.

She blows the stream of smoke against the rearview mirror, it bounces back into her face but she takes no notice, makes no apology, she merely sucks her drug and admires the view. Only a few yards away a flock of pearly gulls are scavenging through trash, they scatter when a hound rushes forward, they circle overhead, backpedal their wings, throw their feet forward and alight again on the mound of broken seashells.

"Drive on," I urge the girl, "take me away from here," but she ignores me and I cannot persist, since it was I who made the law and prohibited speech.

The sea, the beach, the plump bathers, the hemp smoke, the heat—all is a perversion of natural order. I know from Gibble how long ago the seashore was a stretch of bog and dune, scattered with isolated lighthouses and small family inns. Well, much has changed since the wife came inland, and if she had lived to see how her homeland was abused she would have stopped pining to return. It is hardly to be believed: this sheet metal stretched before me kept her from ever obliging to be completely mine, this dark water, these heaps of sodden ash strewn with bodies, rows of naked arms and legs cast randomly about as if some nameless creature had risen out of the sea, devoured these bathers, and spit out the excess. And the ocean is but a stretch of thick water lapping weakly at the band of gravel between sand and surf, this great, glorious ocean, coated with red sludge. Children dance at the water's edge, chase the tide back, sprint away as it rushes in around their ankles. The Atlantic yawns, rolls sleepily, spiritless. The view seems designed by some mean painter, scenery more fit to be pasted on a billboard than here before me, and trying to imagine how it used to be is the same as attempting to find the child in the unkempt face of a spinster. Fifty-three years Gibble assured me I was no competition compared to the sea but I wonder whether the wife was ashamed, yes, she was ashamed of this sorry body that inspired her devotion.

The great, glorious Atlantic. If I had known that Gibble's account and the picture postcards were untrue, I would never have come this distance. I do not like to consider all I put up with just to look for myself. So many stumbling along the walk are white-haired, all of them pretending to enjoy themselves, so many with nothing better to do than watch the waves break feebly upon the shore. I doubt no longer that before me is the source of disease, the great parasite eating away at the land, nibbling in such small bites, taking its good time but always pursuing its end. Where are the wading birds, the willets and the plover? Where are the barrens Gibble described? Instead of birds there are dirty children scampering along the sands, instead of stunted junipers there are masts and flagpoles extending from the pack of sailboats offshore. The sky is a plaster ceiling enclosing sea and land, it is no lie to say that a man has more freedom underground than here.

I prefer the mountains, a woodland not so easily ruined by human occupation, I prefer Josiah's Pond to this basin. I would rather be standing at my own back door—the kitchen would be full of the rich smell of suckle, I would survey the uncropped woodland, the timber in its fine summer greenery, I could imagine it all to be mine and forget the influence of industry upon the land, for the countryside does well to camouflage its trash, covering candy wrappers with dead leaves, pop bottles with sumac. The countryside works slowly but sooner or later it digests the rubbish, the earth takes into its bowels deer carcass and cardboard alike, while here the refuse floats upon the water, collects upon the sand, and the people wallow in their waste instead of burying it. Gibble described to me the schools of haddie that are driven to shore by voracious blue, he told me how the haddie collect knee-deep, stranded by the retreating tide. These crowds are comparable to beached fish, they are more dead than alive, expelled by the sea, burning a crusty brown in the sun, while somewhere out there, beneath the glass sea surface, far below the yachters' nets and the trolling lines, the blue are gestating, multiplying, claiming the watery acreage as their own.

The girl smokes her drug until it is hardly more than a finger-nail paring, then she tosses the remainder out the window and drives on along the avenue. On our right the beach is segmented by chicken wire and picket fence, and on our left nightmarish hostels rear out of the lawns—twisting spires, towers of salt-bleached wood crowned with white lattice. There is no reasonable cottage to accommodate a man and his wife, no modest home.

Now without consulting me the girl has parked in front of the largest of the edifices, a huge spiny seashell of a dwelling. "What do you mean to do next?" I ask, but she has no reply other than a winsome smile. I tell you I am more worthy of fear than of pity, yet she has nothing but an uncompromising grin and blood-flecked eyes with which to speak to me.

She reaches to the back seat, snatches for her beauty bag and leaves the Skylark, she crosses the yard and struts up to the porch cluttered with lawn chairs where guests recline lazily. Into the grand hotel sweeps the girl while I remain in the Skylark, flushed from the superior sympathy she spends so lavishly on me—it is enough to make a man feel impoverished though truly I need not be ashamed. I must go after the girl and haul her back and force her to speak out loud again, she shall answer me in a delicate and gracious voice, she shall attend to my directions, for now I choose to turn around, I choose to leave the sea behind me. There is nothing respectable about the wife's past, and I am eager to move inland again, perhaps to journey into the northern clime and dis-cover a wilderness that will receive me, some sanctuary of pine and rhododendron.

How many times I have already tracked the girl I cannot say. I follow her across the lot and up the steps, I hold myself with such majesty that the women on the porch look upon me with their appetite moistened. But I do not return their attention, I do not disdain to glance right or left at the many guests whose eyes are shadowed by cap visors, their hands folded upon their laps. I enter the building as if I had enough money in my wallet to purchase the great Atlantic itself, I stroll through the door left ajar and down the carpeted hallway. The wallpaper is embroidered with felt ivy, the lighting fixtures have huge glass bulbs and dangling crystal chains, the oaken thrones are empty, pushed back against the wall. The ancients rustling past me keep their eyes focused ahead, I am not acknowledged but that makes no matter, it is a scarlet, snow-covered world here, deadened, and I am only passing through, I do not mean to linger. I enter the central domed room where there is a reception desk and a marble fountain misting rubbery tropical vegetation. I pretend a sure purpose, for I do not want to suffer the shame of expulsion; I mean to find the girl—she could be hiding anywhere in the woodwork, in the closets, behind any one of these closed doors. Why has she led me into this antique lodge? Ahead in the hall I see one of the guests sunken into a wheelchair—on top is a scruff of silver hair, on bottom are two slippered feet paddling along the ground, pushing and pulling the chair while the shrunken arms hang useless beside the wheels. It is fast approaching me, so I duck through an archway and hide beneath an empty coat rack while the chair rolls by.

As the creature passes I take a good look at the sunken cheeks, the balding skull, I understand how this is not the grand hostel I had assumed it was, it is instead a seaside institution where ancients come to fade and die, it may be a dressed-up institution, but in truth it is an institution like any other for the weak, the incontinent and incapacitated, an institution, I have arrived at last, baited by that treacherous girl, lured ever forward, I have arrived—an institution and I am trapped. It is the fate plotted by the wife, made known to me by Gibble, it has been my direction all along. I am helpless as a firefly inside some rascal's jar while around me the elderly folk dwindle to ghosts. An institution. But they have not taken me entirely, I am still a capable adversary and if I could make my way home from the Adenburg cemetery through late winter wilderness then I shall find my way out of this sepulchre, this vessel of costly clutter. Like the mermaiden's beauty bag containing scents and soap, this place pretends to nurture elegance while in truth it is harboring the substance of death.

I turn to face the parlor where I have hid—a broad expanse of shining floorboards stretches to a curve of glass doors, a room without furniture except for what looks to be a piano pushed to one corner, covered with drapery. I let my eyes sweep along the edge of the room from wall to curtained glass to an alcove where, on a cushioned ledge in the shadows, there is a body. Dead? Dying, yes, I can hear the rattling breath. I creep cautiously across the room, the bundle does not move, and not until I am right beside the window seat do I see it is a girl in a plum-colored dress and a white bonnet. A young gentlewoman from some lowland tribe. Now I do not forget how on the day my own mam was laid out for the viewing we were visited by dozens of these old-fashioned men and women clad in their somber costumes, I do not forget how none of them had a kind word for me, they moved like shadows, their shoe heels made of cotton, and I thought they had come to take my mam away to their netherworld rather than to bid her goodbye.

This sleeping girl wears the same dull dress meant to hide her shape, though I can see how she is constructed, I tell you I can see, for the dress collar has slid off her shoulder to reveal a portion of her throat, her hands are tucked beneath her bosom, her face is the blushed shade of skin unused to sun but lately exposed. I have not observed one the likes of her for years, and how she has come to be asleep before me I do not know. Can I be certain that she is not a trick, another deceiving dream, and I have fallen under the institution's influence? Her eyebrows are a dusty red, her face blemished, yet how can I be sure that she is not the institution's bait? Someone must know my appetite, someone must have selected a morsel guaranteed to interest me, and the girl is here impaled on such a hook that will hold me fast.

I must leave this place at once! But first I must prove that she exists. I want to know whether she is spirit, flesh, or fancy, I cannot stop myself, my hand has a will of its own as it inches across the empty space, my fingers twitch, quiver, hover over the cheek. If I do not trust my eyes how can I be sure unless I touch her, but if she wakes and finds me here, if she is independent of my vision, what shall I say to her? I dare not land my fingers on her flesh, I dare not whistle softly into her ear. An old-fashioned gentlewoman, pristine, chaste, scarred by the pox but untouched by worldly corruption, she is what my dear mam must have been a hundred years past and I have discovered her again in this house of the dead. It is as though I have come upon my origin, the form that harbored me and dropped me ripe upon the earth.

On a second round I may not choose to be brought so quickly into the world. It must be amply warm inside this gentlewoman's womb, I would sleep when she sleeps and take in the foods she swallows, and although my papa would be disappointed when the birthing day came and went and he still had no son, I would let him suffer my absence as I have in my manhood suffered his. No, I would not choose to leave her on the second round, she is worthy of a close embrace and maybe she would not mind if I dropped my hand gently upon her bosom, maybe she would make room for me upon the ledge, blink her sleep-blurred eyes, she would see how I am an old man in need of comfort, I will spend the day in her arms and I will not let myself pass away from her at nightfall, no, I will not leave her on this second round. If she knew how I was fearing she would not let me go.

She stirs. From the hallway comes a sudden trumpeting of voices: *Beware of the old man, beware!* The chaos is my own, but it is sufficiently loud to disturb this gentlewoman. As I shiver she blinks, her eyes are like jellied eggs, she looks up expecting girl-friend or bellhop, finds instead a hunchback wanting to caress her. She shrinks away, the ruckus inside me is deafening, the world unbalanced. I stagger backward across the room. I do not belong to myself anymore, I am no better than her apparition and will disappear as she wakes.

I would not be locked inside this gentlewoman's dream if the mermaiden had steered our Skylark inland. I turn around and find her leaning immodestly against the door frame, her shirt bundled up so that hideous scar must show itself. Who knows how long she has been watching me? I do not doubt that she will make me pay for what she has seen: an old man wanting nought but to hold this frail gentlewoman in his arms, and to be held by her. Now I have no time to explain myself to the angel, for the hussy has struck off again. I leave the gentlewoman and hurry out of the room and down the corridor, around the lobby fountain, past the aimless guests, and I catch sight of her as she escapes through the door. She must have been to the hotel's privy to freshen herself and discovered the paints gone, the snapshot gone.

By the time I arrive at the entrance she has already run across the road to the wood walk, dissolving into the crowd of strolling bathers. How I shall find her in the multitude I do not know, there is nothing to be done but wait for her to return. As I leave the building I am half expecting a white-robed arm to extend out the doorway and collar me, I am half afraid that I have been convicted, sentenced, condemned to this institution, but no one takes notice of me as I pass along the porch and down the stairs, no one cares, and I remain free.

On the walkway above the beach I take a seat on a slatted bench between two unsmiling fellows who have the same tangled, frosted hair, swollen lips, flattened noses. They are turned away from each other. This is a common feud—two brothers divided by passion, pretending indifference. Together we sit out the murky afternoon, watching the bland amusements before us: children sculpting castles, old women in golf caps shirking flies, flesh basted with sun oil, young bodies wrapped around each other like beef hunks on a spit. We all three look out over the scene and none of us dares comment aloud, I have settled in the midst of an argument and do not want to disturb them, and they have clearly reached the point where words do no good. We wait, and gradually the humidity relents, the wind rises, and the few swimmers tumble out of the surf onto the beach. By late afternoon there is still no sign of the girl, but I have faith that it is merely a matter of time before she will be missing my company.

It seems a trick of the dusk: I see the old-fashioned dame from the institution trotting down the plank steps to the sand, but she has duplicated herself many times over, there are four, five, a half-dozen replicas of the gentlewoman, a troop of them on the sand before me, all wearing bonnets and long dresses so I cannot distinguish one from another, they are barefoot and have come to dip their toes into the surf. I do not mind so much that my girl is absent now that I have so many gentlewomen here—their harsh dresses flutter and snap about their legs, the red-flecked foam wraps around their ankles. I am content to pass the twilight observing the innocents, they are unchanged by passing centuries and have resisted the souring that spoils other youths—consider those boys, for example, the rapscallions who stalk the girls, whistling and shouting vulgar names. But I do not blame the boys for teasing them, who could help but single out such oddities. If I were a spry thing I too might want to game with these somber delicacies, I too might toss fistfuls of sand at their feet, challenging them to undress like other seaside girls. I wonder which female is the one I discovered asleep, the one so like my own mam, I would like to ask her what good she means to do in this infernal town.

Now one of the ruffians has discovered some huge crablike creature at the water's edge. He grips the shell and holds it before his face like some frightful mask, he lunges for the girls and they draw back in a single cluster, their hands extending out, fumbling, clasping for each other's garments. Maybe they are nurses hired to care for the ancients, maybe they are the ones who prepare a corpse for viewing, whatever their task is it must be connected to death. As they file back to the hostel, their faces downcast, their hands hidden in the folds of their skirts, a chill draft seems to rise from them. If I had some authority here I would see to it that these gentledames could take their pleasure for as long as they wished—dipping their toes into the ocean must be a rare treat.

The boy who is clearly the lead tormentor still holds the giant crab by its tail while the other boys squat on the sand. He swings the crab in wide pendulum arcs, another boy swats at it with a twig, and even from here I can hear the boys exclaiming at the wriggling pincers, proof that the animal is still alive. In another situation I might go down and have a look at the living fossil—I know from Gibble how the occupant in such a shell is soft as the inside of my lip, and I would like to see for myself the animal encased in the armor.

The crab is set on its back in the sand, the three boys huddle over it and with a pocket knife they take turns punching the blade through the belly armor, they pry open the crust and dig out the flesh. I do not know the proper method of dismantling these crabs but there must be a more merciful way than this—is that stain on the sand the thick, tarry, naked crab itself, puffing and deflating? Are the boys smeared with carnage? The wicked one has snapped off the tail and he displays the prize, holds it up for all to see, but I have an uneasy sense that he is directing his victory toward me, surely he cannot be addressing the two stony brothers. Well, I will not sit by and applaud such barbarism, I shake my fist at the boy and he shakes the tail in retaliation while the other boys clutch each other and break into a spatter of laughter like drunken gluttons at the height of a feast.

I am luckless. The boy has selected me as his new victim; he rushes across the beach, open-mouthed, a look in his eye I cannot describe, his two small companions capering at his heels. Waving his arms, he flies up the steps as though hurled by a catapult. Now before me are the two choices available to a free man in a

crisis: to stay, to flee. But on this occasion I have no opportunity
to decide, I have no time to spring off the bench and scuttle down
the wooden walk, the boy is already upon me, teasing my neck
and shoulder with his short, deadly whip while the others hoot
and catcall and the brothers slip away into the crowd gathering
to watch an old man beaten publicly. They have no sympathy,
they cannot imagine themselves into this weathered hide, they
cannot feel with me the swipes and humiliation, they think that
because I am toughened by seventy years and more, hardened by
winter cold, blistered by sun, I feel nothing.

I shut my eyes. I shut my eyes to the spectators and fold my
arms over my head. Shameful refuge, this posture of defeat, cow-
ering beneath the whip. And the water has become velvet beneath the dusk, and the night shadow is creeping over the beach,
reviving it after the day's abuse. Fine refuge. Boys laughing.
Crowd murmuring. I want to seal my ears forever, to deafen myself to this world. If I could hear nothing then I would uncover
my face and I would not have to endure the sound of the collapsing waves, I would not suffer the racket of insult and ridicule. I
have no scalding words to fling out, no protests, no prophecies, I
cannot give an account of my suffering that would bring them to
their knees. They have no idea what it is to be an old man set
upon by pint-sized demons, and they go on muttering appraisals
of the battle while I struggle to protect myself and the boy dangles his whip inside my shirt collar and the waves fall lazily, un-
heeding, and the gulls wheel overhead. Where is the wife to de-
nounce crowd and assailants, to accuse them in her quiet voice,
to blame them for the damage done, to warn them that such a
man with such a stock of experience inside is not easily replaced?
Once I am gone I am gone forever. I tell you they will be sorry,
there shall be no opportunity to revive what they have lost, the
damage done is irreparable, and they will suffer the conscience,
all of them, they will be laden with remorse. I do not envy them
their sad lot, such a burden of guilt.

How long I have endured this assault I cannot say. When the

crab tail ceases to tickle, when the boys stop giggling, I peek out like some great turtle that has survived a storm. The crowd has filtered away and none of the pedestrians moving along the walk shows an interest in me now that the boys have left off. With my eyes shut there was a multitude gathered, but now I am not so sure, they are all preoccupied with food, smoke, bottle, and radio, it is hard to think of them distracted. My flesh does not smart from the lashing and I see no sign of the wicked one. Well, I may not have wounds but I have a memory, and I assure you I will not soon forgive these bathers who delight in a man's shame. If I ever have opportunity to repay them, they will not be spared, delinquents and spectators alike, and all the women who deserted me when I was sore in need.

When it is not anger that motivates a man it is nature, and what with this excitement I am compelled to visit the surf. I rise, walk to the steps and lower myself gently to the beach. Sand fleas leap into my trouser cuffs and seagulls trot before me. I stand upon this intermediary filament and splash the giant stretched out before me. Now that the crowds are gone and the horizon empty of sails I understand better how the ocean may be a forbidding sight, and I cannot comprehend the impulse that kept my wife ever longing to return. She never used the ocean for sport, she merely took pleasure casting her moony stare morning to night over what was a terror to her. I spit into the sea. It heaves indignantly, swells, washes over my shoes. I draw back, slop and struggle across the difficult sand and up the stairs, and join the column of pedestrians. I stroll with them along the walk toward the dome of light. The sea growls below, disgruntled, powerless; we are safe from it up here, we may build, decorate, demolish as we please.

Now the walk has widened and on either side of me are food shacks and carnival stands, cartoon freaks painted on billboards, bloated cloth puppies displayed on shelves. In glass cases there are porcelain fortunetellers, and at my feet, such rubbish—hot dog rolls, sucker wrappers, shredded bathing caps, bread crusts, soiled diapers—this is to the land what the bluefish wake must be to the ocean: a stain of gluttonous waste, everywhere there are people gorging and discarding, procuring and gorging, madness truly. But such amusement serves at least to help shelter the town from the ocean, and if I were a seaside dweller I, too, would seek loud diversion to muffle the rumbling that never lets up, never lets up; imagine passing a lifetime in the neighborhood of this incessant voice. I understand why the wife was so eager to come inland when Gibble sent for her.

But here such clanging, jingling, squalling, laughing, are enough to deafen a man. If the mermaiden is anywhere she will be found amidst this circus, so I keep a sharp lookout. I wander along, hoping to recognize her in one group of teenagers or another, I grow hungry again, and so weary.

It must be near to ten o'clock when I feel a gentle tug upon my shirt, small fingers wind around my wrists, lips brush against my chin.

"Tom Trouble!"

Well, it is my vagabond come back for me, I do not think she has ever approached me in this familiar way, it proves she is overjoyed to discover me though I am an unkempt, rancid old man. She is eager to pass over the late disruption in our friendship, we are as before, two travelers shirking the public.

An urgent whisper, "Old Tom," signals the end of our pact of silence.

I welcome her back with an earnest embrace, I squeeze a rousing shriek from her, I hold her by the shoulders and look into her eyes to examine her better. I find the bright, glazed look, the glittery red orbs, unseeing, and I understand how her joy springs not from me but from the carnival, from the drugs and games. Her loosened blouse, frayed hair, and grime-streaked face tell of her exploits.

"Where have you been?" I ask, and she replies, "Old Trouble,

I was looking for a photograph, a photograph of Gus and me. We were standing on this beach—and now I've lost him."

I want to hear no more. If she smells of drug I will say nothing, if she smells of carnal pleasure I will say nothing, it is not my place to keep her sober and now likely she has both hemp and seed inside her, foolish streetwalker, yet she is glad to see me, she kissed me once and another I mean to take.

"Old Trouble, I'll tell you the truth—"

She raises her blouse and before I can look away she has grabbed my hand and is forcing me to touch her heated flesh, to finger the scar, the line of puckered skin dribbling along her rib-cage.

"The truth is that I fell asleep at the wheel. We didn't know where we wanted to go, we were just going away. So the truth is I'm to blame."

Her voice trails off, my fingers rest upon the feathery welt below her bosom. I do not know why she must go back and back again to the day she lost her young Negro, but I tell you I will say nothing, I prefer her beside me and if this depends upon her confession then I will not interfere.

She is tender with me now, she has invited me to touch her. She shakes her head to clear the trance, lowers her blouse and leads me by the hand, away from the surf, through a passageway skirting a fudge shop. I do not know what she wanted me to understand when she showed me her scar, I do not care, a female's past is always a mixture of secret love and tragedy, and a man wastes his time if he tries to uncover her. Now the girl tells me she has found a room suitable for an old man in need of sleep, she insists it will be great fun occupying ourselves eternally in this shore town. I offer no opinion; ours is a delicate bond, a tender gut that will easily tear, and I do not want ever again to unsettle her devotion. She is fondest of me when she is submerged in dream, and I will do whatever I can to keep her glad.

TWELVE

A Reliable Arm, Hold On to It

THREE DAYS, she reads ceiling cracks for parables that will reveal the world's mysteries, she has settled like dust that will not be beaten clean. In our room the walls are a boiled egg yolk shade of lime and the tile floor sucks at rubber soles like liquid cement spread for a walkway. The pipes in the corner knock and rattle through the night, sounding the arrival of cockroaches that ascend through the bath drain to bask in the darkness; in the morning I find clusters of them in the enamel tub, congregating close to the puddle of water dripping from the spout, the plocking rhythm marks time while for full an hour or more I consider the constitution of the metal door handle, the latch and thumb press, the line of shadow cast upon the door.

The girl shares nothing with me but sometimes I dare to steal a look at her, her face is a plaster death mask, her flesh dissolves into the sheets as a deer carcass disappears into the earth. Three days and she ventures no farther than the privy, where she smokes the drug while she ponders her reflection. She knows I shall not chastise her for the indulgence, she enjoys her hemp as the wife enjoyed medicines, and I will do nothing to interfere.

She does not speak of the paints or the snapshot, though surely she knows it was I who did the plundering, I who stole her image. She waits—for what I cannot say—she stares like an ancient bed-ridden woman, but it is enough that we remain together, I tell you it is enough that we remain together, three days, we have found our solitary refuge, seaside.

I dare not raise the question of tomorrow, the fact that our funds will run out does not concern me, I have lost my forward-looking sense. There is nought but the faucet drip, the shadows, the shallow mermaiden breath, the strike of the match head when she lights her drug, sometimes the thud of her bare feet as she heaves off the bed, sometimes the groaning of bedsprings as she shifts positions, draws her knees to her chin, picks at the sediment between her toes. Only once has she surprised me with a display of passion. It was our second motel night and I was making an attempt to entertain the girl with an account of how the ice-water trout came to life upon the chopping block, I tried to have her hear the sound of frozen reeds combed by a February wind, I tried to have her live with me the winter adventure, indeed, I thought I had won her attention. She looked as if she could not wait for me to relate facts of the upland weather, facts of the trophies won with a lively shiner or an arrangement of peacock feathers on the hook.

I thought she had forgotten her private suffering when suddenly, without warning, the girl sprang from the bed, danced across the floor, and slid an aluminum can lid off the counter into her open palm. She had seen some indescribable beast in me and was threatening it with the razor edge of the tin wafer. "Don't you want to touch me?" she invited, though I promise you I had made no suggestion of advance. "Don't you want to touch?" not ranting accusation as she had the night we were packed on the asphalt, instead confronting me with her shameless seduction.

But I understood clearly how it was the drug responsible, she saw me through a distorted lens, she saw not my age inhibiting me but the image of her own terror and there would be no convincing her of my good will when she was under the influence. So I cut short my soliloquy and lifted my hands to signal defeat— a gesture that appeased her, for she set down the lid, approached me, took to coddling me in contrite affection now that I had surrendered, she patted my head, murmured, "Poor old Tom," like I were a stray hound she had befriended, "poor old Tom, lovable pirate." This is her way, she will treat me gently as long as I manifest no spirit and remain her pet, her doll, an old hunchback fresh from the taxidermist.

Three days I have tarried as a passing phantasm. It is I who attends to the motel fees, lifting sufficient cash from the girl's wallet, I who purchases foodstuff and prepares the canned macaroni while the girl indulges in drug. Now though we are in a bedchamber, just the two of us, I have no desire to try advances and she has made no second invitation. I want only to be near; I am at peace when I am stretched beside her, and though I sleep close to the edge and she against the wall, still we share the same mattress. Why this female flesh does not inspire me I cannot say—it is not that I have lost ambition, not that I have lost desire. But we seem to live in a world where touch is impossible, vision all we have, it is enough to embrace her with my eyes. I have been woven tight into this tapestry and as long as I have consciousness I will not be alone, it is enough to cower inside this green room with a child and know she has no one left but me.

We have been hiding like a new-wedded couple in this lowly resort, and daily I have set off on two excursions—one in midmorning to purchase provisions, one near dusk to gaze upon the glassy sea and watch the gentlewomen descend to the beach to splash in the surf while the sand-coated ruffians make sucking sounds and throw fistfuls of sand. You know I would like to handle one, I am not satisfied with the mere sight of these dames as I am with the one who occupies my bed. These girls never approach, they flirt with the water but they will have nothing to do with me, and just when I am gathering courage to call out to them, they grow transparent in the twilight until they are silhouettes of gray, then they file back to resume their chores and I never can be sure they will return on the morrow. When they are gone I rise from the bench, troubled though refreshed, and I wind my way along the crowded walkway back to the motel without stopping to watch the contests between squirt guns and balloons, pop guns and bottles, for I have no interest in these entertainments, I want nothing but to wait out the rest of my days in uneventful contemplation of the innocent and the beautiful.

Three morns, three noons, two dusks. And now the third. I leave the mermaiden to dwindle and I go out into the carnival. Around me minstrel songs are pumped through loudspeakers, clowns inside glass cases howl at the cost of a dime, children spit melon seeds through the slats of the boardwalk, and machinery swings and plummets people fool enough to pay for stomach upheaval. This is a mockery of the scientific effort—here technology is vulgarized in game and ride, there is no forward movement, only spirals and circles, so every passenger is forced to return to his starting point. A great circus of science with a single goal: the greatest happiness for the greatest number. It was Gibble who tried to convince me that technological ambition springs from this generous impulse, but I always knew it was otherwise, I always knew the men in their laboratories were too absorbed in the particular to care about the general, and if cities were truly planned around the democratic principle then this carnival is all we have left, the remnants of the nation meant to be. And always there is the surf in the background, surging forward, cackling back, clawing desperately for a firm hold on gravel and sand, but only those who disdain the amusements will hear its voice.

I know what preoccupied the wife, I have listened to the dirge haunting her though she resolved to keep the song a secret from her husband. *No need to concern the man, no need to repeat the sound aloud, the tide is a woman's burden and must be suffered silently.* Such was her way fifty-three years, she had salt water in her blood, yet she clung to our floating continent, moved away from the sea. Now I wish to call her back and explain to her how we more readily endure when thoughts are not borne solitary, the world is less fierce when we mingle, I wish to have her hear me out, I will invite her to ride in me while I drag my heels along the wooden walk. *Wife, we shall wander the coastline together and no one will notice we are joined, I am two, no one will overhear the echo of one heartbeat upon another. I will keep you safe inside me and together we will pass through the days and never again will the sound of the waves worry you. We have come far, so do not argue for your independence anymore, Wife, exist in me and do not complain.* We will enjoy the carnival together and no one will glance twice at us, no one bothers to take notice of an old widower, no one cares to explain the madness in his eyes. I pity these generations who indulge in drug, gambling, and machine athletics but have not learned to listen through the ears of another, nor have they learned to shirk ambition, nor do they know what it is to come back from the dead.

The evening is not so still and the water not so placid as it has been these prior days. Tonight a thin fog shrouds landscapes and skylines, it is a gauze of mist as delicate as a cataract curtain descending over my eyes. Slowly I make my way along the glistening boards, I step with care for if I fall now I endanger the wife. There are few tourists entertaining themselves tonight, but still the game bells clang, the clowns laugh, the neon colors blind.

Wife, I am sorry to have brought you here, for it is a bothersome carnival, a wet evening, nothing to see. But we will look upon the water, we will wait for the maidens to appear, we will admire their changelessness, their grace. Wife, stay with me, and do not suggest you have better things to do, more important tasks at hand, you have earned your retirement and all along I was promising you this seaside vacation, you will not spoil it for me. Stay.

I fear this mist, for I cannot tell whether it arises from in front

of my eyes or within them. This must be how drug disguises—
it transforms the world into a watery mirage and from that into a
true oasis, first a girl will see what she wants to see, then she will
drink from her dream, how wondrous it must be to float in foggy
twilight where it does not matter whether the water is real or
imagined. I push on through the cloud, I find my bench and settle
on the wet slabs. I wish I had my mackintosh, and if I had kept
my cap with my Parmacheene pinned to the rim I would pull it
low over my ears, I would not be shivering so.

*Wife, hear the buoy bells ring, the foghorns sound the dangerous coast-
line crags, hear the surf.*

It is not hard to imagine myself far from the carnival to a lone-
some boardinghouse built on wood pillars above the marsh, the
wife's home, she abandoned it and I will tell you why: *Because you
feared the water, Wife, that is the truth, you feared it as a child and kept
fearing it all your life. For fifty-three years you hid your fear, you made
yourself into a crusty, steely-eyed woman but I understand what was
inside you, I assure you I understand, so do not try to cover yourself.*

But we do not share together the mist, the night, the ocean,
for long. We have a visitor, a man interrupting our contemplation
with a loud "Evening!" ovaling his mouth to a pea-sized hole and
sipping the air.

His arrival is ill timed, I do not care to have a stranger intruding. He settles beside me, grunting as he lowers his arse, he is a
stiff old salt eager to exchange pleasantries. At another time I
might receive him more congenially—it seems we share the same
plight of age and poverty, he might have been a friend to me if
circumstances were different—but I have my woman to look
after, *how can I be conferring with you, Wife, when there is someone else
wanting my attention?* He is dressed in a rain slicker, yellow
breeches to match and knee-high boots, he looks to be a deep-sea
fisherman. I would like to query him about the sport but I do
not want to open up the subject or there will be no end to our
talk.

226

"We'll have a time of it tonight," he persists, he will not be satisfied until I reply, so I mumble acknowledgment, which he takes as approval. "I prefer the rough weather," he rambles, "it draws the most reluctant to the surface, while when the sun is hot overhead and the waters smooth, you have to sink your line to the deeps."

"Large minnows will take the big fellows," I say, I cannot help myself, I cannot withhold what I know. "Suckers, too."

"You," he barks, "do not have to tell me about bait. No man knows bait better than I. At home, my friend, I have a beetle farm, a thousand and more. The mackerel love them breakfast, lunch, and dinner. No, sir, I need no advice. I will take you to see for yourself my collection of delicacies."

He is a boaster though I tell you I would thrill to see such a farm, but I know well the wife would not approve, so I thank this salty mariner and I refuse, I refuse on the wife's behalf.

"Another time, eh? But the mackerel, how I love their meat. Hard to find these days, with the corporations out there taking just what they please, disrupting the balance."

"I have heard much of the earnest blue."

"Aye, his fame is cheap. The palm for appetite belongs to the deep-water trapmouths, they live some six thousand miles below the surface and will swallow fish much bigger than themselves. It must be a beautiful world below—imagine having a mile of water over your head."

I tell him I come from the hills, he watches me warily a full minute or more, then he asks in a voice so measured, so low, you might think he was demanding my life's secret: "You fish, then?"

I do not hesitate to announce my devotion to the sport, the man has identified my talent in my face, he sees me for what I am, a fresh-water angler away from his element.

"Sport, you say!" He is taken aback. "It is no game and you are no fisherman until you are in your boat before the moon has set seven mornings a week. You are no fisherman until the struggle loses its thrill, becomes tedium, your daily labor, you must learn to despise it, then you may call yourself a true fisherman. You must come see my briny hull. I will take you out to sea, and I promise you, you will never think of it as sport again."

Truly he is a proud skipper and I respect such a man whose life is an endless battle with salt-water fish, but I tell him no, I cannot accompany him, no, my time is short, though if it were not for the wife I would be less quick to decline.

"And do you shoot?"

I, who have never owned a gun, I who have never been inclined to lacerate the pelt of woodland creatures, I, who prefer the doe flashing upon the path ahead rather than dissolving, spoiled flesh, into the soil—I say falsely, "Certainly I shoot," for suddenly I feel in contest with this man, as if my reputation were at stake.

"Ducks?" he asks.

"Positively," I lie.

"Then you, sir, must show me your swing shot, and I will show you my blind, my bird blind, built in a marsh five miles south from here, you must come with me tomorrow, the storm tonight is promising, the fowl will be abundant."

A marsh, he says, the wife's origin, a desolate place. I beg him to describe the land, I demand to know if he can see from his blind a crumbling, shuttered house.

"I take no notice of the land, my friend. I look to the sky."

But I tell you if I ever found my wife's home I would pry open the door, I would make my way across the dark hallway into the parlor lined with moldy tarp covers, I would ascend the rotting staircase, streak my fingers along the banister dust, I would enter the bedroom. What I would find I cannot say, I cannot imagine.

"I built my blind along an established flyway and I have such an arm," he rattles on, "a twelve-bore repeater with a modified choke. The gun has never failed me, I do not exaggerate to say I am a flawless crack shot. I have a heavier rifle for land hunting, but I do not mind shouldering this for a day. You will use my

twelve-bore, I'll use my upland, we must set off before dawn."
He has offered me his gun, he assures me that I have never eaten
as well as I will tomorrow. "But of course if you have brought
along your own arm," he says, "then you don't need to borrow
mine. I know a fellow grows attached to his weapon, and what is
right for one man may not be right for another."

He includes me in his hunting plans though he cannot suspect
I am still seeking the wife in the home she abandoned half a century past. Now I am certain she would have stayed rooted to her
native sand if the ocean had not threatened, if the surf's voice
were not so awful and so constant. She saw how the sea steadily
devoured the sand, she was sure one day it would reach her feet,
she would go under, she saw how her pappy was failing and she
knew she had but one hope left. *Gibble!* she cried out, for he was
near a brother to her, *Gibble, help Pappy and me!* and he sent away
for his cousin, my mail-order bride, my burden fifty-three years.

The man speaks loudly of his blind carefully woven with cat-
tails and swamp reeds, he tells of the birds, their astounding eyesight, and how if a cover does not blend into the landscape then
a man has no chance of surprising fowl. He says he owns two
wool-lined rifle cases, extra solvent and wax, he says he is ready
when I am.

But I have interests other than birds, interests that are just now
gathering at the water's edge, like the flock this shooter is wont to
describe. The gentlewomen have arrived. They stroll to the
empty beach, but this man takes no notice of their beauty, he is
busy describing with his hands how he holds firm to the breech,
uses scope and peep to gauge the deer bouncing through the sage-
brush. There are only three of the dames braving the fog tonight,
they stand where a thin membrane of surf reaches them, washing
over their toes, they perform their water worship silently, three
virtuous maidens, solemn but not in love with the grave, they
face the ocean while I look reverently upon their backsides, truly
a blessed sight, enough to revive a man's spirit.

The duck shooter runs on with his comparison of decoys and trophies, but I have no patience, I prefer to be left in peace. I would trade sporting talk were I in a sporting mood but not tonight, no, not with the gentlewomen outside, the wife inside, the mermaiden awaiting me.

In these late years of my long life the females have been persistently demanding more attention, first it was the wife losing her parts, then it was the girl disgracing herself, now it is the gentledames tempting the water. But do not mistake me, I always reserve a place for women, still I wonder how they have come to preoccupy me so. Well, maybe I am ready to turn to other attractions, maybe this duck shooter would be good company, he has arrived just in time to revive my affection for manly trial. I am not so old that I am incapable. Though my arms may waggle flaccidly and my legs tremble with my weight, still I long for the kill, yes, I will do it, I will accompany this shooter, I will share his gun and his table. I will follow him from boat to blind, we will sit side by side tomorrow morn and take turns blowing ducks into a thousand ragged pieces.

"Man, show me your boat!" I demand, and he blasts fish-rot breath, overjoyed, he slaps his chest, identifies himself as Mister Samuel Fyfe and boasts of his vessel—the barnacled hull does not tell the full story, the battered deck cannot speak of all the storms it has withstood, but I will tour the sloop bow to stern and I will soon be praising its merit.

Now he has caught me by the elbow and I have no opportunity to resist, I must hurry with this wayfarer across the boardwalk and into the narrow street, I must leave behind the gentlewomen and walk the pavement past these great ghostly mansions, across the street and into a dank alley. It is not long before I am regretting this undertaking, I would have preferred to stay put upon the bench, and why I struck out in the company of a stranger I cannot say. I am a sportsman, yes, but I am spent. I have made my exertion, now it is time to take my due retirement. *It was a passing impulse, Wife,* I regret having accepted his invitation. I have come a far distance and had meant to spend my last days as a dandelion head gone to seed, the wind in my hair. I wonder if I have been inhaling the girl's hemp smoke too long, this delirium is drug-inspired, I was thinking myself hearty when in truth I am so tired, why am I so weary after three days doing nothing but admiring, sitting, sitting and admiring? I cannot say, but my exhaustion is a fact, *Wife, it will be most wonderful when the peaches are ripe,* I hope we turn home soon or it will be too late, the fruit will drop to the earth and the red ants will set upon it, all because we dallied in the company of this proud shooter.

Behind the neighborhood we come upon the harbor, an arm of water thrown across the land, a sleeve of an inlet pressed into the belly of town. Looming in the fog are great furled masts and even greater yachting towers, hundreds of boats. There are a few mariners moving about on the decks and in the parking lot. The mist sets a strange pall over their activity so it seems not routine they are busy at but instead grim preparation for war. Fyfe leads down a slippery, near-vertical plank suspended by rope, he holds my forearm to aid my descent and keeps a firm grip as we pass along the floating walkway. As with a suburban avenue that begins with stately homes and ends with bleak, mean abodes, the pier displays its sleeker vessels first, and behind these are worn lobstering boats, and at the back of the row are plywood cabins nailed to rafts, dismal structures chained to iron dock rings. Surely these homes do not go sea-gallivanting, without sail or motor they are fit only for the harbor. Such a vessel is Fyfe's home, a flat-roofed closet with an eye-slit window in each wall and a single door appropriately sized for dwarves and hunchbacks. Fyfe is a man nearly Gibble's height, and he must stoop to enter, he guides me from the dock onto the narrow deck and into his home, a waterlogged crate with electrical bulbs, an oven, even a flush toilet. So he is merely a tale-telling voice, like any fisherman solitary in his habits, lying concealed in the harbor ward though he would have me believe his is a glorious palace, weathered but watertight, enviable, sacred. No, my friend, it is none too easy to remain both proud and honest when faced with the meager trophies collected over a lifetime. With nothing to do but count up his earnings, how can an old man help but pretend to have more than he has? Friend, go over a lifetime spent in diligent labor and indigent accommodations, look backward and *tell yourself lies!* vain lies, rejoice in your scant fare, say it be more than it is.

"You have done good for yourself!" I pump him with false praise and he whoops in agreement, sure as hell he has done good, that is right, nobody can say old Fyfe did not see himself through on his own, no one can say old Fyfe fled the ocean when age overtook him; Fyfe is upon the water seven mornings a week.

But his true love remains the marsh, the whispering wind, the fowl beating their wings against the water, the crack, the strike, the plummeting carcass. He would keep a hunting hound if he had the space, he would buy a third rifle if he had the money. For a moment, only a moment, he lapses, seems on the verge of complaint—stuffy home, stinking water, no furnace, no room for a dog—but he resists such an outburst, instead he winds his way back to the blind, his swing-shooting skill, his twelve-bore with modified barrel. He pulls a carrying case from beneath his cot, unclips the buckles, and tenderly removes barrel and breech. He sets it upon the mattress so I may ponder it with admiration while he pours whiskey and stations himself on the opposite side of the cabin, his elbows resting on the counter top, his fingers sunk into his fleshy jowls.

Wife, I have not forgotten you and please do not utter your disapproval, I know what you must think. But do not blame him, he has no woman who will object to his cheek stubble, no formidable wife who will tidy the house.

"To the deadly game." He toasts his glass while I remain empty-handed, he has poured a second glass but makes no indication that it is mine.

Well, I will not worry over his manners, I will take the drink

232

myself, I will compose some eulogy for his airy home, his epic past, his modified barrel, and then I will be off, *Wife, we will be free of this dullard,* I will return to scope and peep upon the gentle-dames though likely they are gone from the beach now, installed for the night in the home of the dead.

"Listen," says Fyfe importantly, peeling off his raingear until he stands before me in trousers and ribbed undershirt, "the right lead for one man is not necessarily right for another." But this shooter has lost track of our conversation, he is saying nothing when he proclaims so confidently, "Take a woodchuck prone, take a duck upright. Learn your preferences, and use your stance to good advantage. Whether you target what you aim at depends on how you hold your gun and balance."

I see this man has the Gibble quality—he must treat every acquaintance as a subservient, assuming command with his forceful advice. But I have more interest in the rigging strung on the walls, the bottle with a miniature sailing sloop inside, the whiskey, the lobstering traps used to hold his pots and pans, the fog horn wooing boats to harbor, the sloshing of water around pilings—I close my eyes and imagine the deluge.

Wife, do not fear if you lose sight of the shore, we must trust this boat to keep us dry, I will drag a net along the ocean floor and collect a multitude of sea life—squid for frying, bass for broiling, while around us circle the schools of ravenous blue. We will feast and sleep, sleep and feast, and though we will be dashed about by conflicting tides, still we have a ceiling, electricity, planks beneath our feet, a flush toilet, and fish as much as we can eat.

For now there is tart whiskey and an endurable companion. I will pretend a love of the hunt, for it is best to keep his voice and liquor flowing, I am grateful to be here with a worthy shooter instead of at the motel with a young female specter. Another drink, another toast to a lifetime full of natural adventure, *Yes, we have much to be proud of, we have made it this far when all along the way there were perpetual threats, illness or accident to stop us short.*

But he turns to me, he lowers his glass and says solemnly,

"You, sir, have never shot a gun. Not in your lifetime. Not in mine."

So he has uncovered me, it is best to oblige and go by the truth. I lower my head and make no attempt to defend myself. He is quick to forgive—he comes round to rub my back, explaining how any proven hunter would have cradled the twelve-bore, stroked its polished metal, while I did nought but look blankly. Well, he has won this round, there is no denying that I do not love the arm, and now that he knows I do not share his passion he lets loose whole encyclopedias of hunting lore, he wants to fill the single night with his wisdom. I fix respectfully on him while he describes how he kills uniformly at seventy-five yards, though at least half of his success must be attributed to his treasured rifles, bought through a mail-order catalogue some distant year. Luckily he was not victim of wholesale fraud, there are such scandals in the rifle business, a man does not know whom to trust so when he finds a reliable arm, he had better hang on to it.

"Look to the weapon . . ."

Another toast, another drink, I must sit down. This duck shooter is too caught up in the thrill of the hunt to notice my distress, but I tell you I am not fooled into admiration, his talk is artifice, his feverish tone indicates how he is a man rarely heard and never fully tolerated. This crack shot wants to give his own life consequence, he wants to pass on his skill, to be assured that someone will remember him so he can expire with satisfaction, knowing his story is kept by a survivor, at least one survivor. He has selected me to inherit the burden of his life though I am his near equal in age, he is as my own reflection in some warped mirror, I see in him my urgency, and face to face I am stricken by powerful fatigue. I need to sit. This Fyfe has three-quarters of a century contained in him, yet he has no heir, no one to crop and trim his unweeded mind, he has become disordered without a wife to be as his compass, to make certain he has direction, without a wife he staggers and backtracks, repeats, lags, circles around his desires like the park rides orbit around, around an empty center. But I will tell him: spew it out, man, pass it on while there is still time left, for your tongue will fail if not today then tomorrow.

And you, Wife, attend to me, let me know that my voice is not wasted now as it was all those years when you had no interest and my son no understanding, I had advice to share yet he would not learn my language, I wanted only to unplug the blockage and release his reason so he could come into his own.

". . . A slow, steady pull and you aren't likely to overshoot. Fit the stock to cheek. Aim . . ."

Tell me everything you know, man, I will handle your wisdom tenderly, I will enshrine it, carry it to my grave.

"Where are your bugs, you said you had bugs!" I remind him. He slaps his hand upon the counter, and just as I rise to follow him the boat slides over a wavelet, returns horizontal, but I have already dropped my glass. It bounces across the floorboards without shattering—you know I am a man who makes little disruption, I might pull the trigger on this fellow's favorite arm and there would be no sound, no smoke, for nothing I do makes a difference. But this is a fool's concern, a man must not dwell on his shortcomings, this is the influence of drink and I must resist Fyfe's cloying hand that wants to replenish my glass time and again.

"You want to see my bugs? Aye, I have them like I said."

He indicates the cabinet beneath the sink, he motions me to open the door myself, explaining how they thrive in a cool, lightless place, they saturate themselves in shadow, they feed upon each other. So I do as he says, I squat, there is such searing pain in my back but I do not complain, I clasp the cabinet handle and pull it ajar.

Wife, do not look. Too late, you have seen for yourself, I feel you throbbing inside me with womanfear but please, Wife, be silent.

The drainpipe is coated with these beetles, they wrap around the steel like matted fur, the cabinet floor churns with the boiling masses, insects crawl upon each other in an effort to escape the flood of light—some are climbing up the pipe, some hang from the sink and drip in clumps, falling upon the backs of their fellows.

Is this what the doctors found when they opened you, Wife? Was there an assemblage ever expanding? Did you scrub the wainscot and keep the sheets starched to cardboard in an effort to deter the intruders? Is this why you held me off, you were scared I would enter you too deeply and see for myself the evidence?

The beetle proper does not compel revulsion, for it is useful impaled on the hook, but the overpopulation enclosed in the cabinet, the excess, is enough to cause my fingers to tremble upon the door latch, my tongue to waggle speechlessly; it is only when they are too many that I lose appreciation. You know we have sciences sufficient to shatter the hard crust of the earth, but still the cockroach shell resists us.

"You see?"

From behind me he stretches one arm over my shoulder and the other around my waist, presses his barrel chest against my back, he reaches both hands into the breeding cabinet and flakes bugs from the drainpipe into his palm and scoops them from the swarm below. Soon one groping hand is gloved with insects, he draws it out, holds it beneath my nostrils so I can make better observation. Now Fyfe is not taunting me, he honestly marvels at these beings which neither bite nor buzz, which want only to be left in peace. I am reminded of old Gibble's interest in the cricket, an obsession I was hard pressed to understand.

"You see?"

As they drop from his knuckles onto the edge of the cabinet he rotates his hand to give evidence of the pink waxen flesh, unharmed. Now this shooter has an extraordinary ability to shape his values according to his needs, he is an undauntable optimist

236

with earthy spirit, and if he be slightly skewed still I dare not toy with his opinions. If he cannot exterminate his insects he will admire them, if he cannot move from his home he will claim it a castle—and with whiskey to dull his judgment he need not face the truth of his life, he can pretend it has been all manly trial and adventure, he has no fear, so content in his make-believe world, he loves without discrimination. *Wife, I will not disturb his peace of mind*, he is an idle man, tied to a heavy sinker yet fancying himself active and profound; he loves his cockroaches and lusts for hunt and gives no thought to his faults. I tell you I have compassion but little respect for him, and I wish he would brush clean his hands and free me from this absurd embrace and shut this insect aggregate back inside the cabinet. But still he must fondle his pets, push them across his palm, gently press their wings open with his thumbnail—blessed bugs, consolers of this wretched man, they skid blindly across his hand, fleeing the light, ignorant of the devotion spent on them.

"A carefully handled, plump beetle is worth more than the most expensive lure," he advises me, though I know how there are occasions when only the artifice of feather will suffice. A seasoned angler weighs factors of weather and location and even the time of day before he chooses between the fly and the bait, but perhaps it is different in the deep sea, perhaps an impaled bug is all a man needs.

In his better days he must have been fearless in the open water, though how unfortunate that he who has made fishing his life's work does not respect his antagonist and considers the sport a dire chore and has lost track of quality, so he confuses the reward—he thinks a well-bred beetle is a better show than any fish strung upon the line, he thinks his decrepit cabin is testimony to his seamanship and he loves it more than a snail loves its shell. His is a tight-woven, fantastical excuse for pride, and never have I met the likes of such a man who can alchemize the insect into gold, the hovel into shrine, pretending—no, actually *believing*—

that the tattered remains of his profession are worth the hard labor spent on them. Yet still he needs the sound diversion of the waterfowl hunt to keep him spirited, still he needs the whiskey to keep him afloat, because if he had long pauses to reflect he would sooner or later face what he is: a solitary, with immense compassion to spend and no one to care for him through his decline.

He strips the bugs from his hands and closes the door, leaning close enough so he can nibble upon my ear if he pleases, then he rocks back on his heels, pushing against the mound where my shoulder blades meet. There are scattered cockbugs climbing across the floorboards, disappearing into corners and crevices, but Fyfe takes no notice of them, instead he grips my elbow, lifting me upright, spilling whiskey into the glasses, toasting, "Aye. Aim. Pull the trigger! Call the shot!"

He is already back in the desolate land, back in his sanctuary where congresses of birds arise from the marsh grass. *Aim, pull the trigger, call the shot.* "Rifle down. Bring the butt to the shoulder." Boast of your skill, man, dance with the vital spirit! He caresses his rifle, demonstrates stance, speaks of the days to come when he and I will sit mute in the bird blind, anticipating the kill. He has noted my weak posture and advises me to keep prone whenever possible, he tries to pass the gun over to me, warning me to handle it lovingly, for if I find the arm comfortable I may hang on to it, yes, it is mine if I want it, the seal of our friendship. I am made awkward by this ancient's generosity. I decline the gun and pour myself more drink, mumbling gratitude between gulps—*Wife, forgive me but I have such thirst.* "Look to the arm . . ." There is a wind up in the harbor, the mist has changed to driving rain, we will have hard going tonight. "Scope the duck ahead of its flight . . ." He mimics the shot, stares aloft, then sets down the rifle. *Wife, we are adrift, but do not fear: this ark is watertight, we have a long voyage ahead, the line has broke, the shore is far. Two make a multitude.* We are adrift on the open sea, the rocks rise as fangs out of the foam, the blue are near.

I push apart the curtains and see nought but the ocean spray flecking the dark, the rain splintering, it is a sight too awful to dwell upon. I turn back to face this mad solitary, who is proclaiming the joy of the hunt while he bustles with prudish pleasure over the table.

"You must be famished, my friend." He draws goods from the squat Frigidaire, replenishing the glasses, stumbling about as the waves roll beneath this shabby dwelling. "Dinner is served."

The chair, Wife, grab hold the chair!

I plant myself on an overturned barrel, I clutch the table edge to keep my balance and I stare at the open jaw, the black dewdrop eye glinting toward the ceiling. The carcass on my plate is a fish, to be sure, what kind I cannot say, with its belly slit and scales burnt to charcoal, I do not recognize the species. Fyfe waits for me to initiate the gluttony, and I cannot disappoint him after his kindnesses. I lift the fish by its tail, unpeel the skin, pry open the belly, it is ice cold inside but I go at it with my fork, jabbing and tearing, I catch a piece of stringy meat on a prong, place it on my tongue, and nod at Fyfe, who plunges quick into his own fish, holding it against his lips as if it were a stick of buttered corn. Now I do the same, for this appears to be the proper method of houseboat gorging, I tear at the tasteless flesh and when I have nearly stripped the fish I recall the city Negress and her tale of the bird that died in the palm of her hand. I do not know why I must think of her now, but I am overwhelmed by desire to see that underground queen, and with my thoughts wandering I take an inadvertent piece of spine into my gullet. With the next swallow I feel a pinprick near my throat-apple—a splintered hollow bone has stuck firm and will not be dislodged. No matter, it is not a sore irritation. Although I began without appetite, somehow this crude repast has fulfilled me, and soon I am heavy-lidded, warmed by drink, belly full, indifferent to the weather.

He offers me a place to rest, and I am grateful. I thank the skipper for his generosity, he waves me off—"No bother, no bother at all." He directs me to his cot and helps me ease onto the thin slab of mattress, soft and knotty as a bed-tick stuffed with pine boughs. What with the waves below me, the drink inside, I would be tumbling right out of bed if my host did not secure me with his hand flat against my chest, yes, he is a good man however crazed he be, and who knows but that we will run aground upon some paradise where the peach orchards are spread shore to shore, and we will live upon cobbler and let our beards grow untended, our mouths will be like the hermitage back in the woods, an aperture overgrown with vines, yes, the good skipper will keep me safe.

He lies beside me now and there is nothing to fear, neither the storm outside nor the splinter within my throat, a wondrous motion, the soothing waves beneath the hull, Fyfe and I, my brother and I in a watertight urn, with nothing to fear. We are ancient scrolls inside a bottle and someday in the distant future we will wash to shore and a naked child playing at the water's edge will discover us, he will squat upon his chubby haunches, unplug the bottle opaque with sea slime, flatten the paper and stare with uncomprehending eyes at the gibberish of history, he will not understand the strange marks, still he will prize his find and keep the message locked in a casket with other boyhood trinkets dear and mysterious to him.

And so the night passes, the room is soon awash in a ponderous light coming through the blue window sash. Fyfe sleeps with one arm slung across my chest. With the first waking swallow I feel the splinter in my throat. Beneath us the ocean rumbles uneasily but the rain has stopped, the wind has died. Clothes are strewn about, plates have been left untended, and a few rampant bugs crawl up the walls. As I slide from beneath the iron arm the pain in my throat bounces to my temples, throbs in my gullet, it will not be shaken away. My eyelids are swollen, my body aching after this night of foolhardy joy spent in a man's embrace.

Wife, we have sunk low—she is with me still, and though I may be disgraced still I am salvageable, we have come far together, passed over great obstacles, we will not be rent apart so easily.

We must be off before he wakes. He has been holding me through this long night, clutching me as if I were a woman or a fearing child. He is nought but tufts of hair, bits of bone, and I cannot imagine such a pitiable form arising ever again, perhaps our gaming was too much for him and his spirits will not be roused until the final calling; we must be off.

I creep across the boat and do not pause to cast another look over this home, where a man cannot live honestly, a man cannot live with himself as he is, he has to devote himself to insects and spin tales of false adventure in order to find inspiration to pass from today into tomorrow. The shooter has a wealth of unspent passion and will take anything into his arms, he will love whatever he can find. A sorry plight, I am glad I am not he who has never known the pungent wifesmell that fills a home after fifty-three years, he has never taken a strand of hair and dusted it against his lips, he has had no woman to beget in him habits of peace and patience, no, he is all the time indulging in fancy to fill the emptiness.

There is you, Wife, I would find my life unendurable without you so please ready a teaspoon of soda in water to help me pass this fishbone from my throat.

And there is the mermaiden, a lost soul who needs a man's heavy hand, I will teach her what is good, I will rid the room of drug once and for all. *I feel an urge to do right, Wife, we must hurry.*

I follow the boardwalk toward the carnival though I would prefer to be idle, resting upon a bed of ferns with my silk gut wound upon the drying spool, my rod propped against a willow. How I wish I could return to that Easter in November when everything was promising to be right. But I do not need to repeat my life, with the wife contained in me I feel we have such possibilities: *Remember how it was for us, we could not have known what lay in store,* but around us the poisonous activity slithered through air and stream, released by the ambition of science, a poison fancied into the world, *radioactivity*—without substance but with lasting effect upon doe and wife, and now it means to steal away the girl, to dissolve her to bone if I do not go fast to her and hold her in my arms though there is this sproat in my gullet, a hook lodged and tugging, it is all I can do to go forward.

Upon the beach a crowd has gathered by the water's edge. I make out a cluster of plum-colored gentledames mingling with tourists, they are all admiring the furious sea roused by last night's storm, and I am reminded of the ceremony for the wife up in Adenburg. The congregation here on the beach must be exclaiming over the strength of the ocean, a spirit not to be subdued by wire or chemical. Or perhaps some rare leviathan has swum close to shore and the people are marveling. Well, it is time for them to stand in awe before the fish—all of these vacationers who do not know how to make fire or impale a mud minnow on a hook.

Wife, I hurt when I swallow, and I am bored with these civilians, I have a task at hand. The boardwalk is full of people hurrying to have a look at the spectacle, whatever it be, but I go my own way. With eyes swollen, my head aching, the cold chisel twisting in my throat, I go my own way, though I cannot help but keep one watchful eye upon the beach, I cannot help but wonder what it is that absorbs them.

Has there been a drowning, Wife, is there a body floating offshore, arms flaccid, hair trailing like seaweed rope? A body draped in burlap, one of the gentledames stolen away by the tide rip?

I hear someone calling for a boat, someone shouting for police, but no one dares plunge into the angry, tarpaper sea. I want to witness no more disaster, I am an old man and have seen enough tragedy in my time. I will be off—I would be off but for the sniveling boy who has come to bother me, he tugs at my wrist and I recognize him as the same one who dangled the crab tail inside my collar. Well, he has picked the wrong moment to apologize, I try to brush him away but he hops excitedly one foot to the other, draws the back of his hand below his nose, collects snot between his fingers; he is bound to make some meaning, so I shake his shoulder and command, "Tell me what you want, boy, then leave me!"

"Don't you know?" he bursts. "Don't you know what's out there?"

I try rattling the sense from him but he will not make himself clear, he intends to ridicule me again. Well, I will not let him have his way with me a second time, I push past him but he flits in circles around me, demanding, "Don't you want to know? There's a girl out there."

As I thought, Wife, a gentledame, victim to the undertow. It is no secret that the ocean is full of the dead, I am sorry such innocence must drown but the sea will devour without respect, this is the law. I can do no good gaping with the others, I will go my own way.

"I saw her dive!"

I do not want to hear.

"I saw her run into the water and dive."

"Leave me be!"

"I saw her take off all her clothes. Right on the beach. There were people watching her, but she didn't care."

Wife, a girl unclad, a girl without discretion. How many can there be?

"Who do you mean?"

"A girl, she stripped completely naked and went under."

"A girl painted like a porcelain doll, with uncombed hair?"

"A crazy girl!" cries the boy. "She took off all her clothes and dove into the water. She hasn't come up for air."

Around me I hear the gasped exclamations from all the curious rushing to see for themselves, *drowned, drowned, drowned,* the boy has begun to shudder, he tries to stifle it, he cannot help himself, he has seen too much—milky flesh as tender as a living crab inside its shell, sliding beneath the surface of the water. *Drowned, they say, Wife, drowned, but we know better.* The boy curses the girl, so soft and now she is fodder for the blue, for the multitude of sea creatures waiting to avail themselves of such a treat, *but we know better, Wife, yes, we know better.* I am the one who named her, I am the one who predicted she would return to the sea. For an instant I see the spume of water between the gully of waves, her spout, it must be she, *drowned, they say, but we know better,* the spume is evidence, she need not come up for air. We came this far distance together, retired underground to gather our strength, arose, moved on, and she was all the time preparing for this: *to uncover herself and dive.* They think there is a madwoman drowned out there but I know better, *tell me I am not mistaken, Wife, tell me it is she and not another, assure me that she lives.* Even now she must be snaking through coral stems, her hair unraveling, her eyes open. Yes, I gave her the name.

My hand falls upon the boy's head but he slaps me away, darts off, screaming at the heavens that would not spare such delicacy. His is a pathetic rage. Upon the beach the crowd calls urgently for help, but nobody, not even one of the gentledames, no, not even an old-fashioned gentlewoman is willing to leave behind the land.

Wife, I ask you to give proof, they think her drowned but we know better, she has gone out in search of her lost love, the water spout was evidence, *Wife, tell me what you see beneath the surface.* They think her dead but I know better, a woman's longing is not so easily extinguished and were it not for the pitiable sorrow of this small boy I would be praising the mermaiden, were it not for the anguish she has left behind I would be admiring her courage. *I beg you, Wife, answer me!* There is nought but the frantic song of the spectators, the far-off sirens, the wind stirring the water, the waves breaking. I prefer blindness to this vision. I press my hands over my face, *Wife, you have yet to explain yourself to me,* she will not answer, this was always her way. *Wife, what is it that frightened you? Or did you leave me for something better?* but you know she never replied, her mouth was filled with salt water, flecks of foam around her lips.

They say a kiss revives a drowned woman. I did what I could

the day the illness strangled my wife though she was transformed, I have not told you how she was transformed from my
wife into a gutter wench. Fifty-three years she disguised herself,
she had me believing that her hard manner was instinct, while in
truth it was a pose, she had me convinced that the home de-
pended on her untiring attention and that no other wife would
put up with a man the likes of me, while in truth the form could
be easily replaced, for what was she behind her hard work and
preoccupations but a hapless arrangement of womanparts? She
lay upon the floor with her ankles crossed, a busted strap of her
overalls trailing along the leg of the upturned chair, her eyeballs
rolled back into their sockets, one sneaker kicking like the paw of
a distempered dog in slighter and slighter jerks until it moved not
at all, and she was motionless.

So I fell upon her. I did what I could, though her skin was like
wet dung beneath my hands, I put my lips to hers, though she
tasted of spoilt milk, I clutched her, though I was despising the
sight, I breathed for her because it did not matter what I saw, she
was my wife and I wanted her. But she had already gone and in
her place was a carcass, the mouth a funnel, inside a vacuum that
sucked out my soul like a raw egg through a straw. I turned over
and over like a silverfax caught in a whirlpool, I screamed, *Wife!*
and got for reply the echo of my own voice. She was gone from
me. Whether the current stole her or she fled of her own will I
do not know, I cannot say the reason why, she gave no clue.

I have told this much, I will tell the rest of it: when the wife
raised her voice in the final nonsensical song, when she staggered
from the willow chair, she opened her arms. It was the only time
she invited, the only time my wife needed me. But she was gone
before I reached her, I was slow to answer because I did not
understand what she wanted, in truth I remained stock still a yard
away in the very moment when my wife was finally willing to be
mine. It was confusion that kept me from holding my wife in her
last waking moment. *Such confusion.* Fifty-three years I had a sus-

picion my wife preferred Gibble to me, fifty-three years I thought the first place in her heart belonged to her cousin. But at the end it was the husband she required, she took me by surprise with her last-minute plea.

Do not ask me to consider what a wife must think when she calls for her man and he falters. Now my tears are made of flame and ice. I tell you it is not heartache that makes me weep so, not the pain in my throat, nor fear, it is the sight of fury's impotence, a boy's wrath mingled with my own and wasted on indifferent God.

THIRTEEN

How to Do Wonder

BEGIN at a modest pace. Build wind and muscle gradually, from day to day increase the distance. Accustom yourself to staying afoot three, then five, then seven hours, and do not let Age dupe you, she will be all the time trying you out, inviting you to despair. The secret of foot travel is this: face the sea, turn on your heel, and do not look back. Never stumble, never fall, never crash blindly through the bush, never falter, never waste your breath, never fear the night nor revolt against the dawn, never hurry, never drag your feet through dry mulch upon the path, never make fire with willow, go to any extent to procure the best timber and strike your match to the lee of the wind. Never lack a motive, never scorn the portents in a moon—the penumbra foretelling someone's death, a halo of red, your own. Never linger with a tramp, never dismiss a tenderfoot seeking advice, never go too far at once nor go too long and do not pretend stamina, never waste, never spend what is not yours, never curse the sifting snow for the storm will end on the morrow, do not shirk labor nor make the grave your goal, never regret what you have left behind and take pride in the miles come, be sure to keep your grubstake stocked with bacon, beans, and rice, never dally over a familiar haunt, never ridicule a man his faults, never fear a screaming osprey, never close your ears to the music in the water nor your eyes to the light dancing upon the leaves. Show your victim mercy—make the killing quick, wrench him free from the barbed hook, and lay his spiritless form to cool in the bucket. Never game when you are full exhausted, *know your limits*, know what you are and will not be, you see what you see and forgive others their differences, do not equivocate over status or wealth, you have a station so keep to it and wear its flags when you voyage out, hold fast to your original name and never permit such a union that will shatter you upon its dissolution, never love a wife you will lose nor a son you will fell nor dames who will go under, take it upon yourself to calm unquiet thoughts, to moderate the passions, to hold an even keel, you will be content alone if you stay true to your abilities and fight if there is need and rest when you must, be worthy, be just, wary, stoical and fierce, never try to marry opposites and do not consider your living hard so long as you are capable, there is luck contained in the future like petals inside a bud, but do not pluck—be patient, cast your eyes upon the path ahead but do not try to rush and do not try to keep the wife from going where she wants, she is other, you are one, so do not put trust in fidelity vows and never love what has already passed.

I am grateful to leave behind the sea, to walk alone through the countryside. If you had my eyes you would see the deep spring-hole lined with brushy alder, if you had my thirst you would celebrate the mountain with great sucking gulps, if you had my hunger you too would rejoice at the clusters of plump blackberries inside the bramble. I have come along the highway and across the land. Still there is the bone lodged in my throat and though the spring water is cool and the berries sweet, with every swallow the pain shudders through me, hardly to be endured, and I cannot tell whether the black dribble is salty from my blood or is the taste of sea water lingering.

I have been helped. Back in the shore town there was a young fellow who witnessed me making my way by foot along the road. He slowed his car and waved at me, surely he could see I am one of the ancients and should not be left to stray upon the highway, for you know I might distract, I might divert, I might be responsible for accident. An oddity. How long ago was it I set out? "Where shall I bring you?" he had asked. Home. I will be at home again. But I said nothing, and he did not persist. The color of his skin I cannot say, he was as a furnace fire that burns so hot it has no tint, he was a young solitary on his way west—to make his fortune or to forget an injury of love I do not know, I did not ask, and neither did he beggar me with questions. Maybe he believed I had no knowledge of his language or had lost the capacity to hear. So I listened to the traffic, how long we drove I am not certain, and when he stopped at a roadside snack bar and excused himself into the hut, I fled.

This is not right. I did not flee. I slipped, yes, simply so, as if the earth had opened as an envelope flap. I crossed the lot, stepped over the rail, floundered down the hill toward the landfill, sending cascades of gravel to warn of my approach. On a sandy clearing I brushed away two coupling dragonflies hovering above a box turtle. The turtle withdrew his legs when my shadow crossed his shell. I followed a footpath along the rim of the pit that was overgrown with pokeberry and trumpet vine sprouting between mounds of sand. This is how I came to be a woodsman again; the hours since I cannot say.

How shall I cook without an oven to use inside a green-log fire? How shall I build a shelter without a rolled tarp treated with paraffin, how shall I repair without a needle and thread, without rivet or ax? How shall I make fire without flint? There are berries. Green onion ramps. There are squirrels barking noisily, hidden in the tamarack, and if I had a slingshot, if I had stone and swath and sufficient skill, I would knock a choice rodent off the branch as my brother did that night so many years back when we were challenging the wilds. Though I have told of the squirrel stretched upon the rocks, how she looked, how she screamed in the night, I did not describe how we readied her for our meal. Now I am desperate enough to wish that night, that kill, that awful meal, repeated—she was a pretty mess in preparation, but fried she was delectable.

"What do you mean to do?" I demanded when Brother took the limp body into his hand. He had knowledge but no experience in this fine art, and I did not esteem him while he went about the job of dressing the animal, no, I did not admire him while he put the knife to the rodent's neck and struggled to saw off the head, but the stringy ligaments were reluctant so he pulled her apart like a cork from a bottle, twisting the tiny skull free. Next he had a go at the twig feet, which gave more easily, and then he severed the tail and flung it at me, taunting, reminding me how the prior midnight I was a girl, fearing nought but roving animals—as if it were only me and not him, too, who had withered at the unholy sound of the dead squirrel's cry. He set upon the dismembered carcass with such ruthlessness—I have told you this much, I might as well describe all—he slit the body crosswise in several tallies and then tried to rip off the skin but it would not easily give, he hacked and tore at the unyielding hide and removed it in shreds, all but the scalp, which came away mostly whole. Then he had me fetch a bucket of pond water and he dipped the meat in quick, not sufficiently to clean. Next I was assigned the cooking task, he had me prepare the hind legs for him, the front legs for me. I did as best I could, parboiling and then frying with pork fat, I burnt the squirrel to charcoal but still we ate her, we ate her and savored her and by the next day when we were installed at home again I had forgotten how I had been despising my brother while I gnawed upon the fried legs, I had been wishing him dead.

How have I made it to here from there? An arbitrary plot, with no more design than a butterfly's dance. I have a destination in mind and no straight path. If I had muslin I would make a slipcase of moss to use as a pillow. If I had an ax I would make my home right here in the forest—a fireplace, a supping room, a window to the west; if I had wire I would bind together hemlocks to make a broom.

Mine is the only voice, she no longer scolds, *Man, keep it clean!* Keep it clean, she wanted me to keep it pure, to stay respectable, unbearded, scrubbed and soaped, virtuous and diligent. I dare not call out to her nor beckon, they all go under anyway, leaving me alone, with a sproat hook in my gullet; I splash, turn deliberately, pit all my strength against the line, seek a sheltered lair in crag or submerged reef, but there is a very expert hand at the opposite end, slacking then drawing.

Do you wonder where Gibble has got to since I set off the day of my wife's burial? I have told you what I know as best I can, except for this one fact, which I will tell you now: the day I returned to the cemetery with the mermaiden on my arm and saw the figure bent over the wife's plot, it was not me wearing the brown worsted. Yes, it was my brown worsted, but I was not beneath it. Maybe you have already guessed that it was Gibble who had come alone to worship, Gibble who had stolen my cap and taken my place mourning the wife. Gibble has always been one step ahead, he adored my woman, his cousin, my mail-order bride, long before she came inland, he has been in control of my direction all these years. Do not ask me why he chose to waste his cleverness on me, every individual contains a mystery he cannot resolve and Gibble is mine. I assure you he is awaiting me, he has rigged the chair with steel and leather, I know I am walking directly into his hands.

But this is as it should be, for all through my travels I have not wandered outside Gibble's territory, I have been trapped from the start, and a compass would do no good so I might as well turn myself over to the man in charge. I cannot be always resisting, sooner or later my strength will give, and the more determined I object, the faster I will be brought to the gaff. So I am returning whence I came, my throat bleeds, my lungs labor, and when I drop my trousers and squat nothing will excrete—outside I am caked with grime, putrid, inside I am ice.

You know I do not like to think of how *they* stood on the beach amidst the gaping crowd, *they* the gentlewomen, they the cherubs—I would have as soon violated a star as injured them. While *she* swam away beneath the waves. *She* the strumpet, she the streetwalker, leaving me with nought but a snapshot. Now who is left to make sure this old angler does not stray off the path, who will attend to his needs, who will be the attraction drawing him on?

This morning I retreated from the sea, pursued Little Fury to demand more of him: *Is it true what you say? Was it she? What was the look on her face?* though I knew. But I lost him among the beach tourists, they were all of them running toward the surf so they could say to each other tonight, in the dark, in their bedroom privacy, *Thank God it was not you.* They surged toward the sight where they hoped to find a body laid out as a symbol of death that had this time spared them. They wanted to gaze, to shudder lavishly, to clutch their children in their arms. I will not say what it was that kept me stumbling forward long after I lost sight of the boy, but I knew I had looked enough upon the sea. How I came to be back at the motel is a miracle, for I had hardly been able to hold myself to a steady keel, the planks swayed beneath my feet, it was a giant's breast we were stampeding, he had woken, stirred, roused by the tumult, he would rise and we would all slide off this gargantuan into the ocean's mouth.

She was not in the room examining her nails, I did not find her splotched with shadows, wearing an oversized T-shirt and blue panties. By the time I reached the motel I had spent all my sorrow and was as hollow as the room, where no young girl upturned her face slowly, as if two fingers were levered beneath her chin, no one said to me, *Why are you in such a sweat, old man? Is it your heart, are you in pain?*

But I was not alone. Shall I share with you the vision that started a trembling in me, a trembling that will not cease until I expire? Shall I describe what I saw when I took the snapshot from my trouser pocket and held it in my palm? Consider the squirrel, the one that was supper for Brother and me. Consider the tiny skull without its flesh, the face without its skin, and you will know what I saw in place of the girl. But in the photo the boy still kept his arm around the bones, he clung to her, undaunted by the flayed skull, the naked cheek plates, the eyes in their black sockets, the lipless mouth. Now it is not any man who will love the carcass left behind. I left the snapshot upon the pillow, I took nought but the clothes upon my back, and the trembling—yes, I took the trembling with me—and I turned away from the beginning of that fated romance as I had turned away from the sea.

To be as an antelope, rising the full width of my body at every leap. To be as a pike catapulting across the lake. To be as a salmon mounting the falls. The farther an old man travels with the prevailing wind at his back, the harder it will be to retrace his passage. But now I must return. I do not know for certain whether it is the hook compelling me or the vision behind, I do not know whether I am being drawn in or prodded along but I suppose it is one and the same, to wander toward or flee from. The blade in my throat makes me thirst, yet to drink is agony, and when I kneel at the mountain springs I am a parched wanderer beseeching his own mirage to save him. It looks wondrous with the blackberries ripe and the waters clear. I told the wife the warmth would come, the fruit would be plentiful, our days would be without interruption. It is no little task for a man to prophesy in these uncertain times. Now I have seen how the world is dismantled by the hand of science, nothing stays intact what with the laboratories burning, contraptions exploding, the radioactivity traveling wireless from continent to continent—it is all I can do to stay on my feet and predict the weather.

The path I trod has led me away from the landfill into a park.

Around me branches clutch their wind apples, resolute against the wind. A welcome sign at the boundary to the wilderness advises me: *The silent observer sees the most*. But I ask how shall a man be silent when he is in a hurry to be home? That is like commanding the wind to mute its song. I do not forget how once I fancied an impenetrable quiet that had settled over Josiah's Pond, but I know better now—when there is motion there is voice, the very earth groans in its revolutions, and a solitary man if he listens carefully will hear the echo of the globe inside himself, there is music in him whether or not he prefers to hear. The rank beginner will spill out his complaints hither, thither, but the expert will make an even distribution, he will be sometimes lamenting, sometimes extolling, and only in the worst crisis will he let go of his language and emit such a cry that means nothing. I maintain there is no sound but this that does not refer to one thing or another—even now the babbling reveals a creek nearby, the thumping suggests carpenters, perhaps they are restoring a house. I have no wish to be hammered and sawed back to the parcel I was, I will be content if I only keep at a respectable clip, I am a proficient woodsman and know better than to go beyond my speed.

All the while I make headway I contemplate the wilderness, I consider how to use it to my best advantage. The mountain waters do not ease me, the light stimulates no mirth, but when I discover a bottle sundered upon the rock, when I see the advertisement on the weathered shard—a ladle, a woman, an inviting motto—I want nothing more than a draught of the skipper's whiskey to help me fade, dissolve, to sleep. Why must we keep on when the soil yearns to embrace us and we want to root? Because in the dead air space between our feet and the earth there is propulsion, the heat beneath our soles is searing, we cannot stay upright and at a standstill for long while the world's core burns, we are unable to endure arrest unless we have been trained as sentries, and even then who knows what goes on beneath the bulk of a uniform? Surely fingers scratch at groins, boot heels dig at hamstrings, thumbnails find their way into cracks between the teeth. I am not soldier-trained and do not have fortitude to hold a rigid stance, always I must be plodding, laboring, heading out, returning home. I must be in motion and now I am compelled westward, there will be clogged gutters, mold on the wainscot, dirt between the floorboards—surely enough to occupy me—and of course there will be Gibble, preparing the chair. Why is it I have come so far and there is no freedom for me? I have a lifetime's education yet I am passed from wife to industry to enemy, from idiots to waifs and wretched solitaries.

These bits of fractured bottle, these empty cans and paper wrappers are spread before me in such plenitude—you might call it garbage but I will call it treasure. I do not have eyes in vain and will tell you how to earn a nickel: always pocket glass and tin. This old angler, he outwits the undertaker, he is long lasting and bound to rip the sproat clean of his jaw. I do what I have to do. I stoop, I collect a beer can, an unshattered pop bottle, an applejack pint, a jelly jar. There is such rubbish slung alongside the path I do not have arms enough to hold the empty containers so I take off my shirt, next my undershirt, and with this I make a cradle such as might be used to hold fatty pine for tinder. I find a green branch and loop this to make a handle, tucking it through the armholes, knotting the ends. *Excellent repair!* you would say if you could see. Well, I will build up my capital with the tourist waste, I will buy my return journey, at this rate I shall be home before dark, the excursion is saved, the finish, imminent.

It is not easy work, stooping and harvesting, it wearies me but I keep on, and when I have an assortment heaped in my makeshift pouch I head toward the highway with the intention of flagging a bus and trading my collection for a ticket home. I do not have to wander far off the path before I come upon a paved thoroughfare leading out to a state road—there is a trinket store at the corner, the sign declares candles, perfumes, preserves. Now I do not know what good such a store would do me but I will see if I can barter away a portion of my burden. The log bunker is almost lightless inside and pungent with pine incense; my eyes must grow used to the darkness before I make out the man and woman behind the dried fruit display, both in the similar posture of sleep, sitting in canvas chairs, arms folded across their chests. They seem childish figures with their noses hardly reaching above the counter, the silver wispy hair identically mussed. I lack the boldness to interrupt their dreaming, so I retreat from the store, but not without first lifting a package of apricot and a white chocolate bar from the shelf, for regardless of the splinter in my throat, I will die without sustenance, and the picnic fruit should give some spirit to my bowels.

I am nearly free from the room, my treasure-pouch jingling, clacking, I am nearly out in the lot when I hear a voice call weakly after me, "Can we help you, sir?"

Bother, the gentleman and lady have woken, they pretend to pick up the chores they left off, wiping the glass top, arranging packages of berry soaps in baskets. I am able to hide my stolen goods in my trouser pockets before I make the return trip across the store, but they show nary an indication of suspicion, they are simple-minded merchants with no grand ambitions, solid people I can see right off, so I am not long flustered. I lower my bundle to the floor and beckon them to look more closely. Man and woman are both no more than a child's height, with flesh folds like a pug dog, the lady has a weeping eye beneath her spectacles and the man has rust-colored teeth. I unveil my treasures, clearly these folk are baffled, so I go ahead and propose a sum. The man tells me in a modest voice that I might try a mile down the road at the grocery store. The woman interrupts, says surely they will accept my collection, and they do not dispute. The simple man returns to the cash register, rings out the change drawer; the simple woman separates and counts the cans and bottles. They pay me generously. I ask them if this is sufficient to take me to

Clarion; they tell me it is not nearly enough. I ask them where I might catch the bus.

"Across the street," the woman drawls.

"At a quarter to," adds the man.

I do not linger with them. Outside I feel some shame at my theft. I unwrap the candy and drop it between the paws of a scurrilous hound sleeping in the yard. I have to nudge him to stir his interest, he wakes, laps lazily, wakes further, snatches the sweet, tosses it into the air, seizes it between his teeth, then swallows the piece whole. Half the evidence gone. I think I can endure the compunction over dried apricots. I station myself at the autobus sign and scan the asphalt strip, I wait and allow my eyes to wander back to the trinket store, so dark you would hardly think it was inhabited. Now after a string of cars the bus comes by, and just as I am boarding I glance down and notice the white tuft of a tail in the road, the points of two animal ears at the edge of the grass—it is a deer carcass long since bulldozed into the tar, its outline vague as a poor tile mosaic. I cannot say why I took no notice of it earlier when all the time my feet were nearly planted on its back.

"Where do you want to go?" the driver demands, pulling the folding doors closed behind me, so I extend him my hands full of coins and ask him for the destination of this bus.

"North," he grunts, and I ask, "Through Clarion?"

Well, I am lucky today, he nods as he sets the bus in gear and I have nought to do but pay the price and find a seat.

"Then Clarion is where I want," I announce, lurching forward, grabbing for the pole, dropping all my coins into his glass machine. "I shall go as far as it will take me," I say, staggering down the aisle to find an empty seat. Other than myself and the driver there are only a few old women, each occupying a double seat alone, each with the wrinkled tidings of spinsterhood upon her brow.

It will be an easy journey from here, and when I have gone the distance of my ticket I shall descend from the bus, collect glass and tin enough to buy my passage home. I settle back against the cushion. A summer storm is gathering behind us, a black knotted mass in the sky. I have a safe, dry place and can watch without despair as the cloud bundles meet and the hemlocks tremble in the draft. I would like to stretch across the seat but the fish bone still claws at my throat. This must be what it is to hold a babe inside when he is wanting to be out, a son with waxen nostrils and fingernails, a child curled like a centipede—there is no position he prefers, his restlessness keeps you attending to his discomfort.

I recall the sorry skipper, and I cannot help but conclude that the barb in my gullet is his devising—revenge for my indifference. I spit a rusty, foul juice between my knees, it makes a splotch on the floor then dribbles backward as the bus carries us uphill. I tell you whiskey would be better insulation than any bed-tick of matted needles or a brown wool suit, whiskey would douse the flame in me and dissolve the chill so I could watch peacefully the rain that has begun to filter down and the fleshy necks of the women and the meadows lapping to the roadside, alit with violets and green goldenrod. The more land around a man's feet, the higher the quality of his living, this is an indisputable fact, and only in the deepest wood will he live the truly civilized life. Ask the hermit and he will share with you his wisdom, but turn toward the city and see what kind of information you will gather from streetwalkers and hounds, Negroes and mariners. Ask the hermit and he will reveal to you the logic of the seasons, the method of hibernation, the migratory routes, but enter the city and you are lost. I am glad to come home, I will try to forget what I have seen. Believe me when I say I have learned almost nothing.

The driver lets out a few passengers at crossroads stops and takes in others, keeping us in a flux—first we were a cluster of women with myself the oddity, now we are a mixture of youngsters and laborers commuting home. We have come far since I boarded, it seems the driver has forgotten that my ticket does not guarantee a passage to the end, or maybe he is keeping me on out of charity. He sees I have no supplies, no mackintosh, no cap— if I were to be loose in the drizzle for long I think I might drown, yes, it is a watery world looming, I am glad to have a place on this bus. It is not possible to identify the time, somehow day melts into dusk, into eve and night, the moon hides somewhere inside the storm and from my seat I can see the dashboard lights, a comforting glow, the dials indicate we are safe, our speed moderate, our fuel tank full. I am content to let someone else do the piloting. I shall devote my energy to converting the pain in my throat into thoughts, into dream, and soon I shall wake from it, free.

We might be approaching midnight, we might be near dawn— the sky gives no indication of change, it is a ponderous shroud hanging over us and we cannot tell one hour from the next as we rattle over uneven roads. I am happy; all but for the pain I would stay here forever.

Now the bus slithers to a halt like a lizard that has reached a rock summit. We wait. No passengers disembark, none board. We wait. The dashboard glow is abruptly obscured by two trousered columns as the driver lumbers down the aisle. It is so peaceful here but for his belabored breathing and his boots scuffing.

"Clarion." A burly edifice, he fingers his visor, rubs his knuckle in his ear. "Clarion. This is your stop."

How can I ply him for more time when he has been generous, how can I beg, *Keep me to the end,* when I have nothing left to barter? I am a public spectacle. I pretend to gather my belongings when in fact I have only my wad of undershirt. The driver grips just below my armpit, pulls me upright. Have I ever known a hand to be so adamant and yet so gentle? The man, he is good yet cruel to be sending me into the rain, into the night, penniless, alone because of a name—*Clarion*—that I stupidly revealed, my identity fixed, my territory defined, my destination—Clarion—home.

I grope along the aisle, conscious of the accusing eyes peering from the dark, and it comes to me that this begins my execution, the driver has declared both my conviction and my sentence. After this season of flight I am not to be spared, I am expelled. I stand at the roadside, sucking in the stream of exhaust fumes as the bus wrenches away. The rain keeps on, the asphalt is silver with it. I unknot my undershirt and tie it like a bonnet around my head. I am not far from home. My arm still tingles where he held me. I turn as a man cast off from his battery in the middle of war, and I plod homeward, humiliated. I do not complain. I have had hard living but I do not complain. I follow the roads familiar to me. There is need to hurry now with the rain dripping inside my collar, I must move beyond my usual speed and I must pretend to feel nothing. I pass the mailboxes guarding hidden drives—a lifetime spent in the region yet my neighbors remain strangers to me, there are so many who have passed through I never could keep track of the families just arrived or on their way out. No matter. If an automobile stops to offer a ride, I will refuse. I am in exile. Soon I will be home. I do not complain. Why is it the rain must besiege me? I am an old man and have felt sufficient remorse over my wrongdoings.

I veer away from the road and cut into the orchard of five hundred peaches. The peaches are ripe. I yank one from the branch. I press the damp fur against my lips, and I walk through the dark along the path. I know this land so intimately, if I were blind I would need no guide. I hold the globe to my mouth, I do not eat. A vine catches my ankle, I stumble forward, I fall. Flat on my belly I curl my fingers, scratching scallops of mud into my palm. I do not cry out. Neither do I moan. I have lost the fruit. The ground is soft with the rain. I rub my cheek into the mud. In my haste I forgot to keep a reserve of strength, and now I have none to summon. I cannot rise. No matter. The journey is not spoiled. I shall sleep here and the rain will end on the morrow. I slap the earth around me for the peach. I will say now in case I forget: *Excuse my mistakes and I bid you all farewell.*

It will be a story to tell over again if I live to get out of this. I will heap more wood upon the fire. Who will believe me? I will lean close to the flame, letting shadow and light play upon my face, I will be grotesque, with raving eyes and quivering white nostrils. Then they will believe me.

Gibble must have opened the curtains, prepared the home for my return. Across the valley I see my windows aglow. I best not dally. How I rise to my feet I cannot say. I tread toward Josiah's Pond down the path that is overgrown with thicket. I feel nothing but the sproat. A man has a central pain, he numbs to everything else, and so it is with me. Perhaps green lilies carpet the pond. I do not see the Gibble raft, it is too dark to tell shadow from substance. Inadvertently I kick a dead log. Not a log. My muzzled ax. The handle has rotted and breaks in two when I lift it. I toss both blade and stem into the water. The splashing sounds like geese rising. I climb toward the house. I lose the path and stumble over ragweed clumps. The yard has not been tended. The kitchen light is on. Maybe Gibble will be heating dumpling stew in the cast iron kettle. The wind is stiff against my back, it hardly takes an effort to mount the hillock and approach my home, as long as I stay balanced I make good time.

I climb the three wood steps to the back door. I try the handle; the door is barred to me. I never secured this lock, there was no need. I have no key. I knock. Each time my knuckles meet the wood, the sproat hook tugs. I feel the peach against my lips and smell the juice beneath the tender skin, though the fruit is lost. From the corner of the gutter a stringy drool of rain babbles to a puddle. This is where, in the winter, huge icicles grow and thaw and shatter upon the earth. No one receives me. I walk through the mud around the house, clutch the windowsill, and peer into the kitchen. There is no plate set upon the table. No beaker of pear wine. No stew.

There is someone in the willow chair, his back to me. I do not

261

fool myself. That is the wife's chair, that is my son. His shaved head is bent forward. He is not praying. Neither is he idle. From the position of his arms, the angle of his elbows, I can see he is trying to draw thread through a needle. He has no skill, he will not succeed. He pursues the task. I watch his back, for how long I cannot say. I rap upon the windowpane. He does not turn, he does not acknowledge me. I go round to the front door but this too is locked. I return to the window. My son cannot understand how I have suffered. I do not complain. I tell you I will be gentle with him from now on, I will show him how to do wonder on the rapids and in the deepest lakes, I will give expert assistance and he will not have to unlearn a lot of errors later, no, I will be patient, it will take time, we will do good, the wife would be proud. I pound my fist against the glass, the window does not shatter. He is intent upon his task, unaware of me as if he were still a half-pint, curled upon my lap. The kitchen is neat, the counters clean, the floor swept. Who taught the boy his chores and then left him I do not know, maybe the nuns, more likely Gibble. I would not have predicted my son was capable of surviving solitary. I call out to him through the glass—he cannot hear me. Is there a scar upon his brow? Has he forgiven me? He cannot hear me over the rain—this is the reason, there is a foul magic in the night—the sky assaults us, the rain creates a din upon the roof, claps into puddles, strikes the glass, the wind pursues its maelstrom course around the house. We are so close yet I cannot enter, the heavens drown out my voice, he does not know I have come home for him, he need not be alone if he would only turn.